Janice Preston  heartwarming his novels are standal set in the same Re include book-hopp writing she enjoys reading, pottering in the garden when the sun is shining, and travelling when she can. She fuels her imagination with endless cups of coffee, is far too keen on unhealthy food, and is an expert procrastinator.

About the Author

... writes sensual, emotional, and
historical romance. Although all her
... she reads, she loves to write stories
... Regency world, and many of her books
... featuring characters. When ...

His Christmas Wallflower

JANICE PRESTON

MILLS & BOON

First Published in Great Britain 2022
By Mills & Boon, an imprint of HarperCollins*Publishers* Ltd
1 London Bridge Street, London, SE1 9GF

www.harpercollins.co.uk

HarperCollins*Publishers*
1st Floor, Watermarque Building,
Ringsend Road, Dublin 4, Ireland

Special thanks and acknowledgement are given to Janice Preston for her contribution to *The Governess Tales* series

ISBN: 978-0-263-31803-6

MIX
Paper | Supporting
responsible forestry
FSC™ C007454

CHRISTMAS WITH HIS WALLFLOWER WIFE

JANICE PRESTON

To all the readers and reviewers who have taken
the Beauchamp family to their hearts.

Thank you for all your support and
enthusiasm – I'm eternally grateful. Xxx

Chapter One

Cheriton Abbey—early September 1817

Try as she might, Lady Jane Colebrooke couldn't quite suppress her quiver of excitement as her father's carriage passed through the gates of Cheriton Abbey, the Devonshire seat of their neighbour, the powerful Duke of Cheriton. It was Olivia, the Duke's daughter and Jane's childhood friend, who had told Jane that her brother, Lord Alexander Beauchamp, would be home for the first time in over four years and Jane's heart had twitched with the longing to see him again.

Not that him being there would make any difference. She'd long ago accepted he would never return her feelings. They'd last met in London in the spring. He'd even danced with her. And still he never seemed to notice her as a female, let alone a lady worthy of courting. No. To him, she was—as she had always been—good old Janey. She turned from the window and her heart shrivelled at seeing her stepmother's sharp gaze on her.

'Why the sour expression, Jane? You are going to a garden party, not a funeral.'

Jane bit the inside of her cheek, determined not to

retaliate. Defying her stepmother had never borne fruit and life, she had learned, was more tolerable if she allowed Lady Stowford's jibes to pass over her head.

'I hope you will at least be civil to Sir Denzil when you meet him,' Stepmama continued. 'He has been invited... I made a particular point of asking when I saw him at church last Sunday.'

Jane swallowed. Stepmama had been doing her utmost to pair Jane and Sir Denzil Pikeford ever since the man— another neighbour—had begun to show an interest in her. The fact Jane actively disliked the baronet made no difference—Stepmama was so eager to get her just-turned-twenty-three-year-old stepdaughter off her hands she had even persuaded Papa to add an extra one thousand pounds to her dowry.

One thing Jane knew for certain: if she ever *did* marry, she would not meekly accept whatever her husband decreed, as she accepted Stepmama's demands. She would stand up for herself. Right from the start. But it was hard to change the habits of a lifetime with the stepmother who had raised her from a baby and who ruled their household like an empress.

'You do not accuse me of incivility, I hope, ma'am?'

Papa stirred at her words. 'Jane is never rude to people, my dear.' Bless him for one of his sporadic attempts to support the daughter of his first marriage, no matter how unkind Stepmama might be. Jane couldn't blame him for intervening so rarely. Not when she, too, often chose to remain silent rather than setting the household on its ears for days on end.

'You know very well she needs to be *more* than polite, Stowford, if I am to bring Sir Denzil to the point. Really... have you forgotten our dear Miranda is to come out next year? How shameful if her older sister is *still* unwed!'

She raked her stepdaughter from head to toe while Miranda, the elder of Jane's two half-sisters, smirked.

'You had the perfect opportunity to marry—in your *debut year*, no less—when that nice Mr Romsley offered for you. Quite a coup for a girl as plain as you. But, oh, no! *He* was not good enough for *Lady Jane*. I begged you to accept him but, as ever, Lady Jane knows best! And since then, nary a sniff of a suitor until Sir Denzil. You are *such* a stubborn gel. I've always said so.'

It was hot in the carriage, with the family all squashed in together, and Lady Stowford, her face the shade of a beetroot following her outburst, collapsed back against the squabs, fanning herself furiously. Jane turned away, the all-too-familiar pain curling through her. It was so familiar she barely noticed it any more. The pain of unrequited love.

Ha! How naive had she been? In March 1813, the Beauchamp family had attended Olivia's wedding to Lord Hugo Alastair at the Abbey before all heading to London for the Season. It was Jane's debut year and she'd had such high hopes, certain Alex would finally see her as a young lady and not simply the annoying little neighbour who had dogged his footsteps throughout his boyhood.

He was two years her senior and her childhood hero. He'd taught her to ride and she'd willingly followed him into all sorts of adventures, often ending in trouble of one sort or another. But Alex always protected her from the worst of the blame and she'd marvelled at his bravery in the face of his father's formidable wrath.

But at the start of her first Season all her hopes crashed to the ground. London Alex treated her exactly as Devonshire Alex had always treated her—like another little sister. Her hero-worship of Alex might have matured over the years into love, but Alex clearly didn't see her in that way and who could blame him? His reputation as a skilled lover was legendary and unhappily married ladies of the *ton* vied for his attention. Why would he ever be interested in a plain, dull female like *good old Janey*?

Despite that inauspicious start, her love for him—buoyed by her blind hope that, one day, he would open his eyes and recognise her as his soulmate—had persisted and she had stubbornly refused Mr Romsley's offer, for how could she make her vows to another man when her heart belonged to Alex?

She had lived to regret her decision because she'd received no further offers in the intervening years and Alex had not returned to Devonshire since. The only time she saw him was in London during the Season each year and now she accepted he would never see her as anything other than his old playmate. *Now*, she would willingly marry. She longed to have her own household to run and to escape Stepmama and her constant barrage of criticism. But that would *never* be with Sir Denzil Pikeford. In his late thirties, he drank too much, his teeth were rotting, his manners were appalling and his conversation consisted mainly of boasting of his hunting exploits.

Even Stepmama was preferable to a lifetime with *that*.

The carriage drew to a halt. Jane looked up at the honey-eyed stone walls of the old Abbey… It had been like a second home to her throughout her childhood and the memories flooded back…happy childhood memories…

Grantham, the Duke's haughty butler, showed them straight through the huge hall and out to the extensive lawns at the rear of the Abbey, where a footman offered them glasses of punch or lemonade. There must have been fifty guests there already and Jane recognised many faces as her gaze swept the crowd, seeking…

Her heart leapt, then beat a tattoo in her chest. She

might have accepted her love would remain unrequited for ever, but still she could not deny it.

Lord Alexander Beauchamp—tall, broad-shouldered and impossibly handsome, with those strong Beauchamp features shared by all the men of the family: the strong jaw, aquiline nose, lean cheeks, beautifully sculptured mouth and arresting eyes under straight, dark brows. He stood with his older brother Dominic, Lord Avon, slightly apart from the crowd, and Jane recognised that Dominic was attempting to pacify his fiery-tempered brother.

They looked so alike, other than their colouring: Dominic shared the black hair and silvery-grey eyes of the Duke—as did Olivia—whereas Alex had the thick mahogany-brown hair and amber eyes of his late mother. In temperament, however, they were opposite. Dominic had always been the dutiful, responsible son. Alex had, for as long as Jane could remember, rebelled against his father—one of the reasons he hadn't been back to the Abbey for so long. The other, Jane knew, was the painful memory that haunted him whenever he returned...the memory of the day he'd found his mother's dead body in the summer house by the lake.

Alex had never spoken to Jane about that day—he'd been seven years old and he hadn't spoken at all for a year afterwards—but Olivia had long ago told Jane all about it and about the nightmares Alex suffered. Jane's young, tender heart had gone out to him, but she had never been able to penetrate the barriers behind which he retreated whenever anyone ventured too close to his memories of that day, or to his feelings about what had happened.

He kept everyone—family included—at arm's length.

While Dominic talked, Alex's restless gaze swept the crowd and Jane felt the physical jolt when his amber eyes— tiger's eyes, Dominic always called them—alighted on her. He grinned and beckoned her over. A blush heated her cheeks as she walked towards him and she schooled her expression, always afraid her feelings for him would shine from her eyes. A girl had to have some pride.

'Janey! How lovely to see you! You still game for a swim in the lake like we used to?'

'Alex!' Dominic hissed. 'For God's sake, think before you speak, will you? Would you say such a thing to any other young lady of your acquaintance?'

'I'd say it to Livvy.' Alex winked at Jane. 'Janey's just like one of us...she doesn't care about standing on ceremony, do you, Janey?'

Jane shook her head, stretching her lips in a smile. Defeat spread through her, settling like a lead weight in her stomach. There was the proof, as if she needed it, that Alex would never view her as anything other than his old childhood playmate.

'Of course I don't mind. After all, if I'm not accustomed to your teasing ways by now, Alex, I never shall be.'

Alex grinned again. 'There! What did I tell you, Dom?' He slung his arm around her shoulders and hugged her briefly into his side. 'How's the old witch?'

Dominic rolled his eyes. 'I'll leave you to it,' he said. 'Jane—please try to stop my reprehensible brother from upsetting anyone else. He's already enraged Lord Wagstaff by ripping up at him over the state of his horses and I really must go and see if Liberty needs help...she's been gone a long time.'

Liberty was Dominic's new bride—they had met earlier that year in London, fallen in love and married, despite Liberty not being the perfect society lady Dominic planned to wed. Jane had met her in London, where they had married in June, and thought she was, in fact, the perfect match for Dominic, helping him to take life, and himself, a little less seriously.

'Is there something amiss?' Jane wondered why Liberty might need help.

'That dog of hers,' said Dominic. 'Never have I known such a mischief-maker. He cannot keep his nose out of trouble for more than five minutes.'

'Romeo?' Liberty had rescued the dog as a stray in London earlier that year.

Dominic nodded. 'He sneaked into the kitchens again, knocked over a cream jug and helped himself to a crock of butter, just when the servants are run off their feet with preparations for today. Liberty's gone to catch him and shut him away. Why she insisted on bringing him here I'll never know!'

'You can't fool us, Dom. You dote on that dog as much as Liberty does,' said Alex, nudging his brother.

Dominic's jaw tightened. 'I do *not* dote on him. I merely tolerate him.'

'Is that why he was sprawled across your lap last night when I arrived? He was fondling Romeo's ears, Janey, and murmuring sweet nothings.'

'Rubbish! I was doing nothing of the sort. I'll see you both later.'

Alex watched Dominic stalk away, his mouth curved in a smile that managed to be both mischievous and satisfied at the same time, before switching his attention back to Jane. She tore her own gaze from his lips, that telltale heat building again in her cheeks.

'How does it feel being back after all this time?'

Alex's top lip curled. 'Same as ever. I arrive and then I can't wait to leave.'

'You can't mean that, Alex. It's years since you've been

home. And the entire family is here…surely you want to spend time with them?'

His eyes roamed across the crowd as Jane spoke and she noticed them pause as they reached his father, the Duke, his gaze turning wistful as it often did when he watched his father. She suspected he longed to have the same easy rapport Dominic had with their father, but that he simply did not know how to change—their relationship had been tetchy for as long as Jane had known him. That wistfulness didn't last long. His expression soon hardened.

'I do mean it. This is no longer my home. Foxbourne is. Let's not talk about that, Janey. Tell me, how is Pippin?'

Jane's throat tightened, aching at the mention of her beloved mare. 'She died, Alex. Last year.'

Genuine shock and sympathy played across Alex's features. '*Last year?* Why didn't you tell me?'

'When would I tell you? You are never here and, in London…it's not the same somehow.'

'But… Oh, God, Janey. I'm sorry. What are you riding now?'

Horses had always been their shared passion and they were the love of Alex's life. He bred and trained horses at Foxbourne Manor and had built a solid reputation for producing first-class riding and carriage horses.

'Sandy.'

'*Sandy?*' Alex burst out laughing, but quickly sobered. He searched Jane's expression, a frown knitting his brows. 'I thought you were joking, but you're not. How can a plod like old Sandy be a suitable mount for a rider of your quality?'

'Papa said it's not worth me having a new horse when Sandy is there doing nothing.'

'Your *father* said that? Now I know you're gammoning

me—he's always been so proud of your skill as a horse-woman. It was the old witch, wasn't it? What *is* her game?'

Jane burned with humiliation. Her stepmother's game was to make Jane's life so intolerable she would view marriage to Sir Denzil as preferable. But she wouldn't discuss such a subject with Alex of all people.

'Shall I have a word with your papa, Janey? I've got a filly at Foxbourne that would be perfect for you... I'd give him a good price. Half what she's worth.'

Alex hadn't changed. He'd always been ready and willing to take up cudgels on Jane's behalf whenever she was treated unfairly. To see that protective streak still in evidence infused her with a warm glow. She might not have Alex's love, but he did care for her. With that, she must be content.

'I would rather you said nothing, Alex. He'll only tell Stepmama and you know how cross she'll be if she thinks I've been complaining about my lot. It's not worth the upset, but I do appreciate the offer.'

'You're too forgiving, Janey. I've always said so. Look at the number of times you've forgiven me!' He winked at her and they both smiled at the shared memories. 'But I'll not say anything if you prefer me not to. Now, I really ought to mingle. Not that I want to, but I did promise Aunt Cecily and my stepmother I would be sociable.' Alex's father had remarried five years before. 'I'll see you later, I expect.'

Off he strode, leaving Jane deflated and with a headache pinching her forehead. She rubbed it absently. The thought of joining one of the loudly chattering groups clustered around the lawn held little appeal. Stepmama was talking to Sir Denzil Pikeford and Jane turned away before Stepmama could wave her over. She really couldn't face that bore with her emotions in such a raw state.

She slipped through a gate into the apple orchard next to the lawn and on into the copse beyond, on the far side of which was the Abbey lake where, it was said, the monks used to raise fish to supplement their diet. The fresher air by the water would hopefully help her headache. And no one would miss her.

Chapter Two

Tension gripped Alex as he made polite conversation with his father's guests. He didn't belong here. Even in this crowd, even among his family, he felt alone. Separate. For ever the outsider.

He hadn't been back to the Abbey since Olivia's wedding and was only here now because it was the first time in over four years the entire Beauchamp family had all been together under one roof. The rest had been here a month already and he had only finally agreed to attend the annual Abbey garden party because Dominic threatened to drive up to Foxbourne to fetch him. He'd arrived yesterday and fully intended to leave tomorrow.

An hour or more of small talk and sipping cider-apple punch was enough to try any man's patience and Alex had less than his fair share of that. When dealing with people, at least. Horses…now that was another matter. There, his patience knew no bounds. With a smile and a gesture towards the house, he extricated himself from an in-depth conversation about last year's appalling weather—still the main topic of conversation for country folk—and he slipped away, feeling his tension dissipate as he left the crowds behind. Once inside, he hurried through the library, and out on to the terrace that hugged the east wing of the Abbey. Down the steps, along the stone-flagged path that bisected the formal garden, through the arch cut into the beech hedge and out on to the path beyond. It took less than a minute to reach his goal: the small gate that opened into a copse of ornamental trees.

He closed the gate behind him.

Alone. As always. As he liked it.

Nothing but trees. No need to put on a charade. No need for polite conversation about trivialities.

He leaned back against the trunk of a copper beech and closed his eyes. It had been as painful as he feared, coming back. The family had all come out to greet him. Alex had tolerated hugs from his aunts and his sister, but when Father had come forward, his arms opening, Alex had thrust out his hand for a handshake, quashing his guilt at his father's sorrowful expression. He couldn't explain the aversion he felt for his father, but it was undeniable. Every time they met, Alex felt like a cat having its fur rubbed the wrong way and he couldn't wait to get away.

Then last night, in his old bedchamber, the dreams returned. Not as badly as in his childhood, but enough to unsettle him and for him to wake this morning with that old feeling of impending doom pressing down on him.

It was good to see the rest of the family, though. And dear Jane…his childhood playmate: the squire to his knight, the soldier to his general, the pirate to his captain. Shame about Pippin… God knew what her father was about, allowing that old witch to pick on poor Jane the way she did.

Alex pushed away from the tree and shrugged out of his jacket, then rolled up his shirtsleeves. Warm, dry days had been few and far between this summer—although it was still an improvement on last—but today was one of them: the sun high in a cloudless sky and insects humming. Alex wandered through the trees, his jacket hooked over his shoulder, absorbing the peace, disturbed only by the occasional burst of laughter from the garden party, taking little notice of where he was going. It was only when the sun reflecting off the surface of the lake dazzled him that he realised where he was. He stopped, his guts churning in that old familiar way.

He'd had no intention of coming here, to the place where it had happened. His mother's favourite place. And yet his feet had led him there. Unerringly. As they always did. The summer house overlooking the lake was no more— destroyed by his father after his mother died, a weeping willow planted in its place, in her memory.

The willow had grown in the years since he had last seen it, its fronds now sweeping the ground, and the surrounding trees and shrubs—also planted after her death— had matured, isolating the willow in a clearing bounded by woodland and water.

He stood, just looking, the dark memories close, clawing their way slowly, inexorably, out of the chasm of the past. His heart drummed in his chest, nausea rising to crowd his throat as he shoved those chilling memories of his childhood—of that day—back into the depths and slammed a mental lid on them. He'd had enough practice at keeping them at bay. Eighteen years of practice—he'd only been seven when his mother died…when she was killed.

He shoved harder, feeling sweat bead his forehead. He shouldn't have come here, should've stayed with the others, endured their chatter and their laughter, but it was the same every time he returned to his childhood home. No matter his best intentions, this spot drew him like a lodestone.

The sound of a scuffle and a scream, quickly cut off,

grabbed his attention. He scanned his surroundings, still shaken by the past that lurked, ready to catch him unawares. He saw no one, but a muffled cry and a grunted oath sounded from beyond a clump of rhododendrons. His heart thudded. Those sounds… The memories swirled, trying to form. He swore and strode into the copse, rounding the bushes. Whatever he saw would be preferable to the images hovering at the edge of his mind.

'No! Please! Stop!'

Breathless. Pleading. Scared.

No…*terrified.* Alex broke into a run, deeper into the trees, even as the sound of a slap rang out. He rounded another thicket.

Rage exploded through him—a starburst of fury that electrified every single nerve ending and muscle. He hauled the man off the woman beneath him and jerked him around, vaguely registering the stink of alcohol. His fist flew and he relished the satisfaction of the crunch of bone and the bright claret spurt of blood. He cast the man aside.

She was curled into a defensive ball, her back convulsing with silent sobs. Alex knew that feeling…he shoved again at the memory that threatened to burst free. The past needed to stay in the past. He fell to his knees and gathered the woman into his arms.

'Shh…shh. You're safe. He's gone.'

He'd recognised him. Sir Denzil Pikeford, a local landowner, who'd been well into his cups when Alex spoke to him earlier and now stumbled away through the trees, hands cupping his bloody nose. Pikeford would suffer the consequences for this, but he could wait.

He held the woman's head to his chest as he stroked down her back, soothing her, registering the bare skin, the ripped clothing. Her shuddering sobs gradually subsided. Her breathing hitched. Slowed. Hitched again.

'There now. You're safe.'

Alex looked down. And realised for the first time she was a lady…one of his father's guests then, not a maid, or an unwary farm girl caught off guard.

'Alex?'

A quiet, halting enquiry. She looked up, face blotchy with tears, one cheek stark red, eyes puffy, ringed by spiky wet eyelashes. Recognition thumped Alex square in the chest. He recalled the slap and another surge of fury rolled through him. How could anyone single out a girl as kind and inoffensive as Jane?

She pulled away from him with a gasp, frantic hands scrabbling to gather the tattered remnants of her gown to cover her exposed breasts. Then her eyes rounded with horror as voices called out. The sound of feet trampling the undergrowth came closer. Swiftly, Alex reached for his jacket—fallen nearby—and slung it around Jane before, still on his knees, twisting his torso to face her parents.

'By God, sir! What is this?'

Lord Stowford, Jane's father, was mottled with rage. Alex stood to face him, but before he could speak Jane's stepmother reached her husband's side.

'Oh! You *wicked, deceitful* girl! You are ruined!' She turned to her husband. 'Stowford! *Do* something!'

'Beauchamp! You shall answer—'

'Papa! No! Alex saved me. It was Sir D-Denzil.' Jane scrambled to her feet.

'I knew it!' Lady Stowford pressed one hand to her bosom and plied her fan vigorously with the other. 'As soon as I saw you sneaking off with him!'

Alex frowned, glancing down at Jane. Surely she knew better than to be so careless? But…he took in Lady Stowford's expression. The smug smile in her eyes. If she'd *seen*

Jane and Pikeford, why not follow them straight away, and intervene?

Jane swayed and Alex moved closer, cupped her elbow, supporting her. Shivers racked her body and tears rolled down her face. Alex stared in disgust at Jane's stepmother. Cold-hearted witch! What kind of a female…a *mother*… was she? Where was her concern for another female in distress, let alone one she had raised from a baby? But, then…she had always resented Jane.

'I didn't.' Jane was shaking her head in frantic denial. 'I *s-s-swear* it, Papa! I had the headache and hoped a walk by the water would help. He followed me. He *grabbed* me.'

'It matters not! You are ruined!' Lady Stowford's words rang with triumph. 'Stowford! Go and find Sir Denzil at once. He must make an honest woman of Jane. Then all will be well.' She eyed Jane with pitiless disdain. 'I will not allow your disgrace to taint your sisters.'

'Noooo!' Jane sagged against Alex as she uttered a low moan of despair.

'Have you no compassion?' Alex glared at Lady Stowford. A memory surfaced…of Her Ladyship trying hard to promote a match between Pikeford and Jane during last Season. And Jane's disgust at the idea. 'That foul drunkard *attacked* your daughter! He was forcing himself on her and you would have her *marry* him?'

Her haughty gaze raked Alex. 'I would, as would any responsible parent. At least she will have a husband at long last! She should be grateful.' She turned to her husband, his expression that of a man wishing he was a thousand miles away. 'Well, Stowford? Do not just stand there. Go and find Sir Denzil. You *must* see Jane *has* to be wed now she is no longer pure.'

'No! He didn't… I am still… Alex stopped him in time, Papa! *Please*, Papa!'

'Stowford! You must think of our other daughters. *Their* reputations are what is important now. Jane must be wed.'

'Then *I* shall marry her.' Alex released Jane's elbow and wrapped his arm around her waist, hauling her into his side.

'Alex?'

His heart plummeted at that voice. Behind the Stowfords three figures came into view: Alex's father in the lead of his uncles, Vernon and Zach. Father's eyes swept the group. Returned to linger on Jane, then levelled a searching look at Alex.

'What happened? Pikeford? We saw him stagger out of the copse just now.'

Grateful for his father's swift understanding, Alex nodded. He held that silver-grey gaze, his gut churning with the same mix of hopeless love and unwanted revulsion he always felt towards this man he so desperately longed to love unconditionally. Father walked forward, ranging himself alongside Alex and Jane.

'This matter can be contained, Stowford. No one will know but us. There is no need to force Jane to marry anyone.'

The swell of relief was brief. One look at Lady Stowford's expression—even as she was agreeing with his father—was enough to stir Alex's doubts. That old witch wouldn't rest until she had her wish—Jane married off, no matter the circumstances.

Jane was still trembling, like an injured bird…fragile… terrified.

'No,' he heard himself say. He slid his arm from around Jane's waist and grasped her shoulders, manoeuvring her so he could look straight into her swollen eyes. 'Lady Jane Colebrooke…will you do me the honour of being my wife?'

* * *

Jane's head pounded. She shouldn't accept him. She knew she shouldn't—this was just like Alex. Impulsive. Doing things he would later regret. He'd been like it all through their childhood. But Jane had no energy. No strength. No courage. The fear Stepmama would, somehow, force her to marry Pikeford was all-consuming.

She had dwindled until she was a mere husk and, like a husk, she allowed herself to be carried on the wind. 'Yes.'

All she wanted was for all of this—and all of them—to go away. The Duke, she could see, was uneasy. But Stepmama—oh, she was delighted! Not only was her nuisance of a stepdaughter finally off her hands, but the family would now be irrevocably connected to that of the Duke of Cheriton, one of the most powerful and influential men in the land.

Jane's conscience made a valiant late attempt at fairness and she clutched Alex's hand.

'Alex! No… I should not have… I am not thinking straight… You need not…'

Her breathless protest died away as he held her gaze with those gorgeous golden-brown eyes of his. Alex grinned that old reckless care-for-nothing grin that had stolen Jane's young heart years before. He pulled her close and put his lips to her ear.

'C'mon, Janey. It'll be all right. It'll be fun.'

The same words with which he had led her into devilment during their youth—he to prove he wouldn't be confined by rules; she, willing to do anything to escape Stepmama and to please her childhood hero. There had always been consequences, of course, but now—here was her chance to escape Stepmama for good. Never again would she have to bite her tongue as she endured one of Stepmama's diatribes about how plain and useless she was.

'Thank you.'

She caught the Duke's frown from the corner of her eye and quailed inside. But it seemed Alex had noticed, too, because his arm snaked around her waist again and he faced his father, chin jutting, head high, bringing to mind the defiant boy, full of bravado.

'Father?'

His challenge was unmistakable. A muscle leapt in the Duke's jaw, but he nodded.

'If it is your wish, then we will make the arrangements. Wait here.'

He turned on his heel and strode away and Jane felt the tension leach from Alex. She eyed those left in the clearing. Stepmama was already crowing to Papa about the connection and the splendid society wedding she would arrange. Alex's uncle, Lord Vernon Beauchamp, walked over to Alex and Jane, followed by Mr Graystoke—a half-Romany whose father was an earl, and who was married to Alex's Aunt Cecily, but refused to be called 'uncle'. Stepmama—for all she fawned over the Duke—held his brother-in-law in disdain and made no secret of the fact.

'Alex? What can I do to help?' Concern etched Lord Vernon's face as he gripped his nephew's shoulder.

'You can shut *her* up about lavish society weddings,' Alex growled. He looked down at Jane. 'Come and stay at the Abbey, Janey. Don't go back there and let her terrorise you into having what *she* wants. Unless…do you *want* a big wedding?'

Jane shook her head. She could think of nothing worse. 'Stepmama only wants one because she thinks it will help my sisters attract husbands.'

Mr Graystoke's lip curled. He strolled unhurriedly across to where Stepmama was still talking at Papa. Silence descended.

'The young couple prefer a quiet wedding. Family only,' he said.

Papa flushed red as Stepmama visibly bristled.

'Who do you think—?'

Her mouth shut with a snap as Lord Vernon joined them.

'And Lady Jane will stay at the Abbey until Alex obtains the licence,' he drawled. 'I foresee no objection from the Bishop and you may rest assured Jane will be well chaperoned in the meantime.'

'I shall come myself to collect her belongings,' Mr Graystoke added and Stepmama spluttered, spots of outrage colouring her cheeks. 'Shall we say in two hours? If you leave now, that should give you sufficient time to pack her belongings.'

The two men turned their backs on her parents and strolled back to Alex and Jane.

'*That* shut her up,' Lord Vernon said, with a wink.

Over his shoulder, Jane watched her parents leave, Stepmama gesticulating furiously. Even though she wanted them gone, it still hurt to see Papa walk away without a word.

'Maybe you should take her back to the house, Alex, and not wait for Leo,' said Mr Graystoke. 'She's had a shock.' He crouched slightly and tipped up her chin, holding her gaze with his dark eyes. 'All will be well, my dear. You are part of the family now. You are protected.'

The anxiety agitating her stomach settled and stilled. 'Thank you.' She glanced up at Alex, who was frowning at her. 'What is it?'

'You can't go back with your gown all torn like that. I—'

His jaw snapped shut and Jane followed his gaze. Alex's father, a gown draped over one arm, was approaching, the Duchess—Alex's stepmother—by his side.

'Vern, Zach, Alex…come. Let us return to our guests. Rosalind will help Jane. The fewer people who know what happened here, the better.'

'We'd better find a way to stop Lady Stowford from spewing her poison all over the district, then,' said Lord Vernon. 'I believe Zach and I *might* have contrived to upset her. Just a smidgeon, you understand. And *totally* without intention.' The twinkle in his eyes belied his apologetic tone.

'I have already helped the Stowfords to understand it is in their best interests to remain quiet,' said the Duke.

'We met them on their way back to the house,' added the Duchess, 'and Lady Stowford made the mistake of attempting to pull rank on Leo, claiming rights as the mother of the bride. I believe she now accepts it is what Alex and Jane want that is important. Now, off you go, you men, and leave me and Jane to make her respectable. Go on! Shoo!'

Chapter Three

Left alone with the Duchess, Jane found her voice again.

'I shouldn't have accepted Alex, Your Grace. I'm sorry. He doesn't want to marry me. I know he doesn't. Step-mama gave him no choice.' Suppressed tears thickened her voice. Why would anyone want to marry her? She wasn't pretty or even vivacious. Alex had been trapped. 'She *would* keep saying I was ruined and I must marry S-Sir Denzil.'

'Jane…you cannot possibly marry that villain after what he tried to do.' The Duchess took her hand. 'You and Alex have always been friends, have you not?'

Jane nodded.

'Then allow him to help his friend and…' The Duchess paused, a line stitched between her brows. Then her chin tilted. 'And, in return, you can be a friend to him. Alex *needs* someone like you in his life…' she nodded, emphasising her words '…although he would never admit it. Unless, of course, the thought of being wed to him truly repels you?'

Hazel eyes searched Jane's face. She shook her head. No. That thought did not repel her. Not at all.

'Good. Now, come, let us get this gown off you and

make you respectable. I have even brought a comb and hairpins. No one will guess what so nearly happened and Leo has already shut Sir Denzil in one of the outbuildings until he sobers up and can be…um…*"brought to fully appreciate the iniquity of his actions"* were, I believe, Leo's exact words.'

They were all being so kind, but Jane dreaded to think what they really thought of her. *She* knew Alex had stopped Pikeford in time, but did anyone else believe her? She shuddered at the memory of his hand painfully squeezing her breast…his fingers between her legs… Her stomach roiled, pushing the contents up. She ran to a nearby bush, bent double and vomited. Tears blurred her eyes. She could not stop retching, even after her stomach was empty and sore. Gradually, the heaving slowed and she became aware of hands supporting her, holding her hair back.

'Better now?'

'Yes. Thank you, Your Grace.'

'Then let us make you respectable again and return to the house.'

They avoided the lawn at the rear of the Abbey, where the garden party continued, by following the lake around until they met the grass path that wound up through the copse towards the formal gardens leading to the terrace and the library. The Duchess peered through the hedge into the gardens before smiling encouragingly at Jane.

'They're empty. When the Duke told me what had happened, I ordered bath water to be heated and a bedchamber prepared. You must be exhausted. Come.'

She slipped her arm around Jane's waist and they hurried through the gardens and up the steps to the terrace, where one of the French doors into the library stood open. Within minutes the Duchess had whisked Jane upstairs.

* * *

Father, as was his wont, moved swiftly to avert any scandal. Pikeford had already left for Plymouth, escorted by two footmen to ensure he took passage on the first ship bound for the Continent, thus thwarting Alex of the chance to thump the bastard again. But Father did not broach the subject of Alex's impending marriage until after dinner that evening, when he invited Alex to join him in his study.

Alex braced himself for the interrogation, every muscle locked tight, as though his body was preparing itself for physical battle.

'Well, Alex?'

Alex unclenched his jaw with an effort. 'Well… I hope you will wish us happy, sir.'

Father stared at him for several seconds, his eyes troubled, before pouring them both a glass of brandy. He handed one to Alex and gestured for him to sit in one of the pair of wingback chairs either side of the unlit hearth.

'You've had time to think this through, Son. Marriage is a big step—it is not something that should be rushed into on a whim.'

'It was *not* a whim.' As ever, he instinctively opposed Father.

One dark eyebrow flicked high. 'Did you know this morning you would propose to Lady Jane Colebrooke today?'

'Of course not! I—'

'Then it was a whim.'

As Alex opened his mouth to protest again, Father held up one hand. 'Hear me out, Alex, before you shoot me down again.'

Alex subsided. How he wished he could emulate Father's cool, calm control. Nothing ever seemed to rattle him whereas he… Alex…flew into the boughs at the slightest provocation. He must learn to control that tendency with a wife to consider.

His insides clenched. A wife! Marriage! He'd never, ever imagined marrying. He knew himself too well to believe he could ever make a good husband.

'It's not too late to change your mind, Alex. Once you exchange your vows, you will be together for life.'

'My mind is made up,' Alex muttered.

'Nevertheless you should listen to what I am about to say, not only for your own sake, but for Jane's, as well.'

'*Jane's* sake?'

Father didn't reply, but held Alex's gaze with his own.

'Jane will be happy to get away from that witch of a stepmother of hers.'

'Granted. But if I can guarantee you that Jane will never have to return to her father's house, will you reconsider your decision?'

Alex stared at his father. 'How?'

Hope warred with resentment inside. Hope, because marriage *was* irrevocable. His father was right, although Alex would never admit that aloud. Resentment because… well, resentment was his habitual reaction to everything his father said or did.

'I will undertake to find her a decent husband.'

He didn't like the sound of that. How could his father possibly know a man's character, or how he might change? Once Jane was wed, that would be it. She'd be bound for life to some stranger she didn't even know. Every fibre of his being rebelled against that idea… Jane was his friend. He'd always protected her, right from when they were children.

'You think I couldn't make her a decent husband? We've been friends a long time.'

'I am aware of that. But…you're only five-and-twenty, Alex. It's a young age for a man to take such a big step.'

'Dom is only a year older than me. He got married this year.'

'He thought it his duty. But then, thank goodness, he fell in love. Besides, you and Dominic are very different characters.'

Alex scowled, biting back the urge to rip up at his father. The truth hurt sometimes.

'*You* were only eighteen when you married my mother.'

'The circumstances were very different. My father was dying and fretting over the succession of the dukedom. I married for him.' Father thrust his hand through his hair. 'Alex…this is not wise… Allow me to find a good husband for Jane… Don't rush into this. You might both live to regret it.'

Alex drained his glass and rose to his feet. 'And we might not! This is *my* decision. I leave for Exeter first thing to obtain the licence.' He'd already arranged for Dominic to drive him in his curricle. 'The wedding will take place as soon as possible.'

Then he could leave this place with all its threatening memories and go home to Foxbourne where he was happiest.

'I intend to make the same offer to Jane tomorrow.' Father's voice was clipped. 'She deserves to know she has a choice.'

Alex's simmering temper boiled up at that. 'There is no need for you to involve yourself—I don't want you pressuring Jane just because you think you know what is best. You cannot manipulate us to your bidding like you manipulate everyone else. I bid you goodnight.'

His temper raged until he was halfway to his bedchamber when—as so often happened where his father was concerned—it cooled as suddenly as if doused in a bucket of icy water, leaving shame behind. He contemplated rejoining the family downstairs but couldn't face having to act the part of happy brother, nephew and son. Not to mention happy prospective bridegroom. He couldn't face his family. Couldn't face his father again. He continued on to his room, eyeing the bed with disfavour, already anticipating the restless night to come.

Why was life never straightforward?

He'd refused his father's offer, driven by that familiar but inexplicable defiance, but that didn't mean he knew exactly what he did want.

He was torn.

He'd been fully reconciled to life as a bachelor, with no need—or wish—to share his life with anyone. And as for marriage to Jane—she was like his little sister! No. She was more than that. She was, and always had been, his friend. But…marriage? Didn't that mean sharing his feelings and his innermost thoughts? That was unthinkable. He kept those to himself. Always had. He was an island—even when he was out with his friends, carousing, he was always separate, somehow, and that was how he liked it.

But, strangely, now he was faced with it, a part of him—a newly emerging, hesitant and hazy part of him—quite *liked* the idea of marriage. To Jane. At least she knew him and knew about his past. And at least she never looked at him with that infuriating mix of sympathy and pity he all too often identified in his family's expressions. He and Jane were friends—surely they could at least be comfortable together, as long as he learned to suppress his black moods. He could do it with the horses…when he worked with them it was as though nothing else existed. No past. No future. Just him and the horse. Could he learn to do the same for Jane?

And Jane loved horses as much as he did—he was sure she would be as happy at Foxbourne as he was.

It would be a better start than many couples experienced.

Jane must have slept right through to the next morning because she vaguely recalled waking at one point to find it was night-time, but now, as she propped herself up on her elbows, she could see daylight limning the curtains. Memories of the previous day loomed—Pikeford following her, his attack, his *strength*...so much more than she could have imagined. It was frighteningly impossible to fight him off and then, just as she despaired of ever stopping him, Alex had rescued her.

She flopped back on to the mattress, biting her lip against the hot sting of tears. How long had she dreamed of him seeing her as someone other than simply *good old Janey*, the girl next door? How many years had she fed her fantasies with images of him realising, at last, that he loved her...proposing to her...?

But not like this. *Never* like this!

Sick dread clogged her throat. She was in an impossible situation. If she protected Alex against his spontaneous, quixotic gesture then she must go home, to the stepmother who would not hesitate to marry her off to Sir Denzil Pikeford. And *he* would be perfectly willing...

She shuddered, rolling on to her side, curling into a ball, her arms wrapped around her torso. She would die rather than end up as Pikeford's wife. Her stomach roiled in disgust.

I cannot lie here for ever. I must face this some time.

She forced herself to rise, crossing to the window and pulling back the curtains. It was early, the sun still low in the sky. A movement caught her eye and she saw a curricle with two male occupants heading away from the Abbey.

She couldn't be sure, but she suspected the passenger was Alex and she recognised Dominic's matched bays. She frowned. Where were they off to so early? Would Alex leave in order to avoid her? He had run away rather than face unpleasant consequences when he was younger, but she couldn't believe Dominic would aid and abet him.

There's only one way to find out.

After dressing—a trunk containing her belongings had appeared as if by magic at the foot of her bed—she ventured downstairs only to find it was too early for the rest of the family to be up and about. She refused breakfast, too embarrassed to eat when none of the family was present. Ignoring her growling stomach, she selected a book from the library and settled in an armchair to pass the time until someone else appeared.

That someone, to her dismay, was the Duke of Cheriton. Jane shot to her feet, nerves churning her stomach. The Duke had never been anything but courteous to her, but he was a formidable and powerful man and some of Alex's feelings about his father had inevitably rubbed off on her over the years.

'Good morning, Jane.' The Duke gestured, indicating she should sit again. She perched on the edge of the chair. 'Grantham said I would find you in here. Are you well rested?'

'Yes, thank you, Your Grace.'

He pulled another chair across to sit opposite. 'You have a bruise on your face, I see. Did Pikeford injure you anywhere else?'

Jane shook her head, mortified at talking of such matters, nervy at being the sole focus of the Duke's attention.

His eyes narrowed and a groove appeared between his black brows. 'Unfortunately neither the Duchess nor my sister are awake, but I can send for a maid if you are uncomfortable being here alone with me.'

Her face flamed. How rude he must think her, when she had known him all her life.

'It is understandable you are still shaken after the events of yesterday.' He went to the door. She heard a murmur of voices, then he returned to sit again.

'I—I thought I saw Alex leaving,' Jane said.

A smile crinkled the Duke's eyes. 'He has not run off, you know. He outgrew that tendency a few years ago, I'm pleased to say. Dominic is driving him to Exeter, to obtain a marriage licence.'

She struggled to meet his gaze. But she must say this... she couldn't allow Alex to sacrifice himself for her. 'I will not hold him to his promise, Your Grace. I could not forgive myself if Alex married me only to regret it. *Please*. Can you tell him he need not marry me?'

'I have told him already and—'

He fell silent as the door opened and Jane breathed a sigh of relief when Olivia, her old friend and only eight months older than Jane, entered.

'Grantham said you needed me in here, Papa. Good morning, Jane.'

Olivia smiled, pulling a footstool over to sit close to Jane. She clasped her hand.

'Thank you, Livvy. Now, as I was about to say, Jane... Alex understands very well he is under no obligation to marry you and that, if he chooses not to proceed, I shall ensure you never have to return to your father's house. But I want you to understand—this offer I am about to make is for *your* benefit, Jane. Not Alexander's.' The Duke rose and crossed to the window, where the early morning sun lit his face, highlighting the silvering at his temples and the lines of stress around his eyes and mouth. 'You have known my son all your life and you know he is not always an easy man. My fear is that if he feels constrained to go ahead with your union—even by his own decision—then, later, he may well rebel against it. And you would bear the brunt of his resentment.

'You deserve to be happy in your marriage, Jane, and that is why I sought you out this morning...to make you the same offer I made to Alex. There is a third way and you may trust me when I say I shall find a way for you to be safe from both your stepmother and Pikeford.'

He returned to his chair, his silver-grey gaze on Jane's face. She swallowed. She should grab his offer with both hands. For Alex's sake. But the Duchess's words resounded in her head, keeping her silent. Alex *did* need a friend... not the friends with whom he spent his time on the town, but someone who would be there for him, day after day. Night after night. Someone to provide him with a safe anchor during those times the past came back to haunt him. Because haunt him it did. They all knew it. But no one had ever found the way to help him come to terms with the day he had discovered his mother's violated body.

And Jane, God help her, wanted to be that friend to him. If...

'What was Alex's answer to your offer, sir?'

The Duke exchanged a wry smile with his daughter. 'He threw it right back in my face and left for Exeter at first light. I believe his exact words were, "You cannot manipulate us to your bidding like you manipulate everyone else".'

Jane gasped and sympathy for the Duke buried her earlier nervousness. 'I am sorry. I don't understand—'

Olivia moved to perch on the arm of Jane's chair and hugged her. 'None of us understands my brother, Jane— there's no need for you to apologise for him. But you do need to think carefully about what *you* want. Papa will help you find a decent husband, if you decide against marrying Alex, and you mustn't be afraid the rest of us will hold it against you. You will still be our dear friend, whatever you decide.'

'Thank you, Livvy. That means a lot.' Jane pulled away from her friend's embrace, and stood up to face Alex's father. 'And thank you for your offer, Your Grace. I do appreciate it. But…as long as Alex does not change his mind and is still prepared to go ahead, I choose to marry Alex. I—I hope you do not mind? I—I…' She hauled in a breath. 'I cannot quite explain it, but…it feels right.' She laid her hand against her chest. 'In here. It feels right.'

Hot embarrassment flooded her. That was as good as a confession that she loved Alex, but she wanted to soothe any misgivings either the Duke or Olivia had about this marriage.

'I do not mind at all, Jane. In fact, I am delighted,' said the Duke. 'As I hope I made clear, my intervention was not due to any objection to either you or to the match, but merely to reassure you both that you need not feel trapped by what occurred yesterday.'

'And *I* say you are a brave woman to take Alex on,' said Olivia. 'But you know what he is like and you have always been friends. Perhaps you are just what he needs.'

She hugged Jane, and kissed her cheek. 'Welcome to the Beauchamp family.'

Chapter Four

Preparations for the wedding gained momentum throughout the day and Jane allowed herself to be swept along despite the unease that writhed in her stomach like a restless
snake. She needed to speak to Alex. It was all very well
the family assuming the matter was irrevocably settled
but what if, now he'd had time to think, Alex had changed
his mind?

All the frenetic activity infected the Beauchamps' dogs:
the Duchess's wolfhound, Hector, Myrtle, a three-legged,
bull-baiting type of terrier belonging to Mr Graystoke, and
Liberty's Romeo. The three of them became increasingly
excited, chasing one another around the house, in and out
of the rooms, until Romeo darted in front of a footman
carrying a tray of china and he went flying. The resulting
crash brought everyone running.

'This is outside of enough!' The Duchess, her hair
awry, shooed the dogs outside. 'The doors are to be kept
shut and woe betide anyone who lets those animals back
inside!'

Even that added to Jane's guilt. The entire household
had been set on its ears just because she had foolishly decided to go for a walk alone.

* * *

The day wore on and, in the late afternoon, Jane found herself helping Alex's two aunts, Lady Cecily and Thea, Lady Vernon, to arrange flowers in three matching lead-crystal cut-glass vases to decorate the hall.

'These vases were made by Stour Crystal,' Lady Vernon said, her pride clear.

Jane knew Lord Vernon's wife came from a family of Worcestershire glassmakers. 'Is that your father's manufactory?'

'It is. Well, it belongs to my brother now. Papa died two years ago.'

'I am sorry to hear that...but you must be very proud. These are beautiful.'

'They are, aren't they? And yes, I...'

Her voice drifted into silence as the front door flew open and Alex and Dominic bowled in, laughing, the three banished dogs at their heels. Jane stilled, nerves erupting.

'Please leave the dogs outside,' Lady Cecily said to her nephews. 'Rosalind's orders. They are overexcited and have been causing mayhem, with everyone so busy. You're fortunate to have missed the worst of the chaos.'

She looked from Jane to Alex. 'Dominic?'

'Yes, Aunt Cecily?'

'Thea and I would appreciate your opinion on the seating arrangements if you will come to the dining room?'

The three disappeared, leaving Jane facing Alex, anxiety churning her stomach.

'Well, Honeybee, and how are you today?'

Honeybee...the affectionate nickname he had given her when, as a child, she was for ever buzzing around, like a bee around a flower. He sauntered over to the table and picked up one of the lilies still to be placed in the vases.

'I am well, thank you, Alex. You…you've been gone a long time.'

'Oh, I got the licence, all right and tight, if that's been plaguing you,' he said. 'But I must ask you—'

His jaw snapped shut as the Duke and Duchess came into the hall together and Jane's heart sank, knowing Alex wouldn't continue with his father present.

'Alex. You're back,' said the Duke.

'As you see.' Alex replaced the lily on the table, its petals now mangled, and withdrew a document from his pocket. 'With the licence.'

'So, you still wish to proceed?'

'Of course!' Alex took Jane's hand. 'As long as you aren't about to back out on me, Janey?'

She shook her head. Alex grinned, only slightly settling her nerves. She couldn't help but wonder exactly what was going on inside his head.

'We'll leave you in peace.' The Duchess linked her arm through her husband's and they disappeared into the drawing room.

'Sorry about that flower.' Alex nudged the stem of the lily he had destroyed. 'Shall I go and cut you another?'

'No. We already had more than sufficient. But thank you.'

He grinned again, flicked her nose and headed for the staircase. 'I must change my coat and boots. I'll see you later, Janey.'

'What was it you wanted to ask me, Alex? Before your father came in?'

He paused, then turned back to her. 'I just wanted to know if you have everything you need.'

'Yes, thank you.'

She doubted that had been his original question. She watched him bound up the stairs, hope and dread warring in her breast as she wondered what their future held.

* * *

Alex stood in the local church the next morning at eleven, waiting for his bride. He stared at the floor, Dominic by his side, still torn by what was about to happen. Every time his doubts had edged him close to backing out of this marriage, his father had said something that made him leap straight back into those slowly closing leg shackles. And besides...there was Jane to think about. Now she'd been compromised—and the whispers had already started—she must marry someone and quickly. And Alex could not condemn her to marriage with a stranger. That same boyhood instinct to protect her that had spurred him into that rash proposal made sure of that.

'This takes me back,' Dominic whispered. 'Waiting at the altar, fretting that Liberty might not show up, but mark my words...' he gripped Alex's shoulder, and squeezed it '...all your worry will fly away as soon as you set eyes on her.'

Except Dominic married Liberty for love.

Alex half-turned, eyeing the members of his family, sitting in the pews, waiting to witness his marriage to his childhood friend. The only one missing was Olivia, who was attending the bride. Lord Hugo Alastair, her husband, had his hands full coping with their two-year-old twins, Julius and Daisy, helped by Liberty. Alex's father and stepmother were there, with three-year-old Christabel and two-year-old Sebastian—his young half-sister and half-brother—and Susie, their adopted daughter. Further back were Uncle Vernon and Aunt Thea, with their three— Thomas, four, Sophie, two, and one-year-old George— and Aunt Cecily and Zach with three-year-old Florence.

Every one of them had married for love. But Alex, yet again, would be different.

Apart. Alone. Always the outsider.

Except you'll never be alone again. You'll have Jane.

And a whisper of…was that *hope*?…stirred in his heart. He forced down the doubts that clogged his throat, longing for that whisper of hope to be true.

The organ music changed and Alex turned to watch his bride walk up the aisle. Another lump filled his throat… not doubts this time, but concern. She looked desperately uncertain. A wave of protectiveness washed through him. Filled him. She was his responsibility now…her happiness depended on him and he would do all he could to stop her regretting their marriage.

Her gown was beautiful: peach-coloured silk that hugged her slim figure and complemented her mass of shiny conker-brown hair, held back with combs and interwoven with delicate white jasmine flowers, leaving loose tresses to wave down her back—and it was almost as though he were looking at her for the first time, which was absurd because he'd known her for ever. She was two years younger than him, his neighbour and his childhood playmate…he'd known her all her life. Taught her to ride. Led her into plenty of scrapes. And yet, here…now…he seemed to really *see* her. As his friend, Jane, yes…but also as a woman. An attractive woman. Not beautiful, maybe, but her figure was…mouth-watering.

And then all thought and conjecture ceased because she had reached his side and he turned to face the Reverend Padstow, his bride by his side, her sleeve brushing his.

Afterwards, he endured the congratulations and the backslapping outside the church, plastering a smile on his face. He felt like public property. This day couldn't be over soon enough for him. But he kept Jane close by his side, his hand resting at the small of her back. She was part of him now. They were a partnership. She was his wife. And when her father, stepmother and half-sisters approached and he felt her tense, he slid his arm around her waist and held her even closer.

'Well, Jane. This is a happy day indeed.' Lord Stowford thrust out his hand. 'You are a very welcome addition to our family, Alexander. You must visit us whenever you choose.'

Alex ignored the hand and inclined his head. 'I rarely visit Devonshire these days, sir, so you need not fear we will darken your doorstop with any regularity.'

We'll visit you over my dead body.

But it was his wedding day. He was the bridegroom. He must be polite to the guests, even when every nerve in his body craved solitude.

He nodded coolly at Lady Stowford and her daughters, and said to Jane, 'Come, my dear. Our wedding breakfast awaits and our guests must be hungry.'

'Thank you,' she whispered as they walked to the carriage waiting to drive them back to the Abbey. Alex handed Jane in and then collapsed on to the seat beside her, shutting his eyes.

'Are you finding this very trying, Alex?'

He cranked his eyelids open to find her watching him, her eyes filled with concern. They were lovely eyes, now he came to study them properly. Warm brown and thickly lashed and full not only of concern, but of kindness and understanding. And wasn't that typical of Jane? All her worry was for *him*. Even on her wedding day.

'A bit,' he replied.

He straightened. They would be home shortly…except he never thought of it as home any more. Foxbourne was his home now and had been for close on five years. His father had bought the estate, together with its breeding stock, five years before. Alex moved in later that year and, two years later—once he proved he could be trusted to run the place—his father signed it over to him. He loved Foxbourne and he couldn't wait to return. To go home.

He laid his hand against Jane's cheek, registering the softness of her skin.

'Shall you object if we leave here tomorrow? I cannot wait to show you Foxbourne Manor, although I fear it lacks a woman's touch at the moment.'

They would need more indoor staff—he'd led a bachelor's life until now, cared for by only his man, Drabble, and Mr and Mrs Kent, who ran the house.

'I have often longed to run my own household.' Her eyes glowed. 'And I cannot wait to settle into my new home, so I'm happy for us to leave tomorrow.' She smiled, then, and raised her eyebrows. 'And I know you well enough to know you'll be itching to leave here as soon as possible.'

He laughed. 'That I am.' He slipped his arm around her shoulders and hugged her. 'You are a brave woman, taking me on when you know what a moody wretch I can be at times.'

He kissed her cheek and the delicate scent of jasmine wreathed through his senses. Desire sparked through his veins, surprising him.

'Well—' Jane pulled back, capturing his gaze with a teasing smile '—in a straight choice between you and Pikeford I thought black moods a touch easier to cope with than drunkenness and r-r-r...'

Her lips quivered and his heart cracked. He pulled her close, nestled her head to his shoulder. 'Don't, Honeybee. Don't try to be brave and pretend it was nothing.'

She stayed there, trembling, for a few minutes. Then the carriage started to slow and she pulled away from him. Brushed a finger beneath each eye in turn and gave a tiny sniff. Alex handed her his handkerchief without a word.

'Thank you,' she whispered.

They both put on a decent show, Jane probably more successfully than him. To watch her you would never believe anything troubled her, but Alex saw the effort she was making all through that day.

Her family left early—to everyone's relief—and, watching Jane with the Beauchamps afterwards, Alex could see she would fit right in. And why shouldn't she, when she had known them for so long they were like a second family to her?

He watched over her, alert for any hint of distress. None came. And, through the day, Aunt Cecily, too, kept her eye on Jane and often drew her into conversations.

'She will need your patience, Alex.'

Zach joined Alex as the family gathered in the drawing room after dinner that evening.

'I am aware of it.'

Zach turned his dark gaze on Alex. 'She is a woman who was born to lavish care on those around her and she will thrive, given love and care in return. You are a lucky man. I feel you will be good for one another, but do not be surprised if the path is bumpy in the beginning.'

Alex couldn't help grinning. 'Is that your Romany half talking, Zach?'

Zach smiled. 'Perhaps.' He bent to fondle Myrtle's ears. She rarely left his side. 'Or maybe it's more that I know human nature and I know *you*, Alex.'

Alex sobered. Zach was right. He did know Alex—as well as, if not better than, any other member of the family. Their mutual love for and understanding of horses had fostered their friendship and respect. The rest of the family were talented horse riders, but they did not share that natural *feel* for troubled animals, and for horses in particular, that Alex and Zach had in common. Edgecombe, Zach's estate in Hertfordshire, was less than thirty miles from Foxbourne and Zach regularly helped Alex with some of the challenging animals he was sent to 'cure'.

'I know it won't be easy.' He would need patience with Jane, but he suspected she would need even more with him. 'But I'm determined to be the good husband she deserves. We've always been friends. It is a good place to start.'

'Indeed it is.'

Alex noticed his father casting occasional pensive glances at him and Zach as they talked and his stomach clenched, aware Father wanted nothing more than to be as close to Alex as he was to Dominic. He turned away, allowing that same unhappy, unsettling mix of resentment and regret to subside. Why did he always feel that way? The rest of the family loved his father unequivocally and Alex—when he viewed him objectively—saw he was a good man. A good husband. A good father. A good employer. But no matter how he tried to overcome his unreasonable distrust with logic, his emotions always won.

He scanned the room for Jane. She sat with Aunt Thea, their heads together, chatting animatedly—well, Aunt Thea was *always* a veritable bundle of energy—and he wondered, for the first time, if his new wife might help him to change. *Could* he change? Was it possible? Could he, as he longed to do, learn to love his father unconditionally?

That thought unsettled him even more. Maybe he could, in time. But not yet. Now, all he wanted was to leave the Abbey and to return to Foxbourne, where it was safe. He no longer questioned that feeling of insecurity that assailed him at the Abbey. It simply was. It was how he had always felt.

'We are leaving tomorrow,' he said now to Zach.

Zach raised one dark brow. 'That is a pity when you have just arrived. The rest of us plan to remain a little longer—the children do so love to spend time with their cousins.'

'We'll all be sorry to see you go, Son.' Alex stiffened as his father interrupted them. 'But I guessed you would be keen to take Jane to Foxbourne as soon as possible. I've ordered your carriage for nine in the morning, but if you prefer to leave earlier, or later, just send word to the stables.'

'Thank you, Father.'

His father tipped his head to one side and smiled. 'Don't leave it so long to visit us next time.' He reached out and grasped Alex's upper arm. 'We miss you. *I* miss you.'

Alex swallowed, his throat constricted by a painful lump. 'I won't.'

But he knew he would.

He threw a smile at his father and Zach and moved away to join Jane and Aunt Thea on the sofa, wondering again if marriage and, in time, fatherhood might help him relax more around his father. He truly hoped so.

'I've been telling Jane about the children, Alex,' Aunt Thea said.

This was the first time Alex had met baby George, the youngest of Uncle Vernon and Aunt Thea's children. Thomas, with a mop of red curls like his mother's and busy creating havoc wherever he could, and Sophie, a little chestnut-haired poppet, had both grown since he'd last seen them and Alex felt a pang of remorse at missing so much of their childhood. At times like this, he could almost forget those feelings that kept him away. Kept him distant and alone. But then they would rear up, nipping and clawing at the edges of his memories, and he would retreat again, behind his barricades, to safety.

'They're all having such fun here together,' Aunt Thea continued, 'that Rosalind has invited us all to come again at Christmastide. I do hope you and Jane will come—we shall be here from a week before Christmas right up to Twelfth Night.' She looked at Alex hopefully. 'It would be lovely for the entire family to be together.'

'Oh, what a wonderful idea,' said Jane, before Alex could reply. 'I remember coming here at Christmas. How I loved all the old traditions—the Yule log, the Christmas Candle, decorating the house with greenery on Christmas Eve. Do you remember, Alex?' Her eyes turned wistful. 'The fun, the laughter, the games—so different to Christmas at Stowford Place. Stepmama never countenanced those old traditions. To her, Christmas is a religious observance and all about charity for the poor. We never even exchange family gifts, whether on St Nicholas's Day or on Christmas Day as your family did.'

'I remember. I'm sure we'll be able to come.' He said the words, but didn't mean them. Christmas was far too soon—he doubted he would be ready by then to stomach all that enforced gaiety.

Jane smiled happily at Alex. 'I shall look forward to it, especially as we won't be spending much time with you all now—assuming you still wish to leave tomorrow, Alex?'

'I do.' He averted his gaze, guilt at misleading her making him brusque, but there were months to go yet. Time enough to prepare her for disappointment. 'Father has ordered the carriage for nine so, if you'll excuse us, Aunt, I think it's time we retired.'

It was their wedding night. The perfect excuse to go to bed early…no one would question them doing so, especially with an early start in the morning. He stood, helping Jane to rise. Her hand trembled in his as they said their goodnights. If the circumstances had been different and if

Alex had been his brother, or his uncle, there would have been a few pointed, if not ribald, comments made. There were none. It was as though they'd been married for years: no teasing; no winks; no nudges.

He told himself he didn't care. He was used to being the outsider. He read the concern on every face in that room. Well, they needn't worry about him—he was determined he and Jane would be happy together. It wasn't until they were walking side by side up the stairs that it occurred to him the concern was for his bride. He squared his shoulders and hardened his heart. What did he care? He would be the very best husband he could possibly be to Jane. Surely her life with him couldn't be any worse than life with that old witch of a stepmother?

Chapter Five

Jane stared into the mirror. She was ready, clad in her best nightgown, trimmed with lace at the neckline and sleeves and fastened at the bodice with three pairs of blue ribbons. Her hair was loose around her shoulders and Peg, her maid, had brushed it until it shone. She pinched her cheeks and bit her lips to bring a little colour into them. Huge, troubled eyes stared back at her, revealing the dread coiling and writhing in the pit of her stomach. Dread at what was to come.

Eyes...the windows of the soul. What would Alex see in them? Would he even care if she was nervous?

She reached for the scent bottle on the dressing table and dabbed a spot above each collarbone and at her wrists, closing her eyes and breathing in the familiar scent that always calmed her.

Jasmine. Her mother's scent. Not that she remembered her mother but, after she died of childbed fever, Peg had transferred her devotion to Jane, ensuring she grew up knowing about her mother. Peg had even saved a half-used bottle of her mother's scent to give to Jane when she was old enough to understand and, since then, jasmine had infused her with a feeling of peace, even in her most troubled moments.

Except…now…tonight…peace evaded her. Her stomach still swarmed with nerves. She knew what must happen. And she desperately wanted to please Alex. She could not bear for him to regret this step they had taken. But, try as she might, she could not banish the memory of Pikeford.

The weight of him on her. His hands scrabbling at her body. The stink of spirits and of foul, hot breath and stale sweat.

Her stomach lurched and she pressed her fingers to her mouth, swallowing hard.

To give the newlyweds privacy, Jane had been allotted a room in the east wing of the Abbey with Alex in the adjacent bedchamber. The rest of the family slept in the main part of the house, apart from the children who occupied the nursery wing to the west. The quiet weighed on her… no distant murmur of voices, no doors opening and closing, no footsteps coming and going. She could almost believe she was entirely alone…until the sound of the door opening behind her set her pulse galloping.

She swallowed again and stood to face her new husband. Her nerves eased a little. This was Alex. He would not hurt her. As long as she kept her mind on tonight, and the present, and blocked all memories of the other day—surely she could manage that?—then she would cope.

She could hardly believe her long-held fantasy had come true as she gazed at him. He was still half-dressed, his shirt—open at the neck to reveal a tantalising glimpse of chest hair—tucked into his trousers. His thick mahogany brown hair was dishevelled and his amber eyes were fastened on hers, a look in them she had never seen before. She had dreamed of this moment, all those nights she had spent alone in her bed. If only… She thrust that thought away before it could take hold and spoil the night to come. Their wedding night. She clamped her teeth together, determined not to reveal her fear. She forced her lips into a smile as Alex stepped closer, scanning her from top to toe and back again.

'Your hair…it is beautiful. Before I saw you in church, I never imagined…' He lifted a lock that draped over her shoulder, allowing it to slide through his fingers. 'It is so soft, so silky.'

He tipped her chin, tilting her face to his, and his mouth covered hers. A gentle caress. She closed her eyes and concentrated on that. Only that. The warm smoothness of his lips as they moved over hers, unhurriedly. Soothingly. His thumb and forefinger still beneath her chin. No pressure. No force. Her heart lurched, and her breathing hitched.

'Shh…' A whisper of sound.

Concentrate. It's Alex. My love. My handsome hero. This is my dream.

His mouth moved, kissing and nibbling a path from her cheek to her ear. He nipped gently at her lobe, then caressed her neck with lips and tongue, and pleasure… anticipation…tiptoed through her. His arms came around her and tightened, bringing her close, and she relaxed into him. Into his hard body…his lean but muscular form shaping her softer flesh. Then his lips found hers again, moving gently. When his tongue probed her lips, she opened her mouth and let him in.

Alex. Her love. Her husband.

As he explored her mouth, she curled her arms around his waist and then slid her hands up his back, palms flat, learning the size and shape of him through his fine lawn shirt: the muscles either side of the dip of his spine, the wings of his shoulder blades, the broadness of his back, the width of his shoulders, the corded muscles in his arms. The strength of him. The maleness of him.

He murmured, deep in his throat. A sound of appreciation. And a strange, achy feeling gathered at the juncture of her thighs.

His hands wandered lightly over her back, shoulders and arms. Learning her, as she had learned him. They moved lower, cupping her bottom, kneading gently. Without volition, she pressed closer and the ridge of his erection pressed into her stomach. She could not prevent her whimper of distress, and pulled back. He released her bottom, but one hand at the small of her back stopped her moving away completely.

'Shhh, Honeybee. It's all right.'

His warm breath feathered over her lips and then he took her mouth again, deepening the kiss. Despite the anxiety building within her, she responded, kissing him back with fervour and when he again kissed and nibbled her neck, she tipped her head back, exposing it, giving him access, as she clutched at his biceps. She tensed as his lips dipped lower, tracing her collarbone, feeling increasingly helpless and at his mercy as he slowly bent her backwards over his supporting arms. He kissed the upper curve of her breast and then straightened her, soothing her with another kiss even as he played with the lace ruffle at her neckline.

'May I?' His fingers paused at the first of the bows securing the bodice of her nightgown.

She stared into his eyes.

Alex. It is Alex. He won't hurt me.

'Yes.'

She looked down, watching as he untied one bow after the other until all three were undone and her nightgown gaped at the neck, exposing the valley between her breasts. Alex's breath turned ragged, and Jane battled the fear that spiralled within her...the memory that sound evoked...the harsh rattle of Pikeford's breath in her ear as he—

She choked back her cry of distress.

Alex. Alex. It's only Alex.

'Alex… I don't…'

He smiled at her and, in one smooth movement, he pulled his shirt over his head. Distracted, she stared at his torso—the hair covering the curved muscles of his chest and narrowing into a thin line as it dipped below the waist of his trousers. Tentatively, she reached out and touched him. One finger at first, then all five and, finally, she flattened her palm against his warm flesh, the coarse hairs rough against her skin.

She'd be the death of him. When had Jane blossomed into this attractive and desirable woman?

Patience. Patience. We've got all night.

That glimpse of her bosoms was nearly his undoing. How he longed to dive in there and see…touch…taste. But he reined in his passion. A Herculean task when her hand splayed across his chest and her eyes darkened, her tongue flicking out to moisten her lips. He desperately tried to think of something else, to distract him from all that warm, sweet-smelling female flesh within his grasp, but it was nigh on impossible. He was an experienced lover, but this…this was different. It was erotic in a way that coupling with the most beautiful of partners had never been; partly due to her innocence and knowing he would be her first, but mainly—and this surprised him most of all—it was that she was his wife. It was new and it was scary, but it was sensual at the same time. He, who had always prided himself on his independence and his need for no one, was aroused by the bond that now linked them together for the rest of their lives.

A groan tore free from deep, deep within him—and he reached for her again, sliding his hands across her shoulders to hook his thumbs inside the neck of her nightgown.

Gently he slipped the bodice from her shoulders, exposing her breasts—so much fuller than he would have imagined given her slender figure—round and firm, with dusky pink nipples at their peaks. He held the bunched fabric at her waist as his other hand drifted over the soft curve of her breast, his fingers closing around perfection, kneading gently.

'I didn't expect—' He fell silent as Jane tensed, even more drastically than before. This time, she was as rigid as a statue carved from stone. He released her breast and lowered his hand. 'What is it, Janey?'

She shook her head, mute, but he could *feel* her distress.

'I won't hurt you. You know that, don't you?'

She nodded.

But she didn't believe it yet…he could tell. He reined in his rampant desire, curbing his needs.

'Come. Let me warm you.' He tugged her nightgown up to cover her again and then drew her into his arms, holding her until she stopped trembling.

'I'm sorry, Alex.' She stepped back, holding her nightgown close, covering her breasts.

'You have no need to fear me, Janey. I will never force you to do anything until you are ready.'

She searched his face. 'I know. I am being foolish.'

He shook his head. 'You are not foolish.'

She held out her hand and he took it and followed when she led him to the bed, her breaths short and sharp in the silence. He did not fool himself it was passion that quickened her breathing. They lay down, side by side, and he turned to her, resting his hand on her ribcage, beneath her breasts. He leaned over and kissed her, ignoring the clamour of his own body to possess her. To possess his wife. He could be patient. There was no hurry.

He focused his mind and his senses on the pleasure of

kissing. Just kissing. He explored her mouth without haste, teasing responses from her until she was relaxed and following his lead, their tongues dancing, the occasional low moan vibrating in her throat. He stroked her face...her hair, neck, shoulders, arms...until she embraced him, her fingers threading through his hair. Still he held his passions on a tight rein, waiting for the right moment.

Her restless shift on the bed was his cue and he brushed the side of her breast. She turned slightly, pressing into his touch. Her breasts were still covered as he stroked and caressed, slowly nearing her nipple. He pinched lightly and she gasped into his mouth.

'Was that good?'

'Yes.'

She gasped again as he gently flicked, then moaned as he bent his head and licked her nipple through the fabric, turning it transparent, the darker areole visible when he raised his head to look.

'Beautiful,' he breathed.

A word he had never linked with Jane before. She had always been...Jane. But seeing her, lying beside him, a smile hovering around her parted lips and her eyelids heavy over passion-filled eyes...it was the exact word he needed. Of a sudden, his throat tightened and his heart skipped a beat.

Jane.

Beautiful. Sensual. And his *wife*.

But frightened, too.

The responsibility...his obligation to another human being...almost sent him fleeing from the bed. But then...

'Alex,' she breathed and pulled his head back to her breast, her fingers tangled in his hair.

And that fleeting moment of fear...of uncertainty... passed.

He tugged her nightgown down to expose her breasts again and took his time—licking, suckling and nibbling, smoothing and stroking her silken skin until she was moving restlessly and moaning softly. He moved so he half-covered her and gathered her nightgown at the hem, caressing her exposed leg, from shin to knee to thigh to hip. Again, he went slowly despite his throbbing desire to bury himself inside her. Again and again he returned to her thighs, stroking inwards and upwards, inch by tantalising inch. His fingers touched her intimate curls and played for a while, tugging gently and twirling. Then one finger slipped between her thighs, sliding along her cleft.

And she froze.

'Steady, sweetheart. It's all right.'

He went back to circling her lower belly. But as soon as he touched between her thighs again she stiffened, a tiny sound of distress escaping her. He'd expected it, but disappointment still coursed through him. He didn't snatch his hand away, but stroked from between her thighs, across her curls and on to her hip. He kissed her, taking his time, then turned her on to her side to face away from him, unwilling to push her any further tonight. He spooned his body into hers, gritting his teeth against the ache of unfulfilled arousal, and wrapped his arm around her waist, holding her close, knowing she would feel the hardness of his erection against her bottom, knowing she must eventually grow accustomed to him and to his body, hoping she would soon learn she had nothing to fear and that she could trust him to never force her or lose control.

'Sleep, my Honeybee. It's been a long day.'

'Alex?'

'Yes?'

'Aren't we going to…to…?'

'Not tonight. We have the rest of our lives together. There's no hurry.'

He willed himself not to drift off. He would wait until his wife slept and then he would go to his own room to sleep.

He'd thought he was done with those bad dreams that had haunted his childhood and his youth, but they had returned since his arrival at the Abbey. Last night's nightmare had been even worse—prompted, almost certainly, by Pikeford's attack. The vision of that animal ripping at Jane's gown haunted him, as did the sounds—Pikeford's grunts as she tried to fight him off, the ringing slap, her cries of distress.

But behind that memory lurked another.

Bigger. Blacker. Colder.

Waiting to catch him unawares.

Waiting for him to sleep.

Once the soft, even huff of her breathing told him Jane slept, he eased himself away from her warmth and returned to his cold bed to face his nightly ordeal.

Jane awoke with a start. She leant up one elbow, wondering what had disturbed her. The happenings of the day before…and the night…gradually surfaced. She reached behind her, feeling for Alex, but her hand met empty space. She sat bolt upright, throwing back the covers, at a shout. That was Alex's voice, she was sure. She scrabbled on the nightstand for the tinderbox and, with shaking fingers, lit the bedside candle in its silver holder.

She listened for any further disturbance, but heard nothing. She sat on the side of the bed, irresolute. Should she go and investigate? Was she overreacting? What if it was just a bad dream…? Surely Alex wouldn't thank her for disturbing him? And while all those thoughts rushed through her head one bigger, more important question hovered.

Why did Alex leave?

He must be so very disappointed in her, to wait until she slept and then creep away to his own bed. Yet he had been so sweet at the time…his care and consideration for her had filled her with trust and love, and she had vowed to overcome the trauma of Pikeford's attack and to become a wife to him in every way.

Another shout from the next room wrenched her from her thoughts. She shot to her feet, grabbed her shawl and flung it around her before hurrying to Alex's bedchamber. She hesitated outside the closed door, raising her candlestick to illuminate the dark passageway, her heart thumping at the low moans sounding from within the room. She tiptoed forward and opened the door, peering around it.

'No…don't…no…no…stop…please…no…'

'Alex?' Her whisper threaded through his heartfelt pleas.

'No…no… No!'

She jumped at his final yell, her heart clenching at the sob that followed. She shut the door behind her, set the candle on a chest of drawers, then crossed the room to the bed. The blankets and sheet were pushed away, leaving Alex exposed. He lay on his side, shaking, curled into a ball, his arms bent over his face, his hands hooked over the top of his head.

Uncertainty clutched at Jane's throat. What should she do? Was it true one should never wake someone from a nightmare? What was happening to Alex in his dreams? She lowered herself on to the bed, swung her legs on to the mattress and then inched closer to him until her hip butted against his back. The entire time Alex emitted low, eerie moans that set the fine hairs on her arms on edge. Slowly, she eased over to face his back and—as he had done with her earlier that night—she nestled her body into his, like spoons in a canteen of cutlery.

'No...no... Mama...stop...no...'

His cries grew louder and, at the same time, more pitiful.

'Shhh...' Jane laid her hand on his arm. 'It's all right. I'm here.'

Her whispers were barely audible but, somehow, his trembling lessened and his ragged breathing steadied. She continued to soothe, stroking his arm and his shoulder and then, once he uncurled a little, his sweat-damp hair, as he relaxed and the nightmare loosened its grip. She tugged up the bedcovers and listened to his breathing, until she, too, fell asleep.

Chapter Six

'Janey?' A hand on her shoulder, shaking her. 'Janey?'

She stirred. As the voice came again, her eyes flew open. 'Alex!'

They were facing one another, in bed, his face close to hers.

'What are you doing here?'

His tousled hair revived the memory of the boy, but his unshaven cheeks and jaw were all man. Heat coiled deep in her stomach as his scent curled through her. Gradually, the events of the night before unravelled in her still-sleepy brain. She rubbed her eyes and yawned.

'I heard you cry out. You were having a bad dream. So I… So I…'

He was so close it was hard to concentrate on what she wanted to say. Warm pressure on her hip alerted her that his hand had moved there and the memory of his kisses sent hot tingles coursing down her spine.

His lips quirked. 'So you came to rescue me?' He pressed a kiss to her forehead. 'Thank you, Janey.'

'Alex? What were you…?'

'Shhh…don't think about last night. Not now.'

Their gazes fused. His tawny eyes darkened and lowered to her mouth. His hand skimmed up her side...settled at her back, splaying there, holding her still as his lips sought hers in a kiss to melt into. She sighed into his mouth, returning the gentle caress of lips and tongue.

The sound of the door opening ended the kiss. Alex lifted his head.

'Not now, Drabble.' Behind her, Jane heard the door click shut. 'Now. Where were we, Wife?'

Some time later—Jane couldn't quite swear to how long it had actually been—Alex lifted his head from her breast and smiled at her, a devilish glint in his eye.

'You're a bad influence, Janey. The carriage is ordered for nine. We'd better get moving if we're to leave on time.'

Already glowing, Jane felt a hot blush sweep her entire body until it burned in her cheeks. She felt so restless. She didn't want to move. She wanted more... Alex had woven such magic with his clever touch and with his lips, tongue and teeth that a hollow, yearning ache had taken up residence between her thighs. His kisses had awakened a fire in her, but she knew he was cautious for her sake. Not once had he attempted to touch her in her most intimate place, the place that was now in such need. Last night, one touch between her legs had sent her into a panic and she was grateful for his continued patience.

She watched him swing his legs out of the bed and rise. He was stark naked, standing with his back to her, rolling his shoulders back before stretching his arms above his head and she watched, fascinated by the slide of golden skin over flexing muscle and solid bone, the broad shoulders above a narrow waist. He had filled out since the times they had swum together in the lake. Then, he had been a boy. Now, he was definitely all man.

Her eyes lowered. To his buttocks. Firm and round. Her

mouth watered as she recalled touching them, squeezing them. His legs were straight and well shaped, dusted with dark hairs. They were beautiful. Paler than the skin on his back…did that mean he worked shirtless outside at times? Her heart kicked and her pulse raced. Would she ever get used to his chest?

He turned and her cheeks burned even hotter at being caught ogling her own husband and then scorched at the sight of his erection, standing proud. He grinned at her, totally unembarrassed.

'That was very enjoyable, Janey.' His smile faded. 'You will get over what happened, you know, and I will help you. There is no hurry and, in the meantime, you have discovered other pleasant activities we can enjoy, have you not?'

'Yes.' Jane's gaze clung to his face as she strove to ignore his chest and everything below his waist. She sat up, rearranging her nightgown and tying the ribbons into prim little bows, pulses of heat still sizzling through her from Alex's attention to her nipples. Her face scorched even hotter. My, that *had* been an education! 'I had better return to my room and dress if we are to leave on time. It won't do to keep the horses standing too long.'

'That's what I like about you, Janey. You love horses as much as I do. We'll make a good partnership.'

As declarations went, it was hardly romantic. But she didn't expect romance. Not from Alex. At least…maybe in time…? She cautioned herself not to hope for too much. Maybe. Maybe not. For now, she must be grateful she was here, with Alex, and not somewhere with Sir Denzil Pikeford. She suppressed a shudder, the events of two days before sending chills racing through her, effectively smothering those leftover frissons of pleasure.

Alex scooped Jane's dressing gown from the floor and

held it for her. She got up and, as he helped her into her robe, her roaming, random thoughts seemed to crystallise. Her eyes narrowed. She knew Alex of old—he was well practised in avoiding any discussion of subjects he found awkward and uncomfortable. In other words, any subject that threatened to delve too deep into his feelings. He retreated behind his barriers, keeping everyone at a distance, and pretending nothing mattered.

'Alex…?' She pivoted to face him. 'Your nightmare… Do you—?'

'Not now, Janey.' He spun away and crossed the room to tug the bell pull. 'Drabble and Peg'll be up with hot water in a minute. We'll talk later.'

Except they didn't. First there was breakfast and the goodbyes to the family, who all gathered to wave them off, amid hugs and kisses and promises to see them again soon. Jane's father was the sole member of her family to come and say goodbye, bringing with him Jane's beloved satinwood sewing box which had somehow been missed out of her trunk. He put his arms around her and hugged her close. 'I shall miss you, Jane.'

Jane hugged him back. 'I shall miss you, too, Papa.'

The exchange brought hot tears to her eyes and she ducked her head to hide her emotion, conscious Alex had completed his farewells and waited now to hand her into the carriage. 'Goodbye, Papa. You will write to me, won't you?'

'Of course I will, Jane.' He patted her shoulder. 'Hurry along now. You've a long way to travel. God speed.'

To give the newlyweds some privacy the Duke provided an additional carriage, for Drabble and Peg and the luggage and, as soon as they set off on the journey home to

Buckinghamshire, Alex settled back into a corner, crossed his arms over his chest and closed his eyes.

'You don't mind, do you, Janey? I'm tired as a dog.'

What could she say?

She had saved her questions for later, but Alex, it seemed, always had a plausible excuse for not delving too deep into the subject of his nightmares. But she knew they still plagued him, even though he reserved separate bedchambers at the inns they stayed in during their four-day journey. On the first night, when she heard him cry out, she went to his room only to find Drabble already there, tending to Alex.

'There is nothing you can do, milady,' Drabble had whispered as he ushered her away from the door. 'I am used to tending to him.'

Drabble had been with Alex for years and, before that, he was a footman in the Duke's household, since before Alex was born. If anyone knew what demons stalked Alex in his dreams, it was Drabble. All Jane could do was bide her time, until they reached Foxbourne Manor. And even on that—surely innocuous—subject, Alex was less than forthcoming. He fobbed off her questions about her new home, simply telling her to 'wait and see'.

The only subject he willingly discussed was his horses and, as it was a shared interest, they whiled away the journey by talking about how Jane could help by schooling some of the Foxbourne youngsters to side-saddle, to make perfect ladies' mounts. She was grateful for the distraction. Periods of silence inevitably resulted in Pikeford creeping into her brain and fear worming its way through her veins. She battled the memory with quiet determination. She refused to become a woman who trembled at shadows just as she had never allowed her stepmother to destroy her spirit.

* * *

Finally, the carriage turned through a wide entrance flanked by massive stone pillars, topped with eagles cast in iron. They followed a carriageway that passed through ancient woodland, in which Jane identified beech, elm and ash trees, before emerging into sunlight and continuing through parkland, much of it divided into paddocks in which horses grazed. Then the carriageway swept to the right and Jane caught her first glimpse of Foxbourne Manor, her new home. Her heart swelled with joy as she took in the many gabled, russet-bricked Tudor manor house, visible over a neatly clipped hedge. Sunlight reflected off the diamond-paned windows of the upper floor and, as the carriage drew to a halt before the front door, Jane turned to Alex in delight.

'I had no idea Foxbourne would be so beautiful! It looks steeped in history. I cannot wait to explore.'

He grinned at her reaction and hugged her. Other than kissing her—often very thoroughly—he'd barely touched her since their wedding night, telling her he would rather wait until they were home to try again, rather than consummate their marriage in a bed where who knew how many others had slept in the past. She had understood his logic, but the delay had done nothing to quell her nerves whenever she thought about the intimacies to come. She had found pleasure in his touch, but she couldn't help but be afraid she would freeze again if he touched her between her legs. Yet he must if she was ever to put what happened behind her. She was desperate not to ruin the experience for both of them and strove to hide her increasing fears about the night to come.

'I knew you'd like it, that's why I didn't tell you much,' Alex said. 'I wanted to see your face when you first saw it. I remember you always loved exploring the Abbey and complained Stowford Place was modern and boring and lacking in character. I only hope you won't find Foxbourne too old-fashioned, though…it still has much of the original wood panelling and dark beams in some of the ceilings. Or too small. It has only six bedrooms plus a nursery suite— nothing like the size of the Abbey or Stowford.'

That mention of the nursery suite sent hot and cold flushes rolling in waves through Jane. She wanted children, which meant she must overcome her fear and put aside her distaste for what Pikeford had attempted to do. She loved Alex. He had already proved she could trust him and that he understood how difficult it was for her. He, of anyone, knew how memories of the past could rear up at any time and cast ominous shadows over the present. At least his memories of the past were contained, only visiting him in his sleep—proof, surely, it was possible to suppress horrific events with determination.

This—marriage to Alex Beauchamp—was her dream come true, even though she would have preferred to win him in a more conventional way. And she *would* make him happy. Maybe he would never love her, but she had enough love for both of them.

Jane loved everything about Foxbourne Manor, from the minute she walked ahead of Alex into the spacious hall with its gleaming panelling and wooden staircase that rose to a half landing before turning back on itself. Alex had sent word of his nuptials to the Kents, who looked after the house, instructing them to hire in local help to prepare for their arrival, and the house had been cleaned and polished from top to bottom until it gleamed. It was dark, but not a gloomy darkness—it had the warm, glowing richness of well-cared-for and well-loved wood.

Alex's pride was clear as he showed Jane around the

L-shaped manor: the great hall, now an impressive drawing room, decorated in green and gold; the library, its bookcases crammed with books; the parlour, facing east to catch the morning sun; the dining room, with its polished rosewood table large enough to seat six couples; and Alex's business room—remarkably tidy and organised and not at all what Jane had expected of the man whose public image tended towards that of a devil-may-care rebel. The kitchen, butler's pantry, larder, scullery and other offices were housed on the ground floor of the side wing.

Upstairs, as he had said, were six bedchambers, including a master bedchamber linked via an internal door to a feminine, if a little old-fashioned, bedchamber for the mistress of the house. The side wing housed a nursery suite, with accommodation for children, nursemaid and a governess's room. The servants occupied the attics, but Mr and Mrs Kent who had, until now, fulfilled the roles of butler-cum-footman and housekeeper-cum-cook, had a separate bedchamber on the first floor, reached via a spiral staircase leading up from the butler's pantry.

The Kents and Sally, a housemaid, had been at Foxbourne from the time of Alex's predecessor. As well as hiring in temporary help to prepare the house for Jane, Alex had also instructed Kent to hire additional permanent staff in the form of a cook, a footman, a kitchen maid and a laundry maid. Alex's focus had always been on the business and ensuring he had enough grooms to care for and help train his horses, but he'd not once complained or quibbled over the need for a full complement of indoor servants now he was married and Jane couldn't wait to begin turning Foxbourne into a happy and comfortable home for them both.

'Now you have seen inside, would you care to visit the stable yard?'

Alex's attempt at nonchalance was not lost on Jane. What she really wanted, after travelling from nine that morning, was to enjoy a hot cup of tea. But, more than that, she wanted to please her new husband. And he, she could see, was eager to continue her tour of her new home.

'I would love to.'

Alex felt awkward and yet excited in equal measures. Never had he even contemplated sharing Foxbourne with anyone on a permanent basis, yet here he was, married. He suffered no illusions about himself and he'd had no time whatsoever to prepare for this change in his circumstances, but…Jane was his friend. If he had to choose a wife out of all the women he knew, she would always have been the most obvious choice to share his life and, to his surprise, he was more physically attracted to her by the day. How had he never noticed that Jane, the quiet little wallflower, was a flower waiting to burst into bloom?

He would make Jane happy to the best of his ability. He could offer her happiness, but he couldn't offer her love. Love meant letting down his guard…allowing another person closer than he'd ever allowed anyone…and the very thought terrified him.

No. He saved all his love for his horses and now, having shown Jane around the house, he couldn't wait to show her his real love: the stables, the horses, the schooling paddock where he worked with them.

He knew, instinctively, she would prefer to rest first and take refreshment, but… And there was his selfish streak. He had much to learn. He'd never had to consider anyone else's needs other than his own—*he* wanted to show her the stables and so that is what he had demanded.

He hauled in a deep breath and smiled ruefully.

'I'm sorry. You would prefer to rest first—I'll ask Mrs Kent to send a tea tray to the drawing room.'

'No!' She clutched his sleeve. 'No. Really. I am longing to see where you work your magic with the horses.'

And there was the difference between them. Him, selfish. Her, generosity itself. Always eager to please him. It had been the same when they were children. Jane had always given way to Alex's demands. A niggle of shame prompted him to say, 'They will still be there in an hour's time. Come...' he took her hand and led her to the stairs '...we'll have that cup of tea before we go outside', and was surprised by the sense of satisfaction he felt at putting her first.

Later, Jane took his arm as they walked the track leading to the barns and stables where Alex spent most of his time when at home. Jane was every bit as enthusiastic as he anticipated—their mutual love of horses had cemented their friendship long ago.

'She is beautiful,' Jane breathed, as they leant on a post and rail fence and watched an iron-grey filly with a light grey mane and tail float around a paddock at a trot. 'Was she born here?'

'Yes. She's three years old now and was one of the very first foals of my own breeding to be born here.'

'What is her name?'

'Whatever you would like it to be. If you like her, she's yours.' Her gasp of pleasure kindled a warm glow inside him. 'I thought how well she'd suit you when you told me about Pippin. She's already backed and we were about to start schooling her to a side-saddle. Would you like to help?'

'Oh! I'd love to.' Jane turned to him, her hands clasped in front of her chest, beaming. 'Thank you.'

The bright joy in her eyes drew him in and, without volition, he clasped her shoulders and pulled her close for a kiss. An unaccustomed emotion settled over him like a warm blanket and it took him a moment or two to identify it as contentment—surprising him. He'd always been self-sufficient, but now he wondered if his life had been missing something all along. Something he hadn't even known he needed. He'd always thought having Foxbourne was enough—the opportunity to take complete control if Father deemed him responsible had been the lure that saved him from the path of self-destruction in his youth. It had been a struggle to change his life but, despite a few hiccoughs, he had managed and Father had signed the estate and the business over to him three years ago.

That magnanimous gesture and vote of confidence from his father had still not been enough to banish the wariness and distrust he had always felt towards his sire, however. Thinking about his father prompted thoughts of the Abbey, and before he knew it he was puzzling yet again over the past and why his childhood home should still give him nightmares.

Jane pulled away from his embrace, her brown eyes searching his.

'What is it? Is something wrong?'

He knew her concern for him should make him feel good, but he couldn't quite dismiss his niggle of irritation. He might be reconciled to sharing his home and his life, but his thoughts were his and he never discussed those damnable nightmares. Not with anyone.

'Nothing's wrong. I was merely thinking of this place and how fortunate I am to have it. And how happy I am you are here to share it.'

It was no lie. It *was* what he had been thinking, it simply wasn't the whole.

'Oh. Well, that is good.'

Her robust response belied the expression in her eyes. He would have to take care with Jane—she was intuitive and, as she had just demonstrated, would soon pick up on any black moods if he allowed the past to gain a hold. It felt worryingly close to the surface at the moment—the visit to the Abbey had been bad enough, but that attack on Jane… Alex veered away from that line of thought with an inner curse. Not only must he lock that memory away for his sake but also, and more importantly, for Jane's. The sooner he could banish her memories of Pikeford, the sooner those shadows haunting her eyes would disappear.

'What will you call her?' The filly approached them, her head and neck stretched forward, nostrils quivering, as Jane extended her hand so the horse could take in her scent. 'She was black when she was born and her coat should continue to get lighter as she matures.'

'What have you called her until now?'

'Pearl.' He grinned as Jane turned laughing eyes on him.

'You named a black foal Pearl?'

He shrugged. 'We knew she would turn lighter and, besides, there are such things as black pearls, you know.'

'I do know. But, as it happens, I like Pearl so I shall keep it.'

They wandered back towards the barn where the stalls were. As they approached, Jane halted and clutched at Alex's sleeve.

'What is it?'

'Shhh. Can you hear it?'

Chapter Seven

Jane turned this way and that before setting off with purposeful strides towards a lean-to attached to the side of the barn, where sacks of oats and barley were stored.

Alex caught her up at the door. It was dark inside, but he, too, could now hear the pitiful mewling. 'Wait there,' he said and strode to the barn where there was always a tinderbox and lantern on a ledge beside the door. He lit the lantern and carried it to the lean-to. Eyes glowed, reflecting the light, and Jane stepped cautiously forward.

'It's a cat and kittens.' She crouched, crooning quietly. Then she looked back over her shoulder at Alex. 'She's very thin... I doubt she's producing enough milk for her babies. Poor things. They look hungry.'

Alex suppressed a sigh. He knew what this meant. Jane could never resist a creature in need. He squatted by her side and the lantern illuminated the cat.

'That's one of the stable cats.' He recognised its distinctive grey-and-white markings. Five kittens were at her belly, latching on to her teats and suckling for bare seconds before releasing the teat and trying another. 'She's one of the oldest—Lilley says she's been here since he first started work for Sir William.'

Sir William Rockbeare had owned and run Foxbourne before Alex's father bought it, and Lilley had stayed on as head groom.

'What do you want to do? The outside cats are not tame. I doubt she'll allow you—'

He fell silent. Jane had already made friends with the animal, stroking beneath her chin with one forefinger. He shouldn't be surprised. He resigned himself to the inevitable.

'Shall I find a basket for them?'

'Yes, please, if it's not too much trouble. I can feed the kittens with cow's milk—it's not ideal, but it's better than nothing and I shall give the mother some meat. She's very thin.' Alex rose to his feet and now Jane smiled up at him. 'Does she have a name?'

He snorted. 'Of course she doesn't have a name. She's not a pet.'

'She's purring at me, despite everything. I shall call her Dora.' She fixed him with a pointed look. 'Did you say something about a basket? I shall move her closer to the house where I can care for her better, if you don't object? There must be an outhouse or something I can use.'

He tweaked a lock of hair that had worked loose and now tumbled down her cheek. 'Of course I don't object. Anything to make you happy.'

She laughed. 'I shall remember that rash promise, Alex. You may very well regret making it.'

'Not me,' he said, airily. 'I'll be back shortly. You stay there.'

By the time they had carried Dora and her kittens up to the house and settled them into a disused storeroom off the courtyard at the back of the house, it was time to change for dinner.

* * *

The evening flew past and, almost before Jane knew it, it was time for bed. Her stomach roiled, but her determination to conquer her fear was fierce.

I love him. I know he won't hurt me. This *is what I want...what I've always dreamed of.*

They went together to check on Dora and to feed the kittens. Jane fed them with a small spoon, holding each kitten's head still as she dribbled milk into its mouth. She made sure they were satisfied before she left them for the night and left some finely chopped lamb and a saucer of milk for Dora. The entire time she was caring for the animals she was conscious of Alex watching her, his shoulders propped against the door frame, arms folded.

'All done?' he asked when she finally stood up.

She nodded, washing her hands in the bowl of water she'd put there for the purpose. Alex patted her hands dry with the towel, then raised them to his lips, pressing a kiss on first one, then the other. He held her gaze, fire banked in his amber eyes.

'Don't be scared, Janey. You will be in control... I'll do nothing you don't enjoy and I'll stop whenever you say the word. But *you* must tell *me*. If you tense up again, I will not stop. Not this time. Not unless you actually say *stop*.' He brushed a kiss to her forehead, then rubbed the pad of his thumb gently across her lower lip. 'Do you understand?'

It felt strange and embarrassing, discussing such intimate matters with him here, in this storeroom, but she understood why he chose to have this conversation away from the bedchamber. Away from the heat and the passion. Her blood stirred and her pulse quickened. She had already come a long way and Alex...she trusted him. Implicitly. She nodded again and, on impulse, rocked up on her toes and pressed a kiss to his mouth. A different feeling coiled in her stomach, thrumming and growing.

Anticipation. Desire. Excitement.

Her apprehension was still there, but it no longer overwhelmed her. She breathed in. Alex: familiar, loved, tasting of his after-dinner port. She cradled his face and traced the seam of his lips with her tongue, the way she had learned from him. A hum of approval vibrated through him. His lips parted and she deepened her kiss as his arms swept around her and hauled her close. Her body moulded to his and she revelled in his lean, hard-muscled form. Visions crowded her brain—his hair-covered chest…his ridged abdomen…those taut buttocks…his sinewy, hair-dusted forearms and gentle hands with those long, clever fingers—images that crowded out her fear.

She clutched his shoulders as their tongues tangled and their lips clung and that strange sensation once more gathered deep in her belly and in the feminine folds between her thighs. Another image arose—Alex, fully aroused. Very male. And hers! Her heart skipped a beat and her breath seized. Slowly, daringly, she reached down and stroked along the hard length of his erection, rejoicing in his groaned response. Alex swept her into his arms and strode for the stairs.

Once in Jane's bedchamber, Alex paused, his back against the closed door, Jane still cradled in his arms.

'The word is "stop", Honeybee. Not "no". I intend to have you screaming *no* many times before the night is out, but I will only stop if you say that word.'

'S-screaming?'

His eyes never left hers as a slow smile stretched his lips. 'Oh, yes. Screaming. With pleasure. In ecstasy.'

Then his lips found hers again and they were on the bed. Fully clothed still, but that did nothing to slow the explosion of desire that rocked her as Alex kissed, fondled and stroked every inch of her face, neck, shoulders and chest. He was too slow. Too cautious. She pushed him away and sat up.

'Help me,' she demanded as she tried to reach the buttons at the back of her gown.

He unbuttoned her and unlaced her corset. She pushed his jacket from his shoulders and tugged his shirt over his head, impatient to see that magnificent chest. When she was clad only in her shift and he in his breeches, Alex flung himself down on to the bed, smiled and beckoned, heat blazing in his eyes. About to join him, Jane hesitated. *You will be in control.* She caught her lip between her teeth, then slowly released it, rewarded by yet another flare of desire in those beautiful tawny eyes, and an impatient hand patting the mattress beside him.

Control.

Jane approached the bed slowly, holding Alex's gaze the entire time and then, slowly and deliberately, she slid her shift up to her thighs, lifted one leg across him and straddled his hips, her knees bent, hands splayed on his chest. He closed his eyes as though in pain, the planes of his face hardening, his eyebrows bunched.

'Alex?'

He opened his eyes at her whisper and their gazes fused again. The corner of his mouth quirked and he flicked his brows. He rested his hands on her knees, his thumbs rhythmically caressing her.

'Janey?'

'If you want me to stop, you must say the word.'

He burst out laughing. 'Janey—you are a tease!' Then he sobered, his chest rising and falling with his quickened breathing. 'Do your worst.'

She stroked across his chest, the hair crisp to her touch.

His nipples hardened and she bent to catch one between her teeth and gently nipped. His gasp encouraged her to explore further and she leaned forward, the tips of her breasts brushing against his hot skin as she kissed her way up his chest to his neck and his ear—the sensitive zones where the caress of Alex's mouth had provoked such shivers of anticipation. Her reward was a low moan of pleasure and a subtle tension that gripped the hard, male body beneath her.

When his hands settled on her hips, she protested. She wasn't done with exploring yet. But rather than lift her or move her aside, he held her still as he flexed his hips, the hard ridge of his erection pressing against her secret flesh. She tried desperately not to freeze, directing her thoughts to what she was feeling now and away from Pikeford, and before long all memory of his attack faded into insignificance as Alex moved her back and forth, rubbing her against his solid arousal.

When his grip eased, Jane kept moving of her own volition. A low moan hovered in the air. Realising it had come from her own lips, she opened her eyes and met his bright, tawny gaze. He smiled. Seductively. Her blood heated still further, her heart pounding. Alex. Her love. For ever. She reached for the hem of her chemise and, in one swift movement, stripped it off over her head. By the time she discarded it, Alex's mouth was on her breast and the tug on her nipple sent a ripple straight to her core. She pressed down on to his shaft, seeking to ease the need building deep inside her.

Slow, steady and languid turned to desperate. Hands squeezed and stroked…lips locked as tongues did battle… harsh pants filled the air, but now that sound drove her on. She thrust her fingers through Alex's hair and flattened her body to his, gasping into his mouth when he growled and flipped her over on to her back. He tore his lips from hers and stood, dragging his breeches down, kicking his feet free, his eyes pinning her in place. Jane shivered at the look in those tiger eyes…and held out her arms.

He lowered himself over her, and the seductive touch of skin on skin sent her temperature rocketing. Her thighs parted and he settled between them, kissing her, slow and deep. Her fingers dug into solid shoulder muscles as he kissed and licked his way to her breasts, and she shifted restlessly, moaning her impatience. She stilled when he explored her stomach with his mouth, dipping into the hollow of her navel, his body inching steadily down the bed. The first flick of his tongue between her thighs almost shot her off the mattress.

'Alex?'

Surely that can't be right? But… Oh… I want more…

'Shhh, my sweet.' Another lick. 'You taste so good. Like honey.' The words groaned out. Then his whole mouth was on her, kissing, sucking…tongue, probing…

Her body arched off the mattress and she reached for his head, clutching mindlessly at his hair, the muscles in her legs tensing as she pushed her yearning flesh against his mouth. His fingers replaced his mouth as he latched on to her nipple, working magic, driving her into a frenzy as she struggled to reach the unknown goal she sensed awaited her. The sensation of his fingers inside her…his tongue and teeth toying with her nipple…his thumb, circling, between her legs…ooooh…exquisite… She arched, helplessly, her fingers clutching blindly at anything within reach…higher…reaching…a sob gathered in her throat…

That sob shrieked from her and she flew into darkness spangled with a million sparkling stars, ecstasy rippling through her in waves. Gasps echoed around the room. Her gasps.

'Oh! Oh! Oh!'

She reached, found Alex and drew him up so she could kiss him.

'Ooh…' She sighed. 'Ooh.'

She felt his smile against her lips. 'You liked that, Honeybee?'

She nodded, unable to form coherent thoughts, let alone speech. Her eyes flew open then as Alex's weight settled between her legs, the head of his shaft at her entrance. She widened her thighs, welcoming him in. Propped on his elbows, he captured her gaze as he slowly, slowly pushed into her. She wanted him. She wanted more. She wanted hurry and urgency, not this slow, slow torture. She reached, finding his buttocks, tight with control, and she grabbed, pulling him in. A stab of pain, gone in an instant. He kept pushing, filling her, further and further until she couldn't take any more.

Then he smiled down at her. 'Do you want me to stop, sweetheart?'

Jane shook her head. 'Nooo…' The long-drawn-out sigh escaped her lips, like a plea. This felt so right.

He moved slowly at first and she soon caught the rhythm, and matched him, meeting each thrust, steady and controlled at first, but then faster and harder—driving her on, up and up, until she reached the edge again and threw herself over. Alex's roar of triumph mingled with her scream of joy as they soared high together. His weight slumped on to her before he rolled aside to lie on his back beside her, his hand seeking hers as, gradually, their breathing returned to normal. Then he turned to face her, propping himself up on one elbow, and stroked her cheek.

'Well, Janey?' His fingers sifted through the locks of hair tumbling across the pillow. 'Do you think you might eventually grow to enjoy such bed sport?'

She laughed at his teasing, gloriously happy, her confidence in herself as a woman as high as those stars. She kissed him, pouring her heart into it.

'Oh, yes. Although…' she tilted her head '…we might be compelled to practise. A lot.'

Alex laughed. 'I think we might manage that.'

He sat up, and swung his legs out of bed. Jane's stomach clenched. She touched his back, the skin warm and smooth beneath her fingers.

'Don't go, Alex. Please.'

'I don't want to disturb you, Janey. You know I have… that is, you know I'm a restless sleeper.'

This wasn't the time to discuss his nightmares so she let his comment pass, but she was determined to try to help him overcome his childhood demons. She was convinced talking about the past would help, but she knew how hard he would resist.

'I don't mind if you're restless. I would rather you stay— can we not at least try? I like having you here with me.'

'In that case, my sweet, I shall stay.' He lay back again, rolling over to face her. 'I like being here with you, too.' His lips curved into a wicked, teasing smile, his tawny eyes dancing. 'And I can think of no better way to start the day than waking up next to a beautiful woman.' He leaned across, seizing her lips in a slow, drugging kiss. 'Especially a beautiful woman who just happens to be my wife.'

Her heart swelled. Were they mere words, or did he truly think her beautiful? It was not how she had ever thought of herself: Stepmama had lamented her plainness often enough. But this was Alex—never a man to pay lip service—although she did recognise he meant all of her, not only her appearance. Even so, a warm glow of contentment radiated through her at the realisation he did, indeed, think her beautiful. She opened her arms and he snuggled into her, his breathing already softening and slowing as one hand drifted across to cup her breast and one leg settled between hers. He sighed. An upwelling of tenderness brought tears to Jane's eyes as she stroked his hair back and feathered a kiss to his forehead.

''Night, Janey,' he murmured.

Before long his limbs grew heavy and slack and he fell asleep. Jane's eyelids soon drifted shut and she, too, slept.

Chapter Eight

Alex roused, floating up from the depths of a long, dreamless sleep, his brain scrambling to catch up with his slowly awakening body. Gradually, the events of the night before formed coherent images and he smiled, a deep sense of satisfaction pervading him as he became aware his body was folded around another and his right hand loosely clasped a shapely breast.

Jane! His wife…and now they were married in every sense of the word.

He cranked open one eyelid and blinked, surprised by how light the room was, despite the drawn curtains. He frowned. Morning. It was morning. And he had slept right through. He tried hard to ignore the quickening of his blood and his growing arousal as he struggled to make sense of the time—what had happened to his nightmares? He searched his memory. No. There was no bad dream; no restless thrashing about to recall—merely a deep sense of peace and a burgeoning need to sink into his wife's welcoming heat. His arm tightened, drawing Jane closer to him, and he flexed his hips, pressing his erection against her bottom.

She stirred and murmured, her arm moving to lie over

his, her hand covering his, her fingers closing to encourage him to caress her breast.

'Mmm… Good morning, Husband.' She turned and pressed her mouth to his.

Maybe—and his spirits rose at this last coherent thought before passion took control—this was the answer to those nightmares that had plagued him ever since he had witnessed Pikeford's assault on Jane. Make love to his wife every night and sleep in her arms.

Some time later Alex relaxed back against the pillows, Jane sprawled across his chest. He sighed, tightening his hold. She raised her head, propped her chin on her clasped hands and fixed him with a direct look.

He bit back a smile…that look was very 'Jane'. People often thought because she was quiet, it meant she was shy, but Alex knew different. She was something of a rarity among females, in his experience—never one for small talk or gossip, but unafraid to speak her mind and, the more he thought about it, the more he realised he couldn't have picked a better wife if he'd tried. Jane, his best-ever female friend, who was revealing herself to be a far more sensual being than he could ever have imagined. He felt happier and more hopeful than he had for a very long time as he contemplated their future together.

'Thank you,' she said.

He frowned. 'For what?'

'For being patient with me.'

He laughed. 'Me? Patient? Hmm… My family and friends would stare to hear my name and that quality in the same breath.' He hooked his hands under her arms and slid her up his body so he could kiss her. 'But there's always a first time, I suppose. And don't they say patience has its own reward?'

He nipped her earlobe and nibbled his way down her neck.

'I think—' she tilted her head back to allow him better access '—the saying is "patience *is* its own reward"!'

Alex shrugged, distracted by the fluttering pulse in her throat.

'I like my version better,' he murmured, laving that pulse.

His hand wandered down her back to cup one delicious buttock. The blood rushed to his groin and, with reluctance, he rolled her off his chest.

'Alex...?'

The doubt in that one word was underlined by the worry in her lovely brown eyes. She might not be shy, but he knew only too well the toll her stepmother's constant criticism had taken on her self-confidence. He couldn't bear her to think he was rejecting her. He smiled reassuringly.

'You are new to this, my sweet—I don't want you to get sore. Besides...' he brushed her lips with his '...I need to recoup my strength.'

He reared up and flipped her over on to her back—making her giggle—before kissing her very thoroughly indeed.

'Now, my lady, it is time we got up.' He swung his legs out of bed before he could be tempted to take things further again. 'Have you an idea of what would you like to do today?' He stood up, turned to face her and bowed with a flourish. 'I am entirely at your service.'

She laughed up at him—a glint of mischief in her eyes—and reached out, but he stepped back before her hand could close around him.

'Good grief.' He shook his head at her. 'You *are* making it difficult to act the responsible and caring spouse, you wanton minx, you.'

She dimpled at him, her head tilted. 'You shouldn't be so hard to resist, you handsome devil.'

He laughed and grabbed her hands, hauling her from the bed and into his arms.

'Well? Would you like to make a start on Pearl's education?'

Her eyes lit up, but then a fine groove appeared between her eyebrows and she blushed. 'I think I might prefer to wait a day or so.'

He bit back his grin of pure male satisfaction. 'Of course,' he said gravely. 'Maybe later I will drive you around the area so you can get your bearings. Come on.' He released her, gave her a gentle push and swatted her backside playfully. 'Get moving. The day's half over already! I'll go to my room and get dressed and I'll see you in the parlour for breakfast.'

'Well?' Later, after they had eaten, Alex eyed Jane over the rim of his coffee cup. 'Have you any further thoughts about how we might spend the day? I'm completely at your disposal... I've already sent word to the stables I won't be available until tomorrow.'

'Well, first I must check on the kittens. Peg promised to feed them first thing this morning, but I can't expect her to take on the whole burden of caring for them. And I must consult with Mrs Kent on household matters and the new staff we need. And then—'

Alex held up his hand. 'Are you telling me you have no need of me today? You've had your wicked way with me and now I am *de trop* until it's bedtime?'

'No! Oh, Alex, I did not mean...' She stared at him, and pouted. 'You utter wretch! You are teasing me.'

'Of course I am, Janey.' He winked at her. 'Well, while you feed the kittens, and you and Mrs Kent make plans,

I dare say I ought to attend to my ledgers and correspondence. So I shall be in my business room should you have need of me.'

Jane pursed her mouth, shaking her head. 'Now I see why you were so keen to spend the day with me— anything is preferable to completing ledgers and writing letters.' She stood, and rounded the table. 'You never did care for studying and lessons, I recall.'

A dark shadow nudged at his memory. A time when he had skipped lessons with his tutor...the summer house by the lake... He thrust the memory away and forced a smile.

'You caught me out! But now, because my wife is too conscientious, I have no excuse.'

She laid her hand on his shoulder. 'Give me time to get accustomed to the routine of the house and I will help you. I always used to help Papa... I often wrote letters for him and ledgers hold no fears for me.'

Alex didn't need to force his smile this time. He shoved his chair back from the table, grabbed Jane around the waist and pulled her on to his knee.

'I knew I was right to marry you.' He nuzzled her ear. 'It is the best thing I have ever done. We will make a wonderful team.'

He believed every word. This marriage was going to work out far better than he could ever have hoped. After her reaction on their wedding night he'd wondered if Jane would find it hard to banish the memories of Pikeford, but she had surprised him with her determination to conquer her fear. Although...maybe he shouldn't be surprised, knowing Jane. She had never been one to buckle under one setback—she was a quietly determined soul who got things done.

Life looked rosy indeed, with Jane by his side.

'I'll be in the business room if you have need of me.' If

Jane was to help him in future he should at least present her with up-to-date records from the start. He pressed a light kiss to her mouth and lifted her from his knee as he stood up. 'I shall see you later.'

He left the parlour with a spring in his stride.

Later, while Jane changed her gown, Alex headed for the stable yard to collect his curricle and pair, ordered ready for two o'clock. Sure enough, the feisty pair of chestnuts were ready-harnessed.

'They're lively, milord,' Lilley remarked as Alex leapt into the vehicle.

'I'd be disappointed if they weren't. They'll soon settle once we get moving.'

He drove to the front door, where Jane waited for him, clad in a flattering cornflower-blue pelisse over a white carriage dress with deep blonde flounces and a matching broad-brimmed, feather-trimmed bonnet. The day was fresh and bright—a bit like the horses—and, as they set off at a spanking trot, Alex couldn't keep the proud smile from his face.

They drove to Malton, which boasted a church and the adjacent vicarage, an inn, a general store and post office, a bakery and a smithy. Alex had never mingled much with his neighbours, but today, when he saw a familiar face, he stopped to introduce Jane, accepting their hearty congratulations with a smile and a glow of pride. Mrs Phillips, the wife of the local vicar, was especially welcoming and she invited Jane to take tea with her one day. Jane accepted the invitation, her pleasure clear. As they drove on, Alex hid his happiness behind a grumble.

'No doubt we shall be plagued by a never-ending stream of visitors, all keen to make your better acquaintance and to invite us to all manner of entertainments.'

She tipped her head to one side. 'Should you object if we socialise with them?'

Would it be so bad? Getting wed had changed his outlook. Even though he'd never had any intention of leaving Foxbourne, somehow it seemed more settled...more *permanent*...now.

'I suppose not, if it makes you happy,' he muttered in a purposely grudging tone, then bit back his laugh when Jane's lips quirked into a knowing, but fond, smile. She could always tell when he was fudging the truth to hide his true feelings.

He saw they were about to pass the blacksmith's forge and reined the horses to a halt.

'I almost forgot; I have a message for the farrier from Lilley—one of the lads is bringing a horse down to be shod tomorrow. I warn you in advance, though—Benson does love to gossip.'

'Then I hope to learn even more about my new neighbours, but I am surprised you don't have your own farrier at Foxbourne.'

'Sir William always used Benson, so I carried on.' Alex handed her the reins. 'Are you happy holding the horses? They've had the fidgets worked out of them.'

'Of course.'

He jumped down as Benson emerged into the sunlight, wiping his glistening forehead with a grimy rag before tucking it behind the bib of his leather apron. His face creased in a smile as he recognised Alex and his eyes brightened when he noticed Jane seated in the curricle.

Alex relayed Lilley's message and then introduced Benson to Jane.

''Tis an honour to meet you, milady, so it is. We was all agog to hear His Lordship had wed—it's wonderful news, to be sure.'

Jane smiled at him but, before she could reply, Benson barrelled on, his eyes alight with the excitement of a juicy morsel of gossip.

'Have you heard the latest news, milord?'

Alex caught Jane's eye, saw laughter twinkling and he winked in response. It felt good to have someone to share a joke with.

'No. I'm afraid you have the advantage of me there, Benson. What news?'

Benson beamed. 'Halsdon Manor is let at last. You'll have new neighbours by All Hallow's Eve...my missus is hired on to help prepare the house.' He switched his gaze to Jane. 'It's been empty these five years, milady, so it has. And even then, Mr Lascelles only lived there a short while before he disappeared back overseas.'

That name left a sour taste in Alex's mouth—he'd almost forgotten Anthony Lascelles owned Halsdon Manor.

'Quite the mystery, so it was,' Benson continued. 'After all, why would a man buy an estate and then leave the country without a word? I never did—'

His jaw snapped shut as he caught Alex's expression.

'Sorry, milord. I was forgetting Mr Lascelles was a relation. You probably know more about it than me.'

'No. I don't.' Alex leapt into the curricle, taking the reins from Jane, but then paused, eyeing the blacksmith. 'Do you have any idea who has leased the Manor, Benson?'

'Nobody does, milord. We's hoping Mrs Benson'll find out more when she starts working up there.'

'No doubt we'll find out soon enough.' Alex nodded at Benson. 'Good day to you.'

As they drove out of the village, Jane said, 'Who is Mr Lascelles? I have never heard of him. *Is* he a relative of yours?'

'Black sheep of the family.' Alex chuckled as Jane's

eyebrows rose. 'And there was you, thinking *I* was the black sheep.'

'Is he from your mother's side?'

'No.' Alex's throat tightened, as it always did at any mention of his mother. 'Father's, on the distaff side.'

'He's illegitimate?'

'Yes. My great-uncle was the duke, but he never married. He had a long-standing affair with an actress and they had a son together.'

'Mr Lascelles.'

'Yes. And Great-Uncle still refused to contemplate an actress becoming Duchess of Cheriton so the title passed on to his brother, my grandfather, and then through him to my father.'

'So he's your father's cousin?'

'Yes. He hates Father, though. Uncle Vernon says he's eaten up with jealousy because he believed *he* should rightfully be the duke. He's…overseas now.' The story of why he had quit Halsdon Manor so suddenly could wait. 'He's actually lived overseas for most of his life. I only met him for the first time in London five years ago.'

'Perhaps he has returned and the house is being prepared for him?'

Lascelles would be a fool to return, given the way Alex's father felt about what he had done. But it was strange it was suddenly let after all this time. 'We shall soon find out, I have no doubt.'

Alex didn't give the potential occupant of Halsdon Manor another thought as he and Jane settled into married life. He would never have guessed he could experience such contentment; if ever he'd thought about it, he would have said he could never tolerate living cheek by jowl with any other person, but he found himself increasingly seeking Jane out during the day simply because he enjoyed her company. He also appreciated the calm and comfortable home she provided for him, he enjoyed sharing his life and ideas with her and, for the first few nights, he slept right through, dreamless, with his wife held close, waking refreshed and blessing the day they had wed.

The dreams began again after a week or so. In them, he was walking around the lake at the Abbey, towards the summer house. The sound of a scuffle from among the trees lured him into the wood before he reached it. He invariably awoke just as he hauled Pikeford off Jane and he would find himself in her arms, her cool fingers stroking his brow.

'Shh… It's a bad dream. I'm here. Sleep now.'

The images would disperse, leaving him thoroughly ashamed that Pikeford's attack was haunting him while Jane had put it behind her, so he denied recalling any details of those dreams even as he puzzled over why they included the long-demolished summer house. He also had the sense someone was walking with him, which was nonsense; he could only assume it was his brain muddling together different memories, as often happened in dreams.

He was grateful Jane's presence helped keep his old nightmares at bay and that he didn't dream every night. Surely they would eventually stop, as his nightmares had done in the past.

The days fell into a comfortable rhythm and their nights were filled with a passion and a depth of feeling Alex had never before experienced. Jane seemed happy and contented. She had gained so much confidence, now she was out of reach of that old witch with her constant disapproval. Jane even at times instigated their lovemaking. There was so much more to the woman he had always thought of as a little sister…how had he failed to recognise this treasure under his nose his entire life?

As time passed, his habitual guard gradually lowered as he allowed Jane closer than he had ever let anyone, but it seemed as though the more contented his life became, the more frequently dreams disturbed his nights. They took a dark turn, with odd images flashing through them— images that filled him with a deep foreboding. Those nights, he would waken with his heart thumping, but unable to make any sense of those fleeting images.

But Jane was always there to soothe and to comfort and although she often asked about his nightmare in the morning he continued to fob her off, determined not to remind her of Pikeford.

Chapter Nine

Jane was truly happy for almost the first time in her life, without her stepmother's criticisms to drag her down. The first weeks at Foxbourne were filled with fun and work, and gradually getting to know one another even better than before. They spent their evenings in comfortable companionship. If Jane took up her sewing—she was making and embroidering silk reticules as Christmas presents for the ladies of the family and monogrammed handkerchiefs for the men—Alex would read to her. Or they played cards, or draughts, or chess, although she feared she would never make Alex a worthy opponent. It seemed Alex could not do enough for his new wife and Jane's natural sunny nature began to reassert itself. Some evenings, she played the piano and they would sing together, Alex's rich baritone voice sending delicious shivers across her skin as his tiger eyes caressed her with the promise of the night to come.

His loving was sublime. Jane felt like a princess as he worshipped her body every night—and most mornings, too, because he continued to sleep the night in her bed. Her confidence in her allure as a woman grew—she enjoyed their intimacies and felt like the luckiest woman in the world.

Alex was changing. The man who had always been so guarded and self-contained relaxed as days turned into weeks, seeming more at peace with himself than she had ever known him, despite the return of his dreams.

To begin with, they occurred infrequently and seemed milder than before. He would toss and turn in his sleep and she would gather him close and soothe him until he slept again. In the morning he had no recollection of the dream and, because he seemed happy and content, Jane probed no further. Gradually, though, the dreams slid into nightmares until, one night, he shot upright in their bed shouting, 'No! Mama! No!'

Jane sat up and wrapped her arms around his shaking body.

'Shhh…shhh…'

He appeared to rouse, as he always did, but he soon settled back to sleep while Jane lay awake, wondering and worrying.

She waited until they were at breakfast.

'You dreamt again last night, Alex. Do you remember?'

'No. I never do. I've told you before, Janey.'

'You called out this time.'

His chin tilted higher. The planes of his face hardened. Jane recognised the signs—this was the old Alex who resented anyone probing too deeply. But she was his wife and she would not be intimidated into ignoring something that was troubling her husband.

'You shouted out. *"No! Mama! No!"*'

Alex thrust back his chair. 'I don't recall.'

But the way he avoided meeting her eyes suggested he did remember—he just refused to discuss it.

'Have you finished eating?'

She nodded.

'As have I.' He rose to his feet. 'I cannot tell you about something I don't remember. They're not important. I've always had them...they'll go soon enough.' He rounded the table to pull her to her feet. 'Now, tell me your plans for today. Shall we work on Pearl later?'

'I would like that.' She would get no further with him right now, but he'd given her an idea.

'Come to the stables at eleven.' Alex kissed her nose. 'And stop worrying about those silly dreams.'

As soon as Alex left for the stables, Jane went upstairs.

'Drabble—' Alex's valet was in his bedchamber '—might I ask you about His Lordship's nightmares?'

'What about them, milady? I thought they'd gone.'

'They did. At first. But they've come back and they seem to be worsening.'

Drabble frowned. 'That's bad news, but I'm not sure how I can help, milady.'

'I wondered...is it true His Lordship was free of them before he went down to the Abbey?'

'Yes. They disappeared completely when we moved here to Foxbourne, but even before that they were few and far between. He suffered much worse as a child.'

'Thank you, Drabble.'

Jane wandered downstairs, deep in thought. The maids were busy polishing and sweeping so, needing time alone to think, she set off for a walk. She'd had little time as yet to explore the estate, so she headed down the carriage-way, pondering Alex's nightmares. After last night, how could she doubt these latest dreams were linked to his mother's death?

She turned on to a winding path through a wood, still deep in thought. It wasn't until the canopy of the trees thickened, blocking out the sun, that her steps faltered. The outline of a thicket bordering the path ahead sent her heart racing and she was seized by an irresistible urge to look over her shoulder. She told herself not to be stupid, there was no one there, but fear still roiled in her belly. She retraced her steps, breathing easier as she emerged into the sunlight, but exasperated by her fearfulness.

Even when she was back on the carriageway that feeling of vulnerability persisted, so she headed back to the house, her thoughts tumbling. She'd worked so hard to banish Pikeford's memory, telling herself it could have ended so much worse, and she was angry he had undermined her confidence so badly she was too scared to walk on her own through a wood.

Determinedly, she diverted her thoughts to the subject of Alex's nightmares. According to Drabble they had gone away before, so why were they now getting worse? Could it be because Pikeford had attacked her so close to where Alex had found his mother? Had that somehow unlocked his memory of that day? Alex had never been able to remember finding his mother, according to Olivia, and his father had felt it was better for him that way.

How dreadful if the attack on Jane had somehow prompted him to remember it after all this time.

Eleven o'clock saw her at the stable yard and she pushed her worries aside as Alex lifted her up on to Pearl's saddle. When they had finished, they walked together up to the house and she gathered her courage.

'I have been thinking about your nightmares, Alex.'

'I don't want to discuss them, Janey. I told you.'

'But—'

'No!'

His brows lowered, his mouth set in a stubborn line. Jane frowned, considering. She'd had enough of biting her tongue for the sake of a quiet life with Stepmama. She recognised this *mind your own business* Alex of old... it was how he had always kept his family and friends at bay. She'd thought he was improving...that the barriers he erected against the world were slowly crumbling. This felt depressingly like a reversal.

As Alex's friend, Jane had never had the right to probe deeper. But...as his wife...

She grabbed his hand to pull him to a halt. 'Alex... please... I truly think it would help if you—'

'I said no.' He snatched his hand away. 'There's nothing to talk about.'

'But I wanted to tell you about...'

She watched him stalk away, back to the stables, frustration humming through her. They never spoke about Pikeford's attack—each protecting the other, she had no doubt—but she'd decided to tell him what happened in the woods earlier and also that the memory of that attack would sometimes catch her unawares; that the feelings she'd had at the time would burst upon her and it would almost be—just for a few seconds—as though it was happening all over again.

She'd hoped it might help him to confide in her. But he'd given her no chance.

The seething mass of his emotions drove Alex to seek solitude. He threw a saddle on Frost, his favourite gelding, and set off for the nearby hills where he could gallop his frustrations away. Except that didn't work. When they halted, breathless, on the brow of a hill, that cauldron of guilt, shame and resentment still bubbled away inside, making him feel sick.

Jane didn't deserve the way he had spoken to her. That was the guilt. But it wasn't powerful enough to persuade him she needed to know about his damned nightmares. How could he tell her, when they always began with Pikeford? She'd done so well to overcome the attack and it was his role as her husband to protect her not only from that memory, but also from the responsibility she would feel at being—as she would see it—the cause of his nightmares. Because that was Jane—she blamed herself and felt responsible even when the fault lay with other people.

Jane had made his life so sweet and he cared for her so very much…she had crept into his heart in the short time they had been wed and now he simply couldn't imagine his life without her. But that didn't mean he would willingly discuss his nightmares. Hell, he didn't fully understand them himself, so how could he explain them to anyone? Somehow, he must convince her to avoid the subject in future. They would both be happier, he was sure.

He slid from Frost's back and sat on a rock to think while the horse cropped grass.

He was honest enough—with himself—to admit shame at his own weakness also played its part in his reluctance to talk about the nightmares. He was ashamed that *he* had nightmares over that damned attack whereas Jane was not only strong enough to overcome her initial fear of lovemaking, but she also slept like the proverbial babe. Perhaps his family had been right all these years, seeing him as always troubled and needing their help and protection. He'd always resented it and now he was damned if he'd allow his wife to see him that way, too.

It was *his* place to be the strong one.

He swore to himself he would work doubly hard to make Jane happy. He would do anything for her. Anything except talk about his nightmares. They would disappear soon enough, as they did before.

Several days later, Alex strode in the direction of the stable yard, hurrying to beat the shower that threatened, his head full of last night's dream, determined to make sense of the few fragments he could recall in his efforts to banish his nightmares for good. He remembered the colour yellow...but how did that fit in? It made no sense.

Then a memory flared and his breath caught as he slammed to a halt with images filling his head—the lake at Cheriton Abbey, the sound of a scuffle, the image of Pikeford on top of Jane, as clear as the day it happened. But then...those memories were replaced with a vision—a swirl of yellow skirt, polished top boots, voices, low, angry, arguing, the words unclear. Almost as soon as it erupted into his consciousness, it scattered, leaving his heart slamming into his ribs and sweat breaking out on his brow.

He stumbled across to the fence and grabbed the top rail, his breaths ragged and urgent, a vice tight around his chest.

What the hell...?

His fingers thrust through his hair, dislodging his hat, then lingered at the back of his head, his nails digging into his skull as he struggled to recall exactly what that had been a memory of. His viewpoint...he must have been on the floor. But neither a carpet nor cool, smooth tiles. His eyes screwed shut. Another memory whispered—that of rough wooden planks against his cheek. He swallowed, lifting his chin to ease the action. Everything throbbed.

His head. His chest. His throat.

His brain.

Was it a memory…or a remnant of his dreams?

Slowly, steadily, the vice loosened its grip and his breathing eased. A drop of rain splattered on the back of his hand, still clutching the top rail. He tipped his face skyward, welcoming the cool rain on his heated skin. He swallowed again. Everything felt looser. Easier.

The distant recall of a dream. That was all.

Alex turned once more for the stables, thrusting aside the black mood threatening to envelop him—the sort of black mood that used to drive him to excess in his desperate bids to escape. Well, he was that man no more. He was happy. He would do everything he could to stop his demons from sullying his new life. And he would continue to protect Jane from the memory of Pikeford's attack. She did not need reminding of what had happened, not when she was recovering so well and seemed so happy.

Happy with *him*, as he was happy with her—a feeling he cherished and one he would fight to preserve.

Alex's resolution to make sense of his dreams didn't go as planned and he soon reverted to trying to block out his nightmares in the face of increasingly distressing visions and new, disturbing suspicions that taunted him. But those visions proved almost impossible to stop now they had started—it was as though he had opened Pandora's box and, try as he might, he couldn't shut the lid again. The only good part was that the more often the daytime visions occurred the less frequent his nightmares became.

They always began with the memory of Pikeford's attack…but then they would slide into something different.

Something dark and dangerous.

Something his instinct told him he must suppress at all costs.

He dared not reveal even a hint of what his memories—

if they were indeed memories—implied. Because it was no longer simply about protecting Jane from any reminders of Pikeford's attack. Because now, bubbling deep in his past— swirling in a murky cesspool of fear, disgust and horror, and creeping ever nearer—was something so huge…so dark…so dreadful…that Alex fought with every fibre of his being to stop that clouded vision from sharpening and becoming clear.

Because…once it did…once he *knew*…he feared there would be no going back.

Chapter Ten

'I must go into High Wycombe this morning,' Alex said one day as they breakfasted together. 'Would you care to accompany me, Janey?'

'I should like that. Thank you.'

Jane kept the frown from her forehead. Where had the friendly, easy banter disappeared to? She didn't understand it, but she sensed a growing distance between them. She was certain it wasn't her imagination that Alex appeared to be holding her at arm's length. Not physically—he still made love to her most nights with tender skill—but Alex himself, the man, was steadily becoming more unreachable.

He hated her asking if anything was troubling him, but it was hard to stay silent when every instinct she possessed told her *something* was wrong. Was he tiring of married life already? Had she simply fooled herself that the bond between them had been strengthening since their marriage? Had she imagined their growing closeness and intimacy? Was it wishful thinking on her part—the feeble hope her childhood dreams could really come true?

She tried to ignore her doubts as she went upstairs to change into her new yellow carriage gown, admiring herself in the pier glass: the colour really did bring out the colour and shine of her hair. She donned her dark blue spencer and bonnet, picked up her gloves and her cloak, and hurried downstairs. Alex was waiting at the foot of the stairs and Jane saw some strong emotion flash across his face.

'What is it?' Her stomach tightened with the familiar anxiety that had plagued her in the presence of her step-mother. 'Have I kept you waiting?'

His gaze swept her from head to toe, a muscle bunch-ing in his jaw.

'Do you not like my gown?' Jane persisted when he did not answer her. She saw the effort it took him to smile at her.

'It suits you very well, Janey,' he said. 'I shall be the envy of every man in High Wycombe.'

That empty compliment did nothing to reassure Jane as Alex helped her with her cloak. Her thoughts whirled as she tried to understand what had upset him, but she couldn't work it out and to question him further would likely only result in an uncomfortable journey for them both. She wanted to enjoy this outing, so she let the subject drop, suppressing her sigh at her avoidance, yet again, of a contentious subject. She had always known Alex was a complex man—she mustn't expect him to suddenly turn into an easy man to understand. But she would keep trying.

High Wycombe, one of the principal towns of Buckinghamshire, was a leisurely hour's drive from Fox-bourne. The sun was shining, but a breeze kept the weather fresh and Jane enjoyed the journey through the beautiful Buckinghamshire countryside, with its rolling Chiltern Hills and wooded valleys, the trees a stunning autumnal mix of russet, orange and gold as their leaves turned colour before they dropped.

In town, Alex dealt with his business and then escorted Jane along the High Street, a broad thoroughfare where the market was in full swing. Jane, still planning ahead for their Christmas visit to Devonshire, bought a pretty ivory hair comb for Susie and set of brightly painted wooden toy soldiers each for Thomas, Julius and Sebastian. She hadn't yet decided what to make for baby George, but she had enough colourful fabric at home to make ragdolls plus matching hair ribbons for Christabel, Florence, Sophie and Daisy and she'd found some beautiful ruby-red satin in a trunk at Foxbourne with which she planned to make a waistcoat for Alex.

Alex treated Jane to a beautiful shawl of flowered silk, edged with local lace, and, after she admired a pair of the Windsor chairs for which High Wycombe was famous, he bought those, too, arranging for their delivery to Foxbourne where Jane planned to put them either side of the fireplace in the morning parlour. After a pleasant few hours, they returned to the Red Lion, where they had left the horses, and enjoyed a glass of wine and a sandwich before setting off on the journey home.

'Well, Janey? Did you like High Wycombe? It cannot offer the variety of goods you can buy in London, but it does boast a decent collection of shops.'

'I loved it, Alex! Thank you.'

'You don't have to thank me, Janey. We're a married couple. You are welcome to accompany me whenever I go into town.'

'Many married couples spend little time together, Alex. You need not feel obliged to invite me along every time you go into town.' She captured his gaze. 'Earlier, when

I came downstairs, I thought you regretted asking me to accompany you.'

His brow furrowed. Then it cleared and laughter danced in his amber eyes as he grabbed her hand, pulled off her glove and pressed hot lips to her bare skin.

'Of course I didn't regret it, my sweet Janey. I was taken aback—I have never seen you wear yellow before, but I was not merely flattering you when I said it suits you very well. You look lovely and you could not have chosen better for such a pleasant day.'

He tipped up her chin, then, and kissed her. She returned his kiss, but pulled away when he began to deepen it.

'Alex!' She laughed, batting his hand away. 'It is broad daylight! What if someone should see us?'

'What if they should? Why should I not kiss my own wife whenever I choose?'

His teasing soothed her and her worries seemed far away.

'You should keep your eyes on the road,' she said, mock severely. 'What if we should have an accident?'

'My horses are too fly to collide with anything or to run us into a ditch.' But Alex did turn his attention back to his driving, taking the reins in one hand as he slipped his arm around Jane and pulled her in close. She relaxed against him, laying her head on his shoulder, contentment flowing through her as the steady beat of the horses' hooves lulled her.

Alex had worked hard to hide the increasing strain he was under, but it was obvious Jane had noticed something was wrong. She knew him too well—she had always been an observant soul and he had always been hopeless at concealing his moods—his entire family could attest to that—no matter how adept he was at concealing the cause of those moods.

But how could he admit Pikeford's attack was leading to increasingly frequent visions that appeared to be linked to his mother's death, even though he had no conscious memory of finding her body? He knew Jane—she would blame herself for being the cause, even though it was not her fault.

It was taking its toll on him. He couldn't even decide if they were real memories, or whether his imagination was resurrecting those awful visions out of his nightmares. And, if the latter, did it mean he was losing his mind? The very thought terrified him—in his youth he had once visited Bethlem Hospital with a group of friends, before it moved to its current location at St George's Fields in Southwark. He shuddered at the memory.

What if I am going mad?

He swallowed down that fear and resolutely directed his attention to the road ahead. Jane's head grew heavy on his shoulder, her face shielded by the brim of her bonnet, peacefully slumbering as the curricle rumbled over the stony track. That yellow gown *had* taken him by surprise. For a split second, when he first saw her, he had felt nothing but terror and he'd failed miserably to hide his reaction. It was odd. Yellow had never affected him before—he could only think that flash of fear and dread was linked to the yellow gown in his visions.

They drove over a humpback bridge and Alex urged the horses into a trot as they approached the long, slow pull up the lane towards home. Jane stirred.

'Are we nearly home?' Her voice sounded thick. Sleepy.

'Not far now, Janey. Close your eyes again, if you like.'

Jane pushed herself upright and straightened her bonnet. 'I was *not* asleep.'

Alex caught her eye and grinned. An answering smile slowly stretched her lips, but she stuck her nose in the air before turning to watch teams of men and plough horses working in an adjacent field until it was masked from view by a copse.

A scream suddenly rent the air and a vivid image hit Alex with the force of a physical blow, followed by a feeling of such powerlessness, such hopelessness, such panic…a pair of boots…her yellow gown and matching slippers…the colour of daffodils…the scent of roses…the rough wood against his cheek…

His gorge rose to crowd his throat as his mind spun remorselessly in a black, choking vortex of terror and chills racked his body. The sound of ripping cloth… *What…no… please*—a woman's voice…pleading. The vision continued—those boots and the slippers, moving…to and fro…as though in a dance. Two figures, sinking towards the floor…a cry, choked off…his heart beating so hard it might burst…the grunts…

A new image began to form.

'Alex?' It seemed to come from far away, and he focused on that voice…safety…reassurance…hope… He clambered out of the past, back to the present, away from that hazy image of his father's face.

People ran when they heard my screams. They told me. And Father came, too… That's all that means. Isn't it?

'Alex?' Jane's hand was on his, her voice urgent. 'What is it? What's wrong?'

He forced open eyes that had screwed shut. 'The…' His voice croaked. He cleared his throat. Tried again. 'That scream…'

'Scream? You mean the children? They're just playing.'

Jane pointed back along the lane, towards the copse, now fifty yards behind them. Alex, his vision clearing, saw the children—no doubt belonging to the ploughmen—darting in and out of the trees.

It was all normal. Thoroughly normal.

The horses had halted and Jane now held the reins. Alex rubbed his forehead. He had no memory of her taking over.

'The horses took fright,' she said. 'I had to stop them.'

He stared at her, trying to make sense of it all.

'What happened, Alex?' She made no attempt to start the horses. 'One minute we were bowling along quite happily, then you jerked the reins hard and went quite rigid and pale. It was like…you weren't there. I-It was spooky. It frightened *me*, never mind the horses.'

'I don't know what happened.' He felt as he did when he emerged from a nightmare, as though his brain were stuffed with wool. 'I really don't know.'

She offered the reins and he shook his head. 'You drive.'

They drove home in silence, Alex conscious of the many concerned glances Jane sent his way. By the time they arrived, his clenched jaw ached. He'd spent his entire life suffering not only the sympathy and pity of his family, but also their misguided efforts to snap him out of his moods. He was damned if he wanted to undergo the same treatment from his wife—he could only pray she would soon forget about it and he would suffer no further lapses in front of her. All he wanted now was to get away…to be alone so he could think about what had happened.

Jane didn't mention the incident again, lulling him into believing she would let it pass. He should have known better. She waited until after their evening meal, until they had settled in the drawing room by the fire crackling in the huge stone fireplace for, even though the days were warm, the nights were drawing in. Jane settled on the sofa, reached for her sewing box and removed her lucet, with which she was making silk cords for the reticules she'd made. Alex quashed his guilt that he still hadn't told her they wouldn't be going to the Abbey at Christmas. She wouldn't be pleased after she had lavished so much care and attention on gifts for the family, but they could at least be sent on. He promised himself he would tell her soon.

'Shall I continue to read to you, while you work?'

Alex picked up *Waverley*. They were already halfway through the story of the Jacobite rebellion of 1745 and he enjoyed the cosy companionship and even the domesticity of reading aloud while Jane sewed. His younger self would have stared to see how he had changed.

'I would rather you didn't.' Jane didn't look at him, her head bent over her work. 'Not tonight, if you don't mind. I would rather talk.'

Hell and damnation!

He wasn't always the most perceptive of men, but he couldn't miss her resolve. Jane lifted her head and his teeth clenched.

'Very well. How long will it be until the kittens are fully weaned, do you suppose?'

Jane's eyes remained steady on his. 'Not long now, but it is not that I wish to talk about.'

Alex huffed a laugh. 'You sound far too serious for this time of night, Janey.' He sat next to her and trailed one finger down her cheek to her neck, and around her neckline. 'Let's go to bed early, sweetheart.' He nipped her earlobe, then sucked at it.

He thought his distraction had worked. Jane moved her head to capture his lips and kissed him, moving her full lips over his, firing his blood. But she took his face between her palms and eased her mouth from his long before he was ready to end their kiss.

'Alex…you do know how much I care for you, don't you?'

He pulled back, frowning. 'Of course I know, Janey. As I care for you.'

'Do you? Really?' She shook her head. 'How can you care for someone if you do not trust them?'

He straightened, staring at her. 'I *do* trust you!'

'I thought you did. But now...' She paused, chewing her lip, and his heart squeezed, knowing he was the cause of her worry. 'You're hiding something, Alex. What happened to you this afternoon? Are you ill? Ought you to see a physician?'

'I'm not ill and I don't need a physician.'

'But...what happened? You mentioned the scream...did it remind you of what happened with Pikeford?'

He'd thought to protect her by not mentioning that bastard, but it seemed she'd reached that conclusion anyway.

'I think of him sometimes, you know.'

Alex stiffened. 'Who?'

'Pikeford. About that day.'

'You've never said.'

'I didn't want to worry you. But that makes me as bad as you—hiding the truth to protect you.'

'When do you think about him? When we make love?' He loathed the very thought.

'No!' She caressed his hand. 'You have helped me so much, Alex. I never think of him at those times. But it *has* affected me—I went for a walk in the woods and I couldn't go on. I couldn't rid myself of the conviction someone was following me.'

'Janey! I had no idea.'

Guilt and shame swirled through him. What kind of man didn't notice his wife's distress?

'And I've had flashes of memory of what happened. For a few seconds it is as though it is actually happening again.

I can't breathe and I can't move, and the fear…it wells up and, even though I know it's not real, it still *feels* real.'

She swallowed audibly and he squeezed her hand, even as his heart thudded against his ribs. That sounded exactly how he reacted to those accursed visions.

'I wish you had told me sooner, Janey. You must have known I would want to help.'

She stared at him, her eyes serious. 'As I want to help you.'

He could see her willing him to confide in her. But he couldn't. He straightened, holding her hands as he gazed into her eyes.

'You must tell me if it happens to you again, Janey. I will help you to get over it, I promise you.'

She didn't try to hide her frustration.

'But… Alex…what about today? I hate any reminder of Pikeford, but that scream didn't affect me. Why would it have that effect on you?'

An image exploded into his head—his mother…the shadowy figure of a man…a struggle. He couldn't tell her! Hell, he didn't know for sure what he was 'seeing' in those visions. Were any of them true? Had he actually witnessed—?

He swiped that question aside and leapt to his feet, fear he was going mad scorching through him.

'Alex?' Jane stood, grabbing his hand, stopping him from leaving. 'What is it? *Please* tell me.'

'It's nothing. You're imagining it. I have the headache so I shall sleep in my own room tonight.'

She didn't release him. 'No. Please do not. Come to bed with me… I promise I shan't plague you with any more questions.' She pressed her lips to his hand. 'But I do wish you would trust me enough to *talk* to me.'

Dear God! How he wished he *could* confide in her. But

how could he when he didn't even know if they were real memories or a fiction conjured up by years of nightmares? And what if he was losing his grasp of what was real and what was inside his head? What then? What would the future hold?

He quashed his fears and forced a smile.

'There is nothing to tell, Honeybee. Nothing at all. Come to bed.'

Chapter Eleven

Jane was relieved when Alex's funny turn, as she came to think of it, didn't recur, but something was clearly bothering him although he tried to hide it. It couldn't be money… the ledgers confirmed their finances were healthy. She was almost certain it wasn't her… Alex would never manage to hide it if he truly regretted their marriage. She'd be left in no doubt if she was at fault.

She told herself it was her imagination…she was being over-sensitive…but as the days got shorter and the nights closed in those doubts simply would not go away and, rather than reassure her, Alex's lovemaking slowly but surely started to echo everything that was going wrong in their marriage. One morning as they lay together in a post-coital glow, Jane could no longer deny her frustration. Physically, she was fully satisfied. Alex was everything she could wish for. But emotionally… She frowned as she pondered the source of her disquiet. She couldn't deny the suspicion that, emotionally—in bed as well as out of it—he was holding back. Those barriers behind which he had always protected himself—the ones she believed were crumbling—were firmly back in place.

The mattress dipped as Alex rolled over to face her. He

traced between her brows with his forefinger. 'Why the frown, Janey?'

But how could she explain when she barely understood it herself? All she could do was to keep proving he could trust her and hope he would eventually confide in her. His lovemaking was so controlled, reminding her of a rider who put his horse at a hedge, but spent the approach ensuring every aid was perfection. She longed for Alex to release his control and 'throw his heart over'.

She lied. 'I was thinking your nightmares have improved.'

'That's good, though. Isn't it?'

It was his turn to frown now, staring unseeingly across the room as Jane laid her hand against his whisker-rough cheek.

'Have you had any more episodes such as that day we went to High Wycombe?'

She'd not broached the subject since and she hadn't seen anything, but that didn't mean they hadn't happened and she knew Alex would never voluntarily admit it to her.

'Why should the subject of my nightmares cause you to think about that?' His amber eyes turned wary. 'The two are unconnected.'

She cuddled into him, her cheek to his chest. 'I wasn't sure they *were* unconnected.'

She remained convinced he was hiding his troubles to protect her. If only he would talk to her about his mother. About the day he found her body. It couldn't be good for him to keep those memories inside.

'I think that child's scream reminded you of Pikeford's attack and, because it happened in the same place as your mother—'

He tipped up her face and kissed her, his lips moving over hers with practised skill, and her thoughts scattered as she responded to the coaxing caress of his tongue. The kiss ended and Alex rolled from the bed in one smooth movement.

'Come on, lazybones. There's work to be done.'

He tugged the covers from her body and picked her up, kissing her again before allowing her body to slide down his until her feet touched the floor. The cool caress of the morning air shook her thoughts back to their conversation... and his blatant attempt to distract her.

'Wait!'

His eyes narrowed. 'Don't think about that day, Janey. Pikeford isn't worthy of a single second of your time.'

'I know. But...your nightmares...they got worse after—'

'And now they are improving. I'm always the same when I go back to the Abbey...the nightmares were not linked to Pikeford's attack and there's no reason whatsoever why a random scream should resurrect anything.'

Was he trying to convince himself, or her?

'I hope that does not mean we can never go to the Abbey, especially as I've already accepted your stepmother's invitation to spend Christmas there.'

She'd hoped to diffuse the tension shimmering between them, but Alex refused to meet her eyes as he shrugged into his banyan.

'I remember you saying so.'

Jane frowned. That seemed somewhat non-committal, but she was reluctant to pursue the subject. There were enough difficulties already in their relationship without cultivating more.

After a few days of heavy rain when they couldn't continue Pearl's education, they took advantage of a dry morning to work together on schooling her.

'She's ready for you to ride out,' Alex said as they

strolled back to the house together. 'What do you say to taking her out early tomorrow? We can ride around the fields and get her used to all the sights and sounds.'

'I say that sounds perfect.' Jane couldn't wait for Pearl's education to be complete. 'And you haven't forgotten I am to visit Mrs Phillips again today, have you?'

Mrs Phillips was several years Jane's senior, but they had much in common, and Jane had promised her support for the vicar's various charitable endeavours on behalf of the poor of the district.

'I hadn't forgotten. Would you like me to drive you to the village or are you comfortable driving yourself?'

'I can drive myself.' Although still wary of walking alone in the countryside she had no fear of driving. She looked forward to the freedom of riding out alone, too, once Pearl was ready. 'There's no need to waste your time and I know you won't miss the neighbourly gossip.' The very idea of Alex sitting making polite small talk with any of their neighbours, let alone a vicar's wife, was laughable. 'I've asked Lilley to have the pony and trap ready at two.'

Jane had spent a pleasant hour visiting Mrs Phillips, hearing all about the usual Christmas activities in Malton—decorating the Church on Christmas Eve and the morning church service after which the poor of the village were invited to an open kitchen at the vicarage. As she and Alex would be away during Christmastide, Jane promised to arrange for food to be sent to the vicarage to help feed the poor, many of whom, Mrs Phillips said, would afterwards go wassailing around the district, hoping to be given gifts of money, food or drink.

When it was time to leave, Mrs Phillips handed Jane a bunch of silvery-pink roses.

'I hope you will accept these? This rose flowers right

up to the first frost and I thought you might enjoy a few fresh flowers.'

'Thank you.' Jane smiled with pleasure, raising the blooms to her nose. 'The fragrance is glorious.' She frowned. 'Do you know…although the gardens at Foxbourne are extensive, I cannot recall seeing any roses.'

'That's odd. The late Lady Rockbeare definitely grew them. Maybe they had to be dug out?'

'I shall ask the gardeners. Goodbye, Mrs Phillips, and thank you.'

Jane tapped the pony with the reins to drive home, but she had barely left the village behind when she heard someone call her name. Pikeford shot into her brain. Suppressing her quiver of fear, she glanced over her shoulder to see Tommy, the postmaster's son, on his pony. She breathed easier and halted the trap.

'Good afternoon, milady. I have a letter for the Manor.' Tommy grinned at her disarmingly as he withdrew a letter from his shoulder bag. 'You'll save me some time if you don't mind taking it. My other deliveries are out towards Cucklow.'

Jane opened her reticule. 'Of course I don't mind, Tommy. How much is the postage?'

'Sixpence, milady.' Jane passed him the coins. 'It's from St Albans.' He wheeled his pony around and trotted away.

That must surely mean it was from Zach—Alex had written to ask for his help with an exceptionally fast and handsome stallion who had been badly treated and harboured a deep mistrust of humans, biting and kicking anyone who entered his stall. Alex had saved him from certain destruction, hoping to use him for breeding if he could satisfy himself Nelson's viciousness was the result of the ill treatment and not a trait he might pass on to his offspring. The stallion, however, was proving a challenge.

* * *

Back at the stable yard, Lilley informed Jane that Alex was indoors so, one arm full of roses and the letter in her other hand, Jane walked up to the house.

Home. She already felt a deep sense of peace being here and marvelled at her unexpected good fortune. Her heart full of joy, she went straight to Alex's business room. He was at the window behind his large mahogany desk, his back to the room, arms folded across his chest.

'I thought to find you hard at work, but here you are daydreaming.'

Jane crossed the room and rounded the desk, laying the roses and the letter on its gleaming surface.

Alex started as she spoke and faced her. She clasped his upper arms and aimed a kiss at his cheek, but he moved his head so their lips met. He cradled her face as he explored her mouth in a kiss that melted her insides.

Would she ever get used to this? The man of her dreams, now her husband. Hers. Heat pooled low in her belly and, with an effort, she pulled away. He quirked a brow, his tiger eyes aglow.

'Is that it? You've been gone hours and all I get is one measly...'

His face blanked. Jane frowned. His eyes looked... empty, somehow. Unseeing. His lips were tight and his chest rose and fell in a rapid rhythm.

'Alex? What is it?'

He screwed his eyes shut and then opened them again, to look at her. Then his gaze shifted to one side, and beyond Jane—to the roses on the desk.

'Get them out of here,' he growled.

'I... Why? What is—?'

'Do it!'

'But...Mrs Phillips gave them to me. They have the most beautiful scent.'

Jane reached for the bunch and held them up to Alex. He dashed them from her hand and spun to face the window again.

'I said get them out of here. No roses. Ever. Do you understand?'

'But...' Her brain scrambled to understand. 'Why?'

She moved so she could see his profile—jaw muscle bunched tight, lips colourless.

'Alex? I don't understand.'

Her voice wobbled and tears stung. She swallowed to keep them at bay.

'Get rid of them.'

The easy option was to mindlessly obey, but why should he get away with barking orders at her when she'd done nothing wrong? She'd had enough of her stepmother browbeating her...she wouldn't accept that kind of treatment from Alex.

'What is wrong with roses?'

His chest continued to heave and his hands clenched into fists at his sides. 'The smell makes me sick. Take them. Go.'

Jane, still puzzled, sensed she would get no more from him while the roses were in the room. Silently she gathered the scattered blooms and left, vowing this would not be the end of the matter.

'Mrs Kent?' The housekeeper was in the kitchen, sharing a cup of tea with the new cook, Mrs Godfrey. 'Would you care to have these roses for your quarters? It seems His Lordship does not care for their scent.'

'Oh, my!' Mrs Kent shot to her feet and almost snatched the flowers from Jane. 'I am sorry, milady. Mayhap I should have warned you, but I thought you would know, having known His Lordship such a long time. It's a strict rule. No roses in the house. Nor in the garden. He made poor Scully dig them all out. Near broke his heart, it did, destroying Lady Rockbeare's pride and joy that way.'

That might underline the fact Alex hated roses, but it explained nothing. Maybe Alex would tell her the real reason once he had calmed down. Jane smiled at Mrs Kent, handing her the flowers.

'It would be a pity to waste them now they have been cut. And His Lordship will never know you have them unless you tell him.'

Needing comfort, Jane headed to see the kittens, who were now eating and drinking for themselves, although they were still with their mother. In the outhouse, Dora— who could come and go through an open window—was absent. Jane sat on a cushion and distracted herself from what had happened with Alex by rolling a pine cone for the kittens to chase. When they tired of the game they piled on to Jane's lap and fell asleep. The smallest, prettiest and fluffiest—grey and white, like Dora—was her favourite and she decided she would keep Mist, as she called her, as a pet.

'I thought I would find you in here.'

Her stomach tensed at Alex's voice. She did not look up.

He crouched next to her, touching her hand. 'I'm sorry. I should have warned you.'

Not much of an apology.

'Why do you dislike roses so much?'

He shrugged. 'I just do.'

It was the old Alex talking—abrupt and dismissive. The *mind your own business* Alex she had known since childhood. The *I don't need anyone's help* Alex. Had it been too much to hope he had changed? Perhaps it was inevitable their relationship would be two steps forward, one step back to begin with. She suspected that, in some way, his aversion was bound up with the past and the secrets that simmered deep inside him. And all she could do was to keep proving to him he could trust her and hope, in time, he would confide in her.

'Anyway, I have good news.' Alex waved the letter under her nose. 'It's from Zach. He's coming to help me and Aunt Cecily and Florence are coming with him. They arrive tomorrow.'

The carriage drew up outside the front door the following afternoon. Alex was down at the stables, but had promised to come up to the house as soon as their visitors arrived and, true to his word, Jane could see him striding in their direction as she went outside to greet the Graystokes. Myrtle had come, too, hopping around on her three legs, her whole body wriggling in delight.

Aunt Cecily enveloped Jane in an apple-blossom-scented embrace. 'I hope you don't mind us all coming? When Alex wrote to Zach about Nelson we thought it the perfect opportunity.'

Jane hugged her back. 'Of course we don't mind. We're delighted to see you all.'

As Alex kissed his aunt and shook hands with Zach, Jane scooped up Florence and kissed her cheek. Two pudgy arms wound around her neck and dusky curls tickled Jane's nose as Alex watched them, his expression wistful. Would he make a good father? She hoped so, but it was obvious he hadn't had much practice with children, unlike Dominic, who was a natural with their young half-sister and brother, and with their cousins. Never mind. She loved Alex and would help him become the man and father she sensed he wanted to be.

Her arms quickly ached with holding Florence's solid

little body but, before she could put the child down, Zach was there, taking his daughter gently.

'You gradually get used to the increasing weight as your child grows, I find. But it is surprisingly fatiguing when you are not accustomed to it.'

Jane smiled up at him, feeling a little shy. She had only met Zach for the first time in the summer and she found him a little unnerving, with his dark soulful eyes and the glinting diamond he wore in his ear.

'It is a pleasure to meet you again, Jane.'

'And you, Uncle…um… Mr Graystoke.'

'Zach will do, my dear.'

She smiled again. 'Come inside. I will show you to your bedchamber—there will be a tea tray in the drawing room in half an hour.'

Chapter Twelve

It was fun having guests to stay and Jane was in her element, playing hostess in her own establishment—a role she had feared she might never fulfil. Her hopes had dwindled as the Seasons passed, but now—when she had finally lost all hope—her dreams had come true and she was married to the love of her life. Who was proving every bit as challenging as she had thought he would.

But while they had guests, Jane pushed any concerns about Alex to the back of her mind—neither of them referred again to his reaction to those roses and their nights together were still full of passion as he coaxed responses from her body as a talented musician might coax exquisite tunes from his instrument.

Alex, for his part, proved he could play the perfect host. He and Zach spent much of their time at the stable yard, working with Nelson—even when it rained—while Jane, Aunt Cecily and, usually, Florence, went for walks whenever the weather allowed, chatting about all manner of subjects, including the planned Christmas family gathering at the Abbey. The only subject they did not touch upon…the subject Jane longed to broach but did not quite dare…was Alex and his past. Until the day before the Graystokes' departure.

Florence was napping, so Jane and Aunt Cecily walked alone.

No sooner was the Manor out of sight than Aunt Cecily said, 'Alex seems very settled at the moment but...' She sighed and slid a sideways glance at Jane. 'I cannot help but worry about him. He is...complex.'

'He is.'

As Jane pondered how to elaborate, Aunt Cecily continued, 'I hope I have not offended you by my frank speaking. You must say if you would feel it would be disloyal to discuss Alex with me.'

Jane almost laughed. 'No. I do not consider it disloyal to want to help my husband. I know he loves you like a mother.'

It was easier to start with something simple. If anything about her frustrating husband could be deemed simple.

'Do you know why he dislikes roses?'

'*Roses?* I didn't know he disliked them. Why...' Aunt Cecily paused. 'Now I come to think of it...he specified no roses at your wedding. I was so busy I didn't question it at the time. And...your garden. There are no roses. And yet I particularly remember Leo mentioned a rose garden when he described the place to me at the time he was thinking of buying it.'

'Apparently Alex ordered the gardener to dig them all up. I only found out by chance—he became quite...well, *agitated*...when the vicar's wife gave me a bunch of roses for the house. I wondered if it might be linked to his discovering his mother's body?'

'Oh!' Aunt Cecily halted. 'That could be it. Margaret... the perfume she always wore was rose-scented and smells *do* prompt memories, do they not? At least, they do for me. Mayhap roses remind him of that day?'

More than ever Jane believed Pikeford's attack *had* revived Alex's memory of that dreadful day.

'Poor little boy,' Aunt Cecily continued. 'He didn't speak for nigh on a year afterwards. I was so afraid he would never talk again…and he clung to me so…he wouldn't even trust his own father. I suppose he was afraid he might lose me, too, like he lost his mother.'

'Did he ever tell you about discovering his mother's body? After he regained his speech?'

'No. I tried to talk to him about it, but he became so agitated Leo decided we should leave it in the past. He thought it would be better for all three children to look forward, not back, so we rarely spoke of Margaret unless one of the children mentioned her. And that was seldom.'

Jane could believe that. As long as she had known Alex, he'd avoided the subject of his mother.

'How sad he avoids all memories of his mother because of that one day. Surely he must have happy memories of her, too?'

'I think Margaret's death supersedes everything in Alex's mind. Besides, she was not the best of mothers to those children. Although…' Aunt Cecily linked her arm through Jane's and they resumed walking '…she *was* attempting to change. Leo stopped her frequent jaunts up to London and, not long before she died, she told me she wanted to become a better mother.'

They let the subject drop, but it left Jane with plenty to mull over. Alex's dislike of roses was something she could accept, but she would love to help him overcome his aversion to his father and to the Abbey. His wistful expression sometimes when he saw Dominic or Olivia with their father was all the encouragement she needed to believe that there, at least, she could help. Perhaps Christmas at the Abbey could be a turning point.

They emerged on to a lane, turning in the opposite direction to the village.

'Halsdon Manor is up here,' Jane said. 'There's been great excitement in Malton because it will soon be occupied, for the first time in over five years. Alex tells me it is owned by your cousin, Mr Lascelles.'

'Oh, heavens. Now *there* is a name from the past. Has he returned to England?'

'Nobody knows for sure, but they say it's been let, so that must mean a tenant.'

'Just as well,' Aunt Cecily muttered.

'Why do you say that?'

'Has Alex not told you the story?'

'He told me Mr Lascelles is your illegitimate cousin and he resents your brother being the duke, but nothing more.'

'Probably because he doesn't know much more, other than what happened five years ago. I doubt he remembers him from his childhood because Anthony has lived overseas for most of his adult life, apart from a couple of brief returns. But he came back and bought Halsdon Manor five years ago and Leo and Vernon came here to try to mend the breach between Leo and Anthony. But I believe that resentment runs too deep for them to ever get along. That trip proved worthwhile, however, because Leo met Rosalind, and he also discovered Foxbourne Manor was for sale and, now, here you are.'

'In that case, I am grateful they at least attempted to heal that breach. This Mr Lascelles sounds unpleasant, to transfer his father's sins on to the Duke.'

'I always tried to give him the benefit of the doubt because I understand his frustration that his life might have been very different. But he *is* a troublemaker. When Leo and Rosalind were courting he took a shine to her and when she rejected him, he abducted Susie in an attempt to force Rosalind to marry him.'

'Abducted Susie? How evil! She must have been terrified.'

'She was only eight when Rosalind took her in—although she seemed younger, a poor little scrap of a thing—and I don't think she understood much of what happened. Luckily, Leo found out and averted disaster, with Alex's help, and Leo persuaded Anthony he would fare better out of the country for a while.'

As he did with Sir Denzil. It clearly doesn't pay to make an enemy of such a powerful duke.

They reached the entrance of Halsdon Manor and paused to gaze at the house, at the head of a straight drive.

'I confess to some relief he won't be returning himself.'

'You probably need not worry even if he did, Jane. Anthony never bore any resentment towards the rest of us, only Leo. But you'd still be wise to be cautious, should you ever meet. He has a great deal of charm, but he *is* clever and manipulative.'

They continued back to Foxbourne, their path taking them past the paddock where Alex and Zach were working with Nelson. Zach strolled over to join them when they paused by the fence to watch.

'Did you have a pleasant walk, my dove?' He stroked his wife's cheek with his forefinger, his dark eyes on her face.

A touch of envy stirred inside Jane. She was content with Alex, but would he ever look at her in that way, with his heart in his eyes? She loved him so much, but would he ever lower his guard enough to love her in return?

'Very pleasant, my darling. I love to walk with Florence, but it was nice to have the chance to talk in peace, was it not, Jane?'

'It was.' Jane's gaze strayed to where Alex—holding out an apple—approached the stallion, who was watching him, head high, the huge muscles in his haunches bunched. 'Is Alex safe in there, Zach?'

'Nelson no longer attacks, now he is not in a confined space. He *wants* to trust us, but he suspects a trick.'

Nelson wheeled around and trotted away from Alex who, rather than continuing to coax the stallion, turned his own back and walked to the opposite end of the paddock. Nelson stood stock-still, ears pricked, before lowering his neck and shaking his head. He took a tentative step towards Alex, followed by another. When he drew near, Alex walked away again, following the fence around. Nelson shadowed him.

'Ah…' Zach breathed. 'He won't be coaxed, but he'll follow of his own accord. He wants to trust Alex, but on his own terms.'

Nelson continued to follow Alex, slowly nearing him until his nose was mere inches from his shoulder. Alex halted and before very long Nelson was crunching an apple contentedly, juice dripping from his lips, as Alex stroked him, murmuring praise.

Having Aunt Cecily, Zach and Florence to stay proved the perfect distraction to stop Alex fretting over his overreaction when Jane brought those roses into his business room. He'd avoided roses over the years, most likely because they prompted memories of Mother, but he'd learned to control that response. Roses, after all, were almost impossible to avoid completely—all manner of social occasions included flowers, and roses were widely used—but his vow to be reasonable and to control his dark moods had shattered the second that smell summoned such a vivid flash of memory. Nausea roiled his stomach whenever that memory edged into his thoughts over the next few days, but although he consciously thrust it aside, afraid of examining it too closely, he could not dismiss it entirely.

This time, as with the child's scream, there had been

no image of Pikeford's attack to warn him, just the instant immersion into...what? The past? A fragment of his old nightmares? He still wasn't sure, but the fear of that vision being true was now equal to the fear he was losing his mind. All he knew was the scent of roses had triggered the same scene—the yellow gown and slippers, and that pair of gleaming boots, the quietly furious voices, the two figures sinking to the floor. But that image had shimmered, fading, and then a new image began to form—something horrifying; something that stole his breath and made his heart thump in his chest and cold sweat gather on his brow. The cries...the grunts...a slender neck...large hands around it...

And he'd panicked, dashing the roses aside, petrified of allowing that picture to fully form, some primal instinct screaming at him that it would be disastrous for not only his own peace of mind, but also the future happiness of his entire family.

Why was this happening to him? Why now? Since Pikeford's attack it seemed a leak had sprung in the barrier between his conscious mind and the deep well of memories of the day his mother died.

These visions were driving him close to despair so he welcomed the distraction of having guests to stay and he strived to behave as normally as possible. The intensity of working with Zach on Nelson helped push his worries to the back of his mind and he genuinely loved having his aunt to stay. Little Florence made him yearn for children of his own—he found himself watching Jane, both with and without Florence, and imagining her with their children. *That* image never failed to bring a smile to his lips and hope into his heart.

I have so much to be thankful for. I couldn't wish for a better wife and I have Foxbourne.

He silently recited the refrain every day, but it never seemed enough to protect against the past that lurked, waiting to leap out and destroy his life if ever he allowed his guard to drop.

He thought he'd done an excellent job of covering his fears and tension, but he might have known Aunt Cecily and, in particular, Zach would not easily be fooled. On the last night of their visit, as Alex and Zach lingered over their after-dinner port, Zach came straight to the point.

'You are troubled, Alex. Both Cecily and I sense it. Have the nightmares continued?'

He supposed it was inevitable. The entire family must know his nightmares had returned at the Abbey—it was impossible to keep such a secret when servants gossiped about their masters so freely. But…he eyed Zach. Could he tell him part of the truth? It would be a relief to let some of his worries out. The other man's calm, non-judgemental attitude positively invited confidences.

'It's not only nightmares.' He strode to the window, gazing out on the night. 'They started again at the Abbey, as you know, but the attack on Jane somehow became muddled into them and they became…worse.'

He walked back to his chair and sat. Myrtle scuttled over to him and laid her head on his knee, staring up at him with worried eyes. Alex fondled her ear. 'I do sleep better now I am with Jane, but…'

He hesitated. How much could he reveal? And would Zach think he was losing his mind? He took a chance.

'It is almost as though, now my nightmares are more bearable at night, they are hovering at the edge of my mind during the day. And something…a sound, a sight, a smell…will suddenly trigger…' He paused, frowning. 'I'm not sure they're even memories; they could just be fragments of nightmares. I don't know what is real and what is imagined any more. And, at times, I fear I am going mad.'

But the greater fear now lurked out there. The fear he had actually witnessed his own mother's murder. And that was a fear he could reveal to no one. Not until he was certain, for how on earth could he voice that other suspicion that prowled around the shadowed edges of his memory? The suspicion fed by those images of his father that followed the visions. He could swear Zach to secrecy, but he and Aunt Cecily were so very close it would be unfair, especially when it could simply be the befuddled recall of a terrified child.

He swallowed past the knot in his throat. Dragged in a breath.

'They conjure up such *feelings*. Feelings that have the power...have the power...' He swallowed again. 'I am afraid of what I will learn if I allow those memories to surface fully, Zach.'

His father's face materialised once again in his mind's eye.

And not just for me. For the entire family.

'If the memories are close and if your mind is ready to remember the past, then perhaps you might be wise to allow them to form fully so you can examine them from a man's perspective,' Zach said. 'At least then you would know exactly what memories still haunt you after all these years. Otherwise, how can you ever move on from the past? Is it not worth facing up to your fears for the sake of your marriage? For Jane?'

'It's not as easy as that. It's all right for you. You've never had—'

'You are wrong.' Zach's dark gaze penetrated Alex. 'I have bad memories that threatened my sanity at times. But I allowed them into the light and they lost some of their power over me. And, with the help and love of your aunt, I confronted my past. Memories cannot destroy us unless we allow them to. They can cause pain and tears and regrets, but once we acknowledge them they are always less powerful than if they are suppressed. If we do not confront our fears, we give them the power to haunt our present and our future. Is that what you want? This dark cloud hanging over you, casting gloom over your life and over your marriage?

'Maybe it is time for you to remember, Alex. You are a man, no longer a seven-year-old child afraid of monsters under the bed. Whatever we speak of tonight will stay between us but, if you will take my advice, you will confide in Jane. She is honest and straightforward. And she loves you.'

'*Loves* me? I...'

He paused, his thoughts whirling. He'd never even considered love, but it made sense of how he occasionally caught Jane looking at him and how, ever since he had known her, she had tried to help him, even when he was being foul to her. He'd always thought love wasn't possible for a man like him, but...he recalled that whisper of hope on their wedding day and the feeling that had grown— the feeling he couldn't imagine his life without her in it. Could it be...?

But even if what he felt for her was love, how could he confide in her? *He* was the man of the house. It was for him to be strong—how could he humble himself by confessing to his wife that the terrors of a small boy still had the power to bring him to his knees? How could she love and respect such a weakling?

Besides, as soon as he admitted he might have witnessed his mother's murder, the questions would start. Who did he see? Who killed her? He couldn't face those questions. He didn't know the answer...he didn't *want* to know the answer. The reason behind those hazy images of his father's face was what scared him the most, threatening his entire family, and the same reason he couldn't burden Zach with the full extent of his fears also applied to Jane.

No. He must deal with this himself.

'Maybe she does,' he said, 'in which case I am a fortunate man. And you are right... If I stop trying to suppress what happened, maybe the truth will not be as dreadful as I fear.' He said the words, but he did not believe them. 'Your advice, as ever, is sound. Thank you.'

Dark, knowing eyes surveyed Alex and his stomach squirmed at the directness of that gaze. Zach always seemed to see what others kept concealed in their hearts and Alex knew he had not fooled him. But he also knew Zach would interfere no further. He had said his piece and he would leave it to Alex to decide whether or not to take his advice.

They finished their drinks in silence.

Chapter Thirteen

A few weeks later Alex again awoke bathed in sweat, his head brim-full of incomplete images and his heart hammering with utter terror.

'Alex?' Jane embraced him, drawing his head to her breast. 'You're safe. It's all right. I'm here. It wasn't real.'

But it *was* real—Mother *had* been murdered. He just didn't know if he'd witnessed it or if his imagination had embellished the truth over the years.

He thrust the memories down and slammed a lid on them.

'Shhh…'

Cool fingers caressed his forehead. His cheek. Combed through his hair. Almost against his will, his eyelids grew heavy and they drifted shut and his unquiet mind stilled as he sank towards blessed oblivion.

It was his first thought when he awoke. At some point in the night they had swapped over, and he lay on his back, Jane slumbering peacefully in his arms, her glorious bosoms pressed to his naked chest and one slim leg flung across his. He was already painfully hard. What better way to start the day and banish the nightmare? He tilted her face to his, waited until her lids flickered and she began to rouse, then kissed her. Gently. One thing he had learned about his wife was that she did not awaken all bright and breezy. She took time to surface. But he knew the perfect way to help her, and he stroked the length of her back, tracing each vertebra, watching her face the whole time.

Her eyes opened, dazed, heavy-lidded. Then widened. She wriggled free and sat up.

'You had a nightmare.'

'Hush. Never mind about that.'

But Jane stared down at him, utterly awake, her expression a mixture of concern and determination. He put his hand on her thigh and caressed her, moving steadily upwards. Jane placed her hand on his and held it still.

'Janey...sweetheart...' Quite apart from now wishing to distract her—as well as himself—from the subject of nightmares, Alex simply wanted to bury himself inside his wife. 'We'll talk later.'

Not likely! But she needn't know that.

But to his dismay, Jane shook her head. 'We *could* talk later, but you forget...I *know* you, Alexander Beauchamp. You will discover a million and one ways to avoid me until you think I have forgotten. However...' she wriggled her way down in the bed until she was also lying flat and wrapped her fingers around his length '...indulge me now and *I* shall indulge you afterwards. To your heart's content.'

She squeezed, and Alex couldn't hold in his moan. God, how he wanted her but he would allow no one, not even Jane, to manipulate him. There was nothing anyone could do to help—the suspicion still haunted him that he had indeed witnessed his mother's murder and, if that was true, he could no longer deny he must have seen her killer.

And only one man's face kept appearing in connection with that day.

His father. The Duke of Cheriton.

Even just *thinking* that made his stomach heave, forcing hot, sour bile into his throat.

It couldn't be true!

That inexplicable aversion towards his father had driven him to rebel throughout his youth but, deep down, he had always *wanted* to love him. Unconditionally. But now... that suspicion gnawed at him endlessly...

He cupped Jane's face, smoothing his thumb over her soft skin. He would feed her a white lie, and then he would bury all thought of nightmares and do what he did best... satisfy them both.

'I don't remember any details—just that I woke up, and you were there.' He rolled to face her, and laid his hand on her waist. 'I went back to sleep and I didn't have another one.' His hand slid up to her breast and cupped it. He leaned across to press his lips to her naked shoulder. 'Thank you, my darling.' He nuzzled her neck, then stopped as Jane's hand landed on his shoulder, preventing him from lowering his torso to hers. He raised his head. Met her eyes. Widened his. 'What?'

Her own eyes narrowed. 'Don't you play the innocent with me, Alexander.' Her face softened. 'Please. I only want to help. Please tell me about it.'

But there was nothing he *could* tell her. He knew how the nightmare began but the rest was still murky, and the thought of allowing those fragments of horror to fully form—as Zach had suggested—was enough to break him out into a sweat again. He simply wasn't ready. Wasn't brave enough.

'What *do* you remember? There must be something.'

He tried not to resent her pushing him, telling himself her intentions were good. Jane was his wife, and she naturally wanted to share his troubles but *he* was entitled to make the decision not to share them.

'I only remember the very start. It is always the same. I hide from our tutor, Mr Brockley, and then I am outside playing. Then I walk towards the summer house, and then I wake up.'

But he couldn't tell her that, in his dreams, his mother walked by his side. Not when everyone believed what really happened was her dead body had been waiting for him in the summer house.

He was afraid to know if that was the truth, let alone where, and how, his father fitted in.

His throat thickened but he forced a nonchalant tone.

'See? It's nothing. I know what happened, because I've been told. But I cannot remember, and I have no wish to, either. The nightmare is the dread of what's inside the summer house. I wake up before I get there, and it's over.'

She held his gaze before releasing his shoulder and moving her hand to his chest. He released his breath in relief as her eyes darkened and her lips parted, and he leaned in to kiss her, his prick springing back into life.

Later that day, Alex found Jane outside, discussing the kitchen garden with Scully.

'Would you care to ride with me, my dear? Nelson is ready to hack out and the men are all busy.' The stallion had come on marvellously since Alex found the key to unlocking his distrust. 'Pearl will set him the perfect example, she's so well behaved.'

Jane beamed. 'I should love to! Give me ten minutes to change my gown.'

They were soon on their way, Jane dressed in a deep red riding habit, her hat trimmed with netting. They rode through the estate and then out on to the local lanes, nattering away, but, thankfully, both avoiding the subject of nightmares. Nelson soon settled, after a few excited jinks at all the new sights and sounds. The weather was cold and dull but dry, and there was little wind—perfect weather to try out a green youngster, with no shadows across the ground to goggle at, and no sudden gusts to upset him.

They stayed out for half an hour and were on their way back, close to home, when they saw a solitary horseman—a stranger, but clearly a gentleman—riding towards them on a rangy black.

'I wonder if that is our new neighbour?' Jane said.

'It's about time, if it is.' Halsdon Manor had been ready since late October, but still no one knew the identity of the tenant and the house remained empty.

'I hope he is a married gentleman with a family. It will be pleasant to have new neighbours.'

They fell silent as the stranger neared. Alex frowned, studying him intently. There was something…

'Hell and damnation!'

'What is it?'

Alex couldn't tear his attention from the other rider, now near enough for there to be no mistake.

'Leave the talking to me,' Alex muttered to Jane. He raised his voice. 'Lascelles. I was unaware you were back in the country.'

Anthony Lascelles inclined his head. 'Alexander. I heard you now live at Foxbourne.' His teeth gleamed in his tanned face as he smiled. 'How do you do?' His dark gaze slid sideways to Jane. 'I also heard about your recent nuptials. My felicitations to you both.' He bowed again, and raised his hat to reveal close-cropped silver-grey hair—a contrast to the jet-black it had been a mere five years before. 'I am charmed to meet you, Lady Alexander.'

'It is Lady Jane,' Alex bit out, his mind whirling at the awkwardness of this meeting after what Lascelles had done. 'She's Stowford's daughter.'

'Ah. The girl next door. How sweet. And how are the family? I regret my failure to stay in touch while I was overseas but, in view of the misunderstanding before I... er...left so precipitously—'

'Misunderstanding?' At Alex's exclamation Nelson sidestepped into Pearl, causing her to bare her teeth at him. Alex smoothed the stallion's neck to settle him. 'There was no misunderstanding, Lascelles. You forget. I was there. And you didn't leave; we *put* you on that ship.'

'You did. And I am most grateful to you.'

'Grateful? Hah! You expect us to believe that?'

Lascelles arched one brow. 'It is the truth, however.'

'Alex...' Jane laid her hand on his arm. 'The horses are growing restless. Maybe now is not the time for this discussion?'

She was right. Both horses were young and green and if Alex was tense it would harm their progress.

'Your lady is correct,' said Lascelles.

Alex longed to snarl at him that it was none of his business but he held his temper.

'Might I...?' Lascelles hesitated, looking uncertain—an uncharacteristic expression for the man Alex remembered. Five years ago, Lascelles had been smooth and assured with, it seemed, the thickest of skins. He was the only man Alex had ever met who openly mocked and challenged his father. Not many dared.

'Well? What is it? I want to keep our horses moving.'

Between his thighs Nelson was quivering with nerves... not helped by Lascelles' horse, who snaked his head in Nelson's direction several times. Although his teeth clashed harmlessly in mid-air, Nelson was on edge.

Lascelles cleared his throat. 'I should appreciate the opportunity to clear the air with you, Alexander, as we are to be neighbours. Might I perhaps accompany you back to the Manor and explain. I am aware I owe you, and your parents, an apology.' He smiled ruefully at Jane. 'A man can change, can he not? Do I not deserve the opportunity to make amends?'

Alex knew exactly how Jane would respond to that—she always wanted to see the best in people.

'Alex?' Her brown eyes pleaded with him.

It went against his better judgement but it wouldn't hurt to hear the man out—they were to be neighbours after all, so they must learn to rub along together somehow. 'Very well. Come to the house. We can talk over a drink.'

Lascelles smiled, and reined his black aside to allow Alex and Jane to ride ahead of him.

'Thank you,' Jane whispered. 'Surely everyone deserves a chance to prove they've changed.'

Superficially, Anthony Lascelles could not have been more charming. Jane had ordered refreshments—a tea tray and Madeira—and they settled down to talk. He declined the Madeira in favour of a cup of tea. Jane poured the tea and passed him a cup.

'Thank you.'

'You are welcome, sir.'

'Oh, you must call me Anthony.'

He surveyed Jane and she suppressed an involuntary shiver. His eye were the nearest to black she had ever seen. They gave the impression of staring into an abyss.

So empty. I wonder what is really going on inside his head.

She scolded herself for that fanciful thought, feeling guilty that she was judging him after such short acquaintance, but she couldn't shake off the odd feeling that assailed her. He looked every inch the gentleman but there was something about him—now he was in her home—

that set the hairs on the back of her neck to rise. Surely, though, it was only Aunt Cecily's warning that was behind her instinctive distrust of the man? She vowed to quash her doubts and to give Anthony Lascelles the chance he had asked for—the opportunity to prove he was a changed man.

Lascelles sipped his tea before addressing Alex directly, giving Jane the opportunity to study him as they talked. Tall, without an ounce of superfluous flesh on him, he was a good-looking man for his age, which she judged to be near to fifty. He was unmistakeably a Beauchamp, with the same cast of features shared by all the Beauchamp men. Lascelles' face and hands were tanned and he looked healthy and vigorous, his silver-grey hair lending him a distinguished air. But there was also a suggestion of arrogance. Well concealed beneath the charm, but there none the less. That was hardly sufficient to condemn him though. Many gentlemen in their world emanated that same air of superiority although, in Lascelles' case, that conceit seemed at odds with his illegitimacy.

Still. His father *was* a duke. Maybe he should be forgiven a little arrogance.

Jane concentrated on the men's conversation.

'I mentioned an apology, and an explanation as to my past behaviour, Alexander. Allow me to offer the apology first—I am sorry for what happened. Events spiralled out of my control. Has that never happened to you?'

His tone implied he knew the answer to that question all too well, for five years ago Alex had been on the brink of losing everything, from what Jane's stepmother had gleefully announced on her return from the London Season. That had been the year before Jane's debut.

'On occasion.' Alex remained brusque.

'The trouble is…your father and I always enjoyed a

similar taste in ladies. I was smitten by Rosalind but the best man won.'

Alex merely grunted as he stared into his glass of Madeira, reverting to the prickly, monosyllabic man he became whenever he was with someone he did not trust. The same man, Jane realised, he became in his own father's presence. She was still hoping Christmas at the Abbey might provide an opportunity to begin healing that rift between the two of them.

'It is humiliating to confess—particularly within hearing of your charming bride—but I became somewhat obsessed by Rosalind and, when it seemed I was to lose her to your father, it became too much to bear. Looking back, I see that I temporarily lost my reason. I became determined to win her at any cost and behaved in ways I now bitterly regret.'

He paused as though hoping for some response from Alex. When none was forthcoming, he continued, 'I hope to offer my apologies to your father and stepmother at the earliest opportunity but, in the meantime, I should deem it a favour if you refrain from telling them of my return. I should much prefer to meet them on neutral territory, such as in London, rather than suddenly appear at Cheriton Abbey.'

Alex raised his head at that. 'You could write to them.'

One corner of Lascelles' mouth lifted in a half-smile. 'I have thought of that, but this is something I need to do in person.'

An awkward silence fell, which Jane felt obliged to fill. 'Where did you go, when you went overseas, Anthony?'

Alex barked a harsh laugh. 'He didn't leave of his own free will, Jane. He had no choice. We put him on a ship bound for China, and Father paid the captain very well to ensure his new crew member had no opportunity to abscond until they reached their destination.'

'Ah…' Lascelles drained his teacup and placed it with its saucer on a nearby side table. He smoothed one hand along his breeches-clad thigh. 'Dear Captain Cheng. We struck up quite a rapport, don't you know, and he—in return for a substantial further payment I was fortunate enough to be in a position to make—allowed me to disembark in Cape Town.'

Alex's eyes narrowed. 'I don't believe you. Where did you get that sort of money?'

Lascelles smiled. 'Alex… Alex…you cannot blame me for making my plight less desperate, surely? Granted, I was imprisoned upon that ship until it sailed, but the Captain understood very well I might have need of replacement clothing and so forth and, as luck would have it, I had planned to leave London that very day. My trunk—containing cash and banker's drafts to cover my expenses—was ready packed. One of the crew went to my house to collect my trunk, for which kindness I rewarded him substantially.'

Alex's mouth twitched and reluctant admiration lit his tawny eyes. He shook his head, and his mouth widened in a reluctant smile. 'Uncle Vernon said you always come up smelling of roses.'

Lascelles smiled back. 'It is a talent. A useful one.'

'Would you care for another cup of tea, Anthony?'

Jane rose to pour a fresh cup for herself.

'I think not, dear lady. I have said what I came to say and I can only hope we might start afresh, Alexander. Just because your father and I have never been on comfortable terms is no reason for us not to get along, I should hope.'

'You've always resented Father.'

'It is true I have always begrudged the circumstances of my birth as, I think, would most men in my position. My father and mother were together for many years and, if he had married her, I would be the duke and my life would be very different. I have never denied my resentment, but these past five years I have realised that to cling on to that bitterness hurts me more than anyone.' His gaze flicked down, and then back to Alex. 'I also blamed your father for your mother's untimely death.'

The colour drained from Alex's face but he made no sound.

'Your father and I might never have seen eye to eye, but Margaret and I were friends long before she wed your father. I didn't know if you were aware of that.'

'No. I know nothing about you, other than what happened five years ago. I don't recall you visiting the Abbey.'

'I visited once or twice in the early days of their marriage but it was clear I was unwelcome and, because your father and I often argued, Margaret asked me to stay away. Shortly afterwards, I went to the Americas. Now,' Lascelles stood, 'I have outstayed my welcome, so I will bid you good day.' He bowed to Jane. 'It was a pleasure to make your acquaintance, Lady Jane. I hope we shall meet again soon.'

There was a slight questioning lilt to his final words and, before she realised what she was doing, Jane said, 'You must join us for dinner some time.'

Lascelles smiled. 'But what a generous invitation. When did you have in mind?'

Jane glanced at Alex, who shrugged. 'Um…well…what about next week?' she said. 'Tuesday?'

Lascelles' smile faded. 'Unfortunately I have a prior engagement.'

Jane's relief was short-lived as he added, 'I am, however, free on Thursday.' His teeth gleamed in a smile.

Jane forced herself to return it. 'We shall look forward to it.'

'I'll walk you down to the stables,' Alex said.

When he returned, Jane expected him to be annoyed she had invited Lascelles to dine, but he merely laughed when she apologised.

'You were right,' he said. 'We're neighbours and I don't want to be on bad terms with him, so it will do no harm. Besides, it will be interesting to talk to someone who knew my mother—none of the family ever talk about her and *my* memories are…'

He trailed into silence, his expression darkening. Jane put her arms around him.

'I'm sure it will help to replace your memories with happier images of your mother, even if they are secondhand.'

She pressed against him, a thrill running through her at the feeling of his lean hard body against hers. His arms wrapped around her waist and he pulled her closer still to graze his lips over hers. Lascelles was soon forgotten as passion overtook them.

Chapter Fourteen

They returned to the subject of their new neighbour over dinner.

'I have been thinking,' said Alex.

'About?'

'Lascelles. I might call upon him tomorrow. I should like to talk to him about my mother and I think he will talk more freely if it's only the two of us.'

Disquiet threaded through Jane.

'I am in two minds about him, Alex. I find him… Oh, I don't know…disconcerting, I suppose.' The word wasn't quite strong enough, but it would do until she knew him better. 'However, I couldn't help but sympathise when he spoke of his father. It would surely be enough to make any man bitter. But…do be careful.' The warning left her lips before she could help it.

Alex stared for a moment, then laughed. '*Careful?* What do you think he might do? Abduct me like he abducted Susie and tried to abduct Rosalind?'

Jane's cheeks burned. He was right. Alex was no child, he was a grown man, but…Lascelles…there was something…

'Your aunt is the least judgemental person I've ever

met, and she warned me to be cautious if we should ever meet. And your father—'

'My father has nothing to say about who I associate with.' Alex scowled as he spooned gooseberry pie into his mouth.

Jane bit her lip against the urge to probe Alex's touchy relationship with his father. He was already irritated with her.

'I am just…uneasy about Lascelles, Alex.'

And now she was irritated with herself. What had happened to her resolve to speak her mind in this marriage?

'And I do not like him asking us to keep his return from your family. Are we meant to keep it secret when we go to the Abbey for Christmas? That will be difficult…and, when your father finds out—'

'Don't start worrying about something that may never happen.'

Jane stared at Alex's sharp tone. What had she said? 'Alex… I—'

'I'm sorry. That was uncalled for.' Alex laid down his knife and fork and reached for Jane's hand. 'You goose. Lascelles is just a man. He's no threat to me, but he *does* give me the chance to learn more about my mother.' He folded his fingers around hers and gently squeezed. 'Dear Honeybee. I can see you're still fretting but please believe me—I know what Lascelles is capable of, and I promise I shall stay on my guard.

'I want you to be happy, Janey—not constantly worrying over me. If you keep this up you'll have me wondering how on earth I've managed all these years without you to watch my back.' His grin took the sting out of the rebuke, but she recognised it as such nevertheless.

She squeezed in return. 'I am happy, Alex. More than you know.'

And it was true. Mostly. But the shadows were there, nipping at their heels. Shadows that hid Alex's past. A past he was no nearer to sharing with her, as far as she could see, and a past that seemed to be steadily widening the rift between them. Against that, the problem of Lascelles seemed trivial.

Alex stood, and tugged her to her feet. 'And I am happy, too, sweetheart. Now, come. I have a wish to listen to music.'

That night, Alex lay on his back staring up through the darkness, mulling over the day's events. Who would have thought Lascelles would return? Father would be furious. That fact alone made his mind up—he would tell none of the family, because it would bring Father straight to Foxbourne to confront Lascelles.

And Alex did not want him here. He had enough to contend with, with these confounded dreams, or memories, or whatever they were. They continued to plague him. More and more frequently. More and more vividly, bringing him nearer and nearer the brink of a place he didn't want to be. Instinct told him Father's presence would make them worse, not better, and then how would he find the strength to hold back the vision that threatened destruction for his family?

He was afraid his suspicions would show in his face.

He simply couldn't face his father at the moment. He recalled Jane's worry about hiding Lascelles' return but that was the least of Alex's concerns. He'd never intended to go to the Abbey for Christmas but now he had even more reason to shun the place and his family. But he must break the news to Jane soon. He really couldn't keep shirking that difficult conversation.

Lascelles, though…he might prove a Godsend. What

if talking to him about Mother could help Alex sort fact from fiction? If he learned more about her life might that help overshadow the day of her death? He had no wish to revisit that day, merely to forget it all together. Was that really too much to ask? He had overcome his nightmares before. Why was he finding it so hard to do so again?

He had so much to look forward to and he'd do anything to stop these terrible suspicions—and the shocking speculation they spawned—ruining the happy future within his grasp.

With this thought, he turned to snuggle close to Jane. Finally, he slept.

The following day he rode Frost to Halsdon Manor, studying the brick-built house as he trotted up the drive, its three-bay central section crowned by a pediment and flanked by symmetrical wings. A flight of stone steps led to the central front door which, as he neared, opened. Lascelles himself emerged.

'Alexander! What a pleasant surprise. Is this a fleeting visit, or will you come inside?'

Alex dismounted. 'I'll come in if I may?'

'But of course, dear boy. Burnley?' A footman appeared behind him. 'Take Lord Alexander's horse to the stables and tell Watkins to do what's necessary.'

Inside the house, Lascelles preceded Alex into the entrance hall where a maid took his hat and gloves.

'Tea?' asked Lascelles. 'Or something stronger? I would value your opinion on a claret I recently discovered, if you care to try it?'

'Claret sounds ideal.'

'Carter! Bring a bottle and two glasses to the salon.'

The maid curtsied. 'Yes, sir.'

Alex followed Lascelles into a salon, lavishly decorated in red and gold.

'The décor is sadly outmoded, I am afraid. I have plans to refurbish the place, however.' Lascelles gestured to a chair. 'Please, do take a seat. I am delighted you have called... I find it so much easier when there are no females around to restrict the conversation, don't you?'

'Indeed.' Alex had come here to establish a rapport with Lascelles so it suited him to agree. He knew many men felt the same, hence the popularity of the gentlemen's clubs in Town.

They discussed general topics—politics, their estates, agriculture—until the claret had been poured and the door closed behind the maidservant. As soon as they were alone, Lascelles raised his glass.

'To neighbourliness, and to new beginnings.'

They touched glasses and then sampled the claret.

'This is excellent,' Alex said, diverted by the quality of the wine. 'You must tell me where you got it.'

'A backstreet vintner in Bordeaux. I returned to England with a couple of cases, and he has agreed to supply more. I shall send a case over to Foxbourne.'

'No! That is far too generous. I cannot possibly accept.'

Lascelles smiled, and leaned back in his chair. 'Oh, but I insist. We *are* family, after all, as well as neighbours. It is the least I can do, for one of dear Margaret's sons, and I dare to hope we, too, might become friends in time. Gifts between friends come with no hidden agenda, is that not the case?' He leaned forward, grasping Alex's knee. 'Allow me to do this, m'boy—it would give me pleasure and I hope before long you will see I have truly changed.' His mouth pursed, and a tiny frown stitched the skin between his brows. 'I do know I have to prove myself to you, Alexander, before I earn your trust. I hope you will give me that chance. Your father might never be able to forgive me, but...' He paused. Shook his head. 'No. I should not ask... I cannot expect you to act contrary to what your father would want. It is unfair of me to even suggest it.'

'My father does not rule *my* life, Anthony.'

Lascelles cocked his head to one side. 'Do I detect a touch of antagonism, m'boy? I do recall there was a— shall we say, a certain tension between you and your father when we met before in London. Have matters between you not improved?'

Alex shrugged. 'My father rarely impacts upon my life. I am my own man.'

'Of course you are, dear boy. It is just…the Duke…he can be quite *forceful*. I have never yet seen any man—or woman—get the better of him.'

'He does not rule my life,' Alex repeated. 'I make my own friends and my own decisions.'

'I am pleased to hear it.' Lascelles sipped his claret, and then raised his glass once more. 'To new friends.'

'New friends.' Alex raised his own glass.

I'll not forget what you did to Rosalind, though.

'Now then.' Lascelles put down his glass and steepled his fingers, propping his chin on them, reminding Alex of Father, who he'd seen in a similar stance more times than he cared to remember.

'I confess to some curiosity, Alexander. Is this merely a courtesy call?' Lascelles cocked his head. 'Or do you have something in particular you would like to discuss?'

He'd wanted to lead into the subject of his mother gradually…almost as an afterthought. This was too obvious. Caution whispered through him: *Don't let him know how much it means to you.* There would be time to talk of Mother, even if he must leave it for another day.

'It is merely a courtesy call, Anthony. And a way to satisfy my curiosity—I've lived at Foxbourne five years now, and this is my first visit to Halsdon.'

'Then you must allow me to show you around.' Anthony rose to his feet. 'At least, around the ground floor. I cannot believe you have any desire to view the bedchambers or servants' quarters.'

'Not likely!'

The first room they entered was a billiards room.

'Do you have a billiards room at Foxbourne?'

'No.' Alex swept the room with envious eyes. 'There's no space. But even if there were, I'd have no one to play with.' The thought of knocking balls around a table on his own held no appeal.

Lascelles raised a brow. 'Jane might learn the game. Your mama was quite an accomplished player, you know.'

'Was she?' This is what he had come for. Knowledge of his mother, of the person she had been. 'You played with her?'

'Oh, yes. Several times, at various house parties at which we were both guests. She was as good as any man, and often won games.' He laughed softly, his eyes far away. 'She could be quite ruthless once she gained an advantage, both in billiards and at the card table. And...' He paused, his dark eyes on Alex. 'And she was a popular young lady.'

Alex frowned. Lascelles had been going to say something different, he was sure. He was aware his mother had had a reputation for taking lovers...of course Lascelles would not speak of that. And Alex didn't want to hear it, either.

'When did you meet?'

'Let me see...it was her debut year. We were both eighteen—you must know she was three years older than your father?'

Alex nodded.

'We were friends from the outset. But, of course, a bastard like me wasn't deemed suitable company for a gently born and bred young lady. But, despite her parents' objections, we remained friends. She confided in me.'

'About…?'

Lascelles smiled. 'Alex… Alex…dear boy. A confidence is a confidence, even if the confessor is no longer with us. But, a marriage made in haste, my boy… I am sure you can fill in the gaps.' His features hardened. 'Your grandfather was sick…fretting over the succession of the dukedom. But if my father had married my mother and made me his heir…' He clamped his mouth shut. 'My apologies. That is naught but ancient history.' His expression softened. 'You remind me of her. You have her colouring. Those eyes…such a tragic waste.' He sighed, and clasped Alex's shoulder. 'You must feel free to come over any time you choose, my boy. *Any* time. We can play billiards, or cards. Or…just talk, if you wish. A man—especially one who has just married—needs male company, I find. Dear Margaret's son will always find a welcome here.'

'Thank you. I might take you up on that.'

'Do. In fact…do you recall that, when your good lady invited me to dine on Tuesday next, I had to decline?'

Alex nodded.

'I am hosting a small gathering—just a few friends to enjoy a day or two hunting and shooting. You must come by one evening for a few games. Billiards and cards… Oh! Have no fear, low-stakes games only. I cannot allow my guests to beggar themselves under my roof! There are more than enough gaming hells in Town should they wish to follow *that* road to penury. Gentlemen only, I'm afraid, so I am unable to extend my invitation to include Lady Jane…but I am sure she will understand if you wish to join us one evening. My guests arrive tomorrow, so shall we say Saturday? Or…' his head dipped to one side again, a ghost of a smile playing across his lips '…might dear Jane disapprove? I should *hate* to be the cause of disharmony between newlyweds.'

'Jane will not object. She doesn't keep me on a leash, you know.'

Lascelles inclined his head, that knowing smile still lurking, setting Alex's hackles to rise. 'Of *course* she does not, dear boy. Acquit me, I beg you…it was never my intention to imply such a thing.'

Chapter Fifteen

'*Tonight?*'

It was Saturday, and Jane and Alex had just returned from a hack on Pearl and Nelson. They had even seen a shooting party on Halsdon land, and Alex had told her Lascelles was entertaining a party of gentlemen at the Manor, but even then he hadn't thought to mention he'd been invited to join them for dinner that evening.

'Yes. You don't mind, do you?'

'But...' Jane frowned. 'When was this arranged? I wasn't aware you had seen Anthony since you went over there on Thursday.'

'I haven't.'

'But you didn't think to tell me he had invited you to dine tonight?'

'I didn't think I needed permission to accept an invitation on my own behalf. I'm sorry you're not included, but it's a male-only gathering.' He grinned at her. 'Not your idea of an enjoyable evening at all, I'll wager.'

He didn't even seem to realise how unreasonable he was being. She tightly folded her arms, as if to keep her anger inside.

'You should have told me. I could have warned Mrs

Godfrey. She'll have prepared a meal for two...if I'd known I would be dining alone, I'd have been happy with only one course.'

Alex scowled. 'Why should the cook care? It's just a meal.'

'And how do you think it makes *me* look, that I didn't even know my husband intended to dine out tonight?'

Alex's jaw set and Jane turned away, hurt he hadn't told her—like he hadn't told her anything about his visit to Lascelles, despite her asking. It was as though he were excluding her, reminding her of the old Alex...going his own way without being beholden to anyone. It made her feel...incidental. Shut out. First his nightmares. Now this.

'Come on, Janey.' He pulled her round into a hug, and kissed her cheek. 'Don't be cross. I'm still learning this husband thing... I dare say I'm too used to coming and going as I please. I'll do better. I promise.'

He held her at arms' length and his rueful smile melted her anger.

'I'm not so much cross as hurt you didn't tell me.'

'I know. I understand. I'll do better. And, to prove it, I should tell you Anthony has invited me over to play billiards any time I like.' He arched one brow. 'Do you mind?'

'No. Of course not.' How could she say anything different now? She consoled herself with the thought he was unlikely to go regularly. 'Although—'

She bit her lip, locking her words inside. He'd already objected when she'd warned him to be careful. Sometimes it was hard not to recall his troubled boyhood and the scrapes he had dived into headlong...hard to relinquish the role of the sensible one who tried to prevent the worst of his excesses. But that was many years ago—their lives had led in different directions: his to school, university and the life of a man about Town whereas she had remained at home, only seeing him when she went to Town for the Season since he stopped visiting the Abbey.

'Although?' His lips continued to smile, but there was glint of annoyance in his tiger-gold eyes.

'Although I will miss you.'

'That's my girl!' He swung her around and, as he set her down again, he kissed her. 'At least you'll have Mist for company.'

Mist had joyfully adapted to her new life as Jane's pet, clearly relishing the life of luxury, while Dora and the rest of the litter had returned to life in the stables. But a kitten was no substitute for her husband. Jane strove to conceal her dismay.

'Do you know who his guests are?' Olivia had told her of the time certain gentlemen had attempted to ruin Alex in order to wreak revenge on his father. What if any of those shady types were among Lascelles' friends? Or what if—and her stomach tumbled at the thought—Lascelles himself harboured thoughts of revenge through Alex?

'Yes and they're all eminently respectable. Anyway. I've enough time to help Lilley work with that team of chestnuts before I need to change my clothes, so I'll see you later, my adorable wife.'

He kissed her nose but his attention was already on the four ready-harnessed horses being led from the stalls.

The walk back to the house was surprisingly lonely and Jane spent the time scolding herself. On their wedding day she had vowed never to be a needy wife, nor to complain if Alex continued his own pursuits, but in the early weeks of their marriage she had grown accustomed to them spending time together. Maybe she had become complacent, believing that was how their life here at Foxbourne would always be, but Alex had led a full life before their marriage and she shouldn't expect him to change his entire life to accommodate her. He had work to do. Although Jane was useful at certain times, it would be odd indeed if she expected to be included in every aspect of Alex's work.

Besides, not only would Alex soon resent being tied too closely to anyone, even his wife, she also had responsibilities. She had the house to run; the staff to manage; she had those Christmas gifts to finish making, and she had also taken over the regular updating of the ledgers.

But those barriers between her and Alex—the feeling of being shut out of parts of his life—troubled her. That was the Alex of old, keeping everyone at bay. Hiding his innermost feelings. The initial happy contentment of their marriage seemed to be slipping further and further out of reach. She suppressed a sigh as she let herself in through the front door. How she wished her husband was easier to understand.

She went straight to Alex's business room. She would work on the ledgers for a while before she changed her riding habit for a gown and her solitary dinner.

That is where Alex found her half an hour later. He breezed through the door, bringing with him the smell of fresh air and horses.

'There you are!' He rounded the desk, took the pen from her and tugged her to her feet. 'No one knew where you were…they all thought you were still outside with me.'

He tilted her chin up as he wrapped one arm around her waist and pulled her close.

'I was worried. I went upstairs and saw you hadn't been up there to change.' His tawny gaze darkened as it fastened on her mouth, and her heart thumped in response. 'I thought you might still be cross with me for not telling you sooner about tonight.'

'Of course I am not.' Love for him filled her heart even

as she warned herself this would not be the only time he would disappoint her. He was a complex man. She already knew that when she married him. If she'd wanted a paragon...an easy life...then Lord Alexander Beauchamp would have been the very last name on her list.

She smiled tenderly. 'I don't deny it was a surprise but I'm not annoyed with you.' The need to speak the words battered at her. 'I love you, Alex. I want you to be happy.'

He blinked, and a slow smile stretched his lips. 'Darling Honeybee.' He possessed her mouth in a slow, dreamy, lingering kiss.

Desire flamed inside, sizzling through her as his lips feathered to her ear and he nibbled her lobe, burning away her disappointment that he hadn't said those three words in return.

'I think it's time you got out of those clothes, Janey.'

He unbuttoned her jacket and pulled her shirt free, deftly scooping her breast from her corset. She gasped, her nipple tightening as Alex bent his head. Hot lips sucked the tight bud into his mouth. His tongue swirled and pure need sparked along her veins. He reached for her skirts, and hoisted them high before slipping one finger between her thighs. She moaned, her core throbbing, already wet for him. She reached between them, unbuttoned the fall of his breeches, freed his straining erection and stroked along his hot, hard length before gently circling the tip.

'Temptress.' The low growl vibrated in her ear.

His hands still full of her skirts, he cupped her bottom and hoisted her up, perching her on the very edge of the desk as he parted her knees and moved between her thighs. He nuzzled her neck and then bit her lobe as he entered her with one swift thrust. She clutched at his shoulders, her head back, her legs wrapped around him as he stilled, his hands supporting her back. She lifted her head to look at him, and found him watching her with a wondering look in those tiger eyes of his.

'Who knew?' he whispered. 'Who could possibly know the fiery wanton lurking inside quiet Janey?'

He started to move. 'Thank you, my Honeybee, for making my life so sweet.'

Later, Jane watched Alex leave for Halsdon Manor with a heavy heart. For all his lovemaking, and all his sweet words, she still couldn't quite shake the feeling that some kind of Rubicon had been crossed. Mayhap it was inevitable—they must settle into a humdrum daily existence. But it felt…*she* felt…as though shadows were starting to close in. She huffed a laugh at such a fanciful thought, and yet she couldn't convince herself it was all in her imagination. There was a growing barrier between them, as though Alex had withdrawn from her—mentally if not physically. And, for her, that diminished the pleasure of their lovemaking.

He shared his body but not his thoughts.

He accepted her comfort at night when he suffered nightmares, but rejected her attempts to help him by bringing those nightmares into the open.

He was a stubborn man. He would tell himself he was protecting her. He would tell himself he was the man of the house and mustn't show weakness. He would tell himself there was nothing she could do to help him come to terms with what had happened the day his mother was murdered.

Jane, however, remained convinced he was wrong. To talk about his memories was, she was certain, the key to stopping them haunting him and, more importantly, the way to stop him retreating behind those impenetrable barriers he had erected against the world, including her.

She must keep trying. She might be defeated for now; she was not defeated for good.

After her lonely dinner, Jane went to the drawing room. She played with Mist, who was turning into an adorable bundle of mischief. When she wasn't running up the curtains, sharp claws scrabbling, she was climbing on the furniture, leaving paw prints on the polished surfaces, much to Mrs Kent's chagrin. Then she worked on the Christmas gift she'd made for Alex—a beautiful ruby-red satin waistcoat which she was embroidering with cream and pale green silk thread.

She meant to wait up for Alex but it grew late and she could barely keep her eyes open. Eventually, she gave in and went to bed where, ironically, sleep eluded her for what seemed like hours. Finally she must have slept because she was roused by Alex stumbling against the bed.

'What time is it?' she asked groggily.

'Late. Gone four. Shhh—go back to sleep.'

A short while later she was vaguely conscious of him lying close behind her, one arm draped over to cup her breast, and then she slept again.

She was woken by Peg opening the curtains to allow light to flood the room. Alex was no longer spooned against her back and, when Jane rolled over, his side of the bed was cold and empty.

'Where is His Lordship?'

'In his own bedchamber; he felt sick in the night.' Peg's pursed lips made her disapproval clear. 'Drabble says he moved so's not to disturb you.' She lifted a tray from the dressing table. 'I brought your chocolate and rolls, milady.'

Jane sat up, tugging the pillow up behind her to lean against. 'Thank you, Peg. Is he awake yet?'

Peg placed the tray on Jane's legs and snorted. 'Not he! I don't doubt he'll still be abed at noon, complaining of his head a-banging. Well, he won't get no sympathy from me, that's for sure.'

'Now, Peg. Do not forget who pays your wages. If Lord Alex hears you talking like that, you'll be out on your ear.'

Peg laughed. 'I've known Lord Alex as long as you have, milady. He'd not dare.' Then she nodded. 'Not but what you're right. Me 'n' Drabble might have a grumble now and then, but you know we wouldn't see no harm come to him. And nor would we say such things in front of them others below stairs.'

'I'm relieved to hear it.'

As soon as Jane finished her breakfast, she tiptoed into Alex's bedchamber. He was lying on his side, curled into a ball, the covers up around his ears. Jane sat gently on the bed and smoothed his hair from his forehead. He looked so angelic she wanted to just hold him in her arms and protect him always.

She smiled as she imagined his horror if he knew what she was thinking. He would be utterly insulted. In his mind—and that of most men—*they* were the ones who did the protecting. She continued to stroke as her thoughts roamed. Perhaps a better word would be nurture. To nurture those they loved came naturally to a woman. Her thoughts drifted on to babies—how she longed to be a mother and to have babies to love and care for.

Alex stirred, mumbling, a frown creasing his forehead. He cranked open one eyelid, then closed it again with a groan.

'Head hurts...'

'Has Drabble brought you anything for it?'

'What...? Who...? Ugh...no. Nothing. Thirsty...'

Jane brushed her lips across his brow. 'There's water here. Let me help you drink, then I'll bring you something later to relieve your head.'

She slipped her arm under his shoulders, helped him up, held the glass to his lips, then laid him gently back. His eyes slitted open.

'You're too good to me, Janey.'

Jane huffed a laugh. 'Yes. I know I am.' She feathered a kiss to his brow. 'Sleep now. I'll bring up the remedy before I go to church.'

Outside the bedchamber door she paused, anxiety that Alex might be lured back into the excesses of his youth churning her stomach. Although surely it was too soon to begin fretting over Lascelles' influence, even if she couldn't trust him—Alex had too much to lose now, with Foxbourne and his beloved horses.

Logically, that made sense. But whenever had Alex and logic walked hand in hand?

She dressed, and then headed downstairs to mix up a remedy to soothe his head, vowing to talk to him about Lascelles as soon as he recovered.

After church, Jane mingled with the villagers.

'Good morning, My Lady.' Mrs Phillips stopped to chat, one of her daughters by her side. 'No Lord Alexander this morning?'

'I'm afraid not. He is unwell.'

'Nothing serious, I hope?'

'No. We think he ate something that disagreed with him.' As the white lie slipped from her lips, she caught sight of Anthony Lascelles, his dark gaze on her. She hadn't noticed him in the church but *he* clearly wasn't suffering the after-effects of last night as Alex was. 'If you will excuse me, Mrs Phillips, I need to speak to Mr Lascelles, but would you care to call at Foxbourne on Wednesday? I am eager to lend more practical help to your charity work for the poor.'

They had discussed the vicar's charity work before, but

had arranged nothing definite, with Jane still settling into her new role. Now, though, she realised if she was to cope with Alex leading his own life some of the time, then she must seek some fulfilment from other sources. It could only help if she cultivated interests of her own.

'Thank you, Lady Jane. I shall be there.'

Jane crossed to where Lascelles was talking to one of the local farmers.

'Good morning.' She encompassed both of them in her smile of greeting.

Lascelles bowed. 'Good morning to you, Lady Jane. Or…might we dispense with the formalities, as we are family?'

'Of course.' She could hardly object—he'd already asked her to call him Anthony.

The farmer mumbled a greeting. 'I'll see what I can do, sir,' he then said to Lascelles. 'You leave it with me. Good day to you both.'

He nodded before ambling away, watched by Lascelles. 'One of my tenants. I need a new estate manager, and he knows of a chap over Cucklow way in need of a new position.'

'I hope he proves suitable.'

Lascelles smiled. 'As do I. I have no wish to spend too much of my time here…its very closeness to London proves far too great an enticement to a lonely bachelor such as myself.' His words eased some of Jane's concern. 'Oh, not that local society is not welcoming, of course. I cast no aspersions. But it consists of families in the main, and I know from experience there is only so much we will have in common.'

'Maybe it is time to seek a wife?' The words came out before she could stop them. 'Oh! I apologise. I did not mean to be impertinent.'

Lascelles smiled. 'There is no necessity to apologise, my dear. You may be right. Perhaps it *is* time I took my chance and experienced domestic bliss. After all, if Alexander can take the plunge… What *were* the circumstances of your betrothal, if you do not mind me asking? I understand Alexander visited the Abbey in the summer but, having been friends for several years, it does seem to have happened without much…now, how can I put it? Without much forethought. A hurried affair, I gathered.'

Shock momentarily stole her breath. Her skin crawled at the thought of Alex discussing anything so intimate with anyone.

'Alex told you about our wedding?'

'No, no. Not in so many words but…reading between the lines, as it were…and me a student of human nature…' He fell silent, his gaze wandering over the people gathered outside the church before turning his attention back to Jane. 'How *is* dear Alexander this morning? I noted his absence. Is his head very sore? I did try to dissuade him from indulging quite so freely but…well, my dear. You know our Alex. He is not easily brought back to heel once he's been allowed off the leash, is he?'

'He has only the slightest of headaches.' Anger clawed Jane at the insinuation she kept Alex tied to her. 'He had urgent business, so he could not attend church.'

'I *see*.' A smile hovered on Lascelles' lips. 'I wonder… when you return home could you remind him Sir Henry will call tomorrow at noon to examine that bay mare he has for sale?' Jane knew the mare he referred to. It was one she had helped to school. 'I am sure it won't have slipped Alex's mind but…just in case, you understand.'

His falsely sympathetic tone and the glimmer of laughter in his eyes set Jane's teeth on edge.

'I shall remind him, sir.'

'Anthony,' he prompted gently.

Jane swallowed her irritation. 'Anthony.'

Their talk had reinforced her feeling there was something distrustful about Anthony Lascelles and she couldn't wait to escape him.

'I must be going. They're waiting for me.' She indicated the members of the Foxbourne staff who had also attended the church service and were now waiting in a huddle by the two vehicles that had conveyed them into Malton. 'Good day to you, Anthony.'

'I shall see you on Thursday, if our paths do not cross tomorrow, dear Jane.' He raised his hat, and his hair shone silver as it caught the sunlight. 'Farewell.' He strolled away, swinging his cane.

Jane watched him go, her feelings in turmoil. Was this instinctive distrust she felt for him unreasonable? It felt as though there was a subtle innuendo in almost everything he said…a hidden message beneath the actual meaning of his words. Or was her imagination playing tricks on her? One thing was for sure, she would be unable to avoid him. She must hope he would tire of country life very quickly, and return to London.

And, in the meantime—should she risk Alex's anger by again voicing her doubts about Lascelles? She walked over to the servants and they were soon on their way home, Jane's head full of ways to warn her stubborn husband against Lascelles without inadvertently driving him closer to the man.

Chapter Sixteen

'Don't worry, Janey. I shan't make a habit of it... I have no wish to repeat the way I feel today.' Alex's head still throbbed like the Devil, albeit less ferociously than earlier. 'All I want is for today to be over, knowing I will feel better in the morning. I fear I cannot hold my liquor as I used to.'

Alex had finally hauled himself from his bed and shaved and dressed. He'd found Jane in the drawing room stuffing strips of fabric into what looked like a purple velvet bag with legs.

'I am relieved to hear that. I do not like to see you in such pain.'

'What *is* that?'

She held it up. 'It's a ragdoll rabbit for baby George. I've made ragdolls for the girls and then thought of making this for George. It's soft so there are no hard edges to hurt him.'

Alex's stomach twisted. He *still* hadn't told Jane they weren't going to the Abbey for Christmas but he couldn't face that conversation now. He would tell her soon, he vowed. 'Very nice.'

He sat beside Jane, and plucked the toy rabbit from her hands. He might appreciate her industriousness in making gifts for the family but, right at this moment, he wanted her undivided attention. He'd barely seen her all day, and he'd missed her.

As he played with an errant lock of hair that had escaped its pin Jane said, 'Anthony came to church this morning.'

Alex grinned. 'Is that a subtle way of asking why I've been fit for nothing for the entire day and yet he was unaffected?'

Jane remained straight-faced as she denied it, but the mischievous glint in her eyes told him he'd guessed right.

'I am out of practice, clearly, although Anthony took his responsibilities as host seriously and limited his intake of spirits. What did he say about last night?'

'Nothing much.'

Alex sensed she wanted to say more.

'He asked about the circumstances that led to our marriage. He implied there was something dubious about it.' She sent him a sidelong glance. 'You didn't let slip anything about…about…' She hauled in a shaky breath. 'About Pikeford, did you?'

'Janey!' Alex wrapped his arms around her and hugged her. 'Do you really think me so crass? I told him nothing, but that didn't stop him asking plenty of questions.' He frowned as a thought occurred. 'I suspect he was using questions about our betrothal and wedding to find out more about the family and the Abbey. That's another thing Uncle Vernon told me about Anthony… He is obsessed not only with Father but also with the Abbey itself. No doubt because he feels it should belong to him! And I can't deny I would likely feel the same in his position. Anyway, enough about him—unless you truly find him riveting as a topic of conversation, in which case…do I need to be jealous?'

'You? Jealous? How absurd.'

The words might mock but, if anything, Jane looked delighted at that idea, and Alex recalled her telling him she loved him. He shifted his shoulders, uncomfortable with the topic; uncomfortable with delving into feelings. That wasn't what this marriage was about, was it? It was a marriage between good friends, borne out of necessity. He'd saved Jane from Pikeford and that witch of a step-mother, and she was already proving herself so invaluable he couldn't quite imagine his life without her now. But jealousy, and love, did not come into it.

'Absurd indeed,' he said lightly, ignoring the stab of guilt as Jane's teasing smile slipped.

'About Anthony, though...' She hesitated, her cheeks colouring.

'Yes?'

Her chest rose as she hauled in a breath. 'I can't *help* worrying about him, Alex... He bears your father an ages-old grudge and Aunt Cecily warned me he is clever and manipulative and to be cautious. I would be happier if we kept our distance from him as far as possible.'

What was it with his family? He removed his arm from Jane's shoulders, resentment bubbling through him. They never thought him capable of managing his own affairs. Could they never see him as a grown man? An adult? Would they always see him as a boy who needed guid-ance and protection? And now Aunt Cecily had infected his wife with the same doubts about his judgement.

'I think I'm old enough to make my own mind up about Anthony, don't you?'

Jane shook her head, and held his gaze, frustration brimming in her brown eyes. 'I am entitled to my opin-ion, Alexander. Or are you suggesting I should always bite my tongue?'

He stared at her frowning face. 'When have I *ever* pre-vented you from saying what you think?'

But you are now, aren't you? Simply by not listening to her, you are dismissing her opinion as worthless.

'I apologise,' he said quickly, before she could respond. 'Of course you are entitled to your opinion, Janey. Go on. I am listening.'

'Thank you.'

She smiled, but it was hesitant and he hated that she felt inhibited. But he didn't hate it enough to allow her to dictate who he might socialise with.

'I am worried, Alex.' She covered his hand with hers. 'There is something about Anthony that makes me uneasy.'

'Why? What has he said?'

'It is not what he says but the *way* he says it…as though everything he says has a hidden meaning.'

It was his turn to frown. 'So you will condemn the man because your overactive imagination has conjured up underlying implications to his every word? That does not sound like you, Jane. You always see the best in people. Let's face it, you must do, to still be friends with me after all these years.' It was true. She was the kindest, most forgiving person he knew. 'Do you know what I think?'

Her eyes widened. 'No. What do you think?'

'I think Pikeford's attack has made you ready to suspect monsters where there are none. You said yourself Anthony has said nothing to cause offence, so why do you insist on taking it? You are being overly sensitive.'

'That is unfair, Alex.' She snatched her hand away, as though his skin was red-hot. 'Don't turn this into an attack on me. I am your wife. I'm trying to help you.'

Of course she was trying to help. It was what she did… helped to heal the sick and wounded. Rescued starving kittens. He gritted his teeth. Was that how she viewed him? As a man who needed rescuing? He leapt to his feet and paced away, then back again.

'I know you only want to help but all I am doing is following *your* advice. You begged me to talk about my mother. Well, be happy. Because I am. To Anthony. He knew her—I'll learn far more from him than going round in circles talking to you about someone you never knew, or about a day…an incident…even *I* cannot remember.'

He hardened his heart as hurt flashed across her face.

'Alex…please…be reasonable… Yes, I think it will help you to talk about your mother, but I am unconvinced a man you barely know—and a man with a dubious past as far as your family is concerned—is the right confidant.'

His jaw locked, and it took effort to release it to say, 'It is not my intention to confide in Anthony, merely to pick his brains to see if it helps restore my memory.'

She searched his gaze. 'Very well. I shall say no more.' She was uncharacteristically abrupt. 'You know your own mind best.' Then she sighed. 'Tell me, how is your headache now? Did the remedy help?'

He was grateful for the change of subject. 'Better. And, yes, it did. Thank you. And, Janey…?' He reached for her hand and raised it to his lips. Her brows lifted. 'I *shall* take care with Anthony, I promise. You are not to worry.'

'Thank you. Oh! I almost forgot… Anthony asked me to remind you about Sir Henry coming to view that bay mare tomorrow. And will you want me to be there, to ride her for him?'

'I didn't need reminding. I wasn't that badly foxed.' Jane levelled one of her looks at him, prompting a chuckle. 'I can't fool you for one minute, can I, Janey? Very well. I confess it had slipped my mind until you mentioned it. And yes. If you don't mind, I should like your help to show her manners and paces.'

'Of course. I shall be happy to help.'

Alex picked up their current book, *Sense and Sensi-*

bility. 'Shall I read to you while you finish stuffing that rabbit?'

He said it with an air of doing her a favour but, in truth, he was as eager as Jane to discover the fate of both Elinor and Marianne Dashwood.

'If you feel well enough and it will not prove too much of a trial for you, that would be lovely.' A smile quivered on her lips. 'Thank you.'

The talk over dinner at the Halsdon Manor gathering had consisted mainly of politics and business, and the presence of Sir Henry Jacobsen, a Member of Parliament, together with several other respectable gentlemen, had helped lull Alex's suspicions about Anthony Lascelles. The one objectionable guest was Colin Theobald—a fellow Alex had known, and avoided, for many years. Alex had never liked him, plus he was infamous for his harsh treatment of his horses—an unforgiveable sin in Alex's book. He'd managed to avoid Theobald on Saturday evening and was dismayed to see him accompanying Anthony and Sir Henry when they came to view the bay mare for Lady Jacobsen.

'I trust you've no objection to me tagging along, Beauchamp?' Theobald's head swivelled from side to side as he took in everything, his eyes sharp with curiosity. 'I'm in the market for a team of four…thought I'd see if you've anything suitable.'

Alex had many objections but he kept them to himself. 'Of course I have no objection. Unfortunately, though, I have nothing currently available.'

He was damned if he would willingly sell any of his animals to Theobald. One look at the horse he rode in on— the dullness of its eyes and the barely healed scars on its flanks—made that decision easy, business be damned.

Jane chose that moment to arrive at the stable yard.

'My wife, Lady Jane,' said Alex. 'She will ride the mare to demonstrate her paces. My dear, this is Sir Henry Jacobsen and Mr Theobald.'

It felt good, to introduce her as his wife. To have someone at his side…a feeling he'd seldom experienced in his life. Her smile warmed his heart and pride suffused him as she greeted all three visitors with the exact degree of courtesy and briskness required for what was, after all, a business gathering.

Lilley led out the bay mare, and Alex cupped his hands to help Jane mount. The mare behaved impeccably as Jane put her through her paces, and Sir Henry looked impressed.

'She cuts a neat figure on horseback,' Theobald commented as Jane executed a perfect figure of eight on the mare.

'She's a talented horsewoman,' Alex replied. 'One of the best I've seen.'

'That is praise indeed, coming from a member of your family,' Anthony said. 'I've never yet met a Beauchamp who is not a skilled rider.'

'That is true.' Theobald smirked. 'And your mother too…she was an *exceptionally* skilled rider, is that not the case, Tony? I remember—'

'She put the rest to shame on the hunting field, for certain.' A muscle ticked in Anthony's jaw, and Alex caught the scowl he directed at the other man. 'And she could handle a horse as well as anyone.'

'Oh, indeed,' said the other man smoothly.

Alex tamped down his anger…he knew damned well what Theobald implied and, although he knew of his mother's reputation for taking lovers, he didn't appreciate having the subject thrust under his nose by some uninvited, insensitive sneaksby. He was grateful for Anthony's intervention… He

wanted to conclude a deal with Sir Henry, not frighten a cus-
tomer away by thumping Theobald on the nose. Anthony had
interrupted Theobald at the perfect moment for Alex to pretend he'd missed Theobald's insinuation. He shot Anthony a
grateful look and received a wink in return.

Jane halted the mare, and Sir Henry crossed the paddock
to examine her. Alex took two paces, then slammed to a
halt as a vision—sudden and shocking in its intensity—
flooded his mind, freezing all coherent thought.

The perfume…roses…voices, arguing. That yellow
skirt flowing around a pair of elegant ankles. The polished boots, back and forth, in step with a pair of yellow
slippers. A woman's pleas. A slap, and the rip of cloth.
Two figures sinking to the floor.

Alex clamped his hands to his ears, desperate to block
those sounds, but they were coming from inside his head.

I will never let you go. You won't abandon me again.

A man's voice. Harsh. Vicious.

A cry…Mother…large hands around her neck…the desperate rasp of choking.

He saw again the blackness when he screwed his eyes
shut. Felt the rough wooden planks chafe his skin. Smelled
again her scent of roses, then felt the burn of his lungs as
he held his breath. Then a heartfelt groan, and the scrape
of boots against the floor, followed by a terrifying silence,
broken only by his own tortured breaths.

He relived the shudder that racked him when he finally
opened his eyes to the froth of her crumpled yellow gown.
Yellow that filled his vision. A naked leg. One hand out-
flung, fingers slightly curled. Still. Oval nails, smooth
and perfect.

Alex's head throbbed as he fought to banish the images,
sounds and smells of the past. Then gorge erupted, forcing
its way up his throat as that horrific scene was replaced by

an image of his father's face. His stomach cramped as he desperately scrabbled his way out of the nightmare vision and back to reality, battling the urge to drop to the ground and curl into a ball, one thread of his mind still linking him to the present and screaming at him to keep it hidden.

An arm landed across his shoulders. 'What is it? You've turned ghostly, m'boy. Are you quite well?'

Anthony's voice. Low. Concerned. Alex couldn't muster a reply, his head pounding with questions.

Why the hell has this happened now?

There was no scream or scuffle. No scent of roses. Nothing. Except a random mention of his mother.

How could any sane mind conjure up such a vision? Am I going mad?

'Alex?'

He forced his attention to Anthony.

'I'm all right.'

He looked across the paddock to where Theobald had followed Sir Henry over to Jane and the mare. Thankfully neither man seemed to have noticed what happened, although Jane glanced over several times even as she responded to Sir Henry's questions. He would face an interrogation later, that was for sure. How much longer could he fob her off? He couldn't tell her about this. It would be utterly unfair, for he could no longer avoid thinking the unthinkable— what if he hadn't just discovered his mother's body all those years ago, as everyone had told him?

What if he had *been* there? Seen and heard what happened?

He felt sweat bead his forehead and upper lip. What if he had seen her killer? His lungs heaved, dragging in breaths that simply did not satisfy his need, as though he had been running full tilt. His vision swam. His legs felt like jelly.

Anthony gripped his arm, guiding him to a nearby fence he could lean against for support.

'Take a minute,' he murmured before calling to the others: 'We'll be with you in a moment.' He lowered his voice again. 'I'll tell them we're discussing business and, if that does not fool them, I shall blame it on your unaccustomed excess of alcohol the other night. Make a jest about you being a sober and upright citizen these days. So very insensitive of Colin to bring up the subject of your dear mama in that way. Such a blow to a young child, to lose a parent to such a heinous crime. I presume your father did tell you what happened to her?'

'I found her.' The words came out before Alex could swallow them. 'I found her body.'

'*You* found her? But...what were you doing there? I... From what I've been told, she was in the summer house. Were you not in lessons?'

'I was meant to be. I hid from our tutor so I could play in the copse. I... I don't remember what happened. They say I found her body. The gardeners heard me screaming.'

'Oh, you poor, poor boy.' Anthony squeezed Alex's shoulder. 'But it was fortunate you did not run into the scoundrel who killed her.'

'Yes. I was lucky.'

He avoided eye contact with the other man as he lied. How could he ever admit his visions of that day? He wished...oh, how he wished it would all go away. He dragged in a deep breath and levered himself away from the fence, the muscles in his legs still shaky. 'I'm sorry. Please forget this—it's in the past. I don't want to think about it. I'm more interested in learning about my mother when she was alive, if you will talk to me about her?'

'Of course I will, my boy. I shall be delighted.'

'When did you last see her? I know you have lived abroad much of your life.'

'That is true. I left England soon after your parents' marriage and returned…now, let me see…it was the year before your mother died. I intended to settle in England but I grew restless and left just a week before dear Margaret's death. I was back in America when I received the shocking news. I have never been so distressed, but I was grateful I'd had the opportunity to renew our acquaintance.'

They headed towards the others, Anthony's hand on Alex's shoulder. 'Your mother was a very special lady; one I fear your father never fully appreciated. But, then, he was so young when they wed… I daresay he would treat her differently now. With greater understanding.'

They left the subject while Alex concluded the sale of the mare to Sir Henry, and then their visitors left, leaving him and Jane standing outside the stable yard, watching the three men ride away.

'What happened?'

No preamble. Trust Jane… No skirting around the subject, but straight in. He wasn't surprised…she'd never been afraid, in her quiet way, to challenge him and hold him to account. But neither did she used to pity him, and he could read that emotion more and more in her eyes. In her voice. In her expression.

In her words.

And he loathed it.

'Nothing. It was the alcohol from the other night.'

'Still?' Jane's voice rang with scepticism. 'Alex…*do* you need a physician? Please…I am worried. These turns you've been having…what if it's nothing to do with visiting the Abbey and your old nightmares but something more serious? Something medical?'

'It's not medical. Stop worrying. I am perfectly well. If

you must know, Theobald made some derogatory remark about my mother, and I had to take a few minutes to stop myself from punching him on the nose.'

He looked at the worry in her kind eyes. Resentment twisted through him even though he knew that was unfair and he despised himself for it. The early part of their marriage, when they had grown closer and closer, seemed a far-off memory and the dangers in marriage to someone as perceptive as Jane were ever more apparent. He knew she was trying to help but he couldn't allow her to stray into those areas of his life where *nobody* was allowed. The distance between them was widening, the barriers between them solidifying, in his attempts to hide the slowly emerging truth of his past because he knew, instinctively, that once those memories fully surfaced the pain they would cause…the heartbreak…would destroy the family he loved more than life itself, even if he couldn't always show that love.

He touched her cheek. 'Janey. If I thought I needed a physician, I would tell you. I promise.' He tried a grin but her expression told him she wasn't fooled. 'You know what I can be like. Unpredictable. You've said it yourself. Can we not count it a success that I *didn't* thump Theobald? You know in the past I wouldn't have hesitated.'

His attempt to reassure her hadn't worked, judging by the worry and, again, pity he could read in her expression. How long would it be before that was all she saw when she looked at him? A mass of troubles…the sum of his past rather than the successful horse breeder and trainer he had worked so hard to become? He had struggled all his adult life to leave the past behind him but his family still watched him, on tenterhooks in case he slipped back into old habits. Must he now expect the same from his wife?

Well, he was damned if he'd let that happen.

'You should thank Anthony for stopping me doing something I might regret, Jane. I for one am most grateful to him.'

Jane's mouth set in a tight line, but he'd spoken the truth. What might have happened had Anthony not been there? At the very least he would've made an utter fool of himself. At the worst… He didn't like to think of the worst.

He was starting to believe Zach was right—if he tried hard to recall that day, would knowing the full truth—the identity of the killer—help? God knows it couldn't be worse than this speculation.

And if his suspicions were true then he would have to learn to deal with it.

On his own. As always.

Chapter Seventeen

After experiencing Anthony's talents as a host on Saturday, Alex was unsurprised he proved an entertaining dinner guest on Thursday. Jane, he could see, warmed to Anthony during the meal and laughed out loud several times as he regaled them with interesting tales of his time living overseas.

'I shall leave you to your port.'

Jane stood to leave the room when they finished eating. Both Alex and Anthony rose to their feet and Alex waited for Anthony to suggest they drank their port in the drawing room rather than leave Jane on her own. He said nothing, however, and Alex felt obliged to follow his guest's lead.

'We will join you shortly, my dear,' he said as Jane left the dining room.

Once the port was poured, Anthony leaned back in his chair and sighed contentedly. 'You keep a fine table, my boy. My compliments to your cook.'

'I'll pass them on.' Alex sipped his port. 'I suggest we finish these quickly and join Jane.'

He found himself the focus of those dark eyes and a knowing smile. 'Yes. I gathered from our conversation after church that your good lady rather expects you to dance attendance on her.'

Alex frowned but, before he could frame a suitable retort, Anthony continued, 'Oh, not that I blame either of you—it is natural for young lovers to wish to spend every minute together, after all.' His head tilted, and he adopted a sympathetic air. 'But it is…disappointing…when the wife of a dear friend… Now, how may I put this? When she seeks to curtail that friend's enjoyment in the company of other gentlemen in the fear he has not outgrown his youthful indiscretions.'

'My *youthful indiscretions*?' Alex found it hard to believe Jane had discussed any such thing with Anthony.

'Dear Jane… It is understandable that she will worry about your welfare, Alexander. I am convinced she will learn to trust you.'

It was true. She constantly worried about him, much to his annoyance. He wondered exactly what she had said to Anthony—he would not lower himself to ask but neither would he rush to finish his drink and join her. Dance attendance on her indeed.

Instead he persuaded Anthony to talk of his mother, and his memories of her youth. Finally, Alex drained his glass and stood up, but then sat again abruptly as he recalled something Anthony said that had been bothering him.

'The first day we met, you said you blamed my father for my mother's death. What did you mean?'

Anthony frowned. 'It is hardly a proper subject to discuss with you, Alex. Leo is your father, and deserves your respect.'

'Allow me to decide who deserves my respect, Anthony. It was a simple question. Did you have a reason for saying that, or was it your dislike for my father that prompted it?'

He held his breath as he awaited the answer although

quite what he expected he didn't know. After a long pause, Lascelles shrugged.

'I was fond of dear Margaret…as a friend, of course. I daresay I am somewhat prejudiced against your father but, over the years, I have often wondered how some vagrant happened upon the summer house, where I understand she was killed.'

Alex suppressed his shudder at the mention of the summer house.

'It was, after all, in the middle of the estate and not so very far from the Abbey itself. How, I wonder, did the killer find his way there? And why? Think of the risk… If he'd wanted to ravage some poor, unsuspecting female he could surely have found a less risky target?'

Alex's mouth dried and his heart pounded. He felt sweat dampen his brow, and he wiped it with his handkerchief.

'There…' Anthony rounded the table to put his hand on Alex's shoulder. 'I've upset you, speaking of such painful matters. Come. Let us join your charming wife.'

'You go ahead, Anthony. I shall follow soon.'

He couldn't face Jane just yet. She would see in a moment he was upset, and she would, of course, blame Anthony. But this was Alex's fault. He *had* asked, after all.

Jane had dreaded Anthony Lascelles coming to dinner, but he'd proved excellent company and she felt quite in charity with him as she waited for the men to join her, although she was disappointed they left her alone for such a long time. Finally the door opened but only Anthony entered. He strolled across to where she sat on the sofa, Mist curled on her knee, and bowed.

'I do beg your pardon, my dear Jane. I suggested we brought our port in here to keep you company, but dear Alex…well, it is natural for a man to crave the release of other male company from time to time, I am sure you agree?'

Jane fought to conceal her hurt. 'Of course.'

'I hope you will forgive us—I should hate for you to be reluctant to extend invitations to me in future in the fear I will always monopolise your husband.'

He tipped his head sideways, with an ingratiating smile that did not reach his eyes. Jane nodded, suppressing her involuntary shiver. No matter how entertaining his raconteur skills, he still made her uneasy.

'There is nothing to forgive, Anthony. I've been quite content with my book and with Mist for company.' She laid her hand on the kitten's soft fur, and was rewarded with a rumbling purr.

'What a sweet kitten.'

'Where *is* Alex?'

'He will join us soon, my dear. He... Ah, here he is now. Alex, dear boy, your good lady has forgiven our lapse in manners in not joining her sooner, and I dare to hope I shall still be welcome in your lovely home in future. I shall look forward to further reminiscences but, for now, I shall say my farewells.'

'Will you not stay and take tea before you leave, Anthony?'

Jane voiced the invitation from obligation, not from the desire to extend the time in Anthony's company. Alex clearly noticed her reticence, darting a glance of disapproval at her, but Anthony appeared oblivious.

'I thank you, dear lady, but I shall decline. I make no doubt you young newlyweds are finding an old man like me distinctly *de trop*.' He bowed and, as he straightened, his dark gaze pinned Jane. 'I shall leave you both to your pleasures...' He paused long enough for Jane to question his true meaning, then—with a flash of teeth—he smiled and added, '…for I am certain you are eager to discover what happens next in your novel.'

Jane stretched her lips in a smile. 'Then I bid you goodnight, Anthony.'

Alex clapped Lascelles on the shoulder, shaking his hand. 'Thank you for answering all my questions—you've been very patient.' He shot another reproachful glance at Jane. '*And* most helpful. I'll show you out myself.'

He said nothing, however, when he returned.

'Shall we go up?'

Jane frowned. 'Will you not tell me what you've been talking about? Did you learn much about your mother?'

'Yes, a great deal but I shan't bore you with it. After all, you didn't know her.'

Jane tried hard not to care. Alex had always been this way—always kept the different parts of his life separate. She didn't doubt he cared for her but she was still excluded from parts of his life…parts of him…and she had no idea how to reach the core of the man trapped behind that barrier.

She swallowed back her disappointment. 'I am tired,' she said. 'I think I will go up now.'

Alex didn't quite meet her eyes. 'Now I think about it, though, I'm not ready to retire just yet.' He helped Jane to her feet and kissed the tip of her nose. 'Sleep well.'

Jane lay awake, staring blindly into the darkness, worrying. Alex was still downstairs and, if she was honest, it was something of a relief. Lately, when they made love, although she was always physically satiated, she ended up feeling flat. Emotionally hungry. Dissatisfied.

And his moods seemed to be worsening. Was it simply pride that kept him from confessing what he was so afraid of? Because he *was* afraid. She saw the fear haunting his eyes, especially since Monday when, whatever he might tell her, she was convinced he'd had another of his funny turns. And that fear, she was certain, was new. He had always been haunted. But he had not been afraid. Rather, he had always been fearless. She frowned. At least, he had always *appeared* fearless. On the surface.

If only he would trust her. He must know she wouldn't think any the less of him, or love him any less, no matter what. But he stubbornly refused to even admit anything was wrong and, try as she might, she couldn't find a way to break through the barrier he had thrown up between them.

Finally, weary of her ever-circling thoughts that appeared to get her nowhere, she rolled over and slept.

My husband is the most frustrating man I know!

The refrain ran through Jane's thoughts a minimum of twice a day in the days and weeks that followed. Alex continued to act all strong and manly, denying there was anything wrong and, despite knowing that pestering him to talk only made him irritable, Jane could not help herself. She was worried sick about him. If only he would trust her…she was certain they could resolve whatever it was that shadowed his eyes and was robbing him of his appetite.

A voice inside Alex's head warned he was in danger of becoming obsessed with finding out everything he could about his mother. Most days, either Anthony visited Foxbourne, or Alex rode over to Halsdon and if, for whatever reason, they did not meet for a few days a panicky feeling would take root in his gut, growing there until the next time he saw their neighbour.

He shoved aside Jane's concerns—this was his problem, and he would find a solution. He couldn't risk giving her even the slightest hint of what was going on inside his head until it was clear in his own mind, and it was a long way from being clear. Talking to Anthony helped, however, and those distressing visions became less frequent—he even coped with the smell of the rose-scented perfume worn by a lady seated in front of him in church one Sunday without making an utter fool of himself. It helped to breathe through his mouth and to concentrate his thoughts on the sermon… It was surely the first time he had *ever* paid so much attention to a vicar's discourse.

Things were improving. Except for that deep dread that assailed him whenever a mental image of his father formed in his mind's eye. But was his father's face linked to his memories of that day because it was he who had carried seven-year-old Alex back to the Abbey or was there a more sinister reason? What if those dreadful suspicions were true? What if his father had killed his mother? That thought alone was enough to make him feel physically sick.

Alex and Lilley were debating which of their young stock to sell to ensure a sufficient stock of winter fodder one day when Anthony rode up to them.

'Would you care to come up to the house?' Alex asked. 'There's a real nip in the air this morning. I dare say you would appreciate a glass of something to counter it.'

Anthony's gaze slid away from Alex, as though embarrassed. 'I should not like to presume. I…' He shook his head. 'No. I am being over-sensitive. Yes. Thank you, Alexander. I accept with pleasure.'

Alex frowned. 'What do you mean…presume? There is nothing presumptuous about accepting an invitation from a man to join him for a glass of wine.'

'No, of course there is not. Ignore me, I beg of you.'

'No. Tell me what you meant. Has…has Jane made you feel unwelcome?'

'Not at all! Please do not think… I am certain she did not mean…after all, I *have* been a frequent visitor. It would be no wonder if a bride resented a friend who distracted her husband. Not that a word of criticism has left her lips, I assure you. She has been all that is civil.'

Civil? Alex had been on the receiving end of Jane's civility when she disapproved of something but it was her duty as lady of the house to make *all* visitors feel welcome, without regard to personal feelings. His inner voice urged him not to fly in and throw accusations at Jane—she'd warned him she didn't care for Anthony, and it was true he visited Foxbourne frequently.

The last thing they needed was even more conflict between them—it was bad enough with her constantly on at him to talk about his mother, and what had happened. She seemed unable to accept it was part of his life separate from their marriage and their life at Foxbourne. Plus, at the back of his mind, was the nagging realisation that he still hadn't told her they wouldn't be going to the Abbey for Christmas. It never seemed to be the right time but he was horribly aware he couldn't put it off much longer.

'Well, you may take it from me that you are welcome to visit any time you choose, Anthony. After all, I visit Halsdon as often as you come here.'

'Thank you, my boy. You have no idea how much that means to me, coming from Margaret's boy. If I had ever been blessed with a son, I would wish for him to be just like you.'

Once indoors, Alex led the way to his business room.

'I do suggest, though, that you might visit me at Halsdon more often instead,' Anthony continued as Alex stood aside for the older man to precede him into the room. 'At least there we can be sure we are not disturbing— Oh! I do beg your pardon, Jane. I am sure neither of us had any notion you might be in here.'

Alex entered to see Jane standing on the far side of the desk, his quill knife in her hand.

'You may rest assured you are in no way disturbing me, Anthony,' she said. 'I have merely come to borrow Alex's knife as I have mislaid my own and I am writing to my father.'

She smiled, but it did not reach her eyes. She rounded the desk and headed for the door, saying, 'Please excuse me. I must go and attend to my correspondence.'

Alex poured them both a glass of Madeira.

After they had settled, Anthony said, 'I am reluctant to broach the subject, but I hope Rosalind is content with your father? I know I forfeited any right to concern after my despicable actions five years ago, but I still care enough to wish her happy in her marriage.'

Alex always tried to avoid the subject of his father but Anthony was persistent in introducing him into conversation.

'Yes. They are happy together.'

'I am glad. She is more fortunate than poor Margaret. Her life with your father was far from happy.'

He'd told Alex that many times, as he'd recounted his memories of Alex's mother. He sipped his wine. 'Speaking of your father...'

Alex tensed. He might have grown closer to Anthony but he was conscious the man had never put aside his hatred and jealousy of Alex's father.

'What about him?' he asked when Anthony seemed reluctant to continue.

Anthony shrugged. 'Oh. It is of no importance. Not really. But I cannot help but wonder why your own relationship with him has not improved? Five years ago, you were

still a headstrong young man, for ever in trouble…as I remember, that is. Forgive me if I have misinterpreted the
events of that year.'

Alex scowled. 'No. Your memory is correct. But I do
not see your point.'

Anthony waved his arm, indicating the room. 'I am curious why—five years later, with you a responsible estate
owner, running a business, and, from my observations, no
longer in thrall to your previous wild existence—you are
still at odds with the Duke?'

When Alex failed to respond, Anthony continued, 'Have
I touched upon a nerve? My dear Alexander, please forgive
me. It is family business. I understand.' He leaned forward,
patting Alex's knee. 'But if you ever need someone to listen, you know where I am. I know you have family loyalty
at heart—and you're aware your father and I can never be
friends—but if anyone can understand, it is I.

'It is hard to be the outsider; the only one, seemingly,
out of step. Your father is universally admired. And the
rest of your…of *our*…family love him unconditionally.'
He shook his head. 'I sometimes wonder why I cannot do
likewise.' He raised his glass. 'You and I, m'boy, are kin-
dred spirits. We should take strength from that. Cheers.'

He smiled, and drank, and Alex automatically responded to his toast although the very notion he and
Anthony Lascelles were alike bothered him. Intensely.
Anthony had always resented and loathed Father. That was
his conscious decision, driven by resentment and jealousy.
It wasn't the same with Alex. He'd always longed to love
his father unconditionally, as Dominic did, but that natural filial love had always eluded him.

And he didn't know why; unless these accursed visions
were trying to expose the reason. The familiar dread coiled

in his gut. He no longer doubted he had witnessed his mother's murder. But…could his father *really* be her killer?

'What is it?' Anthony's voice seemed far away. 'Alexander? You are pale, my boy. Are you unwell?'

'No. I'm all right. It's nothing.' Alex drained his glass and rose to his feet. 'Thank you for calling in, Anthony, but I really must return to the stables…there are decisions to be made.'

Lascelles was soon mounted, ready to leave. He touched the brim of his hat in farewell.

'Don't be a stranger, Alexander. Call upon me whenever you wish…you will always find a warm welcome.'

Later, Alex found Jane in the drawing room, embroidering initials on the handkerchiefs she'd made for Christmas.

'Anthony feels unwelcome here.'

'Does he?' She captured Alex's gaze. 'I am sorry, Alex, but I have said nothing to make him feel that way. I'm aware of my duties as hostess, and I say all the right words. I cannot help it if my inner feelings reveal an aversion to Lascelles, the same as *he* seems unable to prevent his inner…*offensiveness*…from peeking through at times.' Her lips tightened before she added, 'There is something not right about the man.'

'You shouldn't allow Aunt Cecily's prejudice to infect you. You are positively searching for reasons to object to him.'

Jane leapt to her feet, her eyes shooting sparks. 'I am not! You are being unfair, Alex. I am polite to him because he is your guest, but you cannot force me to like him. *I* cannot understand why *you* don't recognise his deviousness.'

'He knew my mother! I—'

'But that doesn't stop him being devious!' He winced as she raised her voice. What had happened to quiet, inoffensive Jane? 'Why do you *always* find time for him yet hardly have any time to talk to me?'

Anger roared through him, partly fuelled by knowing she was correct. He sought out Anthony to talk about his mother, and yet his mother was the very reason he avoided talking to Jane. The irony wasn't lost on him. He paced the room, desperately tamping down that rage. How ridiculous, to allow a neighbour to cause such a row.

'You know I need to find out about Mother.' He stopped pacing and took Jane's hands. 'Let's not quarrel, Janey. I hate it when you're cross with me.'

Jane's face softened. 'I hate it, too. But please don't expect me to mindlessly obey you when it goes counter to what I believe. I *will* continue to speak my mind—but I only ever do it out of love for you.'

Shame now held him in its grip. She was far too good for him. His hands slid up her arms to her shoulders.

'I do know it. But I won't stop seeing Anthony. I cannot. Please accept that.'

'I do.' Her soft hand caressed his cheek. 'But I wish you would trust *me* enough to talk to me, Alex. You are remembering something from the past, but what can be so dreadful that you are unable to tell me?'

He stiffened. He didn't want this discussion. Not again.

'Whatever it is you're afraid of, I can help. Please. Just tell—'

Alex jerked away from her. 'There's nothing. I *have* told you. Time after time. Why won't *you* trust *me* when I say there's nothing wrong?'

He spun on his heel and slammed out of the room.

Chapter Eighteen

Jane picked up her discarded sewing, her throat a painful mass of unshed tears. Her hands shook and, after pricking her finger twice, she gave up trying to control her emotions. She crossed to the window, staring blindly out, as she relived every moment and every word of their argument. Her arms wrapped around her waist, her hands fisting in the fabric of her gown. Should she have apologised, and promised to be less mistrustful of Lascelles? Should she give in, and accept Alex's refusal to talk about whatever was troubling him? She *could* be the easy, supportive wife who never questioned her husband's judgement and decisions but she believed, with her whole heart, that was the wrong path.

Despite Alex's fury. Despite his refusal to confide in her. Despite her distress at his reaction…she still believed she was right to keep encouraging him to trust her.

Or nagging him, as he would no doubt see it.

She hauled in a deep breath, and lifted her chin. She *knew* Alex. She'd seen these tactics time after time, from way back when she first knew him. It was how he kept the world at arm's length—his brother, his sister, his aunt and uncle. His father. He kept them all away, never allowing them to probe too deeply. It was his defence…the way he pretended nothing mattered…nothing could touch him… hurt him. But he *was* hurting, deep inside. She knew it.

And that fear still haunted him. She had glimpsed it too many times, shadowing his tiger eyes before his expression would blank, his jaw tight. It had started with his stay at the Abbey, and Pikeford's attack, and it linked to that day he had discovered his mother's body. The entire family counted it as a blessing he couldn't remember, believing ignorance protected him. Jane wasn't so sure.

Now…was he remembering the details of that day after all? Could he now picture his mother's brutalised body as he had found her? Jane shuddered, the memory of Pikeford close. He'd hit her. He was drunk…she'd been unable to reason with him… How far would he have gone had Alex not intervened? Another shudder racked her body, her skin crawling with gooseflesh and, of a sudden, all she wanted was to turn to Alex, to feel his arms around her, his strength and his comfort.

Her heart ached that he would not turn to her in his distress, but chose to turn to Lascelles. With a muttered exclamation she swiped the tears wetting her cheeks. Crying wouldn't help. She didn't know what would help. Or… yes, she did.

Alex.

She couldn't bear to leave his anger to fester…she hated it when they quarrelled. For her own sake, she would apologise for now but it wouldn't stop her trying again. She'd lived too long with her stepmother—having to edit every word before she spoke—to be prepared to tiptoe around within her own marriage.

She spun on her heel and half ran to the door, which opened as she reached it.

Alex. Contrition on his face.

Jane stepped back. 'I was coming to find you. To say I'm sorry.'

'No. It's me who is sorry.' He hugged her close. 'I'm a brute. I know you are trying to help me, but...' He shrugged. 'I am too used to fending for myself.' He tipped up her chin, searched her eyes. 'Forgive me, Honeybee?'

She bit her lip. 'I forgive you, Alex. But...I still want you to trust me. I really do believe it will help you to talk about whatever is haunting you. Unless, of course, you have already confided in Anthony?'

She couldn't help herself, even though she was aware she was playing with fire by revisiting the very reason they had argued. A myriad of emotions played across Alex's face. Jane braced herself for him to lose his temper again, but he sighed, and Jane released her own breath, knowing he would not fly up into the boughs again. This time.

'Jane...sweetheart...there's nothing to tell. Your imagination is conjuring up ghosts where there are only figures draped in sheets. They are of no concern. Now...come for a ride with me? I want to inspect the two-year-olds in the north paddock. Lilley and I have been discussing which of them to sell and which to keep. I'd value your opinion.'

Jane knew a distraction when she saw one. Alex was a master at deflecting attention from subjects he refused to discuss. She suppressed another sigh as she accepted her husband's latest olive branch.

It was the first day of December, and Jane had just finished writing to Olivia when Kent came into the parlour.

'Mr Lascelles is here, milady—he brought a letter with him. He met Tommy on his way to the village. I told him His Lordship is away from home, and he asked for you.'

Jane stood, her insides clenching. The prospect of being

alone with Lascelles unnerved her, with Alex absent from the house.

'Thank you, Kent. Have you offered him refreshments?'

'Yes, milady. He declined. He said he will not linger but didn't wish to leave without paying his respects. He is waiting in the library.'

'Thank you.'

Jane smoothed her clammy palms down her skirt before she preceded Kent into the hall. The letter lay on the console table and she recognised Liberty's neat hand. Her heart lifted. Liberty's letters were always entertaining— almost as good as chatting face-to-face. They'd become firm friends since their first meeting, before Dominic and Liberty's marriage.

But before she could read it, there was Lascelles to face. She longed to ask for a maid to come and sit with them but was embarrassed to reveal her mistrust in Lascelles.

As she passed Kent into the library, however, he murmured, 'I shall be in the hallway should our visitor change his mind about refreshments, milady. You only have to call.'

Relief coursed through Jane. 'Thank you, Kent.'

She stepped into the room. Lascelles was perusing the titles in a bookcase. A movement on the top of the bookcase caught Jane's eye and, before she could shout a warning, a grey bundle of fluff launched itself, landing on Lascelles' shoulder. Lascelles swore viciously and grabbed Mist, turning back to the room as he did so. Jane froze, her stunned brain scrambling to make sense of what she was seeing, as Lascelles held the wriggling kitten tightly in his hands. His face distorted into a snarl as his grip tightened…squeezing…

At Mist's squeal of pain Jane broke free of her paralysis and charged at Lascelles.

'Let her go!' She shook his arm in her fury. 'You evil brute! *Let her go*, I said!'

'Gladly!'

Lascelles cast Mist across the room. She rolled several times, leapt to her feet and shot out through the door, fur on end, tail fluffed out to twice its normal size. Lascelles smoothed the sleeve of his coat, and stared down at Jane, eyes narrowed. They were so close the woody, sweet and spicy scent of his bay rum cologne filled her nostrils, and her ears detected his erratic breathing. He might look un-ruffled, but she suspected he was a mass of tension beneath the surface. That gave her courage, to realise he might be as rattled as her.

'I *ought* to apologise but I will not. Cats are vicious animals, totally unsuitable as house pets. They belong outside, with the rest of the vermin. That animal *attacked* me.'

Jane fought the instinct to retreat. 'I see no blood.' She forced the words through gritted teeth. 'Get out of my house and *never* come back. Do you hear me?'

Fury flashed in his eyes. '*Your* house? I think your hus-band might have something to say about *that*, my dear. He will not take kindly to you banishing me. Not when *I* have the information he craves.'

'He will not take kindly to you torturing an innocent animal.'

Lascelles sneered. 'Your word against mine, my dear. You are clearly distraught and your imagination is play-ing tricks.'

'Milady? Is everything all right?'

Jane didn't even glance at Kent, determined to hold Las-celles' gaze. 'Mr Lascelles is leaving, Kent. Please show him out.'

Lascelles' gaze hardened. He reached out, lifting her

chin with one finger. Jane refused to flinch. She wouldn't give him the satisfaction.

'Take care, Lady Jane.' His voice was a menacing whisper. He held her gaze for what seemed like an aeon before pivoting on his heel and striding from the room.

Jane squared her shoulders, determined not to succumb to her quivering nerves.

'Thank you, Kent. Please tell the rest of the staff Mr Lascelles is on no account to be allowed into the house unless His Lordship is at home.'

'Yes, milady.'

'Did you see where Mist went?'

'Upstairs, milady. I hope she wasn't hurt.'

'So do I, Kent.'

Jane found Mist trembling under her bed. She coaxed her out and sat on the bed to examine her, petting her and reassuring her. She appeared unharmed physically and, murmuring softly to calm her, Jane carried her downstairs to the parlour, collecting Liberty's letter on the way.

She settled Mist on her lap, smoothing her fur. It was an age before the kitten ceased trembling. Eventually, though, she slept, and Jane also dozed off, having already read Liberty's letter three times, squinting as she deciphered the crossed lines, but reluctant to disturb the sleeping kitten to fetch a book to read to pass the time.

Alex paused inside the parlour door, watching Jane before she was aware of his presence. Her eyes were closed, her lashes a dark crescent against the gentle bloom of her cheeks. Her lips were parted, her chest gently rising and falling with every breath. Her hair had escaped some of the pins, and tendrils stroked her neck, leaving her perfect shell-like ear peeping through. One hand rested on

Mist, curled on Jane's lap, her green eyes on Alex as one ear twitched. In the other was a letter.

Peace warmed his heart. No matter what horrors his visions stirred from the past, Jane was his life now and he vowed to try even harder to make her happy—their disagreement the other day had shaken him more than he believed possible and he had no wish to repeat it. But Jane hadn't mentioned nightmares or the past since, and she hated quarrelling as much as he did, so hopefully they could avoid the subject in future and all would be well.

As he walked towards her Mist suddenly leapt up and shot past him, out the door.

'Ouch!' Jane woke with a start, rubbing her leg. Her eyes widened when she saw Alex. 'I didn't know you were home. Why did Mist run off? Is Lascelles here?'

'Anthony? Why should he be here?' He crouched down next to Jane's chair. 'There's blood on your gown. Did Mist scratch you?'

'She dug her claws in as she jumped off.' Jane tutted as she examined the spot of blood. 'I shall have to change this, and sponge the blood out before it dries.'

'I'll come with you.' He nuzzled her neck, breathing in her jasmine scent, licking the hollow beneath her ear and nibbled her lobe. It was too long since they'd made love, the growing distance between them by day having its effect by night, too.

But Jane pulled away. 'Alex… Lascelles called. I caught him torturing Mist. *That's* why she ran away when you came in.'

'Torturing?' Anger brewed. 'What happened?'

'He was squeezing her. Hard enough to make her squeal. He claimed she attacked him, but she only jumped down onto his shoulder. He…he frightens me, Alex. I've told him not to come here again.'

Alex stood up, torn. He couldn't abide any kind of cruelty to animals, but…he *needed* Anthony. He was the only person who could help him know his mother and ultimately make sense of the past. 'You barred him from Foxbourne?'

'I did.' Her chin lifted. 'I hope you will support my decision. I will not be threatened in my own home.'

'He threatened you?' The anger boiled now. No man threatened his wife.

She nodded. 'Maybe not in so many words, but the threat was there.'

'What did he say?'

'He said, "Take care, Lady Jane".'

Alex frowned, and his anger eased. 'That doesn't sound threatening, Jane. Are you sure you aren't imagining it?'

She'd always been the same with Anthony, reading hidden menace in the most mundane conversation. What had happened to *Everyone deserves a chance to prove they've changed*?

'I am sure.' Jane's mouth settled into a stubborn line. 'It was the *way* he said it. I don't want him in my home again. Please, Alex.'

He folded his arms. 'I'll ask him to stay away. I can always go to Halsdon instead.' Jane's brows snapped together. 'I still need to talk to him about Mother, Jane. You must understand that.'

'But you cannot talk to me about her?'

Alex sighed. 'I will. One day. Once I understand it all.'

'Understand *what*?'

Her cry of anguish wrenched his heart but he turned away.

'Alex? Liberty has written to us.'

He turned back, relieved by the change of subject. Jane held the letter out to him, but the sight of those crossed and recrossed lines made his head throb. 'Perhaps you might paraphrase it?' He was rewarded with a laugh, even though it was strained.

'Firstly, she has shared the happy news that they are expecting their first child. Is that not wonderful? And, secondly, we're invited to stay at Clystfield Court next week, before we all go on to the Abbey for Christmas. She fears otherwise the weather might prevent us travelling.'

His heart lurched. He'd *still* not told Jane they weren't going to the Abbey. He could think of nothing worse, especially now with his suspicions about his father's role in his mother's death.

'No.'

Jane stared. 'No? What do you—? *Pfft!* That's a ridiculous question. I know exactly what you mean by "No". What I need to ask is "Why"? It will only be an extra week away, and Olivia, Hugo and the twins will be there, too. It will be—'

'I mean, no we are not going to the Abbey for Christmas.'

'*What?* But…we accepted…we're expected. Your entire family will be there.'

'Which is precisely why we are not going.'

Jane stood up and grabbed his hands. 'I don't believe you don't want to see your family. You *love* them. Why, Alex?'

He shrugged, pulling his hands from hers.

'Is this what our future holds?' Her voice sharpened. 'What if we have children? Would you deny them the opportunity to know their aunts and uncles and cousins? Not to mention their grandparents.'

'I've made my decision.'

Jane stared at him like he was a stranger. His gaze slid from hers and his insides shrivelled until he felt like an empty, useless shell. But he couldn't face his father. He simply couldn't.

'What about what *I* want? Or does my opinion not count? What *is* it you won't tell me, Alex?'

He couldn't tell her. How could she ever face any of his family again if she knew what he suspected? She would never be able to hide the truth from her eyes.

'If it's the Abbey…if you're afraid your nightmares will return…'

'It's not the Abbey! I can cope with a few bad dreams.'

'Your father then. We could compromise—go to Clystfield and then come home. You wouldn't even need to see your father…'

The rest of her words faded as an image of his father erupted in his head.

He was in profile, his lips drawn back in a snarl. *I will never let you go!* Alex surged to his feet, utterly shaken. He'd accepted he had witnessed his mother's murder. He had suspected his father may have been involved but he had hoped…no…*prayed* it was not so. Prayed that the mental images of his father were simply his child's memory confusing his father—who had indisputably been there in the aftermath—with the man who attacked his mother.

But this was an image that shook his very foundations… the first time he had pictured his father actually playing a part in his mother's death. Not his father as he was now, but as he was then: lean, dark, dangerous. The image of *his* hands around Mother's neck. His greatest dread was true. He'd always blamed himself for his prickly relationship with his father. But now…the fault was not his. And that knowledge shattered him. He couldn't even begin to wonder at the impact of this on the rest of the family.

Nausea roiled his stomach, turning his legs weak and his breathing shallow.

'Alex? What is it? What's wrong?' Jane clung to his arm.

He needed to be alone.

'We're not going to the Abbey. That's my final word on it.'

How could he possibly go, knowing what he did? The very thought made him long to curl up into a ball and sleep for ever now he had the answer to his aversion to his own father. His father the killer.

The nausea rose up his throat: acid, burning, threatening to erupt.

'Alex…please…tell me…'

He must be alone. He snatched his arm free.

'I have work to do.'

He strode from the room before Jane could reply, and ran outside, hoping the fresh air might help clear his head. And defuse his anger. And obliterate that sudden, horrific image of his father, the sound of those words, gritted out through clenched teeth. Words of fury. Alex's stomach knotted, screwing tight, as his breathing grew shallow. He headed for the garden, to the arbour that used to support rambling roses but was now cloaked with honeysuckle every summer, and sank on to the bench, leaning forward, his forearms propped along his thighs.

His throat was thick, aching, and his head throbbed anew as it sank into his hands. He strove to rid his mind of all thought, but the images kept coming. Relentlessly. The yellow dress, the angry voices, the boots and the slippers, the breathless pleading: *'No. No. Please.'*

All while he had cowered beneath the chaise longue, where his mother had loved to recline on warm days. He'd done *nothing* to save her.

His stomach heaved, propelling him out of the arbour to the nearest bush where he retched until his stomach was empty. Tears burned behind his eyes.

I cannot stand this.

The visions were now crystal-clear, and that deep, deep

dread that had plagued his childhood and that he had managed to keep suppressed all these years—firstly with the help of alcohol and drugs and wild escapades and, latterly, by concentrating fiercely and wholeheartedly on his beloved horses—could no longer be ignored.

His stomach heaved again, his muscles clenched in pain. They'd had it wrong. Everyone had it wrong. He'd believed them because it had suited him to believe them…so he wouldn't have to face the truth that he hadn't just found his mother's murdered body, nor even that he had watched her being killed, but that he had watched her being throttled by his own father.

He sank to his knees, oblivious to the sharp sting of the gravel through his breeches. His arms wrapped around his torso as he bent forward and then rocked, images from the past…from that day…tumbling through his thoughts, clearer and sharper and, seemingly, unstoppable. He hadn't been seen. At no point had his father spotted him, cowering beneath the chaise longue, the floor rough against his cheek.

All these years. The truth had been there. Inside him. Waiting.

Again, his stomach clenched, a nest of snakes writhing inside. The lid on that day had cracked, and he had fallen through into a past of horrors. He could never rid himself now of that memory, and he had no choice but to somehow live with it.

He had watched his own father kill his mother.

He swallowed desperately, forcing his gorge back down his throat as chills raced across his skin. He could never admit the truth to a living soul, for it would tear the Beauchamp family apart. He thought about Dominic and Olivia, not to mention Christabel and Sebastian. How could he brand their father a murderer? He could never do that to his brothers and sisters, let alone to Rosalind and the rest of the family.

But how could he allow his mother's death to go unavenged?

'Alex?'

Her call was distant. He couldn't talk to her. Not now. He scrambled to his feet.

'Alex?'

Nearer now. Panic set in. She knew him too well. Would know something drastic had happened. And she wouldn't give up…she would keep pushing him for an answer. And what if that rage roiling his insides should erupt at Jane? He couldn't take that risk, and he hadn't the strength to put on his customary brave face. He wasn't ready to bury it inside and pretend nothing was eating a hole in him. Not yet. Maybe in time…

Because if Jane should learn the truth… *He* also knew *her* too well. She could never dissemble with his family, and God forbid she should ever come face-to-face with his father. No. She must never know. But he must get his own emotions under control before he could attempt to fool her into believing nothing was wrong.

He turned and sprinted for the stable yard, despising himself but helpless to do anything else. He needed time to clear his head, and to work out how he could continue to face Jane—not to mention the rest of the world—with this new knowledge.

Chapter Nineteen

Alex regained some semblance of calm during the ride to Halsdon Manor, painfully aware it didn't bode well for the future of his marriage that he could face Anthony but not his own wife. He should never have wed. He was incapable of making any woman happy for long…his demons were too strong for that. And now he knew why. Anthony was the one person who shared Alex's distrust of his father and, right now, that's exactly what he needed. The freedom to admit there was something wrong. If his disdain for Father showed, Anthony would accept it whereas anyone else of his acquaintance would—as they always had—immediately try to persuade him he was wrong, and to use guilt to lever him into a filial love he had never felt.

And now never could.

He swallowed back a sob.

It would be better if I were dead. They'd all be better off without me.

The thought appeared from nowhere, shocking him. Jane's face materialised in his mind's eye, her brown eyes warm and trusting. She deserved so much better than him but he could see no way of being the husband she wanted him to be. Not now.

Servants were hurrying hither and thither when Alex arrived at Halsdon Manor.

'I leave for London this afternoon,' Anthony said, as he and Alex settled in the pair of wing back chairs in his salon.

'London?' The news hit Alex like a blow to the gut. 'I didn't know you were planning to leave this soon. How long will you be gone?'

Anthony shrugged. 'I had no intention of leaving yet, but I believe it will be for the best after this morning's unfortunate misunderstanding.'

'But…'

What about me? Who can I talk to if you're in London?

Sheer pride kept those words inside but now he felt even more compelled to discover as much as possible about his parents' marriage. To work out how a man like his father could be driven to murder. He was drowning, and Anthony was his lifeline…the only thing keeping his head above water.

Anthony speared him with a knowing look. 'We will talk again on my return, my boy. Never fear.'

Alex swallowed down his desperation. 'And when will that be?'

'I know not. Weeks? Months? It depends how long it takes your lady to forgive me, even though she utterly misread the situation.'

Belatedly, Alex recalled what Jane told him about Anthony and Mist. Shame piled upon shame. What kind of man didn't leap to the defence of his wife? If Anthony hadn't mentioned the incident, Alex would have completely forgotten, so bound up was he in his own troubles.

'How did she misread seeing you torture her kitten?'

'*Torture?* An exaggeration, my dear chap, I assure you. That is the trouble with females, is it not? They are prone to leap to conclusions, allowing their emotions to colour the facts before their eyes.'

Anthony put down his glass, leaned back in his chair, and steepled his fingers, propping his chin on them. The pose brought Father to mind—how many times had he seen both his father and Dominic adopt a similar pose? Nausea again churned his stomach. Would he feel like this every time his father was brought to mind?

Again, that scandalous idea crept into his thoughts. He thrust it aside, concentrating on what Anthony was saying.

'I bitterly regret what happened, my dear chap, but you must believe I had no intention of hurting the little creature. It startled me, leaping upon me from above as I browsed the bookshelves. Those claws are needle-sharp, and they dug straight into my scalp. I didn't know what attacked me—I swiped it away by reflex, and that was what Jane saw. She would not listen to reason, and so I beat my retreat.'

Alex recalled the spot of blood on Jane's gown…proof indeed of the sharpness of Mist's claws.

Anthony leaned forward. 'Surely you can see how that might be misinterpreted? Ladies' sensibilities are so easily upset, are they not?'

Alex did see how a misunderstanding might arise, but Jane was no fool and she was no delicate flower, prone to fits of the vapours. But, whatever the truth, the result was that Anthony was leaving for London and Alex *did* blame Jane for that.

'Indeed,' he said. 'But there is no need to leave on Jane's account, Anthony. I shall talk to her…explain it was a mis- understanding.'

'She has banned me from your house, dear boy.' An- thony's brows rose, and his eyes widened. 'I had so hoped to put to rest all those past disagreements with your branch of the family. I fear there is little hope now. Your lady wife will no doubt confide in the other Beauchamp ladies and, once your father gets to hear of it…' He sighed. 'He is an implacable enemy, Alexander. You will not have seen that side of him, but *I* have. Too often. What your poor, dear mother endured…but… There. I have said too much. Your family loyalty must of course be with your father.'

Tears burned behind Alex's eyes. He held his breath, desperately clamping down on all the emotion threatening to erupt.

'My dear boy! What have I said?'

Anthony's sympathetic tone was his undoing and, once the words began, he could no more stop the flow than he could stop the sun rising every morning.

Alex rode home two hours later, his spirits lighter after letting out all his pain and confusion. And Anthony was the perfect person to talk to—his loyalties never tested because there had never been any love lost between him and Alex's father. He had sworn on his life never to reveal what Alex told him, not to anyone, and Alex had no choice but to believe him for, by the time his brain had caught up with the torrent of his confession, the worst had been said and it was far too late to unsay it.

But nothing he said had persuaded Anthony to change his plans. He was leaving for London that afternoon.

Alex left his horse at the stables and headed for the house under a sky turned pewter by massing storm clouds. His pace faltered, despite the icy raindrops that spattered him. What to say to Jane? What explanation could he offer? His immediate crisis had passed…he was better able to control his feelings now he'd had his chance to vent…but he knew his wife. She would not let this go. She would want to know… He could hear her in his head.

What happened? Why did you run off? Where have you been?

Tension seized him again. He couldn't tell her. How would she ever face his family again? In time, *he* could face them although he would *never* willingly meet his father again. Ever. But Jane would never be able to keep her expression free of such dreadful knowledge.

He met Jane in the hall, at the foot of the stairs, her eyes puffy and pink. She stiffened when she saw him.

'You've come home, then?'

'As you see.'

'Alex…' She put her hand on his sleeve. 'I've been worried. Are you all right?'

'Yes, thank you.' His voice sounded raw to his ears. 'I'm sorry I stormed off.'

'No. *I* am sorry for plaguing you to talk to me. But…you *can* trust me, you know. I wouldn't think you less of a man for talking of your feelings as a child, if that makes sense?'

Her brown eyes were open and honest, warm and caring. She still harboured the hope he would share more of himself…his past…with her, as he'd known she would.

He stretched his lips in a smile. 'I know I can trust you, but there is nothing to tell. I spoke to Anthony, by the way, and you need worry no further. He leaves for London this afternoon.'

Jane stared at Alex. He'd gone to Lascelles? Run from her as though she were the devil incarnate, and gone straight to that evil…? She sucked in a deep breath, desperate to calm herself. The last thing she wanted was another argument but…could she really keep biting her tongue? Was this how she wanted to live her life? She'd had no choice while she was growing up. She did have a choice now.

'You said you had work to attend to.'

Alex scowled. 'I did it for you, Janey. You wanted me to tell him never to darken our doorstep again. That is what I did.'

She scanned his pale face; the shadows beneath his eyes; the deep grooves from nose to mouth. He appeared to have aged ten years since yesterday.

'Alex…please…'

He snatched his arm away. 'I've told you. There is nothing more so please stop nagging me. I cannot tell you what doesn't exist.'

Her hands clenched into fists. Infuriating man!

'Very well. I am going to consult with Mrs Godfrey about dinner.'

She pivoted on her heel and stalked down the hall to the kitchen, not trusting herself to say another word.

Early the next morning, Jane lay awake next to a still-sleeping Alex. He'd been restless, crying out several times in the night, but had not woken. Jane had soothed him each time, longing to shake him awake and demand to know what was troubling him, but she'd resisted, telling herself he needed his sleep. Telling herself she'd talk to him in the morning. But now that morning was here she realised that to badger him again would simply result in the same reaction. And an idea had come to her in the night.

She would agree to not spending Christmas at Cheriton Abbey but—in the hope Alex might confide in Dominic—she would try to persuade Alex to go to Clystfield Court. Today if possible, for hail had clattered against the window in the night and it was noticeably colder. If it should snow, they would be going nowhere.

If that failed, she had no idea what to do next, but she

was close to the end of her tether. Was it really asking too much to be allowed to help him?

She waited until they were at breakfast before broaching the subject.

'Alex. Please may we discuss going to Clystfield Court?'

His expression darkened as he put down his knife and fork. 'We discussed it yesterday. You know my decision.'

'I understand you don't wish to go to the Abbey, but could we not visit Dominic and Liberty? It will only mean two weeks away, including the travelling...surely we—'

Alex leapt to his feet, thumping the table with his fist, making the crockery rattle. 'No! Stop harassing me. I won't go. Let that be the end of it.'

'But *I* wish to go, Alex.'

'Then go, if it's so important to you. Go with my blessing. I'll even order the carriage for you.'

She stared at him, horrified at his implacable expression. He had called her bluff, knowing she would not go without him. But she couldn't give in. Not yet.

'Mayhap I shall.' Jane drank her coffee, holding his gaze.

Alex shrugged, and picked up his cutlery. Jane's cup rattled as she placed it in its saucer and she silently cursed her trembling hand. She wanted to sink her head in her hands so she could order her thoughts, but she refused to reveal her devastation. Her mouth was as dry as a desert, but she picked up her toast and bit into it, chewing as best she could while Alex continued to eat his bacon and eggs. An awkward silence ensued, until they were interrupted by Kent, bearing a note. Alex opened it, and Jane, perplexed, watched utter relief suffuse his expression.

'Who is it from?'

Alex looked up. 'Anthony.'

'What does he say?'

'He didn't leave yesterday after all.'

And Alex's relief not only made sense but it tore at her heart. What was going on? Why was Lascelles so essential to Alex?

Alex thrust back his chair. 'I have business to attend to, and then I'm going out. I shall see you later.'

No words of endearment, no teasing smile, just a stern-faced near-stranger who banged the door behind him. When he went out, would it be to see Lascelles?

Tears bubbled close to the surface.

If only I hadn't nagged him about Clystfield. If he does visit Lascelles, I have no one to blame but myself!

But it was not long before she realised she was doing what she always did—blaming herself when it was Alex who was being unreasonable, laying down the law without explanation. After a short while, she gathered herself together and rose from the table, determined not to allow the matter to rest there. Alfred, their new footman, was in the hall, waiting to clear the breakfast dishes.

'Did you see where His Lordship went, Alfred?'

'No, milady. But he did speak to Mrs Kent…' he pointed to where the housekeeper was talking to Sally on the stairs '…so she might know.'

The housekeeper looked around at her name.

'Mrs Kent, do you happen to know where His Lordship is, please?'

'He's gone out, my lady. I presumed to the stables. He asked me to put a letter in his business room, and then told me he's dining out tonight and not to expect him back till late.'

Jane's heart plummeted. He'd gone already? And he intended to dine out, without even informing her?

'Thank you.'

She marched to the business room. The letter must have

been the one from Lascelles, and she wanted to know exactly what that scoundrel had written.

She found the letter straight away and read it with an increasing sense of disbelief.

I am persuaded you need me more than ever, dear Alexander. You convinced me it is my duty as your friend to remain, at least until I can be of no further comfort in your hour of need.

Come to Halsdon whenever you wish. Stay here as long as you need to. Come tonight to dine! We shall put the world to rights over a bottle of that claret you enjoy so much.
Your loyal friend and confidant,
Anthony Lascelles

Confidant!

Fury raged through her as she stalked from the business room, swung her cloak around her shoulders and strode down to the stables, driven by the urge to follow Alex and challenge him. Except…she knew his stubbornness. Knew the more she reasoned with him, or badgered him…*whatever* tactic she might try to bring him to his senses…he would resist her.

And wasn't that exactly why he had gone to Lascelles now? Her nagging had driven him from her. Her anger seeped away and her shoulders slumped. What was she to do? Going along with whatever Alex decreed might satisfy him, but what if that made *her* unhappy? Yet standing up for herself merely widened the rift between them. If only he would listen—she was worn out with trying to get through to him.

She spent time petting Pearl, feeding her with slices of carrot she found in the feed store, at a loss to know what else to do with herself. Frost was gone, so Alex had definitely left Foxbourne. If he'd already gone to Halsdon, he would be all day and evening with that evil so-and-so, even though she'd told him what he'd done to Mist.

She wandered outside, one slice of carrot left, which she'd saved for Nelson who no longer attacked the men now he was turned out in a small paddock with an open-sided shelter rather than confined in a stall.

Jane tried everything to coax the horse to her, but he merely stared at her from the far fence. She let herself in the gate and approached him slowly, the carrot on her outstretched palm, but paused about ten feet from the horse, sensing he was about to run off.

'You are as difficult and prickly as your master,' she muttered, before walking back to the gate in defeat.

As she reached for the latch, she felt something stir her hair. She stilled, holding her breath. Then whiskers tickled her cheek, and a quiet snort confirmed Nelson had followed her. Remembering how Alex had handled the stallion, she didn't look at him.

'Good boy…you want to be friends, don't you, but you can't quite trust me yet.'

She put the carrot on her palm and held it in front of her. Nelson stretched his head over her shoulder, and whiffled at the carrot, before taking it gently between his lips. The crunch in her ear was loud, and pleasure filled her as she stroked his velvety nose. She let herself out of the gate before she faced Nelson. He moved away, but she didn't mind. He'd trusted her, and she felt a huge sense of achievement.

She shivered. The wind had picked up, sneaking around corners in eddies, and fingering its way through gaps in buildings and clothing alike, so she started back to the house, following the line of the fence. Nelson, still in the paddock, kept pace with her. Of a sudden, Jane halted, a blinding truth whirling through her brain.

All this time trying to persuade Alex to trust her and all she had succeeded in doing was to drive him away, straight to Lascelles. *That* was why he had gone this morning. Not because he desperately wanted to see Lascelles, but because he felt cornered. By *her*.

She shivered again, huddling in her cloak, wondering what to do. Kent had been muttering about winter setting in early and, if he was right, the weather would soon deny them any choice in the matter of travelling down to Devon.

It seemed unlikely they would go. Not now. Unless…

Jane headed back to the stables, where earlier she had heard the murmur of the grooms' voices from the tack room. Silence fell when she entered, and the three occupants stopped polishing tack and stood.

'Lilley, might I have a word, please?'

He followed Jane outside.

'Did His Lordship order the carriage to be prepared?'

'No, milady.'

She'd known his words were bravado. He never thought for one minute she would go without him.

Well, we shall see what you make of this, Lord Alexander Beauchamp.

Jane sighed theatrically, for Lilley's benefit. 'I *knew* he would forget! Have it ready at noon, if you please. I am going down to Lord Avon's estate. His Lordship will follow on later.'

Doubt chased disapproval across Lilley's craggy features. 'You're travelling alone, milady? I'm not—'

'It is all arranged, Lilley. Peg and Alfred will accompany me, so you need not fear for either propriety or for my safety.'

'Very good, milady.'

Jane headed back to the house, new purpose in her step. She didn't want to be apart from Alex, especially when he was so very troubled, but maybe the shock of her leaving would bring him to his senses. It was a gamble, but *he* had told her go. He had given her his blessing, so he couldn't accuse her of leaving him or disobeying him.

But would he follow her?

That was the gamble. But, even if he didn't, at least it would remind him she would not stay meekly at home, waiting for him to decide when—or if—he could trust his own wife.

Chapter Twenty

It was midnight when Alex returned to Foxbourne Manor. The wind had settled into a steady, biting blast from the east, and ragged clouds blew hurriedly across the moon, bathing the landscape alternately in a ghostly glow and a blanket of purple shadows. He really shouldn't have stayed at Halsdon all this time, but every time he had made a move to leave, Anthony had lured him into just one more drink…one more game of billiards…one more hand of cards.

One more story about his mother. His parents. The past.

He should have been stronger. More resolute. Jane would be… His stomach stirred uneasily as he recalled their last conversation. He had slammed out of the house. Again. And it had been easier to stay in the warm and put off facing his wife who would be, quite rightly, angry. And hurt.

He would make it up to her. Somehow.

He shivered as he slid from Frost's back and led him to his stall. Pat, one of the grooms, emerged from the tack room at the end of the row of stalls, yawning and rubbing his eyes, prodding Alex into an apology.

'Sorry to keep you up, Pat. I can see to Frost. You get off to bed.'

'No, milord. I'll do it. Mr Lilley left *me* in charge, so he did.'

'Well, you must catch up with your sleep in the morning.' Alex handed Frost's reins to Pat. 'If Lilley complains you're late tell him it was an order from me.'

Pat grinned. 'Thank you, milord, but I meant he left me in charge until he gets back. He thought you'd want him to drive milady to Devonshire himself, to protect her. Him and Nobby have both gone, sir, and taken the blunderbuss with them, too.'

Alex stilled. Then pivoted slowly to face the groom, his mind whirring as he worked out what conversation they were having. Surely…his brain dredged up that last conversation with Jane.

'But I wish to go.'

'Then go, if it's so important to you. Go with my blessing.'

And she'd done it! She'd taken him at his word and gone to Dominic's without a thought for him, and that he might need her. How could she *do* that to him?

'I am pleased he acted so responsibly.'

His voice remained level. Unconcerned. He wouldn't have the staff thinking he'd been unaware his wife was at this very minute *en route* to Devonshire, despite knowing he didn't wish to go. She would be staying in inns. Alone. That Lilley would take care to stop at only respectable establishments was immaterial. A lady should not travel without a male escort and Jane knew it. What the *hell* did she think she was playing at?

'I trust Her Ladyship got away on time?'

Pat was busy unsaddling Frost. 'Indeed, milord. They left about noon.'

'They?'

For one dreadful instant jealousy stabbed at Alex, even

though he knew damned well Jane would not go away with another man.

'Her maid, sir, and that new footman.'

Peg and Alfred. At least she had sense enough to make sure she had some sort of escort. But it wasn't him. Her husband.

How could *she leave me like this?*

But you told her to go! With your blessing!

Alex shook his own words from his head. He didn't want reasoned argument. His emotions tumbled and churned as he abruptly bid Pat goodnight and strode up to the house.

He stayed up half the night drinking, then slept in the chair, where Drabble found him in the morning. Yesterday's events soon burst upon him but rather than feel sorry for himself, as he had last night, he was angry. How dare she defy him? He thrust aside that same voice which reminded him he had *told* her to go. She must have known he'd said that in the heat of the moment. She must have known he hadn't meant for her to go.

Follow her.

No! He would not go running after Jane the minute she jerked on his leash. She'd no doubt done this believing he would meekly follow but she would learn he was not so easily manipulated.

His spirits dived further as he recalled the memory that had triggered their argument. He'd not given a thought to his father—he had been consumed with Jane leaving. But the new facts of his life were unchanged, and he could no more face any of his family today than he could yesterday.

He distracted himself all day with work. She wouldn't be gone long. She would be back before Christmas, which was only three weeks away. Although…he'd checked, and she'd taken all those Christmas gifts she'd made. But, no… she was making a point, that was all. And she wouldn't stay away for good—Pearl was still here, as was Mist. She would never leave them behind. Besides, Dominic wouldn't help her. They were brothers. Dominic had always had Alex's back, and he would do so this time.

His brave face lasted all that day, and the next. It lasted until he sat down to his solitary dinner on the second evening. He couldn't sustain his anger…all he could feel was pity. For himself. And that was pathetic. But there was guilt, too, that he had hurt Jane. She didn't deserve the way he had treated her…but she didn't understand what an impossible position he was in.

He stared down at his plate, and pushed the food around with his fork. What did he want?

Jane.

The answer came loud and clear as he realised, with a jolt, that he loved her. *Really* loved her. The man who thought he could never love anyone, loved his wife. To distraction. And the idea of following her, persuading her to come home, no longer seemed weak. It was a strong man who could admit when he was in the wrong. How many times had he heard his father say those words? He shuddered. And how long would it be before the thought of his father ceased to make him feel physically ill?

His appetite deserted him, and he rose from the table. He would go to bed early, and set off for Devonshire as soon as it was first light. As he left the dining room, Kent was on his way in, carrying a letter. Alex almost snatched it from him, hope blooming. But one glimpse at the writing on the outside revealed Anthony Lascelles' heavy black script.

'Mr Lascelles's man awaits a reply, milord.'

Alex broke the seal.

My dear Alexander,
I am concerned. I have not seen you for two days
now, and I seek confirmation that you have not sunk
in the doldrums after the shock of such a discovery.
You will note that I have not committed any facts to
this missive, in case the wrong eyes should see it!
I cannot bring myself to call in person after my
unfortunate misunderstanding with Jane but do, I
beg of you, write to assure me you are in good health
in both mind and body, or I shall have to overcome
my reluctance to further upset your good lady and
call at Foxbourne to set my mind at rest.
Your loyal cousin and friend,
Anthony Lascelles

Alex sighed. He should have foreseen this, but he had
been so busy being busy, to prevent himself fretting over
Jane, that he had not given Anthony a thought.

'Tell his man to wait for a reply.'

He sat at his desk. How much to reveal? Anthony knew
about Dominic's invitation and that Alex's refusal had
caused an argument with Jane. Anthony, he recalled, had
tried to persuade Alex to go to Devonshire, to confront his
father. At least Anthony would be pleased he was going,
even if he had no intention of going anywhere near the
Abbey and his father.

He dipped his pen into the inkwell and began to write.

'My lord?'

It was the following morning. Alex looked up from his
plate of congealed eggs. The coming few days would be
fraught. If only he could whisk Jane away from Clystfield
without seeing or speaking to anyone else. If only… It was
an impossible wish. He had the three days it would take

him to travel to Clystfield to decide exactly what to say to Jane. And to his brother. And hadn't Jane said Olivia would be there, too? That would make his task even trickier. Olivia was never backward in challenging any member of the family if she scented trouble, and Alex had made a career out of being troubled.

'My lord?'

'Sorry, Kent. I was wool-gathering. What is it?'

'Mr Lascelles is here, milord.'

'*This* early?' Alex waved at his breakfast, and stood up. 'I've had enough, Kent. It can be cleared away. Thank you.'

Drabble was upstairs, packing for Alex's trip—he planned to leave within half an hour. Jane had the carriage, so Alex must drive his curricle to High Wycombe first, where he could hire a post-chaise. That would be an unwelcome delay—now he'd decided to follow Jane, he just wanted to get on with it.

And now, another delay.

'He awaits you in the hall, milord.'

Anthony—his greatcoat buttoned up, a muffler around his neck, gloves on, and his beaver hat in his hand—smiled when he saw Alex.

'Good morning, Alexander! It is perishing cold this morning, so I have provided hot bricks for the journey. My carriage is outside—if we set off now, we might make it as far as Andover by this evening. I know how eager you must be to settle your differences with dear Jane.'

'I… *We*?'

'Oh, do not think I shall interfere, dear boy, but I simply cannot bear the thought of you travelling such a distance alone. Not with such distressing thoughts to plague you. What kind of a friend would I be to abandon you to such a melancholy fate? I shall accompany you to Devonshire and then I shall return in my carriage while you and Jane will have your own carriage for transport home. She will never know I was there, you have my word.'

Alex ignored the warning in his head. He was exhausted. All he wanted was to see Jane. To talk to her. To bring her home. He had no energy to even think about anything else, let alone talk Anthony out of travelling with him—he was a difficult man to shake once he had set his sights on something. Besides…this would save him a good hour and a half now he didn't need to go to High Wycombe first, and Anthony was right. Left to his own devices, Alex would only brood all the way to Clystfield. At least Anthony would divert him from fretting endlessly over the whole sorry mess of his life.

Stuck in one another's company for three days on that interminable journey, however, Alex began to see Anthony Lascelles in a different light. He'd been tolerable—even entertaining—in small doses but his purpose in accompanying Alex soon became apparent. He was oblivious to Alex's reluctance to discuss his father as he dripped poisonous comments about him into the silence and tried everything to convince Alex to go to the Abbey and confront his father.

'Do you not feel it is your duty to expose your mother's killer?'

'How can you live with yourself if you allow him to get away with your mother's murder?'

'Why don't we travel on to the Abbey first? Once you have charged your father with the truth you will feel so much better, my boy…you will be able to rekindle your marriage with a clear conscience.'

Alex exploded at that. 'A clear conscience? What utter rot. I hid away while he strangled my mother and then

denied the truth for eighteen years. How can my conscience ever be clear?'

'But my dear, dear Alexander…how can you possibly
have prevented such a tragedy when you were only seven
years old? And who's to say you didn't remember, in the
beginning, and that your father convinced you of your
mistake? He is an arch manipulator. What he wants is
what he gets!'

A family trait, thought Alex as he eyed Anthony. *And
one you share.*

And doubts slowly crept in about any similarities in
character between his father and Anthony. The latter was…
sly. He manoeuvred behind the scenes, manipulating people into doing his bidding. *Tricking* them.

Just as Jane warned you!

His father, though. He was a powerful duke…yes, he
manipulated people and situations when he felt it justified,
but he was never sly.

The closer they got to Devonshire, the more dread
weighed on Alex until he was ready to scream. Or to punch
someone. Preferably Anthony.

The only way he found peace was to feign sleep. After
a few attempts at conversation, Anthony would lapse into
silence, leaving Alex to silently plan what to say to Jane.
If he wanted her to forgive him, and to believe he loved
her, did he have any choice other than to tell her the truth
regardless of the consequences?

Was his marriage worth that much to him?

He concluded it was.

The carriage pulled up at an inn a couple of miles from
Dominic's estate at six o'clock on the third evening. Although desperate to see Jane, Alex felt grubby and ex-

hausted and in no fit state to convincingly persuade his wife of his love for her.

One more night. That's all. Then I will see her, and we can put this behind us.

Except they could never properly put it behind them, not now he had decided his only option was to tell Jane the brutal truth.

Another very good reason to delay speaking to her until the morning. It would give him one more sleepless night to plan what he would say. The only positive result of his recent sleepless nights was that, gradually, he'd had no need to feign sleep in the carriage. And Anthony seemed to have finally accepted Alex would not confront his father, lapsing into a sullen silence on the final day of travel. Alex couldn't wait for this evening to be over. He didn't care if he never spoke to Anthony again, and he didn't want to hear any more tales of his mother.

When Alex returned downstairs after washing, and changing his clothes, it was clear from the slurring of his words that Lascelles had been drinking in the taproom the entire time.

They were served roast beef and game pie, which they washed down with a full-bodied red wine, following which they settled in a quiet parlour with a bottle of port. Alex was determined to keep this final evening civil, conscious that Anthony *had* provided the transport even though his true purpose in accompanying Alex had nothing to do with Alex's well-being and everything to do with causing trouble for Alex's father.

'Drink up, m'boy.' Anthony filled Alex's glass, slopping some on to the table. 'You look like a man in need of fort…forti…fortification.'

Alex raised his glass. 'To the end of our journey.'

'What is your plan?' Anthony eyed Alex over the rim

of his glass, his black gaze slightly bleary. 'How shall you win back the fair Jane? What can you possibly say to help her understand the turmoil you were in?'

Alex shrugged. That was between him and Jane. 'I haven't planned it. I shall speak from the heart.'

He sipped his port. Anthony drained his glass, and re-filled it.

'You must tell her the truth,' he said.

Alex frowned. 'What truth?'

'About your father, of course.'

Alex said nothing.

'You will never find peace unless you do, my boy. Even if you fear to confront your father, you must at least re-veal the truth of your mother's death. Your brother Avon, too—he deserves to know. And your sister.'

How could he tell Dominic and Olivia? But, again, how could he not? Their mother was still their mother, no mat-ter how little she had cared for her children. But how could he burden them with the knowledge of their father's part in it? It was an impossible dilemma…never had he felt so conflicted as Lascelles droned on, topping up their glasses time after time.

'Poor Margaret. So vivacious…such a beautiful lady. What a tragic waste—she always looked so vital in yellow, my boy…pretty as a picture… She always had plenty of beaux swarming around her, you know, even after she wed your father.' His face blazed with sudden fury. 'She only married him for the title. All she cared for was the status… being the duchess. But later, when I knew her again…oh, then…' He sighed, his dark eyes distant. 'She tired quickly of the country life…she sobbed in my arms many times…' He sighed again. 'Such a beauty…skin like silk.'

'*What* did you say?' Alex leapt up, grabbing Lascelles' lapels and hauling him upright. Rage scorched through him, erupting like a volcano, shooting sparks, hot swathes of molten anger flowing from him. '*You* were her lover? You utter bastard! She was *my mother*.'

His fist landed square on Lascelles' nose. The older man staggered back, stumbling over his chair, landing hard on the floor. Alex followed, fists clenched, murder in his heart. All this time Lascelles had exuded sympathy…told Alex to treat him as a father…

Father! Sick anger churned his gut. He loomed over Lascelles, his lips drawn back in a snarl.

'When?'

That one question consumed him. Had Lascelles told the truth about going overseas after Mother and Father married, or could Lascelles be Alex's father? Is that why he'd always distrusted the Duke? Was it an inherited trait? The air whooshed from his lungs as he prayed it was not true. He hauled a moaning Lascelles up, thrusting his face close to the other man's.

'I asked you *when*, you bastard! When were you my mother's lover?'

Those dark eyes—still, somehow, mocking—narrowed.

'Never fear, m'boy. Your father made good and sure he sired every one of her children. But, once the girl was born, Margaret made certain she didn't have any more.' He frowned then. 'I was not her only lover—she swore she was true to me, but she lied. She might have had the title of duchess, but your mother was still a common slut!'

The roar began deep, deep inside Alex's chest and it echoed around the room as his fury erupted. He drew his fist back, but came to his senses when a prick to his throat announced Lascelles had a knife. Alex gritted his teeth, slowly releasing the other man's lapels.

'Sensible boy.'

Lascelles stepped back and then, before Alex realised

his intention, he upended the table, knocking Alex to the floor. When he scrambled to his feet, Lascelles had gone.

He was drained. His head hurt and his heart…his heart bled. And yet…the rumours about his mother—the rumours she had taken lovers—were not new. But having it confirmed like this—*now*—made the case against his father even blacker. Bleaker. Despair wrenched Alex's heart but it was the fact he'd misjudged everything that made him truly sick. He'd trusted his mother's former lover with the truth about his father rather than confide in his own wife. How had he been so stupid? He threw himself into an armchair and sank his head in his hands. But the truth still remained of that vision of his father with his hands around his mother's throat.

He gazed dully at the bracket clock on the mantel. Eight o'clock. He was only two miles from Clystfield. He needed to see Jane. He *needed* Jane. Tonight. He sprang out of the chair and thundered up the stairs. A quick glance into Lascelles' bedchamber confirmed he'd already gone. That was unimportant now. He could wait…and yet, what could Alex do about something that had happened so long ago? Beating Lascelles to a pulp wouldn't change the facts.

Downstairs, he rousted out an ostler and paid him handsomely to drive him to Clystfield in the inn's gig.

Chapter Twenty-One

She had only been at Clystfield Court two days but Jane was already weary of pretending Alex had been delayed by business; weary of deflecting probing questions about her absent husband; weary of smiling in the face of sympathetic glances cast in her direction. It was clear they suspected all was not well, and she longed to confide in them—after all, who knew Alex better than Dominic and Olivia? But she could not bring herself to tell them why she was there on her own because she didn't understand it fully herself.

Had it just been a moment of pique? An *'I'll show him'* moment? She was hurt he wouldn't confide in her, but was that *really* bad enough for her to leave without a word of explanation? She was supposed to love him, and yet her leaving would make whatever trauma he was suffering worse, not better. But as soon as she almost persuaded herself that her running off was unpardonable, the other side of the argument would rear its head—was the problem that plagued Alex genuinely so terrible he couldn't bring himself to talk to her about it? Or was this simply the same old stubborn, independent Alex who kept everyone who cared about him at arm's length?

The lengthy journey, and the two days at Clystfield with no word from Alex, had taken their toll on her and her reflection in the mirror confirmed the truth of Olivia's bald announcement that she looked worn to a frazzle. During the day it was easier to keep her thoughts from straying too often to her infuriating spouse, and from fretting about what he was hiding from her. She filled the hours with playing with Julius and Daisy who, although twins, were not identical, and sharing Liberty's excitement at being with child. There was always someone around to chat to, drowning out the arguments raging inside her head. But at night sleep proved elusive as she grappled in vain to find a solution to this impasse.

What if he did not follow her? Would she return, with her pride battered and bruised? Or would she…*could* she…stay strong? She wasn't oblivious to the fact that no one of her acquaintance—and certainly not Papa and her stepmother—would shelter a wife from her husband if he wanted her to return. Apart from, perhaps, the Duke. *He* might very well find a solution for her, but she knew that once he became involved, Alex would be lost to her.

Her throat thickened at that thought.

Alex was all she had ever wanted. But why did he have to be so complicated?

You knew what he was like before you wed him.

Yes, but I—

Would you rather be married to Pikeford?

No, but—

Be grateful for what you've got. So what if it isn't perfect. Life rarely is.

But it was *almost perfect! I just want to understand what went wrong!*

She was *utterly* weary.

That evening after dinner, Jane sat at the pianoforte while the others gathered around a card table but they had barely settled into their game of whist when a thunderous knocking at the front door interrupted them. Romeo, who had been dozing in front of the fire, shot to his feet, barking frenziedly. Jane's fingers stilled, her heart thudding, as Dominic strode from the room, Romeo dashing ahead of him.

'I do hope there is nothing amiss.' Liberty's hand rested protectively on her gently rounded belly.

Voices sounded in the hall—among them a voice that raised Jane's hopes as well as her hackles. Alex. And all her fragmented worries and arguments clarified, as if by magic.

Yes, she loved Alex, but he needn't think she would meekly return home simply because she was married to him. It was time for him to prove he had followed her for the right reasons, and not merely because she was his wife.

I must remain resolute if I want him to respect me and not take me for granted.

Liberty had recognised the voice, too, and she moved to stand behind Jane. She squeezed her shoulder.

'Know that we will stand by you, Jane.'

Jane reached up to pat Liberty's hand, grateful for her quiet support. They waited in silence as the low murmur of voices filtered into the room. Jane had heard Dominic pacifying Alex enough times over the years to imagine what was being said. She waited, her heart beating hard in her chest, her mouth dry. Then he came in, windblown and wild-eyed, and she couldn't stop herself.

'Alex!' She ran to him, taking the hands that reached for her. 'You look…' She stopped, realising the absurdity of anything she might say at this point.

You look distraught?

Of course, he would answer. *My wife left me.*

You look desperate?

The same answer.

You look angry.

The same.

His tiger eyes bore into hers as he moistened his lips. And she saw he was nervous, too, but she dredged up that resolve and hardened her heart. If she followed her usual instinct to soothe and to forgive, nothing would change. She wanted the early closeness of their marriage back but, more importantly, she needed to understand what had changed. And why.

But she knew Alex wouldn't easily share his innermost feelings or relinquish his secrets.

She slid her hands from his. 'You followed me. Why?'

'I missed you.'

She stayed silent, holding his gaze.

'I apologise for my behaviour.'

She turned aside, maintaining her blank expression as her heart sank. Same old Alex. An apology…words…it was too easy for them to be meaningless.

Olivia jumped up from the card table. 'I *knew* there was more to this than you told us, Jane.'

Hugo's arm shot out to restrain his wife. He rose, too, wrapping his arm around Olivia's waist and hugging her into his side.

'We'll leave you two to talk.'

'Hugo—'

'This is not our business, Trouble. Let us leave Alex and Jane to talk.'

Olivia bit her lip. 'Oh, very well. But if we don't see you again this evening, please note I expect you to be here in the morning, Alexander, so no slipping away at dead of night.'

'I'm going nowhere,' Alex said.

Fingers of desire stroked down Jane's spine at the resolve in his voice.

'Berty...' Dominic extended his hand to his wife.

Liberty went to him, but she hesitated as she passed Jane, her deep blue gaze questioning. Jane nodded, flicking her a reassuring smile, and Liberty and Dominic followed the other two from the room, closing the door behind them.

Alex immediately began to pace. Jane watched him a few moments before crossing to sit on the sofa, once more reining in that urge to go to him, to comfort him—such a natural part of her character, especially when it came to Alex. But she did help ease the way into the conversation they must have.

'Mayhap *I* should apologise to *you*?'

'What?'

He sat beside her, tried to gather her hands in his, but she pulled them away, swivelling to face him.

'You owe me no apology, Janey.' His brow furrowed as his tiger eyes searched her face. 'I don't blame you for coming here.'

'I didn't mean that. What I mean is... I am forced to wonder if, in trying to help you, I contributed to this...' she lifted her hands in a hopeless gesture '...this situation. You've been pushing me away, Alex. I could see the more I tried to persuade you to talk to me, the faster you retreated, and I know you felt unfairly harried. But I don't wish to be a wife who meekly accepts her husband's behaviour and can never challenge him. Especially when she is convinced he's in pain.

'I've had time to think in the days since I left. I am so afraid you will never allow anyone close enough to truly help you and I am *exhausted*. I cannot go on supporting you when you clearly do not trust me with what is troubling you.'

Alex leaned forward, propping his elbows on his knees, and thrust his fingers through his hair.

'I wanted to tell you the truth... I *want* to. But it's more complicated than you realise. What I know...it doesn't affect me alone.' He hauled in a tortured breath. 'But...you are right. We should have no secrets between us. I will tell you the truth.'

At last.

'Then tell me. *All* of it. Please, Alex. Help me understand what changed. I cannot bear the thought of going home with you, only for all this to start up all over again.'

'I will.' Alex scrubbed his hands over his face. 'I've been an utter fool, Janey. I thought I could cope with it myself. I was wrong.' He surged to his feet and again paced the room. 'How *stupid* can one man be?' The words spat out. 'I thought I was protecting you...protecting my family.'

'Tell me!'

Her nerves buzzed with the need to do something...to help...but how could she help when she still had no clue what he was talking about? This, surely, had to be about more than him finding his mother's body. Alex flung himself on to the sofa again.

'When the nightmares first returned at the Abbey, all I could recall was the beginning. They're always the same: I hide from our tutor, Mr Brockley, and then I am outside playing. And I find myself near the old summer house and I walk towards it. And then I would wake up.' He dragged in a deep breath. 'Then I realised that, in my dreams, my mother was walking by my side. And I thought it couldn't possibly be right because I knew what really happened was that her d-dead body was w-wait—' His voice thickened, and he stumbled over the words. He scrubbed his hands over his face again, clearing his throat. 'Was waiting for me in the summer house.'

He looked at her, his eyes clouded with pain. As a tear fell, she reached to brush it away.

'I thought my dreams weren't real. I thought they'd become confused with the image of Pikeford attacking you. I thought I knew what happened when my mother died, because everyone had told me. But...but...but...' He shook his head. 'I never wanted to remember what really happened that day, Janey. I convinced myself it was the dread of what was inside the summer house that shaped my nightmares.'

His attempt at a smile wobbled. He dashed one hand across his eyes, but he didn't even try to conceal his tears from her. Her heart opened, like a flower to the sun, and she moved closer, placing her hand on his thigh. Offering comfort.

'Then images began to flash into my mind. When I was awake.' He paused, swallowing audibly.

'She wore a yellow gown...smelled of roses... I remember his boots, moving in step with her slippers... He pushed her to the floor. I didn't understand what was happening at the time but I know now. He forced himself on her and, when she pleaded with him to stop, he put his hands around her neck...squeezing until she was still. I... I thought he would see me. He only had to turn his head, and I would see his face...his eyes...'

He shuddered, and buried his face in his hands as huge sobs ripped from him. Jane cradled him close, stroking his hair, until the storm of emotion passed, his words echoing through her mind. The yellow gown and the roses... Alex's extreme reactions began to make sense.

'You have kept that dreadful truth to yourself all these weeks? *Why*, Alex? Why could you not tell me? I could have helped—'

She fell silent as he turned haggard features in her di-

rection, his red-rimmed eyes dull. She gasped as the full
impact of his words hit her.

'But…Alex…that must mean…'

'I was there, Janey. I saw him kill her.'

She struggled to draw breath. 'Who?'

He buried his face in his hands yet again and Jane put
her arms around him…it was like hugging a tree, he was
so unyielding.

'Tell me. Let it out. It will feel better.'

He gulped—half laugh, half sob. 'That's what Zach
said. He was wrong. I told Lascelles, but the relief was
fleeting.'

A shard of pain stabbed Jane's heart. He'd told Anthony
Lascelles the truth, but he'd been unable to trust her? She
thrust down the hurt and the sense of betrayal to deal with
later. At this moment, Alex was more important.

'Tell me. Come on, Alex. How bad—?'

'It was Father!'

Jane gasped. 'Your—? *No!* Alex…that *cannot* be true.'

'It is. My father killed my mother and I did nothing to
stop him. And now…I don't know what to *do*, Janey. How
can things ever be right, ever again?'

Sobs shuddered through him again. Jane held him,
stroking his hair, struggling to assimilate what he'd told
her. When he finally quieted, she said, 'I cannot believe
you have kept this buried all this time.'

'What choice did I have? I wanted to protect you from
having to face the others, and having to keep it secret. But
now—somehow—you will have to manage.'

'Keep it *secret*? Alex! You cannot mean it. You must
tell the others. Between you…between all of us…we will
work out what to do.' She framed his face, searching his
eyes. 'Are you absolutely certain it is a true memory, and
not a nightmare come to haunt your waking hours?'

He shook his head. 'No. I wish I could believe that—it's what I told myself when I first saw him. But then…that day we argued about coming here… I saw him as clear as I see you now. They were *his* hands around her neck.'

Jane frowned. That was the day Lascelles had hurt Mist. She had told Alex about that, before their argument. Before he had run off. 'And you still went to Lascelles and talked to *him* rather than to me?'

'I regret that now, but I did it to protect you, and to protect my family. I wouldn't wish this knowledge on my worst enemy, let alone you. But…now you do know. And it is to stay between us, Jane.'

Jane leapt to her feet. 'No.'

Alex stared up at her. 'No?'

'We cannot keep this…this *abomination* to ourselves. If it *was* your father…he *killed* another person. He broke the law. We cannot keep that secret.

'Look what trouble you've caused already with your secrets and your conviction that you alone know what is best for everyone,' she added, unable to hide her bitterness. 'You have hurt me; you have shattered *my* trust in *you*, by choosing to confide in a man like Anthony Lascelles rather than in me, when I've *always* been your loyal friend, and—in choosing him over me—you have spoiled our marriage after we were so happy in the beginning…'

She paused, somewhat breathless after her tirade. She fought her burning need to try to resolve their personal differences here and now, guiltily aware this was the wrong time. First they must work out how to deal with this dreadful revelation about the Duke, and she must help Alex and the others find a solution.

'It will not do to keep this secret, Alex. You cannot make decisions of this magnitude on behalf of your entire family. At the very least you need to talk to Dominic.'

Alex slumped back, his brow furrowed. Jane waited. Finally, he pushed himself to his feet.

'Very well. If that is what it will take to make things right between us, we will talk to the others. I only hope you are right and this doesn't rip my entire family to shreds.' He grabbed Jane's hand and towed her to the door. 'Where is my brother?' he asked a passing maid.

The maid curtsied. 'I've just served the tea tray in the parlour, milord.'

Alex strode along the hall, Jane stumbling in his wake, until he slammed to a halt about six feet from the closed parlour door.

'I cannot,' he choked out. 'I don't know what to say... or how to say it.'

Jane placed her hand on his chest, feeling his heart thudding against her palm. 'You will find the words. And I will be there with you.'

He drew in a deep breath, squaring his shoulders, and she glimpsed the old Alex...the lad full of swagger no matter what trouble he was in. The Alex who never allowed doubt or fear to slow him down. The Alex who lived live to the full and to hell with the consequences. He'd changed as he had matured, but that same defiant, cocksure lad was still in there somewhere. It was then she knew he would cope with this, as he had coped with so much throughout his life.

Alex thrust the door open and stepped through it. Jane slipped past him to sit at the back of the room as the murmur of voices died away.

'I have something to tell you.'

Alex repeated his tale, punctuated by gasps of horror and vehement denial from his listeners, but Jane only half listened, her thoughts trapped in ever-circling questions about their future.

Alex had finally confided in her but only, in the end, because he'd been forced into it. She longed for the assurance that he saw her as more than just his wife. His possession. Even though, in law, that is what she was. She accepted she must return to Foxbourne—she had nowhere else to go, especially now with this news about the Duke—but she must stay strong and do so on her own terms.

A low cry jerked her from her thoughts. Olivia's head was bent into Hugo's chest, his arms around her trembling body. Liberty, eyes round with horror, appeared frozen in time. Dominic and Alex faced one another, nose to nose, fingers jabbing, Dominic's face dark with anger. They were so alike, especially in profile as they were now.

'You're wrong! Father would *never*…he's not that sort of man. When have you *ever* known him raise a hand to any of us? Never, that's when!'

Alex's chin jutted forth. 'I know what I saw. I couldn't make it up…the yellow dress, the wooden floor against my cheek. I *saw* it!'

Jane hated them arguing but she wasn't sorry she'd made Alex tell the others. He shouldn't carry this burden alone.

'But what reason could he have?' Dominic demanded. 'Why, Alex? Tell me. *Why* would he do it?'

'She had lovers. You've heard the rumours and innuendo, I know you have. Even Lascelles—'

'*Lascelles?* Anthony Lascelles? What the devil has he to do with this unholy mess?'

'He's back. Living at Halsdon Manor. He let it slip this evening—he was her lover! And he wasn't the only one!' Alex spun on his heel and marched across the room, murder in his eyes.

This evening? Jane's stomach lurched. Lascelles had come down to Devonshire with Alex? She'd thought…

hoped…Alex had come to save their marriage. Why would he bring Lascelles, knowing how she felt about the man?

'Who is Anthony Lascelles?' Liberty asked.

'He's my father's cousin and a slimy, evil scoundrel,' Olivia declared. 'I had no idea he was back in England. Does Papa know?'

'No.' Jane kept her attention on Alex, recognising the effort it was taking for him to pull himself together. 'He begged us not to tell any of the family… He said he wanted to meet your father in London, on neutral ground, in order to make his peace with him and your stepmother.'

'Hah! Make his peace. What a bouncer!' muttered Olivia, as Alex strode back to face Dominic again.

'*There* is your motive, Brother. Jealousy. Rage. He couldn't bear her playing him false. I *heard* him—"*I will never let you go!*"'

Jane started at Alex's words as they triggered a memory…she frowned, grasping for a thought that fluttered just beyond her reach. She put her hands over her ears to block out the raised voices, sifting through conversations about Alex's mother.

Someone… Aunt Cecily…what had she said? She surged to her feet. 'Alex!'

Five pairs of eyes locked on to her.

'Alex!' Her breath came in short bursts as her brain scrambled to make sense of an idea that swirled and swooped. 'Aunt Cecily…she told me your mother had agreed to settle at the Abbey. That she had changed, and wanted to put her children first. So why would your father say that? She wasn't threatening to leave him…she was going to *stay*.'

Dominic frowned. 'She is right. Aunt Cecily told me the same after Liberty and I got married. You are wrong, Alex. That was no motive.'

'You've never told me that before! How do I know you're not making it up?'

'Why would I make it up? And when have *any* of us ever really talked about Mother and what happened? It's been a taboo subject for years.'

They were nose to nose again. Two brothers. So alike—typical Beauchamp features, like their father and their uncle—and yet poles apart in temperament. Jane glanced at Liberty. Saw her concern mirrored in Liberty's expression—what if this caused a rift between Dominic and Alex that could never be healed? Jane's stomach squirmed. It would be her fault, for insisting Alex told the others.

No. It's the Duke's fault. Not mine. He's the one who killed their mother, not me.

And yet, she still could barely credit it. Alex's father, a cold-blooded killer? Now, if he had been like Lascelles, she might believe…

Her breath seized.

'Lascelles!'

Alex and Dominic stopped in mid-argument at Jane's yell, and turned as one to gape at her, as did the other three. She gabbled out her idea in fits and starts, afraid to take her time, petrified they would shoot it down before she could properly explain. When she eventually paused for breath she saw the hope on all five faces in the room.

Chapter Twenty-Two

Alex hardly dared to hope it could be true. He was the first to respond to Jane's blurted out idea.

'So…let me get this straight…you think I could have mistaken Anthony Lascelles for my own father? And that it was Lascelles who killed our mother?'

'Yes. All the Beauchamps have the same features. I noticed the resemblance when I first met Lascelles, even though his hair is grey.'

'It was black when I first met him,' Alex replied, frowning. 'Like Father's. But I still can't believe I would mistake a complete stranger for my own father.'

Lascelles? Could it be? By his own admission he'd been her lover.

While Alex pondered, Liberty spoke. 'Maybe it was easier to mistake a stranger for your father than someone you already knew? I thought you were Alex when we first met, Dominic, even though now I cannot imagine how I came to make such a mistake. Do you remember?'

A slow smile stretched Dominic's lips. 'Oh, yes. I remember being harangued on my father's doorstep by a hoyden with an umbrella.'

Liberty's answering smile at that memory—that private moment shared by her and Dominic—tweaked something deep inside Alex. A longing for the same. With Jane. They'd had it at the start of their marriage, until he'd ruined it. As he seemed to ruin everything he touched. Eventually.

'You and Alex have different hair and different colour eyes but all I saw were those aristocratic features, and that hint of arrogance—'

'Arrogance?'

Liberty laughed at Dominic's mock outrage but quickly sobered. 'I am making a serious point, Dominic.'

'And you were an adult, Liberty.' Olivia pulled away from Hugo. 'Alex was a small boy. A *terrified* small boy trapped in a scary and dangerous situation. Alex…is it possible?'

Dear God, I hope so.

'I don't know. His eyes are very different to Father's, but I never saw them. Mostly, all I saw was a pair of boots. And when…when…' He gulped. He was a grown man. He shouldn't be afraid to say what he saw, even though he hadn't understood it at the time. 'When he raped and strangled her, he was in profile.'

'Luckily for you,' Dominic said. 'If you'd seen the colour of his eyes…'

Alex didn't want to think about what might have happened had the killer spotted him cowering under the chaise longue. He paced the room, thrusting his hand through his hair from time to time. He always thought more clearly when he was active, and the surge of hope he now experienced swept through the foggy tangled mess that had filled his brain for too long. How he wanted this to be true. To be finally free of that baffling mistrust that had dogged his relationship with his father since boyhood.

'If Aunt Cecily is right and Mother did intend to spend

more time at the Abbey, and with us…' He paused. 'She didn't send me back to old Brockley that day. I hid from him, and then sneaked outside, into the copse. She saw me, on her way to the lake.' He glanced around the room. 'She walked by the lake every day when she was home, and she always stopped to rest in the summer house. I thought she would send me back to lessons but, instead, sh-she said I could go with her.'

'You lucky devil!' Dominic said. 'I asked to go with her that day, too, but she sent *me* back to old Brockley. But… I think Aunt Cecily is right. She did seem different—I expected her to snap at me for asking, but she patted my cheek and said maybe we could go out later. She seemed happy, and it's the only time I can remember her showing any spontaneous affection for me. That was the last time I saw her.' His voice hitched. 'Carry on, Alex.'

'We collected all manner of things as we walked—fir cones and pebbles and sticks and leaves—but when we reached the summer house she wanted to read and so I settled down to play behind the chaise longue.' The thought then struck him. 'She wasn't *expecting* any one.'

'So,' said Dominic, 'we know it wasn't an assignation.'

'Lascelles said he learned of Mother's death when he was in America, but we only have his word for that.'

'I wouldn't believe a single word he ever said,' declared Olivia. 'I remember Rosalind was *really* scared of him, even before he snatched Susie. He would lie about anything if it suited his purpose.'

'That's true.' Alex took another turn around the room. 'This is all my fault. I should never have allowed myself to be taken in by him—he was always dripping poison about Father and encouraging my distrust. That didn't surprise me with what I knew of his past but now…how can I know if *anything* he said about Mother was true?'

'Do you believe he was her lover, Alex?' Dominic asked. 'That's surely the most relevant question. If he *was* her lover—and she renounced him to spend more time at home with us, as Aunt Cecily claimed—then that could easily provoke a man such as he into a rage. He could have gone to the Abbey to confront her.'

'Yes. I'm certain that's true…he never meant to tell me. He let it slip when he'd been drinking. He said—'

He stopped. His pulse hammered. Anger and disbelief churned his guts as his jaw clenched tight. He'd had him. He'd had his hands on him, and he'd allowed the slippery bastard to escape.

'Alex?' Jane touched his hand. 'What is it?'

'*"She always looked so vital in yellow."* His words. Last night. I should've killed him there and then.'

He stared round at the incomprehension of the others, sick rage at his own incompetence battering his heart and his mind.

'You don't see it! But I should have realised it there and then. I never told him any details. The only way Lascelles could know Mother wore a yellow gown is if he saw her that day.'

A messenger was sent to Cheriton Abbey—a two-hour ride to the west of Clystfield Court—to warn the Duke that Lascelles was in the vicinity, and to announce the arrival of his three children, their spouses and his twin grand-children the next day.

None of them slept much that night. They paced. They talked. They planned. They occasionally dozed. But all of them were waiting for dawn and the chance to take action.

Jane and Liberty both went to bed at one point but, within a couple of hours, both were back in the drawing room with the others, unable to settle. Jane watched Alex.

His entire focus was on the need to find out exactly what had happened that day in the summer house; the need to find Lascelles; the need to talk to his father.

She recognised his preoccupation; understood it; tried hard not to care that he had no energy left to worry about their marriage, and about her. The threat from Lascelles was immediate. Their relationship could wait. But a small, selfish part of her—a part that, when she thought about it, made her squirm slightly with shame—wanted his full attention and longed for him to make *her* his priority. When he did come to sit by her on the sofa—ousting a grumpy Romeo, who was nestled between her and Liberty—it was only to say, 'Why do you not go back to bed? You cannot do anything here.'

And despite knowing he said it out of concern for her, it also felt as though she were being excluded: as though she wasn't fully a member of the family; as though her support was incidental. Much as she had felt in the last weeks of their marriage, since Lascelles' arrival.

'I cannot sleep, so I may as well be here as anywhere.' She stood up and crossed to the window where there was the faintest lightening in the eastern sky. Soon the servants—who had been sent to bed—would be up and about and, after breakfast, the Beauchamps would set out for Cheriton Abbey.

Alex came up behind her, cupped her upper arms and caressed them through her shawl, encouraging her to lean back into his body. Jane stiffened, resisting him. She couldn't help it.

'Janey?'

The pain in his voice raked her, but she couldn't shake her hurt over his betrayal. The fact he had confided in Lascelles and not her. She faced him, searching his shadowed expression, seeking… She looked away. It mattered not what she wanted from him…it still was no time to make demands. He needed to resolve this business with his father and Lascelles and she needed…*yearned*…to feel more secure in his feelings for her.

When she'd accepted his proposal she'd thought *her* love was enough for them both. She hadn't foreseen how painful that one-sided state would prove to be.

'Why did you bring Lascelles to Devonshire with you, Alex?'

'He invited himself along. He turned up with his carriage that morning and…' He shrugged. 'I was anxious to get going. By accepting his offer it saved me going to High Wycombe to hire a chaise-and-four.' He pivoted away, and paced across the room and back again. 'As it happens, it was fortunate. I might never have discovered the truth had he not let slip about his affair with Mother.'

Jane lowered her voice, not wishing the others to hear their conversation. 'But you knew my feelings about him, particularly after his cruelty to Mist. And yet you still confided in him. You still travelled with him. Are my opinions… my feelings…so very unimportant to you?'

Alex stiffened. 'Of course they're not,' he hissed. 'I came to take you home. I—I *missed* you, Janey. So much.' He thrust his hand through his hair. 'Look. I can barely think straight. You *have* to forgive me, sweet Janey. The alternative…' His brows snapped together. 'The alternative doesn't bear thinking about. I know I've been difficult to live with, sweetheart, but…please, can we just get to the Abbey and sort out this Lascelles business? I promise I'll make it up to you. It's not the time to discuss something as important as our marriage.'

She knew she would forgive him. How could she do

otherwise, when he was her husband and she still loved him? But that didn't mean she would give him an easy ride to her forgiveness. Not this time. Or how would he ever learn he couldn't always twist her around his little finger? But, at least he'd said their marriage was important, and she hugged his words to her heart.

'I know it's not the time to discuss this now, Alex, but please don't imagine you can conveniently forget this conversation, avoid the subject and slip back into the same relationship.'

'Darling Janey. I promise I—'

He fell silent when the door opened and a maid entered, and curtsied.

'Breakfast is served in the dining room,' she announced and, in the hustle and bustle of breaking their fast and preparing for departure, Alex never did finish that promise.

The first snow of winter had yet to fall, but every night brought a heavy frost, and the party set off straight after breakfast, hot bricks at their feet. Alex and Jane travelled with Dominic and Liberty, plus Romeo, while Hugo and Olivia were in their own carriage, accompanied by the twins, Julius and Daisy, and Ruth, their nursemaid.

As the carriage rocked over the frozen ruts of the local lanes, Liberty yawned, saying, 'I am so tired... I feel as though I could sleep for a week. I shall never understand why sleep can elude one all night and yet overcome one once morning arrives.'

The two men were sitting with their backs to the horses, leaving Jane and Liberty facing forwards. Alex caught Jane's eye, and flicked his eyes towards Dominic. She knew in an instant what he meant. Dominic's attention was on his wife, his concern clear in his silver-grey gaze.

'Dominic, why do you not swap places with me?' Jane

shifted until she perched on the edge of the bench. 'Liberty might be able to sleep if she can lean against you.'

'Oh, no! I wasn't hinting for you to move, Jane.'

'I know you weren't—you are far too unselfish. But I don't mind facing backwards, and you need to look after yourself. A nap will do you the world of good.'

Without further ado, Jane stood and Dominic, with a murmured, 'Thank you,' swapped places with her. Within moments, Liberty was settled into his arms and both their eyes were closed.

Alex huffed a laugh. 'We are all totally talked out, are we not?'

'So it would seem.' Jane gazed at the passing countryside, glittering with frost.

'Would you care to…?'

Jane turned to see Alex had shifted position, his arms out, offering to hold her. Uncertainty glimmered in his tawny gaze, and that was enough for her to smile, and to accept by shuffling close to him until she could lean into him, her head on his chest. She breathed in his spicy, musky, unique scent and a feeling of rightness settled over her. This was where she belonged. With Alex. But the air between them still needed to be cleared.

The jolting of the carriage lessened when they reached the toll road and, within minutes, Jane's eyes drifted shut.

'We're here.'

Jane had been awake several minutes prior to Alex's announcement, conscious of the increasing tension in the arms that held her, and of the quickening beat of his heart in her ear. The familiar frontage of Cheriton Abbey filled the window, and the only sound was of the stamp of the horses' feet and the jingle of their bits. The groom opened the door, and they all descended as the Duke himself appeared at the front door, Hector by his side. His tension was clear as he waited unsmilingly for the party to troop past him into the hallway.

'Where's Grantham, Papa?' Olivia broke the silence first. 'I'm sure none of us expected you to greet us personally.'

'I sent him to the kitchen to arrange hot drinks. The rest of the men are standing watch. Here and at the stables.' His silver-grey gaze swept his visitors and paused on the nursemaid. 'Ruth, take the twins up to the nursery, if you please. You will be taken care of up there. The rest of you...' Jane saw his gaze linger for a moment on Alex '... go to the drawing room. Your stepmother is there.'

The Duchess greeted all of them with a strained smile, and a kiss to the cheek. As soon as they were all seated the Duke crossed to the fireplace and rested one arm along the mantelshelf.

'Who will start?' His gaze again settled on Alex. 'You, Alexander? Do you care to tell me why you saw fit not to warn me Lascelles was back in England?'

A muscle ticked in Alex's jaw. 'He asked me not to. He *said* he wanted to make his peace with you both in person.'

'And now you doubt that?'

Alex shrugged, his cheeks a dull red, his lips thinned to invisibility.

Tell him!

Jane exchanged a glance with Olivia and saw her own frustration mirrored on her sister-in-law's face. Old habits... Alex had reverted to the same monosyllabic man he had ever been in his father's presence, despite what they now knew. Or thought they knew. She glanced at Dominic, who was watching his father and brother with a deep frown. Of a sudden, Alex leapt to his feet.

'I should like to talk to you alone, Father.' His gaze swept over the others. 'Please.'

The Duke's eyes narrowed, but he nodded curtly. 'Very well.'

The two men left the room, and a collective sigh whispered through the drawing room as the rest of them released their pent-up breath.

Chapter Twenty-Three

Alex strode ahead of his father to the study. He crossed
to the window, gazing blindly out, as Father shut the door
with a snap.

'What do you have to say to me that you couldn't say
in front of our family?'

He turned to face the man who, his whole life, he had
wanted to love unconditionally but who he had always mis-
trusted. And now he knew why. The others…they thought
they'd worked it all out, and Alex *hoped* they were correct.
But for him to *know* it—to once and for all eradicate that
eighteen-year spell of mistrust and fear—he knew he must
confront his father with what he remembered. Gauge his
reaction. He wanted to believe absolutely, with no room
for lingering doubt.

Ironically, he must do exactly what Lascelles had been
badgering him to do ever since they left Buckinghamshire.
He must confront his father.

And he couldn't do that in front of his stepmother or
his brother and sister. Or in front of Jane—the wariness
he saw at times in her lovely brown eyes when she looked
at him had wrenched at his heart. She was right not to
trust him yet… He must work hard to convince her of his

love and to prove himself. And he would do so. But this must come first. It had to be a private conversation, and he could only pray the answer would be the one he wanted more than life itself.

'May we sit?'

Father nodded, and they sat either side of the fire blazing in the hearth. Alex's gut churned at what he must say.

'I would appreciate it if you will hear me out before you say anything.'

Again, Father nodded.

Alex talked for what felt like hours. At one point, Father rose and poured them both a brandy. Alex kept talking. About when his mother died, what he had believed, the nightmares after his visit to the Abbey and the attack on Jane. The horror when his true memories of that day began to emerge.

His father's silver-grey gaze fixed on him unwaveringly, his expression giving nothing away until Alex spoke of his memory of walking with his mother that day, to the summer house, and of settling down to play behind the chaise longue. Only then did his expression slip, shock gleaming in his eyes, before he masked his emotions again. But, when Alex related the manner of his mother's death, the colour leached from Father's face and he surged to his feet.

'Oh, God, no! *Alex*...'

His name tore from his father's lips. Alex willed himself to sit still. He studied his father's expression...interpreting the emotions that ebbed and flowed in that normally unreadable visage. Anguish. Concern. *Guilt*.

In his younger days, he would have leapt straight to the worst possible conclusion once he recognised that guilt. But...he took his time. And he saw that the guilt could be that of a father whose child had been through hell, the guilt of not being there to prevent the nightmare, the guilt of failure to protect not only his wife, but his son. The guilt flowed towards Alex. It was not directed inwards. There was no hint of shame or of fear that he had been found out.

'I thought it was you,' Alex said.

His father's dark brows snapped together in a frown. 'Me? Who did you think was me?'

'The man I saw.'

He had never seen his all-powerful, supremely confident father at such a loss for words. His jaw slack, he stared at Alex, utterly still.

'The *killer*? You truly thought I could kill *anyone*, let alone the mother of my children?'

Alex nodded. 'When I saw him again, in those visions. In profile. He looked like you.'

Father paced then, thrusting his hand through his hair in an achingly familiar gesture. He halted before him, staring down and Alex squirmed at the desolation in his eyes.

Desolation. Not guilt. Not fear. Hope climbed. He so wanted to believe, but he was almost afraid to…afraid to risk the anguish if that hope proved false.

'Me?' His father's voice rasped. 'Why did you say nothing all these years?'

'I told you. I didn't know. Not until I started having those visions.'

Father paced away again. 'It explains, I suppose, why you have always rebelled against me.' His back to Alex, Father stared out of the window. 'Deep inside you had that memory, even if you were never consciously aware of it.'

He turned slowly, capturing Alex's gaze. 'It was not me you saw, Alex. I swear to you, on the lives of every single one of my children. It was not me.'

Alex swallowed, trust and belief battling their way out of the bleak wasteland where his feelings for his father had been trapped for as long as he could remember.

'We discussed it last night and, between us, we think we have worked out the truth. We think it was Lascelles.'

'Lasc—'

Father swayed, and Alex leapt up, hurrying to his side to catch his arm, steadying him.

'I only ever saw her murderer in profile.' The words rushed from him. 'He has the Beauchamp features we all share, but he also had black hair, like you, and black shiny boots, and…when you came…when the gardeners fetched you…your boots…'

The horror and the fear rose up to claim him and, once more, he was that small boy, shaking with terror, his gaze fixed on his father's black, shiny boots. Alex reined in those emotions…*they* were the lies. He was a grown man now, and capable of sifting facts.

'I must have seen your boots and linked them to the killer's boots. As you said, deep inside, I must have always linked *you*, specifically, with what I saw.'

He was still clutching his father's arm, standing close. He closed his eyes, hauled in a deep breath. 'I am sorry for doubting you, Papa.'

He hadn't uttered that name in eighteen long, lonely years. Emotion rose to clog his throat. Father's arm jerked out of his grip at those words and, before Alex could open his eyes, he was enveloped in a hug.

'No! You have nothing to be sorry for, Alex.' Father choked his words out. 'The fault is mine. I see it now. But… back then…I was so sure I was right. I forbade anyone to discuss that day… I simply wanted us all to forget about it. Cecily…she warned me of the dangers of allowing you to bottle it up, but you didn't speak at all for almost a year and, once that had passed, I suppose we were accustomed to avoiding the subject.'

He stepped back, clasping Alex's shoulders, and his silver-grey gaze swept across Alex's face.

'It is I who must apologise to you.'

The mood at the Abbey was sombre. The entire Lascelles business had been picked over *ad nauseam* until they were all convinced he was the murderer. Alex, however—although awash with relief at his reconciliation with his father—remained unsettled, aware of his unfinished business with Jane. Her dismay at his behaviour mirrored his own disgust. He had allowed himself to be manipulated by a killer...been fooled into trusting him, and had turned to him in his troubles instead of to his own wife. It mattered not that his thoughts had been in turmoil. It was not as if Jane was a stranger...she was his old, trusted friend... the playmate who had been by his side throughout childhood...the girl who had always defended him to the hilt.

And the woman he loved.

Somehow, it was as though a dozen veils had lifted and he could see himself and his life more clearly than ever before. And he saw a blind, stubborn fool.

'Jane?'

She looked up at him, eyebrows raised in polite enquiry, but that same caution in her lovely brown eyes pierced his heart. He had pushed a warm, loving, tender woman into becoming this guarded, cool lady. She was still his wife, and he was sure she wouldn't abandon him—the Jane he knew would not easily dismiss her marriage vows. If he took her in his arms and made love to her, he didn't doubt she would respond physically. But that was no longer enough for him. He didn't want her to stay with him simply because they were married and she had little choice in the matter. He wanted it to be the choice of her heart.

He wanted her to love him again, and to trust him with her heart and her feelings.

But her response to him told him louder than words how much grovelling he must do to banish the betrayal and the bad memories.

'Would you care to come for a walk with me?'

Fear flashed into her eyes. 'What if Lascelles is out there?'

'Father has men out keeping watch but I doubt he is fool enough to come here. You will be safe with me.'

Hugo sat the nearest to the two of them and, at Alex's words, he stood, and brushed the wrinkles from his coat sleeves.

'Dom...you suggested we might go and pay our respects to your mother. I know Livvy is keen to do so.' He fixed Alex with his dark gaze. 'Why don't we all go together? Safety in numbers, after all.'

Alex glanced around the room, realising from their expressions that his family were closing ranks around Jane. Protecting her. From him. But his spurt of anger soon fizzled out, and appreciation took its place.

His family. Protective. Always.

And now Jane was one of them, and they demonstrated their concern as they always did...by being there, as they had always been there for him even though he had given little gratitude for their support. He knew they were concerned he would either sweet-talk or coerce Jane into accepting a lightweight apology. They knew him, knew his easy charm, and they knew Jane was the essence of forgiveness and would seek to understand him first, and to make allowances for him, rather than to think of her own needs. And, in their own way, they were telling him Jane deserved better.

But he knew that. Accepted it.

He wanted better for her, too.

He nodded. He and Jane had time to put this behind them. Now he could truly be part of the Beauchamp family, and was no longer an outsider looking in, they would remain at the Abbey until Twelfth Night. He would spend that time wooing his wife—this time with his heart and mind as well as his body.

'That's a good idea,' he said. 'It is a shame there are no flowers to lay in her memory.'

'They would last no time in this cold weather.' Olivia came to Alex and smiled up at him. She nodded slightly, approval in her silver-grey eyes. 'But that is no reason not to go.'

'There's a holly bush with berries out in the copse,' Father said. 'Rosalind and I will cut a few branches before joining the rest of you.'

As diplomatic as ever. His father would allow the children time to pay their respects to their mother in private before joining them with his second wife.

Alex looked down at Jane. 'Will you accept my arm, Jane?'

She smiled, took his hand and rose to her feet. 'Thank you, yes. I expect it will be slippery in places.'

They swathed themselves in greatcoats and mantles, shawls, scarves and warm hats, gloves and muffs and fur-lined boots, and ventured outside, with Hector and Romeo. The air bit at any exposed skin and their breath condensed in the chill. They huddled together for warmth as they went out through the library on to the terrace and then hurried through the formal garden, to the path and the copse beyond, heading for the lake. Once they were in the copse, Father and Stepmother veered off to look for holly berries, Hector at their heels, and Alex, with Jane on his arm, led the way to the lake and to the weeping willow that marked the spot where their mother had lost her life.

There was no return of that dark dread that had always dogged Alex in this place, just a feeling of peace and an unwavering resolve to find Anthony Lascelles and bring him to justice. Hanging was too good for him, but Alex would be content with that.

But that reminded him...he halted. Jane looked up enquiringly.

'Will you be all right, going back to where it happened?'

'I think so.' A smile flickered around her lips, drawing his attention, heating his blood. How long since he had kissed her? He yearned to hold her in his arms, to show her as well as tell her how much he loved her. 'I must face it sometime and what better way than with my own support army?'

They continued, and soon emerged on to the lakeside path, turning towards the willow, where the summer house had once stood. At first, a thicket of hawthorn, elder and brambles masked the lake from their sight but, as it came into view—ice-covered, glittering where an occasional finger of winter sun poked through the surrounding trees, their naked branches still white with frost—Jane halted, bringing Alex to a stop. The others crowded around them.

'Look!' She pointed at the willow, at the far end of the lake. 'Is that...? Alex! It is him!'

A figure, head bowed, knelt by the willow. His silver-grey hair stood out, even at this distance.

'God's teeth!' Dominic moved to stand at Alex's shoulder. 'How *dare* he come here?'

'Hugo.' Alex glanced at his brother-in-law. 'Stay with the girls. Take care of them.'

He sprinted as fast as he could, slipping and sliding at times on the frosted grass and frozen mud, Dominic by his side. He bit back his roar of rage—no need to alert that bastard to their presence. He sucked the freezing air into his lungs, his air pipe narrowing, his breath whistling, but he kept going. They rounded another thicket of shrubs, bursting into the clearing around the willow tree and only then did Lascelles' head jerk up. He leapt to his feet, backing away, leaving his hat and gloves abandoned on the ground.

'Alex…my dear boy…' He reached out, both hands. 'It was not what you think. You gave me no chance to explain.'

Alex flung out an arm to prevent Dominic launching himself at Lascelles.

'He has a knife,' he muttered.

Alex followed Lascelles, step for step, aware Dominic was moving diagonally to his left, to cut off Lascelles' escape. He wouldn't elude them this time.

'You ran away, Lascelles. It was *you* who failed to explain.'

Satisfaction gleamed in Lascelles' eyes. He plainly imagined he could talk his way out of this, using his usual charm and manipulation. Alex smiled his own satisfaction. The bastard had no clue they now knew the truth.

'I confess I loved your mother and that we were…er… intimate. But our affair was *before* she married Cheriton, you must believe me.'

'Believe you? Why should I believe a single word that spews out of that filthy mouth of yours?'

'But Alex…my boy…it is the truth.' Lascelles halted, his face the picture of innocence. 'And you, I imagine, are here to confront your father?'

'Oh, yes,' Alex said grimly. 'It's done.'

'Oh, my poor, poor Alex! But it had to be done, my boy. Justice must be served.'

At that moment, Romeo bounced into the clearing, distracting Lascelles, giving Alex the chance to move closer. Seconds later he heard the others arrive behind him. He glanced round to see the three women approaching him, and he gestured at them to stop. They could do nothing here, and Lascelles was dangerous. Hugo, he could see, was steadily moving to Alex's right. With the lake at his back, and the three men fanned out before him, Lascelles would soon have nowhere to run.

He clearly thought himself in no danger, because he actually stepped forward, his smiling attention on the women.

'Oh! Dear Jane is here, I see. I am so pleased you two have made up your differences. Do you know...' he spoke directly to Jane now '...poor Alex was quite distraught throughout our journey. It is no wonder he completely misunderstood what I said, and flew into a rage.'

'Would that be in the same way I misunderstood seeing you try to squeeze my kitten to death?' Jane's voice was icily cold.

'You were overwrought, my dear. And who can blame you with Alex's recent behaviour...but we must hope he can put the past to rest now he has exposed his father as a murd—'

'Don't you *dare*!' Rage exploded through Alex and he strode towards his father's cousin, his fists clenched. 'We *know* you did it, Lascelles, so you can save your breath for the judge!'

Lascelles backed away. 'No. No. You have it wrong...'

'*I saw you*, you bastard! I *saw* you!'

'Your father...it was your father...'

'How did you know she was wearing yellow? I didn't tell you, so how did you know?'

'I...'

Lascelles could retreat no further with the lake at his

back. His eyes swivelled from Alex to Dominic, then swept back across to Hugo, his panic now showing.

'She only married him because she wanted to be a duchess. *I* should have been the duke, but your father took my title and stole the woman I loved. And then, when I returned to England…our passion…it was as strong as ever. We *could* have carried on. We could have been happy. But then…then…' He gulped. 'It was a moment of madness.' Tears glittered in his eyes. 'I didn't mean to. I was overcome with passion… surely you understand?' His hands reached towards them, beseechingly. 'She drove me to it…she *rejected* me…all for the chance to be a better mother…'

'And you *robbed* her of that chance,' Olivia yelled, her voice cracking. She had moved forward to stand in line with the men. 'Just like you robbed *us* of our mother! And now you'll *hang* for it!'

Lascelles's eyes widened at that. Before any of them could guess his intention, he spun on his heel and ran on to the ice.

'No! You'll not get away! You'll hang for it, you bastard!' Alex charged to the edge of the ice, dodging around Dominic as he tried to head him off.

'Alex!' Dominic's roar chased him across the frozen lake as he slid and skidded after Lascelles. 'No! Don't be a fool!'

Alex ignored him, intent on closing the gap between him and Lascelles until, with a loud crack, the ice gave way and Lascelles dropped through into the lake. Alex skidded to a halt, his heart racing. The red mist that had propelled him on to the ice dissipated as he assessed the danger. He heard Jane scream his name from the shore but the urge to bring Lascelles to justice…to see him swing on the end of a rope…was irresistible. He had cowered out of sight like a coward while Lascelles had throttled Mother…he had done nothing to save her. But here was his chance to assuage some of the guilt that had haunted him his entire life.

Lascelles resurfaced, scrabbling desperately at the jagged edges of the ice.

Alex shrugged out of his greatcoat, flinging it behind him, and unwound his neckcloth as he inched forward. It was all he had to try to reach Lascelles although he doubted the other man would have strength enough to hold on while Alex hauled him out. He edged forward, testing the ice with each foot before putting his weight on to it.

'Alex!' His heart clenched at the anguish in his father's voice as it echoed across the lake. 'Come back! Please!'

But he couldn't. Lascelles slipped below the surface a second time then rose again, trying to hold on as he gasped for breath, his face blue.

Alex took another step. His stomach dived at the slight give in the ice beneath his feet. He must lie flat…distribute his weight over a bigger surface…he glanced back at the shore. His father was on the ice, closing the distance between them.

'Father!' Alex roared, his gut churning. He must make amends for his mother, but it would all be for nothing if anything were to happen to his father. His throat tightened with fear. 'Father. Go back! It's not safe.'

'Then come back. He's not worth it. *Please*, Alex.'

A scant second later an ominous crack reached his ears. He was too late to even lie down.

Water so frigid it seized his breath as he plunged into the dark depths.

Chapter Twenty-Four

'Alex!' Jane screamed, her heart bursting. 'No!'

Hands grabbed her, hauling her away from the edge of the ice. Dominic held her tight as she struggled to free herself.

'Oh, God. Oh, dear God. Please, God. Oh, God.'

The words babbled forth as the Duke lay flat and pulled himself along the surface of the ice. Too quickly for safety. Too desperate for caution. Alex resurfaced and clutched at the edge of the ice but the Duke stopped. Mere feet away.

'A rope! Something!' Sheer desperation in the Duke's voice.

'Jane!' She tore her eyes from the drama on the ice. Dominic gripped her shoulders hard. 'Do *not* go on to the ice. Do you hear me? Let us concentrate on saving Alex.'

She nodded, one sane corner of her brain acknowledging she could only make matters worse. Dominic pushed her towards where the Duchess—her eyes huge—stared out across the lake. Liberty and Olivia stood either side of her, and they parted to let Jane back into their group.

'Hurry!' The Duke's roar resounded across the lake.

Then Hugo was among them. 'Your scarves! Quick now!' His own neckcloth was already in his hands, and Jane saw Dominic—his hands shaking—untying his. Hugo began to knot the lengths together. There was *something* she could do…she ran to help him, noticing he'd tied one of the neckcloths to form a loop.

'Livvy—run and get help,' ordered Hugo.

'But—'

'Now, Liv. Rope. Blankets. Men. A cart.'

Olivia turned and ran. Jane had never seen this side of the normally easy-going, fun-loving Hugo. He sounded like a general barking orders at his men.

'Hector.'

The dog loped across to Hugo, who tied the looped end of their makeshift rope to his collar. And then the Duchess was there, taking Hector to the edge of the ice.

'Find Leo, boy. Go to Leo.'

Hector's ears pricked and then he was on the ice, running, his long legs splaying out at odd angles.

'It won't be long enough, but the ice is safe enough near the edge.' Dominic stepped on to the ice as Hector reached the Duke.

'No!' Hugo stopped him. 'I'm lighter than you. Let me go first. We'll form a chain. It's the only way. If anyone else goes in, at least we'll have a chance of saving *them*.'

'I'm lighter than all of you,' said Jane. 'Let me go first.'

'You haven't the strength,' Hugo said.

Jane stood, feeling helpless and useless, her mind as numb as her body. Across the lake, Alex's head and shoulders were visible, his forearms on the ice.

Please be in time. I can't lose him. Not now.

The Duke untied the makeshift rope from Hector's collar by which time Hugo, on his belly, was already close behind him. The Duke then skimmed the loop towards Alex.

'Alex! Put both arms through the loop!'

Hugo's shout was audible from the shore and, heart in

her mouth, Jane watched as Alex—excruciatingly slowly—did as Hugo said.

Please God. Please God.

'Bend your elbows. Bring your hands to your shoulders.'

Liberty joined Jane on the shore, and hugged her.

'Don't worry, Jane. They'll get him out.'

The words and gesture freed Jane from the awful numbness gripping her. She began to shake. Her throat ached with fear, and hot tears crowded her eyes. Furious, she blinked them away. She must be able to see.

Hugo anchored the Duke's booted ankles into the crook of his elbows and Dominic was on his knees, gripping Hugo's ankles. He was tantalisingly close to the shore, but not close enough.

They began to pull. It was agonisingly slow, difficult to get any purchase on the ice, but they inched backwards and Alex slowly emerged from the hole in the ice. Dominic's muscles bulged as he pulled but his knees kept slipping from under him and he seemed as far away from the edge of the ice as ever.

Jane straightened. Wrenched away from Liberty, and ventured on to the ice.

'Jane! No!'

She ignored Liberty's scream. She hadn't ice-skated for years but, even without skates, she kept her balance. She reached Alex's discarded greatcoat, grabbed it, then slid her way back to Dominic. He glared at her, sweat beading his forehead.

'Don't waste your breath scolding me.' Jane spread the coat behind Dominic, the hem closest to him. 'Lift one knee.'

She slid the edge of the coat underneath his knee. He glanced down, then back at her, hope lighting his face. He knelt on the coat and then lifted the other knee, and Jane quickly manoeuvred herself behind him, grabbing hold of the sleeves of the coat, but she was still on the ice and she knew Alex's only hope was for someone to anchor on to the land. She lay flat, as the men had done. Luck had played its part...she had placed the greatcoat lining side down and she could push her arms into the sleeves up to her elbows. Her hands alone wouldn't have the strength to grip and pull but this would help. Hands grabbed each of her ankles and she knew then that the Duchess and Liberty had guessed her plan. She glanced over her shoulder. Both of them knelt on the grass. Not the ice.

'Pull!' she screamed. 'Pull!'

She sent up another silent prayer, then gritted her teeth against the agonising wrench as her arms felt like they were being pulled from their sockets. But they were moving and then, of a sudden, the strain eased and Alex was out of the water, his body sliding rapidly towards safety. And first Jane, and then Dominic, were on solid ground, watching as the Duke and Hugo hauled Alex unceremoniously over the ice and on to the shore.

Fear clawed at every inch of Jane, but she refused to give way. Alex needed her now, and she would not fail him. She dropped to her knees, ripped off her gloves and began to unbutton his jacket.

'Help me,' she gasped.

Between them, they stripped Alex out of his freezing, sodden clothes and wrapped him in hastily donated coats. He lay still. Unresponsive. Barely breathing.

'It's not enough. He's too cold. It's not enough.'

Jane had never seen the Duke look so broken. So helpless. The Duchess, shivering in her gown and shawl, had her arms around him, her expression bleak.

'No! There must be a way to warm him. We're not giving up!' Jane lay next to Alex, putting her arms around him. The coats were a barrier, and she burrowed into them, nestling into him, thrusting down her despair at the iciness of his skin.

A shout sounded.

'Livvy's on her way with help.' Hugo squatted beside Jane. 'You're doing the right thing, Jane. Share your body heat. I learned that when I was a boy in Northumberland. Stay with him until we get him indoors.'

That was all the encouragement she needed. She closed her eyes and stayed tucked close as they were further wrapped in blankets and placed on a hand cart and taken back to the Abbey. Alex was then placed in a tub of warm water—*Not too hot*, Hugo ordered—and Jane sat by his side, as servants hurried in and out, dipping out buckets of cooling water and replacing them with warm for what seemed like hours.

He was breathing. His heart was beating. His skin began to regain colour. That was what she concentrated on, murmuring her love for him into his ear, begging him not to give in…to come back to her…not to die.

He'd not inhaled any water—a blessing the doctor said when he arrived. He confirmed Alex could be moved into a warmed bed, and told them they must be patient and allow Alex to wake up when he was ready.

Alex came to his senses slowly, gradually becoming aware he was in bed, in his bedchamber, with a fire in the hearth. Two figures sat at his bedside, one either side. To his right, his father. He frowned, and looked left. Relief enveloped him. Jane.

She was all he needed.

But there was something…he racked his brains…something he must say to her. Before it was too late. Something he'd regretted…something he'd wanted to say to her…when he was cold…so cold…when he was sure he'd left it too late. He shivered involuntarily, and she stirred, her eyes meeting his. Eyes filled with the love he had taken for granted until it was almost too late.

The memory shot to the surface… Lascelles…the ice… the cold…

Alex reached for Jane, and she took his hand, smiling tenderly. 'All I could think…' his voice was a hoarse whisper '…when I thought I would die…' She whimpered, and tightened her hand around his. He squeezed back. 'All I could think was I would never get the chance to tell you— and to *prove* to you—how much I love you, Janey.'

Her glorious, beloved smile was all the response he needed. He felt his eyelids droop. Everything seemed such an effort…all he wanted was to sleep again but he was loath to close his eyes, needing the reassurance Jane was with him. He was vaguely aware his father had stirred, and he wrenched his gaze from Jane.

'Welcome back, Son.' Tears shone in Father's eyes. 'We thought we'd lost you. Thank God you've lived to plague us all for a few years yet.' His smile wobbled. 'I'll say goodnight, and we'll talk in the morning.' He switched his attention to Jane. 'Thank you, Jane, for all you have done. Goodnight.'

Alex barely noticed him leave the room. He pulled the eiderdown aside. 'Come to bed, Honeybee. I need to hold you. To know I am not alone.'

She smiled again, slipped off her robe and slid into bed, wrapping her arms around him.

'Silly,' she whispered. 'You'll never be alone while you have me and your family. Now sleep.'

The following day he learned Lascelles had drowned but he found it impossible to summon up either guilt or regret. The need for revenge no longer consumed him—all he wanted, with his whole being, was to be a good husband to Jane and to share everything in his life with her. No longer would he keep parts of his life separate…he no longer needed to. He was reconciled with his father. There were no more past secrets hanging over him.

But he must talk…properly…to Jane, and set their problems to rest.

But that, frustratingly, proved almost impossible, with a houseful of people constantly asking him if he was well and wanting to share their experience of the drama with him. On doctor's orders, he was to rest and stay warm. He'd already refused to remain in bed, and compromised by agreeing to sit by the fire in the parlour but there was no privacy for what he wanted to say to his wife. She had told him, repeatedly, she was happy not to talk about it yet, but that made him more determined to clear the air. He'd spent too much of their marriage avoiding awkward conversations. It was time to put that right.

Eventually, at the end of his tether and sick of being treated as an invalid, he took action.

'Alex?' He'd taken advantage of her brief absence to order William, one of his father's footmen, to take a message to the stables to prepare his carriage. Now, Jane burst in, her eyes huge. 'William said you've ordered the carriage. Are you…are you going home?'

Her uncertainty tore at him. Still she feared the worst.

'No, sweetheart,' he said. 'I'm going nowhere without you by my side. *We* are going for a carriage ride so *I* can set your mind at rest once and for all, and without interruption from well-meaning members of my own family.'

'But you aren't strong enough, Alex. The doctor said—'

'Stuff the doctor.' Alex threw aside the rug Rosalind had insisted he wear over his legs and stood up.

'But, Alex—'

'No more "buts", Janey. I am going. Will you come with me?'

He held out his hand. Jane stared at it.

'Half an hour…that's all. I promise. We won't even leave the estate.'

Jane smiled, taking his hand. 'Very well. But you must also promise that if you start to get tired, or feel ill, or—'

'Yes, yes.' Alex laughed as he swept her into his arms and kissed her. 'I promise I will tell you. But you ought to know, my darling wife, that it will take a lot more than a dip into an icy lake to keep me down. Now, make sure you wrap up warm—I don't want you distracted by the shivers while I am eating humble pie. At least…' he captured her gaze '…not *that* sort of shivering!'

He was rewarded by her blush, and a loving smile.

He handed Jane into the carriage to find fur rugs, blankets and hot bricks already inside and he realised William must have arranged them before he relayed Alex's request to the stables.

'Thank you, William.'

William bowed. 'It would never do for Lady Jane to catch a chill, milord,' he replied, with a grin.

'Now. Janey.' Alex faced Jane as the carriage set off at a sedate walk. 'I only know to start by saying I am sorry.'

She pressed her fingers to his lips.

'I am sorry, too, Alex. If I had known what burden you were suffering under, I would never have left the way I did. I couldn't imagine *anything* so awful you couldn't share it with me. I was wrong.'

'I never meant to tell anyone about my suspicions, Jane. I certainly never intended to tell Lascelles but it somehow blurted out. Oh, Janey, I've been such a fool. You warned me how manipulative he was, but I wouldn't listen and I stepped straight into his web. All I could think of was finding out more about my mother and trying to stop the fear that my father had killed her from surfacing.'

'I still find it hard to understand how you believed it. You know your father is an honourable man—how could you ever believe he could assault and strangle his own wife?'

Alex thrust his hand through his hair. 'I didn't even know that memory was lurking in the depths of my mind. All I knew…all I have *ever* known…is that I did not dare allow my memory of that day to fully form, knowing instinctively it would spell disaster for my family. And so I kept it suppressed. I didn't even realise I'd witnessed my mother's murder. I believed what they believed, and what they told me…that I had found her body.'

He hauled in a deep breath, and took her hands in his. 'But that's not why we're here, Janey. We are here to talk about us. About our marriage. About…' and his pulse gave that little kick he felt whenever he looked deep into her beautiful eyes '…about how much I love you.'

'Do you, Alex? Truly?'

'I do,' he vowed, solemnly. 'And I shall tell you so every day. You need never doubt me again…you *may* accuse me of being a slow learner, however, for I did not realise how far you had burrowed your way into my heart until after you left.' He drew in a shuddering breath. 'I *never* want to feel that way again. Ever. I have learned my lesson.

'Darling Honeybee…' He pulled her close, and kissed her lips, but he didn't allow himself to deepen it even though his blood hummed with the need of her. He still had things to say. 'I didn't even realise how deeply I hurt you by not telling you what was in my head. It was never that I didn't trust you, please believe me. I only thought to protect you—to protect them all. And I thought I could manage it alone, as I always have. But when I found you gone…when I realised how badly I'd hurt you—only then did I realise how deeply I love you, and that I no longer want to manage *anything* alone.'

Jane smiled at him, and put one hand against his cheek. 'I love you, too, Alex. I always have, even when I was that annoying little girl for ever buzzing around and driving you mad.'

'Then I am doubly all kinds of a fool for not recognising the treasure under my nose all this time.'

His lips feathered over hers…once…twice…then he angled his head to deepen his kiss and to dip his tongue inside, tasting her sweetness as she melted in his arms.

Epilogue

The entire Beauchamp family descended on the Abbey for Christmastide. It was chaotic. And Alex loved every minute of it.

The two weeks between Alex's accident and Christmas day had been sweet beyond measure. The woman he loved was by his side—and she was happy...*he* was making her happy! And, for almost the first time in his life, he could relax enough to allow his love to shine forth.

He could finally enjoy being a member of the Beauchamp family.

His family.

His wonderful, funny, joyful family.

Dominic and Olivia and their spouses were there from the start, of course, together with Julius and Daisy. But the fun really started once Uncle Vernon and Aunt Cecily arrived with their respective families, a week before Christmas.

Remembering Aunt Cecily's reaction when she saw him still made his throat ache with emotion. Nothing, it seemed, could stem her flow of tears as she tumbled from the carriage. She'd run to Alex, hugging him as though she would never let him go...as she used to when he was a boy, until he outgrew such nonsense. Then, over the top of her head, he caught sight of first his father, his silver-grey eyes shiny, and then Uncle Vernon with his own eyes sheening and, before he could blink them away, tears rolled unchecked down Alex's cheeks.

He'd soon found himself in great demand as a fun-loving big brother to Christabel and Sebastian and as uncle to the rest of the nippers, and he discovered it wasn't only Dominic who had a natural rapport with the children. At first he hung back, expecting one of his black moods to rear up, driving him to his usual role of watching with envy as everyone else made merry. But his moods had vanished and he no longer needed to retreat behind his barriers and keep everyone at bay.

And now, the ribald comments missing from their wedding night started...teasing remarks about it being time for Alex to add to the Beauchamp clan by filling the Fox-bourne nursery.

How long had it been since any of his family had ribbed him like this?

It felt good.

The only sour note had been their visit to Stowford Place. After a stultifying hour sipping tea and making polite conversation, Jane had suggested to her father that in future he might prefer to call upon them at the Abbey. He had gratefully agreed.

The six men of the family spent Christmas Eve morning collecting greenery: branches of holly, ivy, laurel and fir from the woods, rosemary and bay from the gardens, and mistletoe from the apple orchard. The women then decorated the house, adding candles and fir cones, clove-studded oranges, ribbons and silver and gold paper flowers. In the afternoon, the men then took all the children to help haul the Yule log back to the house, even George, who couldn't yet walk—Zach showing Uncle Vernon how to twist a shawl into a sling, as the Romany mothers did, to carry his baby son. The others took turns at giving shoulder rides to the younger children when they grew tired.

The log fit snugly in the huge fireplace in the drawing room, where it should burn from Christmas Eve right through to the end of Christmas night. The fire was ceremoniously lit using the remnants of last year's log, and the Christmas candle was placed on the windowsill to burn through the night.

Christmas morning dawned bright, albeit with a heavy frost. From the way the clouds were gathering—lowering and merging until the sky was uniformly white—snow looked likely by nightfall. The family attended the traditional Christmas morning church service and, on their return, were greeted by the three dogs who, with the delicious smell of roasting meat pervading the whole house, could hardly contain their excitement. Even the normally serene Hector was lolloping around, barking, tail waving like a flag, while Myrtle bounced around stiff-legged, like a barrel on springs, emitting shrill yips of excitement. Romeo hared into the drawing room and then streaked back into the hall, a slender fir branch, completed with red satin bows, trailing in his wake. He rounded the table in the middle of the hall and darted between Father's legs, evading all attempts to catch him. Liberty grew tearful, but Dominic hugged her better, reassuring her that it all added to the fun.

The family exchanged gifts. Alex immediately donned his waistcoat and Jane went all teary-eyed over the gold locket containing a lock of his hair that Alex had bought her on a quick trip to Exeter. The whole family then played riotous games of Hoodman Blind, Shoe the Wild Mare and Bob Apple—Aunt Thea proving herself almost unbeatable, much to Uncle Vernon's chagrin—until Grantham announced Christmas dinner was served and informed them it was snowing.

In accordance with Beauchamp tradition, once the meal was on the table, the servants were free to eat their own dinner in the servants' hall. That included the nursemaids, and thus all the children, even George, joined the family around the dining table…after they had all crowded at the windows to exclaim at the beauty of the familiar landscape now shrouded in white.

The snow, to Alex's mind, simply added to the magic of the occasion.

The meal was chaotic. But fun. And Susie, bless her—barely out of childhood herself at thirteen, quiet and serious and still looking much younger than her age—took charge of George, freeing Aunt Thea and Uncle Vernon to cope with Thomas and Sophie.

Finally it was over. Everyone was full of roast goose and plum pudding and the nursery maids returned to take their eight exhausted charges upstairs to get ready for bed. Susie went, too, after being begged by Thomas to read them a bedtime story, while the adults trooped out of the dining room to head for the drawing room, Alex and Jane in the rear.

Alex grabbed Jane's hand as they crossed the hall, tugging her around to face him. 'We've barely had a minute to talk all day, Janey. And I haven't kissed you since this morning.'

Jane gazed up at him, her eyes full of love. He brushed one glowing cheek with the back of his fingers and then tucked a stray tendril of silky conker-brown hair behind her ear.

'Would you have it any other way?' She tipped her head, a teasing smile on her lips. 'Is this not what you have longed for—to be happy in the bosom of your family?'

He smiled, contentment flooding him. Anchoring him. Finally he belonged.

'Yes, and it would not be half as sweet without you by my side to share it, Honeybee.' He put his arms around her slender waist and breathed in her jasmine scent. Her hands slipped up his chest to rest on his shoulders as their gazes fused. 'More importantly, have *you* enjoyed yourself?'

Words weren't even needed. The beam that lit Jane's beautiful, beloved face told him all he needed to know.

'This,' she said, 'has been the best Christmas I can ever remember. I didn't know it was possible to be so happy. I love your family, Alex. And I love you most of all.'

He lowered his lips to her ear. 'Have you seen where we're standing?'

They looked up into the forked green lobes of mistletoe, glistening with white berries.

'That is a lot of kisses.' Jane's eyes darkened.

'Better get started then.'

He gently cupped her chin. 'Merry Christmas, Janey.' He caressed her lips with his, the sweet need building inside him. He would never tire of this.

Sweet Janey. His Honeybee. His wife.

Delicate fingers slid around his nape and through his hair as a purr of pure satisfaction hummed in her throat. The blood quickened in his veins as desire rippled through him.

Footsteps on the tiled floor broke the spell.

'Don't forget to remove a berry.' Aunt Cecily indicated the mistletoe, smiling indulgently. 'But make haste. Your father sent me to hurry you along.'

Alex pressed a kiss to Jane's palm before leading her into the drawing room where the family sat on sofas and chairs grouped around the fire. Father, his arm resting along the mantelshelf, was talking to Hugo, sitting with his arm around Olivia.

Alex's stepmother smiled as Alex and Jane entered. 'Leo! Here they are.'

Father looked up. 'Splendid. Alex, pour a glass of champagne for you and Jane, would you please?'

The rest of the family already held full glasses and Alex sensed the air of expectancy in the room. As soon as Alex and Jane were settled, Father cleared his throat.

'This Christmas marks the end of a very special year for our family. We welcome both Liberty and Jane, and I, personally, should like to thank you both for making my sons the happiest of men.

'Dominic—you are to be a father yourself before long. I know you and Liberty will make wonderful parents, and Rosalind and I cannot wait to meet our next grandson or granddaughter.

'I also have Hugo and Olivia's permission to announce the happy news that the twins can expect a little brother or sister in the summer. Again, I cannot wait to meet him or her. Congratulations to you both.'

A murmur of excitement rippled around the room. Olivia blushed, and Hugo simply looked immensely proud.

'Which brings me to Alex.' Father paused, and Alex felt the full force of his penetrating silver-grey gaze. 'Welcome home, Son. For too many years you have been a stranger, but now you are back in the family fold and *nothing* could make me happier.

'Jane…' Again he paused, and when he spoke again, his voice was choked. 'Jane. Thank you. From the bottom of all our hearts, thank you. Without you, I do not believe the last few months would have had a happy ending.'

'So,' Father raised his glass high, the cut glass sparkling as it reflected the firelight, 'I now propose a toast. To us.

'To the Beauchamps.

'May we continue to go from strength to strength. From our generation,' his gaze rested in turn on Stepmother, on Uncle Vernon and Aunt Thea, and on Aunt Cecily and Zach, 'to yours,' and it was the turn of Dominic and Liberty, of Alex and Jane, and of Hugo and Olivia, 'and to the generation to follow—our beloved children upstairs, and those yet to be born.

'May they grow healthy and may they prosper and, most important of all, may they be as blessed as their elders in finding the precious gift of love.'

'To the Beauchamps.' Every voice joined in that toast.

Alex felt as though his heart might burst with joy as he looked at each member of his cherished family in turn. Finally, his gaze reached Jane and lingered, lovingly. They shared a tender smile as their glasses clinked together.

'To the most treasured gift of all,' Alex whispered. 'To love.'

* * * * *

THE GOVERNESS'S
SECRET BABY

JANICE PRESTON

To my fellow authors Georgie Lee, Laura Martin
and Liz Tyner:

It's been a pleasure collaborating with you,
ladies, and I hope I've done justice to your
characters in the epilogue.

Prologue

Early October 1811

Nathaniel Pembroke, Marquess of Ravenwell, threw a saddle on Zephyr's back, mounted up, and pointed the black stallion's head towards the fell, the words of the letter searing his brain and his heart. As Zephyr's hooves flashed across the ground the tears spilling from Nathaniel's eyes evaporated in the wind and his roar of rage was heard by no man. The fells above Shiverstone Hall were avoided by local villagers and farmers alike, and that was precisely how Nathaniel liked it.

The great black's pace flagged and, reluctantly, Nathaniel steadied him to a trot. The anger and the grief burning his chest had not eased—the hollow place where his shrivelled heart had struggled to survive this past nine years was still there, only now it was cavernous…a vast, stygian void. He should know by now grief could never be outrun. It cleaved to you like lichen clung to the rocks that strewed the dale below.

Hannah. Tears again clouded his vision and he blinked furiously, gazing hopelessly at the gunmetal grey of the sky. Dead. Never again to see his beloved sister's face, or to hear her laugh, or to feel the rare human contact of her arms around him, hugging, reassuring. And David, Hannah's husband of eight years and Nathaniel's loyal and steadfast friend…his only friend. Also gone.

The raw lump in Nathaniel's throat ached unbearably as the words of his mother's letter—delivered as he had broken his fast that morning—reverberated through his brain: a carriage accident; Hannah and David both killed outright; little Clara, their two-year-old daughter, the only survivor.

> *You are named as Guardian to the child, my son. If I can help you, you know that I will, but I cannot, at my age, shoulder all responsibility for her upbringing. Neither will I live in that Godforsaken place you please to call home in order to help you with the task.*
>
> *I urge you to come home to Ravenwell and we shall raise Clara together. It is time you took your place in the world again.*
>
> *If you choose not to, however, then you must come and collect your ward. It is your duty and you owe it to your poor, dear sister to take charge of and care for the child she loved more than life itself.*
> *Your loving*
> *Mother*

Nathaniel turned Zephyr for home, the realities of his dilemma bearing down on him. He could not deny the truth of Mother's words—she was getting no younger and she would never be happy living at Shiverstone Hall—his cadet estate near the border between the North Riding of Yorkshire and Westmorland—nor would it be healthy for her. She lived most of the year at Ravenwell Manor, his main estate in the far more civilised countryside that surrounded the town of Harrogate, on the far side of the Dales.

But…he considered those alternatives, neither of which appealed. Go home to Ravenwell? He shook his head in dumb denial. Never. He could tolerate neither the memories nor the looks of sympathy from those who had known him before. Still less could he stomach the recoil of strangers at the sight of him.

By the time he rode into the yard behind Shiverstone Hall, his decision was made. He had one choice, and one choice only. He must fetch Clara and bring her to Shiverstone to live with him. His courage almost failed at the thought—what did he know about children, particularly one as young as Clara?

'You have responsibilities, Nathaniel. You cannot continue to hide away. How are you ever to produce an heir otherwise? Not every woman will react like Miss Havers.'

Nathaniel bit back a growl at the reminder of Miss Havers. He had suspected how that would end as soon as his mother had told him of the woman who had agreed to a marriage of convenience. Even the lure of his wealth and title was not enough to compensate for his scars. Miss Havers changed her mind after one meeting and Nathaniel had retreated to Shiverstone Hall, resolving to live a solitary life. She hadn't been the first woman to react to his altered appearance with horror: Lady Sarah Reece—with whom he'd had an understanding before he was injured—had lost no time in accepting another man's proposal.

He did not miss his former carefree life as one of society's most eligible bachelors: such frivolous pleasures no longer held any allure for him. Nor did he miss his erstwhile friends. He would never forget the shock on their faces, nor the speed with which they had turned their backs on him after the fire.

He was *happy* with his life, dammit. He had his animals and his hawks—*they* did not judge him by how he looked.

His mother forked a morsel of roast grouse into her mouth and then placed her knife and fork on to her plate whilst she chewed, watching Nathaniel expectantly.

'I am but thirty, Mother. There is more than enough time to produce an heir.'

'Would you pour me another glass of wine, please, Nathaniel?'

He obliged. They were dining alone in the dining room at Ravenwell Manor, the servants having been dismissed by Lady Ravenwell as soon as the dishes had been served. That had prompted Nathaniel to suspect their conversation would prove uncomfortable and his defences were already well and truly in place.

'Thank you.' His mother sipped her wine, then placed her glass on the finely embroidered tablecloth. 'Do not think I am ignorant of your plan, son,' she said. 'You arrive here after dark, at a time you know Clara will already be asleep. What is your intention? To snatch her from her bed before dawn and be away before you need to see anyone, or be seen?'

He hated the sympathy in her eyes but he also knew that behind that sympathy there existed a steely belief in duty. *His* duty: to the estate, to his family, to the memory of his father, and to the future of the marquessate. Her jibe about snatching Clara from her bed sailed too close to the truth.

'I came as soon as I could after reading your letter, Mother. My late arrival was because I did not want to wait until tomorrow to travel, but I *am* afraid I must return in the morning.'

'Must?'

'It will not do to expect a two-year-old child to travel late into the night.'

'Then stay for a few days. At least give the poor child a chance to remember you.'

He had last seen Clara four months before, when she had come up to Shiverstone with Hannah and David from their home in Gloucestershire. They had stayed with him for a week. Thinking of his sister and his friend brought that choking, aching lump into his throat once more. He bowed his head, staring unseeingly at the food in front of him, his appetite gone.

'I could invite a few neighbours for dinner. Only people you already know, not strangers.'

I can't... Bile rose, hot and bitter in his mouth.

He shoved his plate from him with a violent movement. Mother jumped, her fork clattering on to her plate and her face crumpled, the corners of her mouth jerking down as her eyes sheened. Guilt—familiar, all-encompassing—swept through him and he rounded the table to fold his mother into his arms as she sobbed.

'I'm sorry, Mother.' She had lost her precious daughter and he had been concerned only with his own selfish fears. 'Of course I will stay for a few days.' A few days would be all he could endure of his mother's efforts to reintroduce him into local society, he was certain of that. 'But no dinner parties, I beg of you. Do not forget we are in mourning.'

Mother's shoulders trembled. 'You are right,' she whispered. 'But…please…stay with me a short time.'

He dropped a kiss on her greying head. 'I will.'

Poor Mother, left with only him out of her family. He was no substitute for Hannah. Why couldn't it have been he who died? Hannah had so much to live for, whereas he… He batted that wicked thought away. No matter how black his future had seemed, he had never been tempted to take his own life. He was content enough with the life he led. The villagers avoided him and he had his dogs and his horses and his hawks: they provided all the company he needed.

Nathaniel resumed his seat, but did not draw his plate towards him again.

'What about Clara's nanny?' He remembered the woman from Hannah's last visit to Shiverstone. At least she was not a complete stranger. 'I assume she is here and will stay with Clara?'

His mother's gaze skittered past him. 'I am afraid not.

She has family in Gloucester and does not want to move so far away. You will need to appoint a new nanny and then, later, she will need a governess.'

He battled to hide his dismay, but some must have shown, for she continued, 'You must put Clara's needs first. She is two years old. What do you know about taking care of such a young child? Of any child? And Mrs Sharp has enough to do with running the Hall. You cannot expect her to take on more responsibility.'

She's right. I know she's right...and yet every fibre of his being rebelled against the notion of not one, but two, strangers coming into his home. He eyed his mother. *Perhaps*...

'And do not think I shall yield if you try to persuade me to raise Clara on your behalf.'

His mother—one step ahead as usual. He must accept that, once again, he had no choice.

'I will advertise for a governess,' he said. One person—surely he could cope with one person. Once she was used to his appearance, all would be well. He need not see much of her. 'Then Clara will not have to adapt to another person in her life later on. She needs consistency after losing her parents.'

Poor little soul. Unwanted by her own mother—an unfortunate girl in trouble—and now losing her adoptive parents. And she was a sweet little poppet. Too young to react with horror to his scars as other children had done in the past, Clara had accepted her uncle and she, in turn, had delighted him with her gurgles and her first attempts at speech. An unaccustomed tingle warmed his chest. She would be his. She might only be two, but she would provide some human contact apart from his servants.

'You must do as you deem right for Clara.' Mother's sceptical expression, however, suggested that she was completely aware of his real reason for choosing a governess rather than a nanny. 'And for darling Hannah.'

A lone tear spilled over and tracked down her lined

cheek. How had he never been aware of those wrinkles before? His mother had aged. Grief, he thought, did that to a person and poor Mother had faced more grief than most.

'I will,' he vowed.

He owed it to his sister, who had tackled her own heartbreak of trying and failing to give birth to a healthy baby with such dignity and grace. She had been besotted by Clara from the very first moment she held her in her arms and impotent anger raged through Nathaniel that she would now miss the joy of seeing her adopted daughter grow and mature. Hannah had been one of the few constants in his life since the fire that had taken his father and changed Nathaniel's life for ever. He would not let her down now. He would write to the editor of the *York Herald*, with instructions to run an advertisement for a trained governess who was willing to come and live at the Hall.

For the first time he felt a sliver of doubt—what sort of woman would agree to bury herself in such an isolated place?

Chapter One

~~~~~~~~~~~~~~~~~~~~~~~~~~

Early November 1811

Grace Bertram breathed easier as she reached the edge of the dense woodland, with its mossy-trunked trees and its unfamiliar rustles and groans, and the barely glimpsed scurrying of invisible creatures through the undergrowth. The track she had followed from the village of Shivercombe—past the church, across a meadow and a river, and then through that spooky wood—emerged on to the edge of bleak moorland and she stopped to catch her breath, and look around.

Moorland—or, more correctly, fells according to the local villagers who had tried so hard to dissuade her from venturing to Shiverstone Hall—rose ahead of her before merging mistily with the overcast sky. She could just about make out the slate roof and tall chimneys of a house squatting in a fold of land ahead, the only sign of human habitation in that forbidding landscape.

Grace's pulse accelerated in a fusion of anticipation and fear. That must be it. Shiverstone Hall. And there, beneath those glistening black slates, was Clara. Her baby, who now lived in this isolated place with—according to those same villagers—a man who was fearful to behold and who breathed fire and brimstone on any who ventured on to his land: the Marquess of Ravenwell. Grace would not...*could* not...allow those warnings to deter her. She had survived that creepy forest and she would survive Lord Ravenwell's wrath. She would not turn back from the task she had set herself two years ago.

She owed that much to the daughter she had given away at birth.

Grace swapped her portmanteau into her left hand and glanced down at her muddied half-boots in disgust. Her left foot already squelched in her boot and the right felt suspiciously damp too. What sort of *lord* lived out here in the middle of nowhere and did not even take the trouble to build a bridge over the river between the village and his house? An uncivilised sort, that was who, in Grace's opinion. There was a ford for horses and vehicles, but the only place for a person to cross the river was by using huge, wet, *slippery* rocks set in the riverbed as stepping stones. She was fortunate it was only her left foot that had been submerged.

Grace trudged on, muttering under her breath, still following the same track. At seventeen, and a pupil at a school for governesses, she'd had no choice but to give her baby away, but she had regretted it each and every day since then. She had promised herself that one day she would track her daughter down and make sure she was happy and loved and living the life she deserved. And now it was even more urgent that she find her daughter and make sure she was well cared for—and *wanted*—since her discovery that the couple who had adopted Clara as their own had perished in a carriage accident.

But doubts still plagued her as she walked, despite her resolve to see her mission through. She might be bold, but she was not stupid. What if this Marquess would not allow her to see Clara? What reason could she give him for seeking out the child? Not the truth. He would send her packing. No. She must find another reason.

And what if Clara is not happy and loved?

What on earth could she—a nineteen-year-old newly trained governess with no home and little money in her pocket—actually *do*? She pushed the thought aside with an impatient *tut*.

She would deal with that when and if it became necessary.

She plodded on, skirting the worst of the puddles that dotted the track. Finally, she crested the rise ahead of her and there it was. She paused. It was bigger than that first glimpse had suggested, but its appearance—grim and grey with creepers adorning the walls—and location were hardly that of a dwelling in which one might expect a wealthy lord to reside.

A shrill cry echoed through the air and she whirled around.

Nothing.

At least she wasn't still in the forest—that unearthly sound would then indeed have unnerved her. She scanned the bleak landscape, but nothing moved. Another plaintive cry brought her heart into her mouth. She looked up and caught sight of a huge bird—bigger than any she had ever seen—gliding and soaring. It then circled once, before pitching into a dive: a dark blur silhouetted against the low clouds until it disappeared behind the hill that rose behind the house.

Grace swallowed, hunched her shoulders, swapped her portmanteau over again, and soldiered on. Her upbringing at her uncle's house in Wiltshire and, since the age of nine, at Madame Dubois's School for Young Ladies in Salisbury had ill-prepared her for such nature in the raw.

Twenty minutes later the track passed through a gateway in a stone wall, at which point the surface was reinforced with gravel. A broad drive curved away to the left, only to then sweep around and across the front of Shiverstone Hall. A footpath, paved with stone setts, led from this point in a straight line to the house, bisecting a lawn. Grace followed the path until, directly opposite the front door, it rejoined the gravelled carriageway.

She paused, her heart thudding as she scanned the stone-built Hall with its blank, forbidding windows, and its massive timber door, just visible in the gloomy depths of a central, gabled porch.

There was no sound. Anywhere. Even the air was still and silent.

It is as though the house is lying in wait for me—an enchanted castle, sleeping until the fairy princess awakens it and frees the inhabitants. Or a monster's lair, awaiting the unwary traveller.

Grace bit her lip, shivering a little, castigating herself for such fanciful thoughts, worthy of one of those Gothic novels Isabel used to smuggle into school and then pass around for her awestruck friends to read. A wave of homesickness hit Grace at the thought of Isabel, Joanna, and Rachel. Her dearest friends. What were they doing now? Were they happy? Grace shook her head free of her memories: the three friends she might never see again and her heartache when the time had come for her to leave Madame Dubois's school. For a few years she had belonged and she had been loved, valued, and wanted—a rare feeling in her life thus far.

Resisting the urge to flee back the way she had come, Grace crossed the carriageway, wincing as the crunch of the gravel beneath her boots split the silence. She stepped through the arched entrance to the porch and hesitated, staring with trepidation at the door looming above her.

I have come this far...I cannot give up now.

She sucked in a deep breath and reached for the huge iron knocker. She would make her enquiries, set her mind at rest and return to the village. She had no wish to walk through that forest as the light began to fade, as it would do all too early at this time of year. She only had to knock. And state her business. Still she hesitated, her fingers curled around the cold metal. It felt stiff, as though it was rarely used. She released it, nerves fluttering.

Before she could gather her courage again, a loud bark, followed by a sudden rush of feet, had her spinning on the spot. A pack of dogs, all colours and sizes, leapt and woofed and panted around her. Heart in mouth, she backed against the door, her bag clutched up to her chest for protection. A pair of wet, muddy paws were planted in the region of her stomach, and a grinning mouth, full of teeth and lolling tongue, was thrust at her face, snuffling and sniffing. A whimper of terror escaped Grace despite her efforts to silence it. In desperation, she bent her leg at the knee and drummed her heel against the door behind her. Surely the human inhabitants of this Godforsaken place couldn't be as scary as the animals?

After what felt like an hour, she heard the welcome sound of bolts being drawn and the creak of hinges as the door was opened.

'Get down, Brack!' The voice was deep and brooked no disobedience. 'Get away, the lot of you.'

Grace turned slowly. She looked up…and up. And swallowed. Hard. A powerfully built man towered over her, his face averted, only the left side of it visible. His dark brown hair was unfashionably long, his shoulders and chest broad, and his expression—what she could see of it—grim.

She could not have run if she wanted to, her knees trembled so. Besides, there was nowhere to run to, not with those dogs lurking nearby.

'You're late,' he growled.

Time seemed to slow. The man continued to not quite look at Grace as her brain examined and rejected all the truthful responses at her disposal.

'I am sorry,' was all she said.

'You look too young to be a governess. I expected someone older.'

Governess? Are there other children here apart from Clara? The parallels with her own life sent a shiver skittering down her spine. She knew the reality of growing up with cousins who did not accept you as part of the family.

'I am fully trained,' Grace replied, lifting her chin.

Anticipation spiralled as the implications of the man's words sank in. If Lord Ravenwell was expecting a governess, why should it not be her? She was trained. If his lordship thought her suitable, she could stay. She would see Clara every day and could see for herself that her daughter was happy and loved. That she was not viewed as a burden, as Grace had been.

The man's gaze lowered, and lingered. Grace glanced down and saw the muddy streaks upon her grey cloak.

'That was your dog's fault,' she pointed out, indignantly.

The man grunted and stood aside, opening the door fully, gesturing to her to come in. Gathering her courage, Grace stepped past him, catching the whiff of fresh air and leather and the tang of shaving soap. She took two steps and froze.

The hall in which she stood was cavernous, reaching up two storeys into the arched, beamed roof. The walls were half-panelled in dark wood and, on the left-hand side, a staircase rose to a half-landing and then turned to climb across the back wall to a galleried landing that overlooked the hall on three sides. There, halfway up the second flight of stairs, a small face—eyes huge, mouth drooping—peered through the wooden balustrade. Grace's heart lurched. She moved forward as if in a dream, her attention entirely focussed on that face.

Clara.

It must be. Love flooded every cell of Grace's being as she crossed the hall, tears blurring her vision. She was real.

A living little person. The memory—a tiny newborn baby, taken too quickly from her arms—could now be replaced by this little angel. A forlorn angel, she realised, recognising the sadness in that dear little face, the desolation in those huge eyes. Given away by her birth mother and now orphaned and condemned to be raised by—

Grace spun to face the man, who had followed her into the hall. His head jerked to one side, but not before she glimpsed the ravaged skin of his right cheek, half-concealed by the hair that hung around his face. Impatiently, she dismissed his appearance. The only thing that mattered was to ensure her daughter was properly cared for.

'Who are you?'

A scowl lowered the man's forehead. 'I am the master of this house. Who are *you*?'

The master. Clara's uncle. The Marquess.

Well, title or not, scarred or not, you will not frighten me.

Grace drew herself up to her full five-foot-three. 'Grace Bertram.'

'Bertram? I don't… You are not who I expected—'

'I came instead.'

'Oh.' Lord Ravenwell hesitated, then continued gruffly, 'Follow me. I'll need to know something about you if I'm to entrust my niece to your care.'

Grace's heart skipped a beat. This was the moment she should tell him the truth, but she said nothing. Could she…*dare* she…follow her heart? She needed a job and it seemed, by some miracle, there might be a position for her here.

'Clara—' Ravenwell beckoned to the child on the stairs '—come with me.'

Clara bumped down the stairs on her bottom and Grace committed every second to memory, her heart swelling until it felt like it might burst from her chest. She blinked hard to disperse the moisture that stung her eyes.

'Come, poppet.'

The Marquess held out his hand. Clara shuffled across the hall, feet dragging, her reluctance palpable. She reached her uncle and put her tiny hand into his as her other thumb crept into her mouth and she cast a shy, sideways glance at Grace. She looked so tiny and so delicate next to this huge bear of a man. Did she fear him?

'Good girl.'

The Marquess did not sound cruel or unkind, but Grace's heart ached for her sad little girl. At only two years old, she would not fully understand what had happened and why her life had changed so drastically, but she would still grieve and she must miss her mama and her papa. In that moment Grace knew that she would do everything in her power to stay at this place and to care for Clara, her daughter's happiness her only concern.

She felt Ravenwell's gaze upon her and tore her attention from Clara. She must now impress him so thoroughly he could not help but offer her the post of governess.

'You had better take those boots off, or Mrs Sharp will throw a fit.'

Grace glanced down at her filthy boots and felt her cheeks heat as she noticed the muddy footprints she had left on previously spotless flagstones.

So much for impressing him.

'Mrs Sharp?' She sat on a nearby chair and unbuttoned her boots.

'My housekeeper.'

Grace scanned the hall. Every wooden surface had been polished until it gleamed. She breathed in, smelling the unmistakable sweet scent of beeswax. Appearances could be deceptive, she mused, recalling her first view of the Hall and its unwelcoming exterior. Although…looking around again, she realised the impeccably clean hall still felt as bleak as the fells that rose behind the house. There was no fire in the massive stone fireplace and there were no homely touches: no paintings, vases, or ornaments to brighten the place. No rug to break up the cold expanse of stone floor. No furniture apart from one console table—incongruously small in that huge space—and the simple wooden chair upon which she now sat. It lacked a woman's touch, giving it the atmosphere of an institution rather than a home. Grace darted a look at the Marquess. Was he married? She had not thought to ask that question before she had travelled the length of the country to find her daughter.

She placed her boots neatly side by side next to the chair and stood up, shivers spreading up her legs and across her back as the chill of the flagstones penetrated her woollen stockings.

Ravenwell gestured to a door that led off the hall.

'Wait in there.'

Chapter Two

Grace entered a large sitting room. Like the entrance hall, it was sparsely furnished. There were matching fireplaces at each end of the room—one lit, one not—and the walls were papered in dark green and ivory stripes above the same dark wood panelling as lined the hall. On either side of the lit fireplace stood a wing-back chair and next to each chair stood a highly polished side table. A larger table, with two ladder-back wooden chairs, was set in front of the middle of three tall windows. At the far end of the room, near the unlit fireplace, were two large shapes draped in holland covers. Her overall impression of the room was of darkness and disuse, despite the fire burning in the grate.

This was a house. A dwelling. Well cared for, but not loved. It was not cold in the room and she stood upon polished floorboards rather than flagstones, but she nevertheless suppressed another shiver.

Lord Ravenwell soon returned, alone and carrying a letter.

'Sit down.'

He gestured at the chair to the right of the hearth and Grace crossed in front of the fire to sit in it. Ravenwell sat in the opposite chair, angling it away from the fire, thus ensuring, Grace realised, that the damaged side of his face would be neither highlighted by firelight nor facing her. His actions prompted a desire in her to see his scarred skin properly. Was it really as horrific as he seemed to believe?

'Why did the other woman—' Ravenwell consulted the letter '—Miss Browne, not come? I expected her three days ago.'

His comment sparked a memory. 'I believe she found the area too isolated.'

The villagers had regaled her with gleeful tales of the other young lady who had listened to their stories, headed out from the village, taken one look at the dark, ancient woodland through which she must walk to reach Shiverstone Hall and fled.

'And did our isolation not deter you?'

'I would not be here if it did.'

His head turned and he looked directly at her. His eyes were dark, deep-set, brooding. His mouth a firm line. On the right side of his face, in a broad slash from jaw to temple, his skin was white and puckered, in stark contrast to the tan that coloured the rest of his face. Grace tried not to stare. Instead, she allowed her gaze to drift over his wide shoulders and chest and down to his muscular thighs, encased in buckskin breeches and boots. His sheer size intimidated her. How furious would he be if he discovered her deception? Her heartbeat accelerated, thumping in her chest, and she sought to distract herself.

'Will Mrs Sharp not scold *you* for wearing boots indoors?' she said, before she could curb her tongue.

His shoulders flexed and a muffled snort escaped him. 'As I said, I am the master. And *my* boots,' he added pointedly, 'are clean.'

Chastised, Grace tucked her stockinged feet out of sight under her chair. She was in an unknown place with a strange man she hoped would employ her. This was not school. Or even her uncle's house, where she had grown up. She was no longer a child and she ought to pick her words with more care. She was a responsible adult now, with her own way to make in the world. Ravenwell had already commented on her youthfulness. She must not give him a reason to think her unsuitable to take care of Clara.

She peeped at him again and saw that the back of his right hand, in which he held the letter, was also scarred.

Like Caroline's. One of her fellow pupils had similar ravaged skin on her legs, caused when her dress had gone up in flames when she had wandered too close to an open fire as a young child. She was lucky she had survived.

Is that what happened to Ravenwell? Was he burned in a fire?

As if he felt her interest, the Marquess placed the letter on a side table and folded his arms, his right hand tucked out of sight, before bombarding Grace with questions.

'How old are you?'

'Nineteen, my lord.'

'Where did you train?'

'At Madame Dubois's School for Young Ladies in Salisbury.'

'Where are you from?'

'I grew up in my uncle's house in Wiltshire.'

'What about your parents?'

'They died when I was a baby. My uncle and aunt took me in.'

Ravenwell unfolded his arms and leaned forward, his forearms resting on his thighs, focussing even more intently on her. Grace battled to meet his eyes and not to allow her gaze to drift to his scars. It was just damaged skin. She must not stare and make him uncomfortable.

His voice gentled. 'So you know what it is like to be orphaned?'

'Yes.'

It is lonely. It is being second-best, unimportant, overlooked. It is knowing you are different and never feeling as though you belong.

'I do not remember my parents. I was still a babe in arms when they died.'

Like Clara, when I gave her away.

He sat back. 'I hope Clara will remember her parents, but I am not sure she will. She is only two.'

'She will if you talk to her about them and keep their memory alive,' Grace said. 'My uncle and aunt never spoke to me of my parents. They had quarrelled over something years before and they only took me in out of what they considered to be their Christian duty.'

Silence reigned as Ravenwell stared, frowning, into the fire. Grace knitted the strands of her thoughts together until she realised there were gaps in her understanding.

'You speak only of Clara,' she said. 'You said you will need to know about me if you are to entrust her to my care. Is she not rather young, or do you and Lady Ravenwell have need of a governess for your other children, perhaps?'

Her question jerked Ravenwell from his contemplation of the flames. 'There is no Lady Ravenwell. Clara would be your sole charge.'

'Would a nanny, or a nursery maid, not be more suitable?' The words were out before Grace could stop them. *What are you trying to do? Talk him out of employing you?*

Ravenwell scowled. 'Are you not capable of looking after such a young child? Or perhaps you think it beneath you, as a trained governess?'

'Yes, I am capable and, no, it is not beneath me. I simply wondered—'

'I do not want Clara to grow fond of someone and then have to adjust to a new face in a few years' time. She has faced enough disruption. Do you want the position or not?'

'Yes...yes, of course.' Grace's heart soared. How could life be any sweeter?

Ravenwell was eyeing her, frowning. 'It will be lonely out here, for such a young woman. Are you sure?'

'I am sure.'

Joy bubbled through her. *Real* joy. Not the forced smiles and manufactured jests behind which she had concealed her aching heart and her grief from her friends. Now, her jaw clenched in her effort to contain her beaming smile, but she knew, even without the aid of a mirror, her delight must shine from her eyes. She could not fake nonchalance, despite Madame Dubois's constant reminders that unseemly displays of emotion by governesses were not appreciated by their employers.

'I will fetch Clara and introduce you.'

Grace's heart swelled. She could not wait to speak to Clara. To touch her.

Lord Ravenwell stood, then hesitated and held out his hand. 'Give me your cloak. I will ask Mrs Sharp to brush it for you.'

Startled by this unexpected courtesy, Grace removed her grey cloak—warm and practical, and suitable garb for a governess—and handed it to him. Doubts swirled. Until this moment she had not fully considered that accepting the role of governess to Clara actually meant becoming part of this household and living here with Ravenwell. She thought she had learned her lesson of acting first and thinking about the consequences second, but perhaps, deep down, she was still the impulsive girl she had always been. Her entire focus had been on the lure of staying with Clara. She swallowed. Ravenwell—who had not smiled once since her arrival and who appeared to live as a recluse in this cold, isolated house—was now her employer. This terse, scowling man was now part of her future.

It will be worth it, just to be with Clara. And what kind of life will my poor little angel have if I do not stay?

There was no question that she would accept the post, even if she had not considered all the implications. She would bring sunshine and laughter and love to her daughter's life. Clara would never doubt she was loved and wanted. Grace would make sure of it.

'How many servants are there here?' she asked.

'Three indoors and two men outdoors. We live quietly.'

And with that, he strode from the room, leaving Grace to ponder this unexpected path her life had taken. What would Miss Fanworth say if she could see Grace now? Doubt assailed her at the thought of her favourite teacher. It had been Miss Fanworth who had come to her aid on that terrifying night when she had given birth, Miss Fanworth who had advised Grace to give her baby up for adoption and Miss Fanworth who had taken Grace aside on the day she left the school for the final time and revealed the name of the couple her baby daughter had been given to.

'It is up to you what you choose to do with this information, Grace, but I thought you deserved to know.'

Grace had left school that day, full of determination to find the people who had adopted her daughter, knowing nothing more than their name and that they lived in Gloucestershire. When she eventually tracked them down, it had been too late. They were dead and Grace's daughter had been taken to live with her uncle and guardian, the Marquess of Ravenwell.

Undeterred, Grace had travelled to Ravenwell's country seat, south of Harrogate, where—after some persistent questioning of the locals—she had discovered that the Marquess lived here, at Shiverstone Hall. And, finally, here she was. She had succeeded. She had found her baby.

She could almost hear Miss Fanworth's measured tones in her head: *'Do take care, Grace, dear. You are treading on very dangerous ice.'*

Those imagined words of caution were wise. She must indeed take care: her heart quailed again at the thought of the forbidding Marquess discovering her secret.

I am not really doing wrong. I am a governess and he needs a governess. And I will protect Clara with the last breath of my body. How can that be wrong?

The door opened, jolting her from her thoughts. Raven-well entered, walking slowly, holding Clara by the hand as she toddled beside him, a rag doll clutched in the crook of her arm.

'Clara,' he said, as they halted before Grace. 'This is Miss Bertram. She has come to take care of you.'

A tide of emotion swept through Grace, starting deep down inside and rising…swelling…washing over her, gathering into a tight, aching knot in her chest. Her throat constricted painfully. She dropped to her knees before her little girl, drinking her in…her light brown curly hair, her gold-green eyes—*the image of mine*—her plump cheeks and sweet rosebud lips.

Oh, God! Oh, God! Thank you! Thank you!

She reached out and touched Clara's hand, marvelling at the softness of her skin. How big that hand had grown since the moment she had taken her baby's tiny fist in hers and pressed her lips to it for the last time. She had tucked away those few precious memories, knowing they must last a lifetime. And now, she had a second chance.

She sucked in a deep breath, desperately trying to suppress her emotion. Ravenwell had released Clara's hand and moved aside. Grace could sense his eyes on her. Watching. Judging.

'What a pretty dolly.' Her voice hitched; she willed the tears not to come. 'Does she have a name?'

Clara's thumb crept into her mouth as she stared up at Grace with huge eyes—too solemn, surely, for such a young child?

'She has barely spoken since she lost her parents.'

Powerless to resist the urge, Grace opened her arms and drew Clara close, hugging her, breathing in her sweet little-girl scent as wispy curls tickled her neck and cheek.

She glanced up at Ravenwell, watching her with a puz-

zled frown. She dragged in a steadying breath. She must
not excite his suspicions.

'I know what it is l-like to be orphaned,' she reminded
him. 'But she has us. W-we will help her to be happy again.'

She rubbed Clara's back gently, rocking her and revelling in the solid little body pressed against hers. She was
rewarded with a slight sigh from the child as she relaxed
and wriggled closer. The tears welled. She was powerless
to stop them. A sob shook her. Then another.

'Are you crying?'

The deep rumble penetrated Grace's fascination with
this perfect being in her arms. Reluctantly she looked up,
seeing Ravenwell mistily through drowning eyes. He was
offering her his hand. Grace blinked and, as the tears dis-
persed, she saw the handkerchief he proffered. She reached
for it and dabbed her eyes, gulping, feeling a fool.

She prised her arms loose, releasing Clara. There would
be plenty of time to hold her, as long as Ravenwell did not
now change his mind about employing her. Grace's head
rang with Madame Dubois's warnings on the necessity of
staying in control of one's emotions at all times.

*It's all very well for Madame. She hasn't a sensitive
bone in her body.*

The words surfaced, unbidden, in Grace's mind but,
deep down, she knew she was being unfair to the principal of her old school. If rumour was true—and Miss Fanworth's words on the day Joanna had left the school, as
well as Rachel's discovery of Madame weeping over a pile
of old letters suggested it was—Madame had suffered her
own tragedies in the past. Thinking of the stern Madame
Dubois steadied Grace. The knowledge she had let herself
down set her insides churning.

Would Ravenwell be thoroughly disgusted by her dis-
play of emotion? Would he send her away? She pushed herself—somewhat inelegantly—to her feet, hoping she had
not disgraced herself too much. She must say something.

Offer some sort of explanation. Not the truth, though. She could not possibly tell him the truth. She mopped her eyes again, and handed him back his handkerchief. His expression did not bode well.

'Th-thank you,' she said. 'I apologise for giving way to my emotions. I—'

Her heart almost seized as she felt a small hand creep into hers. Clara was by her side and, with her other hand, she was offering her dolly to Grace. Tears threatened again and Grace blinked furiously, took the doll, and crouched down by the child, smiling at her.

'Thank you, Clara. N-now I can see your dolly properly, I can see she is even prettier than I first thought—almost as p-pretty as you.'

She stroked Clara's satiny cheek and tickled her under the chin. She was rewarded with a shy smile. Heart soaring, Grace regained her feet and faced the Marquess, holding his gaze, strength and determination stiffening every fibre of her being. She would give him no opportunity to change his mind. She was staying, and that was that.

'As I was about to explain, I was overcome by the similarities between Clara's situation and my own as a child and also by relief at having secured such an excellent position.' She raised her chin. 'It was an unforgivable lapse. It will not happen again, I promise.'

Chapter Three

Nathaniel felt his brows lower in yet another frown and hastily smoothed his expression, thrusting his doubts about Grace Bertram aside. Would he not harbour doubts about anyone who applied for the role of governess simply because, deep down, he still rebelled at the idea of a stranger living under his roof?

He loathed this sense of being swept along by an unstoppable tide of events, but, from the very moment he had read his mother's letter, he had known his fate was sealed. He was Clara's legal guardian and he must…no, he *wanted* to do what was right for her, both for her own sake and for Hannah's. The familiar ache of loss filled his chest and squeezed his throat, reminding him it was not mere obligation that drove him, but his love for Hannah and David, and for their child. He had vowed to make Clara's childhood as happy and carefree as possible, but the three weeks since his return from Ravenwell had confirmed he needed help.

But is she the right woman for the job?

Those doubts pervaded his thoughts once more.

There were all kinds of very good reasons why he should not employ Grace Bertram as Clara's governess. She was too young and, he had silently admitted as he had watched her with Clara, too pretty. Mrs Sharp would disapprove on those grounds alone—his housekeeper had made no secret of her opinion he should seek a mature woman for Clara's governess. Nathaniel knew her concern was more for his sake than for Clara's and it irritated him to be thought so weak-willed he could not withstand a pretty face in his household. He had learned the hard way to protect his heart and his pride from ridicule and revulsion.

Miss Bertram also wore her heart on her sleeve in a manner most unsuited to a woman to whom he must entrust not only his niece's well-being but also her moral character. And, in the short time she had been here, she had demonstrated an impulsiveness in her speech that gave him pause. Did she lack the sense to know some thoughts were best left unsaid, particularly to a prospective employer? Take his boots off indeed! But, in fairness, this *would* be her first post since completing her training and she was bound to be nervous.

There were also very compelling reasons why he would not send Grace Bertram packing. She was pleasant and she was warm-hearted. With a young child, that must be a bonus. He refused to relinquish the care and upbringing of his two-year-old niece to a strict governess who could not—or would not—show her affection. More importantly, Clara appeared to like Miss Bertram. Besides, if he was honest, there *was* no one else. He had no other option. He had interviewed two women whilst he was still at Raven-well Manor, hoping to find someone immediately. Neither wanted the job. And that other woman, Miss Browne, had not even arrived for her interview.

He eyed Grace Bertram as she faced him, head high. Despite her youth, he recognised her unexpected core of steel as she threw her metaphorical gauntlet upon the ground. She wanted to stay. Her eyes shone with determination as she held his gaze.

She does not recoil at my appearance.

She had not flinched once, nor stared, nor even averted her gaze. It was as though his scars did not matter to her.

Of course they do not, you fool. You are interviewing her for the post of a governess, not a wife or a mistress.

That thought decided him. They would spend little time together, but her acceptance of his appearance was a definite point in her favour.

'Come,' he said. 'I will introduce you to Mrs Sharp and she will show you around the house.'

He swung Clara up on to his shoulders, revelling in her squeal of delight, and led the way to the kitchen, awareness of the young woman following silently at his heels prickling under his skin. He needed to be alone; he needed time to adjust. By the time they reached the door into the kitchen, his nerves were strained so tight he feared one wrong word from his housekeeper or from Miss Bertram might snap them with disastrous consequences. He pushed the door wide, ducking his knees as he walked through the opening, to protect Clara's head. Mrs Sharp paused in the act of slicing apples.

'Was she suitable, milord?'

Miss Bertram was still behind Nathaniel; he stepped aside to allow her to enter the kitchen.

'Yes. Mrs Sharp—Miss Bertram.'

Mrs Sharp's lips thinned as she looked the new governess up and down. 'Where are your shoes?'

Nathaniel felt rather than saw Miss Bertram's sideways glance at him. He should ease her way with Mrs Sharp, but he felt the urge to be gone. Miss Bertram must learn to have no expectations of him: he had his own life to live and she would get used to hers. He lifted Clara from his shoulders, silently excusing himself for his lack of manners. She was only a governess, after all. He would be paying her wages and providing her with food and board. He need not consider her feelings.

'I'll leave you to show Miss Bertram the house: where she is to sleep, the child's new quarters and so forth.'

He turned abruptly and strode from the kitchen, quashing the regret that snaked through him at the realisation of how much less he would now see of Clara. The past few weeks, although worrying and time-consuming, had also revived the simple pleasure of human company, even though Clara was only two. She'd been restless at night and he'd put her to sleep in the room next to his, needing to know someone would hear her and go to her if she cried. Although the Sharps and Alice, the young housemaid who had travelled back with him from Ravenwell, had helped, he could not expect them to care for Clara's welfare as he did. Now, that would no longer be necessary. A suite of rooms had already been prepared for when a governess was appointed and Clara would sleep in her new room—at the far side of the house from his—tonight.

He snagged his greatcoat from a hook by the back door and shrugged into it as he strode along the path to the barns. The dogs heard him coming and milled around him, leaping, tails wagging frantically, panting in excitement.

'Steady on, lads,' he muttered, his agitation settling as he smoothed the head of first one, then another. His favourite, Brack—a black-and-tan hound of indeterminate breeding—shouldered his way through the pack to butt at Nathaniel's hand, demanding attention. He paused, taking Brack's head between his hands and kneading his mismatched ears—one pendulous and shaggy, the other a mere stump following a bite when he was a pup—watching as the dog half-closed his eyes in ecstasy. Dogs were so simple. They offered unconditional love. He carried on walking, entering the barn. Ned, his groom, emerged from the feed store at the far end.

'Be riding, milord?' Ned was a simple man of few words who lived alone in a loft above the carriage house.

'Not now, Ned. How's the mare?'

'She'll do.' One of the native ponies they kept for work-ing the sheep that grazed on the fells had a swollen fetlock.

Nathaniel entered the stall where she was tethered, smoothing a hand down her sleek shoulder and on down her foreleg.

'Steady, lass. Steady, Peg,' he murmured. There was still a hint of heat in the fetlock, but it was nowhere near as fiery as it had been the previous day. He straightened. 'That feels better,' he said. 'Keep on with the good work. I'm off up to the mews.'

'Right you are, milord.'

The dogs, calmer now, trotted by his side as he walked past the barn and turned on to the track that led up to the mews where he kept his birds, cared for by Tam. There was no sign of Tam, who lived in a cottage a few hundred yards further along the track with his wife, Annie. The en-closures that housed his falcons—three peregrine falcons, a buzzard, and a kestrel—came into view and Nathaniel cast a critical eye over the occupants as he approached. They looked, without exception, bright-eyed, their feath-ers glossy, as they sat on their perches. He had flown two of them earlier and now they were fed up and settled.

Loath to disturb the birds, he did not linger, but rounded the enclosures to enter the old barn against which they were built, shutting the door behind him to keep the dogs out. Light filtered in through gaps in the walls and the two small, unglazed windows, penetrating the gloomy interior. A flap and a shuffle sounded from the large enclosure built in one corner, where a golden eagle—a young female, they thought, owing to her size—perched on a thick branch.

The eagle had been found with a broken wing by Tam's cousin, who had sent her down from Scotland, knowing of Nathaniel's expertise with birds of prey. Between them, he and Tam had nursed the bird back to health and were now teaching her to fly again. Nathaniel had named her Amber, even though he knew he must eventually release her back into the wild. His other birds had been raised in captivity and would have no chance of survival on their own. Amber, however, was different and, much as Nathaniel longed to keep her, he knew it would be unfair to cage her when she should be soaring free over the mountains and glens of her homeland.

Nathaniel selected a chunk of meat from a plate of fresh rabbit on Tam's bench, then crossed to the cage, unbolted the door, and reached inside. His soft call alerted the bird, who swivelled her head and fixed her piercing, golden eyes on Nathaniel's hand. With a deft flick of his wrist, Nathaniel lobbed the meat to the eagle, who snatched it out of the air and gulped it down.

Nathaniel withdrew his arm and bolted the door, but did not move away. He should return to the house. He had business to deal with: correspondence to read and to write, bills to pay, decisions to make over the countless issues that arose concerning his estates. He rested his forehead against the upright wooden slats of Amber's cage. The bird contemplated him, unblinking. At least she wasn't as petrified as she had been in the first few days following her journey from Scotland.

'I know how you feel,' he whispered to the eagle. 'Life changes in an instant and we must adjust as best we can.'

The turning point in his life had been the fire that destroyed the original Ravenwell Manor. It had been rebuilt, of course. It was easy to restore a building—not so easy to repair a life changed beyond measure. He touched his damaged cheek, the scarred skin tight and bumpy beneath his fingertips. And it was impossible to restore a lost life. The familiar mix of guilt and desolation washed over him at the memory of his father.

And now another turning point in his life had been reached with Hannah's death.

As hard as he strove to keep the world at bay, it seemed the Fates deemed otherwise. His hands clenched, but he controlled his urge to slam his fists against the bars of the cage—being around animals and birds had instilled in him the need to control his emotions. He pushed away from the bars and headed for the door, turning his anger upon himself. Why was he skulking out here, when there was work to be done? He would shut himself in his book room and try to ignore this latest intrusion into his life.

Grace winced as the door banged shut behind the Marquess. She tried not to resent that he had left her here alone to deal with Mrs Sharp, who looked as disapproving as Madame Dubois at her most severe, with the same silver-streaked dark hair, scraped back into a bun. Grace tried to mask her nervousness as the housekeeper's piercing grey eyes continued to rake her. Clara, meanwhile, had toddled forward and was attempting to clamber up on a chair by the table. Grace moved without conscious thought to help her. Clara didn't appear to be intimidated by the housekeeper, so neither would she.

'Well? Your shoes, Miss Bertram?'

'His lordship requested that I remove them when I came inside,' Grace said. 'They were muddy.' She looked at the bowl of apples. They would discolour if not used shortly. 'May I help you finish peeling those before you show me where my room is? I should not like them to spoil.'

Wordlessly, Mrs Sharp passed her a knife and an unpeeled apple. They worked in silence for several minutes, then Mrs Sharp disappeared through a door off the kitchen and re-emerged, carrying a ball of uncooked pastry in one hand and a pie dish in the other. As she set these on the table, she reached into a pocket of her apron and withdrew a biscuit, which she handed to Clara, who had been sitting quietly—too quietly, in Grace's opinion—on her chair. Clara took the biscuit and raised it to her mouth. Grace reached across and stayed her hand.

'What do you say to Mrs Sharp, Clara?'

Huge green eyes contemplated her. Grace crouched down beside Clara's chair. 'You must say thank you when someone gives you something, Clara. Come, now, let me hear you say *Thank you*.'

Clara's gaze travelled slowly to Mrs Sharp, who had paused in the act of sprinkling flour on to the table and her rolling pin.

'Did his lordship not say? She has barely said a word since she came here.'

'Yes. He told me, but I shall start as I mean to go on. Clara must be encouraged to find her voice again,' Grace said. 'Come on, sweetie, can you say, *Thank you*?'

Clara shook her head, her curls bouncing around her ears. Then, as Grace still prevented her eating the biscuit, her mouth opened. The sound that emerged was nowhere near a word, it was more of a sigh, but Grace immediately released Clara's hand, saying, 'Clever girl, Clara. That was nice of you to thank Mrs Sharp. You may now eat your biscuit.'

She glanced at Mrs Sharp, but the housekeeper's head was bent as she concentrated on rolling out the pastry and she did not respond. Grace bit back her irritation. It wouldn't have hurt the woman to praise Clara or to respond to her. But she held her tongue, wary of further stirring the housekeeper's hostility.

Once the apple pie was in the oven, Mrs Sharp led the way from the kitchen. They went upstairs first—Grace carrying Clara—then crossed the galleried landing and turned into a dark corridor, lit only by a window at the far end.

'This is your bedchamber.'

Grace walked through the door Mrs Sharp indicated into a plain room containing a bed, a massive wardrobe and a sturdy washstand. The curtains were half-drawn across the windows, rendering the room as gloomy and unwelcoming as the rest of the house. Grace's portmanteau was already in the room, by the foot of the bed.

'Who brought this up?' she asked, bending to put Clara down. The thought of the burly Lord Ravenwell bringing her bag upstairs and into her bedchamber set strange feelings stirring deep inside her.

'Sharp. My husband.'

'So he works in the house, too?'

'Yes.'

Thoroughly annoyed by now, Grace refused to be intimidated by the older woman's clipped replies.

'His lordship mentioned three inside servants and two outside,' she said. 'Who else is there apart from you and your husband?'

A breath of exasperation hissed through Mrs Sharp's teeth. 'Indoors, there's me and Sharp, and Alice, the housemaid. She's only been here three weeks. His lordship brought her back with him and Miss Clara from Ravenwell, to help me with the chores.

'Outside, there's the men who care for his lordship's animals. Ned is unmarried and lives in quarters above the carriage house. Tam lives in a cottage on the estate. His wife, Annie, spins wool from the estate sheep and helps me on laundry days.

'Now, I have dinner to prepare. I don't have time for all these questions.' She headed for the door. 'Hurry along. There's more to show you before we're finished.'

'I shall just find my shoes.'

Her stockinged feet were thoroughly chilled again, after standing in the stone-flagged kitchen. Ignoring another hiss from the housekeeper, Grace unclasped her bag and pulled out her sturdy shoes, part of the uniform deemed by Madame Dubois to be suitable for a governess, along with high-necked, long-sleeved, unadorned gowns, of which she had two, one in grey and one in brown.

She hurried to put on her shoes whilst Mrs Sharp tapped her foot by the door. As soon as Grace was done, Mrs Sharp disappeared, her shoes clacking out her annoyance as she marched along the wooden-floored corridor. Grace scooped Clara up and followed.

'This is the eastern end of the house,' the housekeeper said, opening the next door, 'which will be your domain upstairs. Your bedchamber you've seen, this is the child's room—there's a door between the two, as you can see. Then there's a small sitting room, through that door opposite, for your own use, and the room at the far end will eventually be the schoolroom but, for now, it will be somewhere Miss Clara can play without disturbing his lordship.'

All the rooms were furnished in a similar style to Grace's bedchamber and they felt chilly and unwelcoming as a result. Clara deserved better and Grace vowed to make the changes necessary to provide a much cosier home for her.

'Is his lordship wealthy?'

Mrs Sharp glared. 'And why is that any business of yours, young lady?'

Chapter Four

Too late, Grace realised how her question might be misconstrued by the clearly disapproving housekeeper.

'No…no…I did not mean…' She paused, her cheeks burning with mortification. 'I merely meant…I should like to make these rooms a little more cheery. For Clara's sake.'

Mrs Sharp stiffened. 'I will have you know this house is spotless!'

'I can see that, Mrs Sharp. I meant no offence. You do an excellent job.' She would ask the Marquess. Surely he could not be as difficult to deal with as his housekeeper? 'Perhaps you would show me the rest of the house now?'

They retraced their steps to the head of the staircase. 'His lordship's rooms are along there, plus two guest bedchambers.' Mrs Sharp pointed to the far side of the landing, her tone discouraging. 'You will have no need to turn in that direction. Alice, Sharp, and I have our quarters in the attic rooms. I will show you the rooms on the ground floor you have not yet seen and then I must get back to my kitchen. The dinner needs my attention and Miss Clara will want supper before she goes to bed.'

Grace followed Mrs Sharp to the hall below, helping Clara to descend the stairs. She bit her lip as she saw the trail of mud from the front door to where she had left her half-boots by the only chair in the hall and was thankful the housekeeper did not mention the mess. The longcase clock in the hall struck half past four as Mrs Sharp hurried Grace around the rest of the ground floor: the drawing room—as she called it—where Ravenwell had interviewed her, a large dining room crammed with furniture shrouded in more holland covers, a small, empty sitting room and a morning parlour furnished with a dining table and six chairs where, she was told, Lord Ravenwell ate his meals.

Grace wondered, but did not like to ask, where she would dine. With Clara in the nursery suite? In the kitchen with the other servants? Clara was flagging and Grace picked her up. The house was, as her first impression had suggested, sparse and cold but clean. She itched to inject some light and warmth into the place, but realised she must tread very carefully where the prickly housekeeper was concerned.

They reached the final door off the hall, to the right of the front door. Clara had grown sleepy and heavy in Grace's arms.

'This,' Mrs Sharp said, as she opened the door and ushered Grace into the room, 'is the book room.'

Grace's gaze swept the room, lined with glass-fronted bookcases, and arrested at the sight of Lord Ravenwell, glowering at her from behind a desk set at the far end, between the fireplace and a window.

From behind her, Mrs Sharp continued, 'It is where— oh!' She grabbed Grace's arm and pulled her back. 'Beg pardon, milord. We'll leave you in peace.'

'Wait!'

Grace jumped at Ravenwell's barked command and Clara roused with a whimpered protest. Grace hugged her closer, rubbing her back to soothe her, and she glared at the Marquess.

'Clara is tired and hungry, my lord,' she said. 'Allow me to—'

'Mrs Sharp. Take Clara and feed her. I need to speak to Miss Bertram.'

'Yes, my lord.'

Grace gave her child up with reluctance, her arms already missing the warmth of that solid little body. She eyed Ravenwell anxiously as the door closed behind Mrs Sharp and Clara. His head was bowed, his attention on a sheet of paper before him.

Has he found me out? Will he send me away?

Her knees trembled with the realisation of just how much she wanted…*needed*…to stay.

'Sit!'

Grace gasped. She might be only a governess, but surely there was no need to speak to her quite so brusquely. He had not even the courtesy to look at her when he snapped his order, but was directing his attention down and away, to his right. Was he still attempting to hide his disfigurement? Grace stalked over to the desk and perched on the chair opposite his.

He lifted a brow. She tilted her chin, fighting not to relinquish eye contact, determined not to reveal her apprehension. After what seemed like an hour, one corner of his mouth quirked up.

'Did you think I meant you?'

'I…I beg your pardon?'

'I was talking to the dog.' He jerked his head to his right.

Grace followed the movement, half-standing to see over the side of his desk. There, sitting by his side, was the rough-coated dog that had jumped up at her when she first arrived at Shiverstone Hall.

'Oh.' She swallowed, feeling decidedly foolish and even more nervous; the dog was very big and she had little experience of animals.

'Now, to business.' Any vestige of humour melted from Ravenwell's expression as if it had never been and Grace recalled, with a thump of her heart, that she might have a great deal more to worry about than a dog. 'I cannot under-stand how your letter applying for the post can have gone astray but, now you are here, we must make the most of it. You said this is your first post since finishing school, is that correct?'

Grace swallowed her instinctive urge to blurt out that she had written no letter of application. 'Yes, my lord.'

'Do you carry a reference or—?'

'I have a letter of recommendation from my teacher, Miss Fanworth,' Grace said, eagerly. Mayhap she was wor-rying about nothing. He did not sound as though he planned to send her away. 'It is in my bag upstairs.'

'Go and get it now, please. I shall also require the name of the principal of the school and the address.'

'The…the principal?' Grace's heart sank. 'Wh-why do you want that when I already have a letter from Miss Fan-worth?'

Out of the four friends, she had been Madame Dubois's least favourite pupil, always the centre of any devilment. *You are the bane of my life*, the Frenchwoman had once told Grace after a particularly naughty prank. Of course, that was before Grace had Clara—thank goodness Ma-dame Dubois had never found out about *that* escapade—and Grace's behaviour had improved considerably since then. Perhaps Madame would not write too damning a re-port about Grace's conduct at school.

The Marquess continued to regard her steadily. 'I should have thought that was obvious,' he said, 'and it is not for you to question my decision.'

'No, my lord.'

Grace rose to her feet, keeping a wary eye on the dog as she did so. His feathery tail swished from side to side in response and she quickly averted her eyes.

'Are you scared of him? Brack, come here, sir.'

Ravenwell walked around the desk to stand next to Grace and she quelled her impulse to shrink away. She had forgotten quite how tall and intimidating he was, with his wide shoulders and broad chest. He carried with him the smells she had previously noted: leather, the outdoors, and soap. Now, though, he was so close, she caught the underlying scent of warm male and she felt some long-neglected hunger within her stretch and stir. His long hair had swung forward to partially obscure the ravaged skin of his right cheek and jaw, but he did not appear to be deliberately concealing his scars now and Grace darted a glance, taking in the rough surface, before turning her wary attention once again to Brack. The dog had moved closer to her than she anticipated and now she could not prevent her involuntary retreat.

'It is quite all right. You must not be scared of him.'

There was a hint of impatience in Ravenwell's tone. Grace peeped up at him again, meeting his gaze. He might be intimidating in size, and brusque, but she fancied there was again a hint of humour in his dark brown eyes.

'Try to relax. Hold out your hand. Here.'

He engulfed her hand in his, eliciting a strange little jolt deep in her core. Her pulse quickened. Ravenwell called to Brack, who came up eagerly, sniffed and then pushed the top of his head under their joined hands, his black-and-tan coat wiry under Grace's fingers. The dog had a disreputable look about him, one ear flopping almost over his eye whilst the other was a ragged stump. Grace swallowed. Ravenwell wouldn't keep a dangerous animal indoors. Would he?

'All he wants is some attention,' Ravenwell said, his warm voice rumbling through her.

Grace's chest grew tight, her lungs labouring to draw air.

'Where are the other dogs?'

'Brack's the only one who is allowed inside.' Ravenwell released Grace's hand and moved away, and Grace found she could breathe easily again. 'I reared him from a pup after his mother died.'

Grace stroked along Brack's back, feeling very daring. 'I am sure I will get used to him.'

She imagined telling the other girls about this: how they would laugh at her fear of a simple dog. Then, with a swell of regret and sorrow, she remembered she would never again share confidences with her friends. They could write, of course, but letters were not the same as talking face to face—sharing their hopes and fears and whispering their secrets as they lay in bed at night—or as supporting and comforting each other through the youthful ups and downs of their lives. And those friends, her closest friends—her dearest Joanna, Rachel, and Isabel—had supported and comforted Grace through the worst time of her life. Theirs had been the only love she had ever known.

She longed to hear how they all fared in their new roles as governesses and she knew they would be waiting to hear from her—wondering if she had found the baby she had vowed to trace. But they would not know how to contact her—none of them, no one from her former world, knew where she had been since she left the school or where she was at this moment in time.

She must let them know.

'My lord…if you are to write to Madame Dubois, do you think…might I write to Miss Fanworth too? I should like her to know I arrived safely.'

'What about your aunt and uncle? Will they not also wish to know you are here?'

'Yes, of course.'

She uttered the words, but she doubted they would concern themselves one way or the other as to her welfare, as long as she did not end up back on their doorstep, costing them money. She had visited them before starting her quest to find Clara. They had made it clear their home was no longer hers, now she was an adult.

'I shall write to them as well.'

'You may write your letters in here. Ned rides into the village most mornings with the post.'

'Thank you.'

Grace ran upstairs to fetch her letter of recommendation, deliberating over her strange reaction to the Marquess. There had been a moment…when he had been standing so close…when he had taken her hand… She shook her head, dismissing her reaction as nonsense. It was fear of the dog, that was all. Nevertheless, she would avoid using the book room to write her letters whilst he was present. She would wait until her disturbing employer was elsewhere in the house.

Nerves knotted her stomach when she returned downstairs and handed him Miss Fanworth's letter.

'I must go now and see to Clara.' The words tumbled from her, and his brow rose. 'I shall write my letters later, so they will be ready for the morning. Thank you.'

She did not wait for his response, but hurried from the room, feeling her tension dissipate as she closed the door behind her. She went to the kitchen, where Clara was eating some bread and butter with a bowl of broth. The room was warm, and steamy with a mouthwatering aroma that made Grace's stomach growl in protest, reminding her she had not eaten since her breakfast that morning.

A man with ruddy cheeks, small blue eyes and sleeked-down mousy hair sat beside Clara. He was helping her to spoon the broth into her mouth, in between supping from a tankard of ale. He grinned at Grace, but Mrs Sharp—sitting on the opposite side of the scrubbed table—scowled as she entered.

'What did his lordship want with you?'

Grace tilted her chin. 'I suggest you ask him, Mrs Sharp,' she said. 'If he wishes you to be privy to our conversation, I am sure he will enlighten you.'

Mrs Sharp's eyes narrowed, but she said nothing more.

Grace switched her attention to the man, whose grin had widened, his eyes almost disappearing as his face creased.

'Good afternoon,' she said. 'My name is Grace Bertram and I expect you already know I have come to take care of Clara.'

The man bobbed to his feet and nodded. 'Pleased to meet you, miss. I'm Sharp—husband of this one.' He winked at Mrs Sharp, whose lips thinned so much they almost disappeared. 'I look after his lordship, such as he'll allow, bring in the wood and coal and tend the fires, and do a bit of gardening.

'I'll wager this little one—' he ruffled Clara's curls '—will be happy to have you here. As am I,' he added, with a defiant look at his wife, who huffed audibly and got up to stir a pot suspended over the range.

Sharp's eyes twinkled as he raised his tankard in a silent toast to his wife's back. He tilted his head back, drinking with evident enjoyment.

'Sit yourself down, missy...' he put the tankard down with a clatter, earning him another irritable look from his wife '...and tell us a bit about yourself while Miss Clara finishes her meal.'

Grace took care to tell the Sharps no more than she'd already told his lordship. It was not lying. Not precisely. She merely omitted certain facts. Sharp—as garrulous and inquisitive as his spouse was taciturn—continued to interrogate Grace until, the minute Clara finished eating, Grace shot to her feet.

'I must take Clara upstairs now, so she can become accustomed to her new room before it is time for her to sleep.'

She smiled at Sharp to soften her abruptness and picked Clara up, hefting her on to one hip. She couldn't wait to have her little girl all to herself, nor to get away from Sharp's questions and Mrs Sharp's suspicious looks. Quite why the housekeeper disliked her she could not begin to guess, unless...

'Will Mrs Sharp miss looking after Clara?' she asked Sharp. His wife was rattling around in the pantry and Grace kept her voice low so she would not hear. 'Is that why she does not care for me being here?'

'Bless 'ee, no.' Sharp's words, too, were quiet and he darted a glance at the pantry door before continuing, 'It's his lordship she's protecting. She's worried he'll—' He clamped his lips and shook his head. 'Nay, I'll not tell tales. You'll soon find out, if'n you don't already know.'

'What?' Grace hissed. Why would a housekeeper worry about a marquess? And protect him against whom? Her? That made no sense. 'What were you going to say?'

Mrs Sharp chose that moment to emerge from the pantry and Sharp smirked at Grace. She couldn't question him further now.

'His lordship dines at six,' Mrs Sharp said. 'And we have our meal after he's been served. Do not be late.'

Nasty old crow. Grace left the kitchen and carried Clara upstairs.

'Alone at last, sweetie,' she said, as she shut the nursery door firmly behind them.

She shivered. There was no fire lit and the only illumination was from the single candlestick she had carried up to light their way. The room had bare, polished floorboards, a large cabinet, two wooden chairs and a small, low table.

Grace lowered Clara to the floor. 'We shall have to do something about this, Clara. This is simply not good enough.'

She glanced down at her daughter, who was gazing up at her with worry creasing her forehead and her mouth drooping. Grace's heart faltered and she crouched down.

'Don't look so sad, little one,' she whispered. 'I am not cross with you.'

The enormity of the task she had undertaken dawned on her. What did she know about caring for such a young child? Had she thought, because she was Clara's mother, she would magically know what to do and how to raise her properly? All her training had been about older children. She cupped Clara's face between her palms and pressed a kiss to her forehead.

'We shall learn how to go on together,' she said. 'But first, I shall talk to your uncle and I will make sure you want for nothing. And the first step will be a lovely cosy room where you can play and have fun.'

'Unc' Nannal.'

Grace froze. 'What did you say, Clara?'

Clara—eyes wide, thumb now firmly jammed in her mouth—remained silent. Grace gently pulled Clara's hand from her face. 'Say it again, sweetie.'

'She said *"Uncle Nathaniel"*.'

Chapter Five

Grace's heart almost seized in her chest. She twisted to look over her shoulder, then scrambled to her feet to face the Marquess, who filled the open doorway. How long had he been there? What had he heard? Her thrill at hearing Clara speak faded, to be replaced by anxiety. She could barely remember what she had said out loud and what she had thought.

'I did not see you there,' she said.

'Evidently.'

Her heart began to pound as he continued to stare at her, frowning.

'You shall have a fire up here tomorrow and Mrs Sharp will show you where there is furniture and so forth in storage. You may make use of anything you need to make these rooms comfortable for you and for Clara.'

He does not seem to think of Clara as an unwanted burden. He accepts her as though she is truly his niece.

'Thank you, my lord.'

He looked at Clara and his expression softened. 'You are a clever girl, saying my name. Will you say it again? For me?'

'Unc' Nannal,' Clara whispered.

Ravenwell beamed. 'Well done, poppet. Now, where's my goodnight kiss?

Clara toddled over to the Marquess, her arms stretched high, and he swung her aloft, kissing her soundly on her cheek. Her arms wrapped around his neck and she kissed him twice, firstly on his left cheek and then—crooning softly and chubby fingers stroking—she kissed him on his scarred cheek. Ravenwell's gaze flicked to Grace and then away. He turned from her, Clara still in his arms.

'Come.' His voice was gruff. 'Let Uncle Nathaniel see your new bedchamber.'

He strode from the room, leaving Grace to ponder that scene. She had thought Clara was scared of her uncle but— picturing again her first meeting with Clara, she now won-dered if her daughter's reluctance as she bumped down the stairs and dragged her feet across the hall was not wariness of the Marquess, but of Grace. The stranger.

That will teach me not to make assumptions.

A chastened Grace hurried from the room to join Raven-well and Clara in the child's bedchamber, which adjoined Grace's.

Grace froze by the door. Here, a fire had been lit—pre-sumably by the elusive Alice—and the room had taken on a warm glow. A rug lay before the fire and there, stretched full length, was Brack. He lifted his head to contemplate Grace and his tail thumped gently on the floor. Twice.

'I do not think...'

Grace's objection drifted into silence as Clara squirmed in her uncle's arms.

'Brack! Brack!'

The Marquess placed her on the floor and, squealing, she rushed over to the dog and launched herself on top of him, wrapping her arms around his neck as his tail con-tinued to wag.

Grace watched, open-mouthed.

'You do not think…?' Ravenwell's voice had a teasing note she had not heard before.

'It does not matter. Clara is clearly fond of Brack.'

'And *she* is not scared of him, despite his size.'

Grace bristled at his emphasis on *she*. 'No, but I did not know he was friendly when I first saw him.'

'That is true. And as you said earlier, you will soon become accustomed to the dogs.'

'I will try.'

Watching Clara with Brack warmed Grace's heart and she could not help smiling at the sight. She turned to the Marquess to comment on Clara's delight but, before she could speak, the good humour leached from Ravenwell's expression and he averted his face. It was only a fractional movement, but she did not miss it.

'Come, Brack.'

He stalked from the room.

Nathaniel sought the sanctuary of his book room. He stood by his desk, staring unseeingly at the surface, tracing with his forefinger the pits and scratches that had accumulated over the years, pondering his gut reaction to Miss Bertram.

Specifically, to Miss Bertram's smile.

Clara needed a governess. That was an irrefutable fact.

Grace Bertram had appeared on his doorstep at a time he was beginning to fear he would never find anyone willing to move to Shiverstone Hall and care for his niece. The alternative—moving back to Ravenwell Manor—had begun to haunt him. So, despite his reservations, he had offered Miss Bertram the post, secured her behind a door marked *Employee* in his mind and banished any thoughts of her as a female. She was as welcome or as unwelcome as any woman taking that post. Her looks were…*must be*… immaterial.

And then she had smiled. And the memories had swarmed up from the depths of his mind, overwhelming him with images from his past: the flirtations, the fun, the laughter.

Memories of how life had used to be.

Unwanted memories of pretty girls who would smile spontaneously at him.

An aggravating reminder of his world before he chose this reclusive life.

With a muttered curse, Nathaniel hauled his chair from under his desk, sat down and pulled a ledger towards him. He flipped it open and forcibly applied his mind to business until it was time to dress for dinner.

He always dined at six and he always—despite dining alone—dressed for dinner. It was the one custom he continued from his former life, allowing him the illusion he was still a gentleman. He contemplated his appearance in the mirror as he wound his neckcloth around his neck and tied it in a neat knot. Would Miss Bertram think he made this effort on her behalf?

And if she does, why should it matter? You are not answerable to her. You are answerable to no one.

The pit of his stomach tangled into knots as the evening ahead stretched before him. Something about the thought of sitting at the table with her, eating and talking, fuelled his vulnerability. But he was sure, once the meal was underway, those knots would untangle. Miss Bertram had already demonstrated a welcome lack of disgust at his scars and that would help him become less self-conscious.

And those memories that glorious smile of hers had awoken? They were just that. Memories. They could wield no power over him as long as he banished them from his mind.

He tugged a comb through the knots in his hair—the winds out on the fells had, as usual, played havoc with it. Should he ask Sharp to cut it? He ran his hand over the side of his face, feeling the now-familiar roughness, as though twists of rope lay beneath the surface. His hair helped to hide the worst of the ravages the fire had wrought, particularly into the hairline where some of his hair had not grown back, but it could not completely conceal it, so it served little purpose.

The sound of his bedchamber door opening jolted him from his musings.

'Sorry, milord,' Sharp said. 'I thought, with the time...'

'No, do not apologise,' Nathaniel said. 'I am late, but I am going down now, so you may continue.'

It was Sharp's custom to tidy Nathaniel's bedchamber and bank up the fire when Nathaniel went downstairs to eat his dinner.

Nathaniel ran down the stairs. The parlour door was ajar and he entered, stopping short on seeing the table was only set for one. He spun on his heel and made for the kitchen. Mrs Sharp was there, ladling food into a serving dish, whilst Ned—who ate all his meals at the Hall—and Alice both sat ready at the table, awaiting their supper, which would be served when Sharp finished upstairs.

'I heard you come down the stairs, milord. Your dinner is ready. I—'

'Why is there only one place set in the parlour, Mrs Sharp?'

The housekeeper frowned. 'I did not think you would want to dine with her, milord.'

Nathaniel bit back a terse retort. This was his fault. He had not specified where Miss Bertram would dine. He had made an assumption.

'A governess would not expect to dine in the kitchen,' he said, 'and it would be too much work for her to dine upstairs in her room. Be so good as to lay another place in the parlour, Mrs Sharp.'

'But...milord...'

'*Now*, please.'

The sound of a throat being cleared delicately behind him had him whirling to face the door. Miss Bertram stood there, hands clasped in front of her, fingers twisting together. She had changed into a dowdy grey dress and the slight blush that tinted her cheeks was the only hint of colour on her person.

'I do not mind where I eat, my lord,' she said.

He did not want a debate. 'I do,' he said. 'You will dine with me in the parlour. Set another place, Mrs Sharp.'

He gestured for Miss Bertram to precede him out of the kitchen. In the morning parlour, he pulled a chair out for her—choosing the place to his left—and then sat in his customary place at the head of the table.

Silence reigned.

Mrs Sharp came in, set a plate and cutlery in front of Miss Bertram and left again, spine rigid.

'Clara went to sleep without any problems.'

He grunted discouragingly.

'I thought you might like to know that.'

Mrs Sharp returned with a tray of serving dishes, saving him from further response.

'It is venison stew, milord.' She placed the first dish in the centre of the table. 'And there are potatoes and some of the pie from yesterday, warmed up.'

Miss Bertram smiled at Mrs Sharp. 'Thank you,' she said. 'It smells delicious.'

'Thank you.'

It was said grudgingly at the same time as the housekeeper darted a worried glance at Nathaniel. The Sharps had been with him since before the fire—had cared for him when the emotional pain had outstripped any physical pain resulting from his injuries, had remained loyal, burying themselves here at Shiverstone without complaint. They clearly worried over the choices he had made for his life.

'Yes, it does,' he said. 'Thank you, Mrs Sharp.'

And he meant for more than just the food. He understood

her concern and the reason why she had not set a place for Miss Bertram in the parlour. She was afraid for him.

Thank you for caring.

She treated him to a fleeting smile before she left the room to fetch the rest of the food.

Nathaniel glanced at Miss Bertram, who was watching him, a glint of speculation in her eyes. He quashed his instinct to avert his face. He could hardly fault her for being curious and he knew he must overcome his natural urge to hide his scars, as he had with his servants. They were impossible to hide; she would see them often enough and, to her credit, her reaction so far had been encouraging. The sooner she accepted his appearance, the sooner he could also forget about it and then his awkwardness would fade.

He reached for her plate to serve her some stew.

As they ate their meal, Nathaniel watched Miss Bertram surreptitiously. Why would such a young, beautiful girl choose to travel all this way north for a post in a bleak place like Shiverstone? She struck him as a sociable sort. It made little sense, but she was here now and he did not doubt she would care for Clara. Whatever the reason, he must count it as a blessing for his niece. He was certain Hannah and David would approve of Miss Bertram.

The thought of his sister and brother-in-law brought the usual swell of anguish, followed by another thought. Miss Bertram had shown no curiosity whatsoever about how Clara had come to be orphaned. She had not enquired once about Clara's parents. Would it not be natural to have some curiosity over how they had died?

Then his conscience pricked him. He had actively discouraged her from conversation, never stopping to consider that if Miss Bertram failed to settle at Shiverstone, she might leave. And then what would he do about Clara? Besides, no matter how he had chosen to live these past nine years, he was still a gentleman and this prolonged silence at the dinner table went against every tenet of his upbringing.

'What made you choose to come to Shiverstone?'

There was a slight choking noise from the woman to his right. His fault, surprising her with a sudden question whilst she was eating.

'Were there no positions closer to where you grew up? Wiltshire, was it not?'

Miss Bertram cleared her throat, then sipped her wine. 'My uncle encouraged me to look for a post outside the county.' She directed a wry smile at her plate, avoiding eye contact. 'He did not want the embarrassment of his niece working for someone he is acquainted with.' There was a hint of disgust in her tone. 'I was the last of my friends to leave the school after our training finished, but when I went back to my uncle's house it was clear I was not welcome. My father had bequeathed me a little money, so I took a room in a lodging house in Cheltenham…and…and I heard about this post and I thought it would be interesting to see the North Country.'

'It is certainly a long way from Salisbury. And Cheltenham. Does it meet your expectations?'

'I…I…no, if I am to be honest. It is wilder than I imagined, but it is very…impressive, also.'

'And do you think you will grow to like it?'

'Oh, yes.' Her vehemence surprised him. 'I am certain of it.'

Nathaniel chewed another mouthful of venison. Was she running from something? Is that why she was content to bury herself out here? He had not yet penned his letter to this Madame Dubois. He would ask her, couching his question in discreet terms.

'If I might ask…' Miss Bertram hesitated. Her head was bent, her concentration still on her plate of food. 'I have no wish to revive painful memories, but I should like to know a little of Clara's parents. So I may speak to her of them.'

Almost as though she senses my suspicions.

'The memories are not all painful.' He closed his eyes, allowing his thoughts to travel back. 'Hannah was a year younger than me and we were very close growing up. There is a portrait of her in the dining room, painted by David, my brother-in-law, if you would care to see it. It is under a dust cover.'

He told himself he covered the picture to protect Clara, but he knew, deep down, it was because he could not bear seeing Hannah's likeness after her death, so he had removed it from the drawing-room wall.

Out of sight, out of mind. Except that did not really work.

'David was a fine artist and painted landscapes for the most part, but he painted Hannah and they presented the result to me when they were last here in June.'

Under the pretence of sipping his wine, Nathaniel swallowed his burgeoning pain. *Concentrate on the happy times.* 'Hannah loved to sing and to play the pianoforte.'

'She sounds a lovely lady. Let us hope Clara will remember something of her and her father.'

'I hope so. She had a fine character and she always remained positive, even in the face of heartache.'

'Heartache?'

The question dropped into the silence. He had said more than he meant to. They had both finished eating and Miss Bertram leant forward, her gaze intense.

'She was unable to bear children. Clara was adopted.'

There was another silence. Miss Bertram pressed her lips together and her lashes swept down, casting a lacy shadow on her cheeks as she fidgeted with the knife and fork she had placed neatly on her empty plate. Her hands were small and delicate, with slender fingers and beautifully shaped oval nails.

She cleared her throat. 'I…I did not know that.'

'As far as Hannah and David were concerned, Clara was theirs. They doted on her. She was such a happy little girl. So very much wanted and loved.'

She raised her head, her large gold-green eyes shimmering as they reflected the candlelight. 'She will be again. I promise you that.'

Chapter Six

Nathaniel's heart lightened at the sincerity that shone through Miss Bertram's words. Here was someone who would help him. The responsibility—he would never call it a burden—of raising Clara and making her happy was no longer his alone. Only now did he recognise the deep-seated worries that had plagued him ever since he read his mother's letter. Only now could he contemplate the coming months and years with a sense of peace and control.

'Thank you.'

Her fine brows drew together. 'Why do you thank me, my lord?' Her eyes searched his.

Nathaniel spoke from his heart. 'I am grateful you are prepared to live out here in order to help me raise Clara. I pray you will remain for a very long time. I do not wish my niece to suffer any more abandonment in her life.'

She stared at him, wordlessly, then dropped her gaze to her plate again. He had to strain to make out her next words.

'I will never abandon her a—'

Her jaw snapped shut and Nathaniel wondered what she had been about to say. Then she hauled in a deep breath, looked up and smiled, driving further conjecture from his mind. The glory of that smile, once again, hit him with the force of a punch to his gut. How long had it been since a woman had smiled at him…genuinely, and not forced or with disgust in her eyes? For the second time that evening, he battened down his visceral reaction. Miss Bertram was his employee. It behoved him, as a gentleman, to protect her, not to lust after her. He made himself imagine her likely reaction to any hint of an approach from him and the thought of her disgust had the same effect on his desire that a sudden squall might have on a summer's day. The resulting chill chased over his skin and his insides shrivelled, as though by shrinking away from his surface they might protect him from the result of his momentary lapse.

The door opened and Sharp ambled in, bringing with him the smell of a brewery. Nathaniel did not grudge him his weakness. At least the man did not overindulge through the day and he deserved some compensation for moving to Shiverstone and leaving his friends and his favourite alehouse in Harrogate behind. Normally garrulous in the evening, Sharp cleared the dishes in silence and, shortly after he left the room, Mrs Sharp came, carrying a warm pie—apple, by the smell of it—and a jug of cream.

Nathaniel took advantage of the distraction to study the newest member of his household even further. So very delicate and pretty, with fine cheekbones and clear skin and silky, blonde hair…no wonder he had been momentarily attracted to her. Familiarity would help. He would cease to notice her appearance, much as she would cease to notice his scars. At least Clara would be cared for and happy.

'I am pleased to hear you say that,' he said, resulting in a swift sideways glance from Mrs Sharp, whose long nose appeared to twitch, as if to say, *What are you talking about?*

Miss Bertram pursed her lips, her eyes dancing, as she watched the housekeeper.

'Mrs Sharp—' amusement bubbled through her voice '—the stew was delicious and the pie smells wonderful. I can see I shall have to restrain my appetite if I am not to increase to the size of a house.'

'Hmmph. I am sure it matters not to anyone here if you should gain weight, miss.'

Miss Bertram's gaze flicked to meet Nathaniel's and this time he was certain she was biting back a smile. A conspirator's smile. He had talked overmuch. Given her the impression they were allies. Even that they might become friends. Every instinct he possessed told him to beware.

'When you have finished your dessert, you may use the book room to write those letters we discussed,' he said.

He steeled his heart against the hurt that flashed across her face. Better she did not get the wrong impression. He was not here to be her friend.

'Mrs Sharp, please be so good as to serve tea to Miss Bertram in the book room. Shall we say in fifteen minutes? And tell Sharp to bring my brandy here.'

'Yes, milord.' Such satisfaction communicated in just two words.

They finished their meal in silence.

What to write?

Grace brushed the untrimmed end of the quill pen against her cheek as she pondered how much she should reveal to Miss Fanworth.

The letter to her uncle had been easy: an enquiry after his health and that of the rest of the family, the news that she had obtained a position as governess to the niece of the Marquess of Ravenwell and her address, should they wish to contact her. She decided, with an inner *hmmph*, that it would be unwise for her to hold her breath waiting for that last to occur.

But… Miss Fanworth… She bent her head and began to write.

My dear Miss Fanworth,
I hope you will be happy to know that I found my
child. She is happy and loved, and I am reassured

that she is well cared for, so I am content. Thank you so much for trusting me with the names of her new parents. I shall be in your debt for ever.

I must also acquaint you with my good fortune in securing a position as governess for the Marquess of Ravenwell. He has the intention of writing to Madame for a reference—despite your letter of recommendation—and I am hopeful that she will find it in her heart to dwell less upon my early escapades and more upon my later years at the school when she pens that reference!

My new address is at the top of this letter and I would count myself fortunate if you might write to me once in a while to tell me how everyone at school fares. Please, also, should you write to them, communicate my address to my dear friends Rachel, Joanna, and Isabel. Might I also request that you send on any letters addressed to me that may have arrived at the school?

Please convey my most sincere regards to Madame and to the other teachers and staff.
Your very grateful former pupil,
Grace Bertram

Grace read and reread her effort anxiously. No, she had not lied, but she had successfully masked the truth. If Madame was to discover the actuality of her new position, she would surely inform his lordship and he would banish her immediately.

She could not fathom the brusque Marquess. His initial reluctance to converse over their meal had disappointed, but not surprised her—no one would choose to live such a reclusive life if they craved company. But the man was not shy and, in Grace's opinion, it was plain bad manners not to make the smallest effort at civilised conversation. Although—she had told herself as she concentrated on her meal—she must remember she was only the governess and not a guest to be treated with due deference.

But then he began to talk and she had relaxed, thinking he was merely unused to company. And her thoughts had raced ahead and, in her imagination, she helped him to overcome his awkwardness and taught him to enjoy socialising, for Clara's sake, and the house would be filled with light and laughter…but then Mrs Sharp—that wicked old crow—had come in and jerked her back to reality and Ravenwell had pokered up all over again.

The prospect of the evenings to come filled her with dismay, but at least she would not lack company entirely at Shiverstone Hall. Sharp was as affable as his wife was hostile, Alice, the newly arrived fourteen-year-old housemaid, was a plump chatterbox and Ned, although he had little to say, did not appear unfriendly.

And there was always Clara. A warm, comforting glow spread through Grace. Her child. The days ahead would be filled with Clara, and the Marquess and his moodiness, and Mrs Sharp and her meanness could go to… Grace squashed that thought before it could form into the word in her brain. She was a mother now, with responsibilities. She was no longer a rebellious girl with a penchant for trouble.

Her letter would suffice. She would leave her letters with his lordship's, on the console table in the hall, for Ned to take to Shivercombe village in the morning.

She leaned back in Ravenwell's chair, her lids heavy. It had been an exhausting day, both physically and emotionally. The homesickness for her school days and for the companionship, laughter and love of her friends welled up, and hot tears prickled. She blinked furiously. Life had taught her that self-pity was not an option. It achieved nothing. She and her friends were grown women now. She'd wager *they* were not wallowing in nostalgia, but embracing their new lives with hope and confidence.

Well, she was sure Isabel and Rachel would be doing just that, but what of gentle, reserved Joanna, abandoned on the doorstep of Madame's school as a baby? She had been taken in and brought up by Madame and the other teachers and it had been a lonely existence until the age of nine, when other girls her age were taken in as boarders. Grace, Isabel, and Rachel were the closest to family Joanna had ever known and she prayed the family who had employed her would be kind.

As for Rachel, there was no doubt in Grace's mind her independent, self-sufficient friend would be in her element with the opportunity to travel to exotic places after she had been employed by a sheikh, in the kingdom of Huria. The girls had found the country on the map—beyond the furthest reaches of the Mediterranean Sea—and Grace had marvelled at the distance Rachel must travel. Journeying as far as Shiverstone Hall had been quite far enough!

And Isabel—a momentary disquiet sneaked through Grace. There had been something about Isabel and her insouciance when she left the school. Her meek acceptance of her future as a governess had seemed out of character, when they all knew her great ambition was to become a famous singer. Would she settle in her new life? Or would she risk everything in her bid for excitement?

She longed to hear all their news and hoped that, as promised, they had written to her care of the school as she had not known where she might eventually find employment. Selfishly, she was relieved she had mislaid her friends' addresses during her travels for, even if she *could* write to them today, how much of the truth would she dare reveal? Could she admit the reality of her new situation? She had never kept secrets from them before, not even the greatest secret of her life, when she discovered she was with child, but…would they understand what she had done, or would they condemn? They would worry about her, of that she was certain.

* * *

That brief interlude, when Lord Ravenwell had reminisced so movingly about his sister, might never have happened. Over her first few days at Shiverstone Hall, Grace barely saw her employer. He only appeared at dinner, dressed in his black tail coat and meticulously knotted neckcloth, adorned with a ruby pin. He remained distant and, after another few abortive attempts at conversation, Grace gave up. Her days were long and full, and by the evening she was exhausted, so she followed her employer's lead and ate in silence.

The quietness and calm of their meals gave her time to think. Time to wonder why he lived as a recluse, what had caused his scars, why he had talked that one time on her first night and then clammed up. He was a puzzling man.

The silence also gave her time to observe. He had been a handsome man. Still was, if one ignored the scarring. The skin of his jaw and up the side of his face on the right-hand side was uneven and pale in contrast to the rest of his face, which was lightly tanned, no doubt from exposure to the sun and the wind out on the fells.

Then, one evening when he was in his cups and his wife was out of earshot, Sharp had told her how his lordship had been burned nine years ago in a fire at Ravenwell Manor. A fire that had killed his father. Before that Ravenwell had been one of society's most eligible bachelors and had led a carefree life filled with fun and pleasure. The fire had scarred more than his skin, Sharp had slurred. It had scarred the very essence of the man. Grace's natural sympathy had been stirred, but she knew the Marquess would not wish for pity and so she said nothing. But still she wondered at the reclusive life he led. He must be lonely.

His size no longer intimidated her, but his silence did. And his dogs—other than Brack, to whom she was slowly becoming accustomed. Ravenwell spent much of his time outside and, although Grace and Clara ventured into the fresh air almost every day, they remained close by the house and they saw nothing of Clara's uncle. Grace's heart bled for Clara. For all his lordship's fine talk about not wanting his niece's life disrupted, what did he think he was doing now by avoiding all contact with her every day? He might just as well not live here, for all Clara saw of him.

Grace kept her counsel. For the time being. For now, she was content to expend her energy in making their upstairs rooms more homely and in coaxing smiles and more words from her daughter.

Chapter Seven

'Good afternoon.'

It was the fourth day of her new life at Shiverstone Hall. Grace and Clara had been playing on the lawn in front of the house and now Clara was chirruping away to herself as she gathered pretty stones from the carriageway, piling them into a heap. Grace tore her attention from Clara, shielding her eyes against the low-lying sun. A young man, clad in a black coat and black, low-crowned hat, stood a few yards away, smiling at her.

'Good afternoon. Mr...?'

'Rendell. Ralph Rendell.' He raised his hat, revealing a mop of curly light brown hair. 'I am the curate at St Mary's.'

Grace's ignorance of the existence of St Mary's must have shown in her expression for Mr Rendell laughed, and said, 'The church in Shivercombe village.'

'I am pleased to meet you, Mr Rendell. Are you a frequent visitor to the Hall?'

The curate's smile broadened. 'And that, I surmise, is a delicate way of enquiring the purpose of my visit.'

Grace bit her lip against her answering smile.

'My visit,' he continued, 'appears to have already achieved its purpose.'

'Which was?'

'To satisfy myself as to your safety, Miss...?'

'Oh, I am sorry. I am Miss Bertram. Miss Grace Bertram.'

Mr Rendell bowed. 'I am delighted to make your acquaintance, Miss Bertram. Am I correct in assuming you are the young lady who enquired for directions to the Hall in Shivercombe last Tuesday and has not been seen since?'

'Yes, indeed,' Grace replied. 'I came in response to an advertisement for the post of governess.' She felt her face heat and, unable to meet his eyes after such a blatant lie to a man of God, she lowered her gaze to Clara, who now stood watching them, her thumb jammed in her mouth. Grace bent and gently tugged at Clara's hand. 'No, sweetie. Your hands are dirty.'

'To this little one? So the rumours *were* true. I did not know the Marquess had a child.'

'Clara is his lordship's niece. She is an orphan.'

Except she still has me, even though she will never know it. Poor Clara: her adoptive parents dead, her father killed at the Battle of Bussaco and me, her real mother, never able to tell her the truth.

Grace buried the sorrows of the past as Clara crouched down again to continue piling up stones. She was here now. That was all that mattered.

'Why should you have a concern for my safety, sir?'

'There was a certain amount of disquiet in the village after you failed to return. Lord Ravenwell is something of an enigma to the good folk of Shivercombe and—in the nature of filling the vacuum resulting from his servants' most unsatisfactory refusal to gossip about him—the villagers have developed their own theories and stories about this place and its master.'

Grace laughed. 'Yes. I recall. When I asked for directions, I was earnestly advised not to risk coming here. But I am pleased I did.'

Those tales had strengthened her resolve to find her daughter.

'And I am pleased to discover you safe and well, Miss Bertram.' Mr Rendell smiled, his hazel eyes creasing at the outer corners. He squatted next to Clara and handed her an attractively veined stone to add to her pile. 'And to make the acquaintance of this little treasure.'

Clara smiled at the curate. 'Fank 'oo.'

'She has beautiful eyes,' Mr Rendell said. 'A most unusual colour.'

Grace strived to sound nonchalant. 'They are lovely indeed.' She bent to take Clara's hand. 'Come, sweetie. It is time we went indoors.'

Mr Rendell stood up and brushed at the hem of his coat, before smiling at Grace. 'And it is time I took my leave of you. I have achieved what I set out to accomplish.'

Guilt over her abruptness prompted Grace to say, 'Would you care for a cup of tea, Mr Rendell? Did you walk all the way here?'

'No, I drove. I left my gig at the stable yard with Tam.' He stared up at the Hall, scanning the frontage, then returned his gaze to Grace. 'Yes, I should welcome a cup of tea, Miss Bertram. Thank you.' His reply was laced with determination.

Grace puzzled over the curate's tone as she led the way to the front door. He had given the impression of a man waging an internal battle...no doubt he was fully aware her enigmatic employer discouraged visitors. But good manners dictated she should offer her visitor some hospitality. After all, he had come all this way, merely to assure himself of her well-being.

Conscious she might be violating an unwritten rule that strangers were not to be invited inside the Hall, Grace lifted the latch and, straightening her spine, marched into the entrance hall. Mrs Sharp was descending the stairs and Grace's courage almost failed at the sight of the hostile housekeeper. Almost, but not quite, for Clara must meet and socialise with others if she was not to grow up shy and awkward in company. And did not she... Grace...deserve to have some friends outside the Hall?

'Mrs Sharp,' she said, 'this is...' Her words faded into silence as Mrs Sharp smoothed her hair back with both hands before hurrying down the remaining stairs, a welcoming smile on her face.

Well!

'Mr Rendell, how very good of you to call. Miss Bertram, please show our visitor into the drawing room and I will bring you refreshments.'

'You have been here before?' Grace asked the curate as she sat down.

'No, never. Mrs Sharp is a regular at church, however, so we are acquainted, although it must be a month since her last attendance. I confess I am a little bemused by her welcome—such visits have been positively discouraged in the past.'

'Does Lord Ravenwell attend church as well?'

'No. We have never seen him in the village. All the servants come to church, when the weather permits, for the track between here and the village can become treacherous in inclement weather. They do not mix with the villagers, however. That fact, in itself, spawns even more speculation about his lordship.' He leaned forward, suddenly intense. 'You are happy here, Miss Bertram? You must know you can rely upon me to help if ever you need it.'

'I am...content enough, sir.'

Was she happy? She was thrilled to be with Clara and nothing would tear her away. But happy with the rest of her situation? With her brusque employer and the taciturn housekeeper—although Mrs Sharp had been surprisingly helpful with Grace's efforts to refurbish the nursery wing upstairs once she accepted there was no criticism of her housekeeping skills. Or with the regularly tipsy Sharp and friendly but unsophisticated Alice? It was too soon to say. And yet, what choice did she have? She had nowhere else to go. And Clara needed her.

'But I thank you for your concern and you may rest assured you will be the first person to whom I shall apply should I ever need help.'

'Then I am satisfied. And I shall look forward to seeing you on the morrow in church, together with this little one.' He reached out and ruffled Clara's curls and she tilted her head to stare at him from her seat on the rug. 'It is never too early to educate a child in the ways of the Lord.'

'I shall be there.'

Grace's heart lifted. It might only be a church service, but it would break the monotony of life at the Hall. So far, she had ventured no further than the kitchen garden to watch Sharp digging the soil in preparation for planting in the spring.

'If not this week, then next,' she continued, 'for I have no idea how we might get to the village. Clara cannot walk that far.'

'You may ride in the carriage with Annie and me.' Mrs Sharp had returned and was pouring the tea. She passed a cup to Mr Rendell and then one to Grace. 'Ned usually drives us and Sharp sits with him up on the box whilst Tam rides.'

Grace stared at the change in the housekeeper—was this all to impress the curate with her good Christian values?

Before she could respond, the sound of boots on the flags of the hall floor rang out.

Clara scrambled to her feet. 'Unc' Nanniel,' she said.

Nathaniel strode through the hall, Brack at his heels. A morning out on the fells, flying Amber, had given him a raging appetite. He was delighted with the eagle's progress. Her wing was growing stronger and she was becoming accustomed to hunting again, in preparation for her release back into the wild.

A scuffle from the direction of the drawing room distracted him. He stopped, then forgot his hunger as a beaming Clara erupted from the room, arms aloft.

'Unc' Nanniel!'

'Clara!'

He bent to catch her up in his arms, then swung her in a wide circle, revelling in her giggles. He hugged her close and kissed her cheek. How he had missed her.

Your fault, came the silent riposte.

It was true. He had deliberately avoided Miss Bertram—and thus, by association, Clara—since her arrival. That first evening, he had found himself relaxing…talking too much…*revealing* too much. He did not want a friend. The danger of becoming dependent upon her company, upon *anyone's* company, disturbed his sleep. What if she did not stay after all? He could not bear to become accustomed to her company and then lose it, leaving him to endure the agony of readjusting to his self-imposed exile.

It was bad enough having to dine together every evening. The silence—yet again, his choice—gave him too much time to think. And to remember. Miss Bertram, with her delicate lily-of-the-valley scent, her prettiness and her femininity was a constant reminder of what he had given up and an ever-growing challenge to his male instincts, kept suppressed for so very long. Not that he would ever risk an overture towards her. A beauty like Miss Bertram would be disgusted by the mere thought of intimacy with a man like him. Besides, the standards he expected of himself would not allow him to take advantage of an innocent woman in his employ.

But…he was increasingly irked by his own behaviour. It smacked of cowardice. If Miss Bertram should decide to leave, then he would simply have to deal with it. He had dealt with worse things. Hannah's face floated into his mind, and his heart clenched. *Far worse.* He would put his caution aside and accept Miss Bertram's presence in his household. He could not run away for ever. He strode towards the drawing room. Clara had come from there. Ergo, Miss Bertram must be in there.

It was time he changed.

He walked in through the door and slammed to a halt as he took in the three faces turned towards him. Of the three, both Mrs Sharp and Miss Bertram wore identical expressions of consternation. The third—a young man— smiled as he rose to his feet and extended his right hand.

'I beg you will forgive my intrusion, sir. Ralph Rendell, curate of St Mary's, at your service.' The young man did not approach Nathaniel, but remained standing with his hand thrust out, a confident smile on his face. His clear-skinned, handsome face.

Nathaniel put Clara down and walked towards the young curate, fighting the urge to twist his neck to shield his scars from Rendell. He shook the proffered hand, steeling himself not to flinch as the other man's fingers closed around his hand, touching the scarring on the back of his hand, even though it gave him no physical pain. The curate showed no flicker of reaction and some of Nathaniel's tension dissipated.

'Ravenwell.'

He gestured to the other man to sit, aware he now had two choices. He could stalk out. It was common knowledge visitors were not welcome at the Hall and no one would be surprised. Or he could be a gentleman. Only moments ago he had accepted it was time to change. Out of the corner of his eye he saw Miss Bertram chew at her bottom lip, worry creasing her brow. Her clear unease settled the matter.

'Mrs Sharp, be so good as to bring another cup, will you?' And he sat down.

Clara immediately clambered on to his lap and settled into the crook of his arm, sighing contentedly.

'Clara is happy to see you, my lord.'

He caught the hint of reproach. 'I have been busy these past days,' he said. It was true. Gradually accustoming Amber to flying and to her new freedom had taken much of his time. He bent his head, rubbing his cheek against Clara's. 'I am happy to see you too, poppet.'

Clara pulled her thumb from her mouth with a pop. 'Unc' Nanniel,' she whispered.

Nathaniel turned his attention to Mr Rendell. 'It is seldom we get visitors to the Hall, Rendell.'

'Indeed.' Light brown eyes regarded him steadily. 'I came to ensure myself of Miss Bertram's well-being.'

Nathaniel heard Miss Bertram's stifled gasp and felt his brows snap together in a frown.

'Well-being?'

Rendell continued to hold his gaze. 'Yes. She was known to have come out to Shiverstone on Tuesday last. I came to make certain of her safe arrival.'

Tactful wording. Nathaniel could not but be impressed by the young man's courage in braving Nathaniel's carefully nurtured reputation to ensure the safety of a stranger.

'Most commendable.'

Mrs Sharp bustled in with another cup and a plate piled with slabs of fruit cake. Nathaniel's stomach growled at the sight, his hunger pangs resurfacing with a vengeance. He accepted a slice of cake and bit into it as Mrs Sharp poured him a cup of tea.

'I have promised Mr Rendell that Clara and I will attend the church service tomorrow,' Miss Bertram said. 'That is, if you are happy to give your permission, my lord?'

With his mouth full of cake, Nathaniel could not immediately reply.

'I am sure his lordship will not stand in the way of your moral enlightenment, Miss Bertram,' Rendell said.

Nathaniel swallowed his food. 'I would not dream of objecting to your attendance at church, Miss Bertram.'

'And,' Rendell continued, 'I would deem it an honour if you would call upon us at the rectory if you can spare the time to visit Shivercombe, Miss Bertram. The rector's daughter is a similar age to yourself, and...' he leant over to tickle under Clara's chin, causing her to squirm with delight '...we have a litter of kittens this young lady might enjoy meeting.'

'Kittens, Clara! How exciting.' Miss Bertram switched her attention from Clara to the curate. 'I am sure she would love to see them, sir. She already takes great delight in his lordship's dogs. But will you not be too busy, with tomorrow being Sunday?'

'Oh, I did not mean tomorrow. You will surely welcome an excuse to visit your neighbours on occasion. After all, living in seclusion is not everybody's choice.'

Nathaniel bit back an angry retort. How dare Rendell chastise him in his own house, and back him into a corner like this?

Outmanoeuvred, by God...and by a man of God, at that.

Then his exasperation subsided, to be replaced by an impulse to laugh. What was he thinking? Was it his intention to keep Miss Bertram a prisoner at the Hall? He had chosen not to mix with his neighbours, but had no justification for forcing her to do likewise. And it would be good for Clara.

'You are right,' he said. 'Can you drive?' he added, to Miss Bertram.

'No.' It was said with regret. 'My uncle did not think it worth having me taught. I thank you for your offer, Mr Rendell, but I am afraid I am unable to accept your invitation.'

'Your man rides or drives in most days, does he not, my lord? Surely Miss Bertram and Clara could come in with him?'

'They could, but he normally leaves here very early and returns immediately. It would not be long enough for a social visit.'

The stubborn tilt of the curate's chin suggested he would

not easily give in, prompting Nathaniel to add, 'You may drive yourself to the village in the gig, Miss Bertram. Our old cob, Bill, is perfectly safe.'

She gasped, pink infusing her cheeks, her green eyes sparkling with excitement. Was she so very eager to get away from the Hall? No sooner had the question formed in his mind than he realised its absurdity. Of course she would be eager to meet other people. What fun was it to be isolated out here with a two-year-old, an employer who barely spoke to her and a bunch of servants?

'That would be…but no. I…I do not know if I could. I am not used to horses.'

'Nonsense. Bill is an old hand. He knows the way to and from the village with his eyes shut and he never gets above a slow trot. I will teach you. You will cope admirably, I am certain.'

As he spoke, Miss Bertram smiled at Rendell with such pleasure Nathaniel's stomach twisted tight. He eyed the curate's clear, handsome countenance and experienced a sharp pang that no woman would ever again look at him in such a way.

No woman or Miss Bertram, specifically?

He surged to his feet and handed a dozing Clara to Miss Bertram, goaded by that snide voice in his head.

I am not jealous of Rendell. I merely do not want people here, in my house.

His reputation had kept visitors at bay for almost nine years and yet, less than a week after Miss Bertram's arrival, his home was already invaded. It was more than a man should have to bear.

See the effect of a pretty face on a man? You do right to keep your distance. Would Rendell be here if the governess was an old harridan?

He thrust aside the thought he was being unfair to Rendell. He was in no mood to be reasonable—he did not want people here. He preferred his animals and his birds for company.

'Thank you for calling.' He forced a pleasant tone. 'I apologise, but I have urgent matters needing my attention.'

Rendell stood and Nathaniel shook his hand.

'I am pleased to have made your acquaintance at long last, my lord. Dare I hope we might see you in church one of these Sundays?'

Nathaniel stared at him, then turned on his heel and stalked from the room.

Impudent devil!

Chapter Eight

'Mrs Sharp.'

The housekeeper paused in the act of serving the evening meal. 'Yes, milord?'

'On Monday morning I shall require you to set aside an hour or two to watch Clara, if you please.'

'Yes, milord.'

He waited until Mrs Sharp left the room before saying, 'On Monday I shall instruct you on harnessing and driving Bill, Miss Bertram.'

He was tempted to relegate the task to Tam but, once the idea of teaching her himself had taken hold in his head, he could not relinquish it. She finished chewing her mouthful of food, then turned to look at him, her green eyes glittering. She was so beautiful, whereas he…he fought his usual battle not to move his head to hide his scars. Stupid, mindless reaction. She knew he had scars so what point was there in turning away?

'I am grateful, but there is no need for Clara to stay with Mrs Sharp. She can come with us. She will not be in the way.'

'Clara likes Mrs Sharp. You need not think she will be unhappy staying in the kitchen with her. Besides, it will do Clara good to be watched by someone other than you, in case—'

'In case what? In case I leave her?'

Nathaniel put down his knife and fork to give himself time to think. Why had she almost bitten his head off? Her head was bent, a muscle twitching in her cheek as she pushed her food around her plate with her fork.

She flicked a glance at him. 'I apologise. I did not mean to interrupt.'

'If you had allowed me to finish my sentence, I was about to say in case you are ever ill or indisposed,' he said. 'Mrs Sharp may be a little…sharp, for want of a better word, but she is fond of Clara.'

'I am aware of that. It was not for that reason I spoke as I did. I should not have done so, but…'

She had begun speaking with such resolve, but now she hesitated, her eyes searching his, the golden flecks in her irises reflecting the light of the candles. Nathaniel's nerves jangled a warning that he might not care for what she was about to say. He waited for her to continue.

'When I first came here, you said Clara had faced enough disruption in her life.'

'You cannot believe that staying with Mrs Sharp constitutes disruption.'

'No, of course I do not. But…your inference was that Clara should not have to cope with losing anyone else from her life.' Her head tilted and she raised her brows. 'What about you?'

'Me?' His voice deepened into a growl. 'What the dev… deuce do you mean by that?'

Her indrawn breath sounded loud in the silence. 'Her parents died. She has been here only a few weeks, getting used to you, and then I arrive. Other than this afternoon, she has not set her eyes on her Uncle Nathaniel since last Tuesday.'

He liked the way she said his name. *Nathaniel*. He thrust

that wayward thought aside and concentrated on her meaning. And, with a sense of shame, he realised she was right. That afternoon he had accepted he must change, but he still had not recognised the effect of his behaviour on Clara.

He recalled Miss Bertram's gentle rebuke: *'Clara is happy to see you, my lord.'*

In his efforts to shield himself he had failed to protect Clara from the very thing she must fear—losing someone else she loved. No wonder she had been so delighted to see him earlier and no wonder she had clung to him later, when he had said goodnight to her as she was about to go upstairs to get ready for her bedtime.

Miss Bertram continued to eat her meal, but her attention did not waver, stirring…what? Not discomfort. Not any more. Already he was becoming accustomed to her presence. And he wasn't annoyed by her presumption. Rather, he was intrigued by her pluck and determination. He could not condemn her concern for Clara's happiness.

'I stand chastised,' he said. 'And I thank you for pointing out my dereliction of duty.'

Her eyes blazed, shooting golden sparks. *'Duty?'*

He stiffened. 'You forget yourself, Miss Bertram.'

She took no notice. 'A child does not require *duty* from those upon whom she is entirely dependent. She requires… *needs*…love. And…and *time*. And—'

Nathaniel held up his hands, palms facing her, fingers spread. 'Enough! I concede. It was poor phrasing on my part and you are right. I shall ensure I spend more time with Clara in future. In the meantime, I hope you can accept she will not suffer if Mrs Sharp cares for her on Monday. Bill is docile, but I do not think harnessing a horse to a carriage should be undertaken with a young child underfoot. She will be much better off in the warm kitchen.'

Miss Bertram bowed her head. 'Agreed.'

They finished eating in their now customary silence but, as Sharp brought in the brandy at the end of their meal and

Miss Bertram stood to withdraw, an unexpected yearning for company beset Nathaniel.

'I shall take my brandy in the drawing room tonight, Sharp. And please tell Mrs Sharp to send in an additional cup with the tea tray.'

'Very well, milord.'

'Do you play chess, Miss Bertram? I have a fancy for a game.'

'I do not, my lord.'

'Would you care to learn?' He easily interpreted the doubt in those gold-green eyes of hers. 'There is no compulsion. I shall not dismiss you from your post if you refuse. We could as easily play a hand or two of cards.'

'I should like to learn the game. I have been told in the past that chess is a game the female mind cannot comprehend.' Her lips firmed, then she smiled, raising her chin. 'I viewed that as a challenge, but had no opportunity to discover whether he spoke the truth.'

'He?'

Grace did not immediately respond. They walked side by side to the drawing room and a sideways glance revealed a frown line between her brows and a wash of pink across her cheeks.

'He was an old friend.' There was the slightest tremble in her voice. 'He went away to be a soldier.'

A suitor, perhaps?

She had told him the barest of bones of her life before she had come to Shiverstone Hall. Would she ever reveal the flesh of her past? He would not ask. Why would he need to know about her life before? She was a governess. That was all he needed to know. That, and how well she cared for his niece.

They entered the drawing room.

Ah. He halted.

'The chess table,' he said. 'I forgot. It was stored away.' There had been no need to keep it out: gathering dust, creating work for Mrs Sharp, reviving painful memories for him. David had been his only opponent since he had moved here after the fire. And now...with David gone...

He tamped down the stab of pain and regret, turned on his heel and strode towards the dining room, grabbing a candlestick from a table as he passed. A patter of feet followed him.

'I can manage,' he said.

'It will be easier with two of us,' she said, sounding a touch breathless.

Nathaniel shortened his strides and a gurgled laugh reached his ears. He glanced down at Miss Bertram, now by his side.

Her eyes twinkled. 'It is hard work to keep stride with you, my lord. You have very long legs compared to mine.'

Nathaniel grunted at that naïve remark, his imagination delving under her ugly brown dress to the slim legs he suspected were hidden beneath. It took no effort to recall that glimpse of shapely ankle on her first day here. He tried to empty his mind of such thoughts the second they surfaced, but it was too late—his pulse had already accelerated. And the picture his wayward mind painted was not easily dismissed.

He directed his thoughts to the whereabouts of the table in a room filled with numerous unrecognisable items draped in holland covers.

'There.'

He pointed to a shrouded shape near the window. He tugged at the sheet covering it, revealing the chess table, a gift from Hannah and David. He smoothed his hand across the cool surface of the chessboard, created from sixty-four squares of attractively veined Italian marble set into a fine rosewood surround. Memories of a very different kind flooded his brain, dousing that inappropriate surge of lust.

'It is beautiful.'

He started as she copied his action, stroking the table

with reverence. The sight of her elegant hand, with its slender fingers and perfect oval nails, next to his ugly skin churned his stomach and he snatched his hand away.

He sensed her quick glance, but kept his eyes averted.

'How can you bear to hide such craftsmanship away?'

He bent to lift the table. 'It is not heavy. I do not need your help.'

'Where are the chess men?'

'Inside the table. The top is hinged.'

He carried it to the door, then hesitated, looking back. Miss Bertram stood stock still, gazing around the room, a speculative look on her face.

'Do not forget the candle,' he said.

She snatched up the candlestick and hurried after him.

He set the table near the window and dragged the two wooden chairs close so they could play. As he did so, Miss Bertram lifted the top of the table and peered inside.

'Draughts! We used to play draughts sometimes at the school, my friends and I.' At first delighted, her tone became wistful. 'Isabel taught us.'

'Isabel?'

'One of my best friends at school. There were four of us.' Her head snapped up, her eyes sparkling. 'May we play draughts? I do know how to play that game.'

'Are you backing away from that challenge you spoke of, Miss Bertram?'

She blushed. 'No, of course not.'

'Good. I shall teach you the basics tonight: what the pieces are called, how they may be moved and the aim of the game, which is to trap your opponent's king in such a way he has no safe square to move to.'

'And then you can kill him?'

She said it with such relish, he was startled into laughing.

'I trust you refer to the king and not your actual opponent?'

'For the moment.' She peeped saucily at him through her lashes, triggering a tug of response deep inside him.

How long was it since he had enjoyed a joke? He concentrated on keeping their conversation to the rules of chess.

'No, the king can never be removed from the board. It is sufficient to have surrounded him. Your opponent then surrenders his king and you have won the game. It is called checkmate.'

Her fine brows gathered into a frown. 'That seems very odd to me. I should rather kill the king. Then there would be no room for doubt.'

Nathaniel listed the different pieces on the board, explaining how each man could be moved and how important it was to plan several moves ahead and guard against losing the most valuable men.

'So…this one…' she reached out and picked up the black knight '…can move like so?' She put the piece on the wrong square.

'No, no. The knight's movement is the trickiest of all the moves to remember. He can move in an "L" shape. So—' he used his left hand to demonstrate '—from this square, this knight can move to here…and here…and…'

'And here!'

Her hand darted out and, before he could withdraw his own, she grasped his hand and tugged, sliding hand and knight together across the board to the fourth possible position. Her skin was warm against his, her fingertips soft. Fierce concentration creased her brow as she studied the board.

She pulled his hand again. 'And here!' She looked up, beaming. Then her mouth opened. 'Oh!' She snatched her hand from his. 'I am sorry. I…' Her cheeks bloomed beetroot red.

'You were carried away with enthusiasm?'

'Yes!' Her lips stretched in a tentative smile. 'Do you think I am ready?'

Nathaniel swallowed hard. She was so young. Naïve. 'Let us leave all that information to sink in,' he said. 'If you have time tomorrow, you might come in here and try to remember what each man is called and how he moves and then, in the evening, we will play.'

Her face clouded.

'And now…I shall challenge you to a game of draughts,' he said.

Her expression cleared. 'Oh, yes. That will be fun.'

Fun. An alien word to use in connection with himself and his life. He cleared the chessmen away and set out the draughtsmen whilst Miss Bertram poured the tea, brought in several minutes since by Mrs Sharp.

'You talked of your school friends earlier.' Nathaniel moved his counter in his opening gambit. 'Are they also governesses?'

What happened to your 'I don't want to know'? Or does that only apply to former beaux? Nathaniel dismissed that sneering voice as Miss Bertram played her opening move and he replied. He owed it to Clara to know more of the woman who would be raising her.

Didn't he?

'Yes. I am longing to hear how they go on.'

Miss Bertram studied the board, the tip of her tongue playing with her top lip, stirring long-suppressed needs deep inside Nathaniel. He forced his gaze to the board, but time and again it drifted back to the woman sitting opposite him.

'I asked Miss Fanworth to pass on my address to them so I hope they will soon write to me.' She moved another man, before adding, 'Although Rachel's letter might take a long time to reach England.'

'She has gone overseas?'

'Yes. She went to be the governess to the children of a sheikh, in the Kingdom of Huria. It is in the desert.'

'That does sound exotic. Did you not hanker after a similar adventure?'

She hesitated. 'No,' she said, finally. 'I think the North Country is enough of an adventure for me. Rachel's parents travelled much of the time, leaving her behind, and I think that is where her dream of travelling to faraway places began. She loves teaching children, so I am sure she will be happy.'

Silence fell whilst Miss Bertram again studied the board. She reached out and moved a man, jumping one of Nathaniel's, and grinned triumphantly as she made great play of removing it.

The devil. He would have to pay more attention to the game and less to his beautiful opponent.

'Isabel,' Miss Bertram said, as Nathaniel contemplated his next move, 'was the only one of us who spent much time with her parents as a child. Her papa taught her to play draughts and she taught us. She has gone to a family in Sussex, and Joanna, my other friend, has gone to a place in Hertfordshire. She is…she has no family and was brought up by Madame at the school.'

'You must miss your friends.'

'I do.' There was a pause. 'Do you not miss yours?'

'No.' Nathaniel kept his gaze on the game during the ensuing silence. Finally, he looked up. 'I no longer yearn after that frivolous way of life and my former friends crave nothing else.'

Irritated as much by his compulsion to explain as by her question, he studied the board again. There. A move he had overlooked. He moved one of his men, putting two of Miss Bertram's under threat. She peered more closely at the board.

'Hmmph. I cannot save both but, equally, you cannot take both. So I shall do this.' With another triumphant smile she moved a third man, reaching Nathaniel's side of the board and earning a 'crown' to turn her man into a king. 'Now I can move it forward *and* backwards.'

Nathaniel secured one of her men and they played on, the conversation on the safer territory of the game. When they finished, Nathaniel found himself the target of a pair of accusing green eyes.

'You allowed me to win.'

He had not. He had been too distracted to give the game his full attention.

'I thought it only fair to give you a taste of what you will be missing once we embark upon our chess challenge,' he said, looking down his nose at her. 'I want you to re-call the taste of victory even as the memory of it fades on your tongue.'

Miss Bertram laughed, revealing pearly white teeth. Nathaniel responded, but the stiff pull of the skin at the side of his face soon jerked him back to reality. What the hell was he doing?

'Come. The hour grows late.' He pushed to his feet and scooped the draughtsmen from the board. 'Open the top, if you please, Miss Bertram.'

She did as he requested and he returned the pieces to their place inside the table.

'Will you...will you be joining us at church tomorrow?'

Nathaniel reined in the temptation to snap a reply. She meant nothing by it. She was young and new to his house-hold. She would come to accept his decisions and Shiver-stone Hall would settle into a new routine.

'No.' He had no need to explain. He crossed the room to the door and opened it. 'Goodnight, Miss Bertram.'

He held the door wide as she passed through with a mur-mured, 'Goodnight, my lord.'

Chapter Nine

On Monday morning Clara sat happily at the kitchen table, helping Mrs Sharp knead dough.

She barely looked up when Grace said, 'Goodbye, sweetie. Be a good girl for Mrs Sharp.'

Despite the wrench of leaving Clara, even for so short a time, anticipation for the morning ahead fizzed through Grace's blood. She hurried from the kitchen and promptly collided with a wall of solid muscle. She teetered backwards and two hard hands gripped her arms as the scent of shaving soap and musk weaved through her senses. Her heart leapt and her pulse skittered.

'Oh!'

'Steady.' A finger beneath her chin tilted her head up and two deep brown eyes studied her, provoking a flush of heat through her body and into her cheeks. 'I had not thought you quite so eager to commence with your driving lesson, Miss Bertram.'

'I am sorry, my lord.'

Her voice sounded shaky. She cleared her throat and stepped back, tugging her upper arm free of his other hand. His hand fell away and her pounding pulse steadied.

'I did not want to keep you waiting.'

He held her gaze for a long moment, then smiled. 'Well, you have not, so you may relax.'

They left the house and, as they walked to the stables, a howl rent the air. Grace stopped, scarcely daring to breathe. 'What was that?'

'Brack.' Ravenwell kept moving. 'He objects to being shut up with the other dogs. I thought you might concentrate better with only Bill to worry about.'

Grace hurried to catch him up. 'It is not my fault I am unused to animals. I shall become accustomed to them, I promise you.'

It was the Marquess who stopped this time. 'I am sure you will. And to the human inhabitants also, I trust.'

'Everyone has been welcoming. Except—'

'Except Mrs Sharp. Yes, I am aware and I have spoken to her. It is not that she dislikes you but, as you must accustom yourself to the animals, so she must become accustomed to new people.'

Grace darted a look at him. It was not only Mrs Sharp who must grow accustomed to newcomers.

Inside the barn, Ravenwell entered a stall, slapping at the huge, rounded quarters of a grey horse who obligingly stepped sideways.

'Miss Bertram…' Ravenwell untied the horse and backed him from the stall '…meet Bill.'

Grace pressed back against the wall. Bill was not as tall as some horses, but he was wide and looked very strong. The head end was not as intimidating as the rear and Bill eyed her with a gentle eye and stretched his nose out, whiffling through his whiskers.

'Take off your glove, so he can learn your scent,' Ravenwell said.

Grace removed her glove, reached out a hesitant hand and stroked Bill's nose.

Ravenwell presented a chunk of carrot on his palm and

Bill picked it up delicately with questing lips and then crunched, eyes half-closed in contentment.

'Here.' Ravenwell passed Grace another piece of carrot. 'Hold your hand flat, like this.'

He supported her hand underneath with one hand and with the other he straightened her fingers. A pleasurable shiver darted through Grace, and she had to force herself to concentrate on his words.

'Never bend your fingers or thumbs. He would not mean to bite, but he might easily mistake them for a carrot. And horses have strong teeth.'

Ravenwell showed Grace the harness and how to tack up Bill, who stood patiently whilst she fumbled with straps and buckles and struggled with the notion she must open his mouth to put a metal bit between those long, yellow teeth.

'You may never need to harness him on your own but, if you should wish to go out and the men are out on the fells, it will be useful for you to know how to do it.'

They led Bill from the stable and backed him between the shafts of the gig, Grace gaining confidence all the time. Bill was so docile, how could she be scared of him? But she took care to keep her feet away from his huge hooves.

'Why does he have such hairy legs?' she asked as Ravenwell handed her into the gig and passed her the reins.

'They are called feathers. They protect the horse's legs against water and mud.'

He climbed into the gig and settled beside her, his thigh warm and solid next to hers, producing, once again, a shiver of awareness. He was so big, so male. She felt safe by his side.

'Now…' he reached for Grace's hands '…you hold the reins like so and Bill just needs a small shake to get him moving.'

Bill walked forward and the gig jerked into motion.

'Keep a light contact with his mouth—that is how you steer him—but you will find he is so familiar with the way to the village, you will hardly need to do anything. We will drive as far as the ford, so you can drive across the river, and then we will return home.'

Grace's confidence increased as the lesson continued. Her nerves dissipated and she began to enjoy both Ravenwell's company and the scenery. The weather was mild for the time of year: the sky a bright blue with white clouds scudding across it, although there was little wind at ground level. This was now her home. The isolation and wildness of the landscape fascinated her and she was surprised by a sudden impulse to take up her paints and attempt to capture its grandeur. At school, her skill and talent had been in portraits and miniatures and the art master, Signor Bertolli, had often despaired of her lack of aptitude in executing landscapes. Affection warmed her at the memory of her messy and disorganised but always encouraging teacher. It would be hard to find the time to paint, with Clara to care for, but she would enjoy the challenge of improving her skill and Clara would benefit in time, when Grace could use her knowledge to help her daughter acquire the accomplishments expected of a young lady.

'Thank you for teaching me to drive,' she said, on impulse. A skill was a skill, whether it was painting or driving. 'It will be agreeable not to have to rely on anyone else if I wish to visit the village.'

'Did you enjoy the church service?'

'Why, yes. As much as one ever enjoys being preached to.'

'I doubt Mr Rendell would appreciate hearing you say that.'

'Oh, he is not at all prosy, I assure you. He is just like any other young man. I told him you were teaching me to play chess and he said he might challenge you to a match one day.'

Silence. Grace peeped sideways. Ravenwell was frowning, his brow low and his mouth tight. She had thought he might be pleased—he must be lonely, living out here with no friends.

He has chosen to do so. You know he will not appreciate your interference.

She had spoken without thought and now the easy atmosphere between them had changed. She could not unsay those words, but she could smooth the moment with inconsequential chatter to distract him from his thoughts. From his fears. Although why such a powerful and wealthy man should fear anything was beyond Grace.

'Miss Dunn has invited me and Clara to call at the rectory next week. With your permission, of course, and if you think I can safely drive Bill?'

He glanced down at her, his frown lifting, to Grace's relief.

'I am sure you will cope, but I shall send Ned with you the first time to make sure.'

'Can you spare him from his duties?'

'Yes. Your and Clara's safety must take precedence. It will be pleasant for you to have a friend in the village.'

'Thank you.'

She sensed reservation behind his words. Was he concerned her visits to the village might result in callers at Shiverstone Hall? She could find no words to reassure him without openly mentioning his dislike of strangers. She still did not understand his choice to live this way. Was it embarrassment over his scars? He was a grown man and a lord. Could he not just brazen it out? Or was there something else. Something deeper? Sharp had hinted as much on her first night at the Hall. She vowed to find out more.

They had reached the river—Shiver Beck—and Grace drew Bill to a halt.

'Why do you not build a bridge? I got wet feet using those stepping stones on the day I arrived.'

She glanced at Ravenwell as she spoke and caught him biting back a grin.

'It is *not* funny.'

'Of course not.' His eyes danced, giving the lie to his words. 'No one normally *walks* from Shiverstone into the village. Drive on, Miss Bertram. You will not get wet feet in the gig.'

Grace shook the reins. Bill crossed the ford without hesitation but, as soon as they emerged on to the far side, Ravenwell showed Grace how to turn the gig for home. It was clear he had no intention of going anywhere near the village.

Grace drove back to Shiverstone and Ned emerged from the barn to unharness Bill and rub him down.

'Should I not learn to do that as well?' Grace asked.

'Very well. Ned, you may leave him to us.'

When they had finished, Grace looked up at Ravenwell to see him studying her with an amused smile. He removed one glove and reached to rub gently at her cheek.

Grace stilled at his touch, a *frisson* of awareness skittering down her spine and setting her insides a-flutter.

'You have a smudge,' he said.

His eyes wrinkled at the outer corners as he smiled and Grace's knees seemed to weaken, causing her to sway towards him. Horrified by her involuntary response, she braced her spine, even as every nerve ending in her body tingled and her breathing quickened.

'Now, as you have proved such an able pupil, I have another challenge for you.'

Grace swallowed. Hard. It was not the thought of a challenge that so unnerved her, but his intimate gesture and the way her pulse had leapt when he touched her, and her sudden awareness of how lovely and kind his eyes were when he smiled—not at all what one would expect from this normally terse man. Her response scared her a little. He was so very…*male*.

Ravenwell, in contrast, appeared oblivious to both his gesture and to Grace's reaction.

'I shall introduce you to the dogs,' he said.

Those words vanquished her embarrassment. A horse was one thing. Bill had stood obligingly still most of the time—he had been either tethered or in harness and thus under control. The dogs... She backed away a step.

'Come...you must not fear them or they will sense it. How shall you manage with Clara when she wants to visit the kennels?'

'Are they shut in? They will not be...' she swallowed, trying to quell her fear '...jumping around?'

Ravenwell laughed. 'I will not allow them to jump around.' He crooked his arm, proffering it to Grace. She hesitated and he raised one brow. 'The track up to the kennels is stony. I should not like you to turn your ankle. Come, you may meet them one at a time. They will make a noise, but they will not harm you.'

It felt odd, placing her hand on the arm of her employer. It was rock solid under her fingers and, again, she was reminded of his powerful build as his aura of masculinity pervaded every sense. She felt vulnerable and yet protected at the same time. A peculiar mix, but not unpleasant. Side by side they followed the path to the kennels.

'How many dogs do you have?'

'Nine, plus Brack. They are an assorted bunch—I use them mostly for hunting, except for Fly and Flash. They are collies and they work the sheep out on the fells. You can meet them first.'

Ravenwell and Grace headed back to the Hall some time later, Grace's head spinning with the names and purposes of the various terriers, spaniels, and the one pointer as well as the sheepdogs. Brack, sulking after being shut in the kennels, was at their heels.

'Why is Brack allowed indoors and not the other dogs?'

'I cannot imagine the chaos of living with that lot under one roof. No, they are happy enough in the kennels; they have known no different from when they were pups. Brack…his mother was a terrier—a big lass and a total hoyden she was. She went missing once for two weeks and, when she came home, she was in pup. Tam reckons she'd been visiting over towards Kendal. There's a pack of otter hounds out that way and when the litter came the pups had that look about them. And Brack certainly loves water. It might be hard to believe it now, but he was the runt of his litter. He failed to thrive and his mother rejected him. So I took him in and hand-reared him and he's lived in the Hall ever since. Eight years now.'

Grace reached out and patted Brack's rough head, aware that most men, given those same circumstances, would have destroyed the weak pup.

'What happened to his ear?' She fingered the ragged stump on the left side of his head.

'His mother bit it off when she rejected him. He may not be the most handsome dog in the world, but he is loyal and trustworthy.'

'Looks are not everything,' Grace said, opening the door to the kitchen, 'and he is very patient with Clara.'

A warm fug of air, filled with delicious smells, assailed them as they entered the room. Clara looked up, then scrambled from her chair as Grace removed her hat and her cloak.

'Ma Berm. Ma Berm,' she shouted, arms lifted as she ran to Grace.

'Miss Bertram,' Grace corrected, even as her heart skipped. It had sounded so like Mama. But she must never allow her guard to waver. She was Miss Bertram. Not Mama. She dropped her outer garments on a nearby chair as she lifted Clara and hugged her close. 'What have you been doing, little one?'

Alice looked up from her task of peeling potatoes.

'She's helped us with the baking, ma'am, and now Mrs Sharp has gone to the parlour to set out refreshments. She said as you'd both be famished after all that fresh air.'

'Uncle Nanniel!'

Clara squirmed in Grace's arms and then launched herself towards her uncle, arms outstretched. Grace, caught unawares, staggered with the shift of weight in her arms and found herself for the second time that day pressed up against the Marquess. His arms came around her, steadying her, whilst Clara's arms encircled her uncle's neck, hugging him tight, locking them into a three-way embrace. For a few wonderful moments Grace leant into Ravenwell's solid, muscular body. Her lids fluttered closed as his musky scent enveloped her and she relished the sensation of being held...of feeling safe. Then, aghast at the yearning such feelings invoked, she wriggled. After a couple of failed attempts, they eventually parted. Grace sneaked a glance at his lordship, to find him regarding her with laughter lighting his eyes.

'You will no doubt wish to refresh yourself before eating, Miss Bertram.'

A teasing note warmed his words, conjuring a silent *hmmph* from Grace. Whatever her instinctive response to his lordship, he clearly did not see her as anything other than an amusing diversion. Without volition, her hand lifted to her hair which had, she discovered, fallen from its pins. At that moment Mrs Sharp returned to the kitchen.

'There you are, milord. I have been to—'

Her mouth snapped shut and she raked Grace with a look of such suspicion Grace's cheeks fired up all over again. Then she raised her chin. She had done nothing wrong. What right did the housekeeper have to look at her as though she'd caught her in some misdemeanour?

'Alice was just telling us about the luncheon,' Ravenwell said into the sudden fraught silence. 'Thank you, Mrs Sharp. I am afraid Clara was a little over-enthusiastic in her welcome, so Miss Bertram is about to go and attend to her hair.' His lips twitched and Grace suspected him of holding back a laugh.

'You may leave this little miss with me, Miss Bertram, and we shall see you in the parlour when you are ready.'

Ten minutes later, having hastily washed her hands and face and brushed out and repinned her hair, Grace came downstairs, her steps slowing as an unfamiliar shyness at the thought of facing Lord Ravenwell came over her. She pressed her hands to her fluttering stomach as she reviewed the morning. What would his lordship think of her foolish reaction whenever they touched?

You are being ridiculous. He cannot know what you feel.

A high-pitched squeal sounded, quashing any remaining awkwardness, and she hurried to the parlour, where she stopped dead at the sight of Ravenwell crawling around the room, Clara perched on his back like a monkey, giggling as she wrapped her small fists in his hair, clinging tight.

Brack stood aside, tail wagging furiously.

'Ride Brack!'

'Ride Brack?' Ravenwell laughed, reared up on to his knees and reached behind to swing Clara from her perch. 'As you have asked so nicely, Miss Clara, you may ride Brack once around the room.'

He sat her on the dog's back, holding her and—Grace could see—supporting much of her weight.

'Miss Bertram, would you please lead Brack around the room?'

Grace started; she had not thought him aware of her presence. She came forward and took Brack's collar.

'Come, Brack.' She was thrilled when he moved at her command.

They completed the circuit, and Clara shouted, ''Gain! 'Gain!'

Ravenwell laughed, scooping her from Brack's back.

'You will tire Brack out and Miss Bertram and I are hungry.' He pulled a chair out for Grace. 'I shall think about buying a small pony for Clara next year. I am certain she will enjoy learning to ride. And you can learn at the same time.'

A simple statement to give so much pleasure. For the first time since she arrived at the Hall she truly felt she belonged. She had a settled place in the world and a family, of sorts. She sat, murmuring her thanks, her emotions welling as she resolutely ignored her earlier disquiet over the feelings stirred by his lordship.

Ravenwell plonked Clara on the chair next to Grace, handing her a slice of buttered bread.

'This will keep madam quiet whilst we eat,' he said. 'Oh, by the way…' he reached into his pocket '…Mrs Sharp gave me this after you left the kitchen.'

Grace took the letter from the Marquess and read her name on the front in a familiar hand. Isabel. It had been addressed to her at the school and the address scratched out and readdressed to her at Shiverstone Hall. She turned it over and on the back was a short note from Miss Fanworth, thanking Grace for her letter and promising to write very soon. Excited, Grace began to break the seal, but then stopped. She should not read the letter at the table. Besides, she wanted to savour every word in private, with no one watching and able to interpret her thoughts and feelings from her expression.

Grace spent much of the next half an hour trying to deter Clara from snatching a sample of every morsel of food upon the table and then discarding it after one nibble.

Ravenwell watched her efforts with a sardonic lift of his brow.

'And this illustrates perfectly why children should take their meals in the nursery.'

Grace bristled. 'She is just excited by being in here and eating with us.'

He laughed, holding his hands up, palms facing her. 'There is no need to leap to her defence, Miss Bertram. It was merely an observation. I am not about to chastise her for doing what children do.'

Grace bit her lip. She should not speak so boldly to her employer. 'I am sorry. And I concede your point. It does not make eating my own luncheon particularly easy.'

'At least you will not have to fret about the effect of Mrs Sharp's cooking on your waistline.'

Grace relaxed at the teasing glint in Ravenwell's eyes, then grabbed at Clara as she stood on her chair and prostrated her torso across the table in her determination to reach a plate of macaroons, despite the half-eaten one already on her plate.

'That is true.' Grace stood up, hoisting Clara on to her hip. Clara squirmed, protesting vocally but unintelligibly. 'Now, this little girl appears to have eaten her fill so I shall take her upstairs for her nap.'

Ravenwell had also risen to his feet and a warm tingle flowed through her at his gentlemanly gesture to a mere governess.

'And you, Miss Bertram? Have you satisfied your appetite after your exertions?'

She smiled. 'I have had sufficient, thank you, my lord. Thank you for teaching me to drive—I shall be sure to take advantage of my new skill.'

He cocked his head to one side. 'And dare I think you are becoming used to our countryside? You appeared to derive some enjoyment from the views.'

Grace untangled Clara's fingers from her hair. 'Oh, yes. I confess I found it somewhat bleak and intimidating at first, but I very much enjoyed it today. In fact, it has awoken a desire in me to get out my sketchbook, although I doubt I have the talent to capture its full glory. I have also resolved to take Clara for a walk every day, weather permitting.' She smiled at him. 'I might even take Brack.'

'Well! Today has been a success already and it is only half over.'

Grace headed for the door.

'Do not forget your letter, Miss Bertram.'

Isabel's letter! How could I forget?

Grace turned and Ravenwell was there, very close, the letter in his hand. She looked up, past the broad expanse of his chest, into his smiling brown eyes and awareness tugged deep in her core as, again, her pulse leapt and her breath quickened. His eyes darkened and grew more intense, then Clara pressed her cheek against Grace's and the moment passed.

'Thank you.' Grace took her letter, forced a quick smile and left the room, the meaning of that exchanged look teasing her brain.

Chapter Ten

Clara eventually dozed off and Grace escaped to her sitting room to read her letter.

It was concise, almost terse, and the news it contained shocked Grace to the core. Isabel, married? Her happy, joyful friend—who had loved to sing and had long dreamt of the passionate love with which she would one day be blessed—trapped in a marriage of convenience with the son and heir of a viscount?

Her marriage to William Balfour was, Isabel wrote, a joining of '*two sensible people in exact understanding of each other*'.

How Grace's heart ached for her friend. The letter sounded totally unlike the lively girl Grace loved like a sister. How she wished she lived closer and could offer her support and comfort. The date at the top of the letter told her it had been written way back in August. Poor Isabel. Wed over two months and Grace had not even known. She wondered how Isabel had fared since.

She would write back immediately and hope Isabel would be bolstered by her support. Although…her burst of enthusiasm faded. How could she write and burden Isabel with the truth about Shiverstone Hall and Clara?

Isabel asked in her letter if Grace had tracked down her baby and, if Grace wrote a reply, she must lie.

But to lie would be a betrayal of their friendship.

She would wait. She would write to her friend later—after a few more weeks, when she was more settled here at the Hall and hopefully Isabel would be in a happier frame of mind and Grace would have come to terms with her own deception.

That decision—really no decision at all, merely a putting off of the inevitable—fretted at Grace for the remainder of the day.

'You have been remarkably quiet this evening, Miss Bertram,' Ravenwell said as they sat opposite one another at the chess table after dinner. 'I hope your letter did not bring bad news?'

Grace's attention jolted back to the drawing room in which they sat. 'Not bad news, precisely. But unsettling.'

She gathered her thoughts and tried to focus on the game. She studied the board, then leaned towards it, peering at the chessmen as though a closer perspective might conceivably improve her position.

I know I'm a beginner, but how have I ended up in such a predicament after so few moves?

The Marquess was watching her, a small smile playing around his lips.

'Quite,' he said, as though she had spoken aloud. 'Your attention is clearly not on our game.'

'I am sorry.'

'No need to apologise. It takes practice, and one's full attention, to play well.' Ravenwell began to move the pieces back to their starting positions. 'We will play another night, when you are not so preoccupied.'

He pushed back his chair and stood up, brandy glass in hand. He was going. Probably to his book room to work on his ledgers. Her surge of disappointment shocked Grace as she anticipated a long evening alone with her thoughts.

Ravenwell, however, did not move away from the table.

'Would you care to talk about whatever is bothering you?'

Grace recognised the effort it must cost this private man to make such an offer—she had seen and appreciated his efforts to change since she had pointed out that his avoidance of her was punishing Clara. She was no longer intimidated by his brusqueness, which she now knew concealed a gentle man who loved his niece and was kind to his animals.

'Isabel's news seems to be all I am able to think about. Mayhap saying it out loud will help me make sense of it.'

He gestured to the chairs by the fire. 'Come, then.'

Where to start? But the Marquess was—or once was—a man of the world in which Isabel now found herself. He might be able to ease some of Grace's worries.

She told him about Isabel and her arranged marriage with William Balfour.

'Balfour... I know of the family, but I cannot recall a William. He is no doubt younger than I. But why you are so worried for your friend? She has made an excellent match. She will be set up for life.'

'You do not understand.'

How could he possibly understand when he had never met the free spirit that was Isabel?

'Isabel's parents doted on her...she dreamt of singing in the opera and she thrives on being adored. How will she survive with a husband who does not love her?'

Grace cringed at Ravenwell's huff of amusement. *He thinks me a romantic ninny now.* 'You do not believe love is necessary in a marriage?'

'I do not. You, on the other hand, expose your youth and naivety in believing such poetical nonsense.'

If only he knew...

The veil had been swept from her eyes long ago. In her mind's eye she saw Clara's father, Philip, tall, lean and handsome with his ready smile, charm personified, who had flirted with her sixteen-year-old self and persuaded her of his love—Philip, whose immaturity sent him fleeing to join the army when Grace had told him she carried his child. Philip, who had been dead nigh on fourteen months, killed in action.

She felt the familiar wash of sorrow over Philip's death on the battlefield, but she had long since accepted that what she had felt for him had been infatuation, fed by his flattery and her foolish pride that such a handsome youth should take notice of her and make her feel important. Every trace of her naïve, youthful love had been wiped from her heart as she saw him for precisely what he was: a self-serving youth who thought sweet words were a sufficient price to pay to get what he desired.

And he was right, wasn't he?

A shudder shook Grace at the memory of that terrifying period in her life when she had succeeded in concealing her condition from everyone other than her best friends but, despite everything, she would not allow her experience with Philip to sour her.

'I cannot accept that love can be dismissed as mere poetical nonsense.'

'You make my point for me. You have no experience of the real world. Indeed, how could you have? You have been secluded at your school since the age of...what...ten?'

'Nine.'

'Nine. Precisely. Naïve nonsense. You should do yourself a favour and rid your brain of such romantic drivel.'

He could not hide his bitterness. Was it because of his scars, or had he unhappy experiences of love? Well, she would not allow him to sully her opinion of the world. She had always—like Isabel—believed in true love.

'Your friend will do very well in her marriage,' he continued, 'and it is a waste of your time to be fretting about her.'

'That is—' Grace stopped.

'That is what, Miss Bertram?'

His eyes were dark and unfathomable. His jaw set.

Sad. But she did not dare say that. She must not be lulled by this new, friendlier Ravenwell. He still paid her wages and he could still dismiss her if she forgot her place.

'That is no doubt wise advice,' she said instead. 'There is nothing I can do to help Isabel. Besides, she has a strength and determination that I am sure will help her cope.'

Ravenwell stood. 'Now your mind is at rest, I have work to do. I shall bid you goodnight.'

He strode from the room, leaving Grace staring after him.

What is going on inside his head? He cannot be happy, living like this.

She switched her gaze to the fire, watching mindlessly as the embers glowed red, emitting an occasional tongue of flame and sending intermittent sparks up the chimney. Her heart went out to the Marquess. How lonely he must be. She would love to see him smile more often and relax. There and then she swore to do all she could to bring more light, life and laughter to his life.

'What have you been saying to put his lordship in such a tear, missy?'

Grace started. She had not heard Sharp come in.

'I am not sure. We were talking about love and marriage…concerning some news I had from a friend,' she added hastily, in response to Sharp's smirk. 'He told me to rid my mind of romantic drivel and thoughts of love, then said he has work to do and left.'

Sharp tidied their empty cups on to a tray, then picked

up Ravenwell's abandoned brandy glass—still half-full—and drained it with a single swallow and a wink at Grace.

'Ah.' He placed the empty glass on the tray and shook his head. 'No wonder.'

'Why do you say that?'

Sharp tapped his finger against the side of his nose. 'I'm not one to gossip.'

'You are admirably discreet, Sharp, but you *understand* his lordship and that is why I ask you rather than any of the others—'

'The others? They do not know the half of what I know.'

'I'm certain *they* do not know the real reason his lordship cuts himself off from his friends and family.'

'No, they don't.' Sharp sat in the chair opposite Grace and leaned forward. 'Only me and Mrs Sharp know the whole truth. We was all at Ravenwell then, living at the Dower House while the manor was being rebuilt. His lordship had been courting Lady Sarah before the fire, but when he went to London to see her, she'd have nothing to do with him. She wed someone else soon after.

'He came home, and never went down south again. Even at Ravenwell, the stares and the whispers were so bad he'd barely leave the estate, but he still suffered from the guilt.'

Guilt? Grace longed to probe, but feared if she interrupted Sharp now he might clam up.

'And then his mother took it into her head to arrange a marriage. To Miss Havers. Desperate for a title and money, she was. But the little bi—beg pardon, *witch*—took one look at his lordship and swore that neither title nor wealth were sufficient to entice her to wed a monster. 'Course, that was soon after the fire. His scars were still raw then. They look better now.'

Ignorant women! Scorning an injured man in that way, destroying his faith in love. If I could get my hands on them...

Sharp's gaze rested on Grace's hands—curled into fists

on her lap—and he smiled. 'Now you see why my missus is so protective of his lordship,' he said softly.

'After that—' his voice was brisk again '—we came to live here and we've been here ever since.'

It was as Grace suspected. Ravenwell had cut himself off from society to protect himself from rejection. And yet…that didn't really explain it. A man such as he…if he wanted to mix with others, surely he was strong enough to withstand a few stares and pitying glances?

'And the guilt?'

Sharp's eyes narrowed. 'I've said too much. Never you mind, missy, 'tis none of your business.'

Grace halted the gig and tied off the reins, as Ravenwell had taught her, delighted and proud at having successfully accomplished her first drive to Shivercombe. They were in the lane outside the rectory and she looked round as the front door was flung open.

'Miss Bertram!'

Mr Rendell—tall, slender, and handsome—hurried down the path to the front gate, beaming. There had been a time, Grace realised, when the attention of such a man would have set her heart soaring but now, although she was pleased to see the curate again, her heart remained stubbornly unmoved.

In her mind's eye an image of a very different sort arose—dark, brooding, attractive in an altogether different way—the difference between a boy and a man. She tried hard to ignore the *frisson* of desire and need that trickled down her spine.

'Good afternoon, Mr Rendell.' She accepted his hand to assist her from the gig and then lifted Clara down. 'As you can see, I have braved my first drive to the village, albeit with Ned in attendance to ensure Clara and I come to no harm.'

Ned had ridden behind the gig and now came forward to take charge of Bill.

'In that case, I shall congratulate you upon the success of your first outing and express my delight in finding you both unscathed by the experience. The weather is currently kind and it would be wasteful not to take advantage.'

'It would indeed. Miss Dunn did invite us to call upon her, but—because of the weather—we did not specify a day. I do hope this is not an inconvenient time? We shall not stay above half an hour, but having a purpose for my drive made it all the more enjoyable.'

'Alas, I am on my way to visit a parishioner, but Miss Dunn is at home and I make no doubt she will be delighted to see you. With your permission, I shall escort you to her and then I must be on my way.'

'Thank you, sir. Ned, we shall not be long.'

'Go round to the kitchen door when you have secured the horses, Ned,' Mr Rendell said, 'and Cook will find you some refreshments.'

The curate picked up Clara and led the way into the square, stone-built rectory. He showed Grace into a smart drawing room and went in search of Miss Dunn.

The first person to come into the room was the Reverend Dunn, his twinkly eyes creased into slits by his cherubic smile.

'Miss Bertram, what a pleasant surprise. Elizabeth asks if you will join her in the parlour where there are some little friends young Clara might like to meet.'

He winked at Grace, held his hand out to Clara, who took it without hesitation, and ushered Grace before him, indicating a door at the end of the passageway.

'It is not as grand as the drawing room and we would not normally entertain visitors in here, but I am sure you will take us as you find us.'

Grace pushed open the door and stepped into a much cosier, if somewhat shabbier, room. The thought flashed through her mind that here was a home in which one could feel comfortable, in stark contrast to the dark, unwelcoming reception rooms at the Hall. The idea of effecting some changes—sparked initially by the beauty of the chess table—grew stronger.

'Good afternoon, Miss Bertram.'

The voice shook her from her thoughts and she gazed around what appeared to be an empty room.

'Go on in,' urged the Reverend Dunn from behind her.

Grace walked forward and there, shielded from the door by a sofa, was Miss Dunn, sitting on a rug before the fire with two kittens scrambling over her lap whilst a third pawed at a length of string being dangled in front of its nose. A large tabby-and-white cat sat to one side, assiduously washing itself whilst keeping one eye on the youngsters.

Grace laughed as the kitten pounced on the string and tumbled on to its back.

'Good afternoon, Miss Dunn,' she said. 'I had forgotten about the kittens you mentioned on Sunday. They are very pretty.'

'Please, call me Elizabeth, for I am sure we are destined to be bosom friends.' She gestured to a chair and bade Grace sit. 'I hope you do not object to being received in our family parlour, but Mama has banned these little ones from the drawing room. Quite rightly, given the havoc they wreak. Please forgive me for not rising but, as you see, I am serving the useful purpose of providing a soft lap for their play.'

'Of course. And you must call me Grace.'

Her spirits rose. How lovely it would be to have a friend so close to her new home; it would help to ease the pain of missing her school friends.

'Look, Clara. See the kittens? Are they not sweet?'

Clara ran forward, all eagerness, and the kittens scattered.

'You must take care if you are not to frighten them, Clara,' Miss Dunn said, gathering her on to her lap. 'Sit here with me and we shall see which of them is bold enough to come and meet you.'

An hour later, Grace tapped the reins on Bill's broad back and they set off on the drive to Shiverstone Hall, Ned riding behind. Grace waved goodbye to Elizabeth and to Mr Rendell, who had not long before returned from his visit and joined them in the parlour, along with Mrs Dunn and a tea tray. Watching her new friend and Mr Rendell together—catching the occasional shared glance and the resulting pink tinge of Elizabeth's cheeks—Grace suspected there was more to their friendship than they might wish anyone to suspect.

As they left the village, Grace glanced at Clara, sitting quietly for once, one hand clutching tight at the handle of a covered wicker basket wedged on the seat between them. Doubts surfaced. Had she presumed too much, accepting this gift for Clara? Then Clara looked up at her, shining eyes huge in her beaming face, and all doubts shrivelled.

Ravenwell loved Clara.

He would not begrudge her a kitten.

Would he?

Thinking about the Marquess set up those peculiar nervy sensations deep in the pit of Grace's stomach once again. They had plagued her ever since the moment he had wiped that smudge from her cheek. Ridiculous thoughts and longings flitted in and out of her mind, no matter how hard she tried to quell them. She did not need to concentrate on driving. Bill, as Ravenwell had promised, needed no guidance to find his way home. Instead, she diverted her wayward thoughts by admiring the beauty of the day and of the surrounding scenery, imagining in her mind's eye how she might capture it on canvas.

Chapter Eleven

Nathaniel trotted Zephyr steadily down the track that led through the forest towards the village as Brack ranged through the trees, nose to the ground. He was concerned about Clara's safety. That was the only reason he couldn't settle to anything this afternoon, after he learned that Grace had driven them both in the gig to Shivercombe. Never mind that Ned was there to keep them safe. That was his role. He would only go as far as the river and he would await them there, if he did not come upon them beforehand. Sharp had assured him Miss Bertram only intended to stay at the Rectory for half an hour before returning and they had already been gone an hour and a half.

He emerged from the forest and followed the track as it curved towards the ford in the river. Here, large slabs of rock—smoothed by centuries of erosion by the flowing waters of Shiver Beck—had been laid across the riverbed to create a place for carriages to cross. The only time it became impassable was after heavy rain when—although not very much deeper—the swiftness of the current rendered the ford treacherous. At least the water level fell as quickly as it rose, so they were never cut off from the village for long.

Nathaniel reined Zephyr to a halt as they reached the

ford and slid from the saddle, pulling the reins over the horse's head so he could crop the grass whilst they waited. Brack, as usual, could not resist the lure of the water and swam into the deeper water, downstream of the ford. It was a beautiful, crisp November day, but Nathaniel was in no mood to appreciate either the weather or the natural beauty of his surroundings. He crossed his arms and tapped his foot, his attention fixed on the track that led from the ford and soon disappeared from view as it wound into the village.

Finally, as he was beginning to think the unthinkable—that he must go into the village and make certain they were safe—he heard the *clip-clop* of horses' hooves and the rattle of wheels. His heart returned to its rightful position in his chest as Brack exploded from the river and shook himself thoroughly, sending sparkling drops of water arcing through the air. Nathaniel mounted Zephyr, sending him splashing through the ford as Bill plodded into view, towing the gig, and he heard Miss Bertram say, 'Look, Clara. There is Uncle Nathaniel.'

'Uncle Nanniel! See kitty!'

Bill halted beside Zephyr. Clara bounced up and down on the bench seat whilst Miss Bertram...he focussed on the governess. Miss Bertram did not quite meet his gaze. She looked sheepish. Guilty, even. What had happened in the village?

'Ned, you may ride on ahead,' Nathaniel said. 'There is no need for us both to accompany the gig.'

Even while he was speaking, he was chewing over the meaning of her expression. Had she met with Rendell? Did she feel guilty for meeting him whilst she was meant to be looking after Clara? He tamped down the spiral of anger that climbed from deep in the pit of his stomach, knowing he could not begrudge her some independence or the opportunity to make friends. He might choose to live the life of a recluse, but he could not insist that others—even if they worked for him—follow suit.

Besides—he took in Clara's joyous expression—it was good for Clara.

He reined Zephyr around, called Brack—who appeared strangely eager to clamber into the gig—to heel and nudged the stallion back into the river. A glance behind showed Bill following behind, splashing through the crystal water that reached halfway to his knees as he negotiated the ford with the ease of long familiarity. Once they reached the other bank, Nathaniel rode alongside the gig.

'Did you visit Miss Dunn?' She had said they would visit the rectory, to call upon the vicar's daughter.

'Yes, indeed, and we agreed we are to be friends and I am to call her Elizabeth and she will call me Grace.' She threw a huge smile in his direction, but it did not distract him from the tinge of anxiety in her eyes or prevent him from noticing her hurried speech. 'We had an exceedingly pleasant visit and then Mrs Dunn joined us, and Mr Rendell, and—'

'Kitty!' Clara half-stood in her effort to interrupt Miss Bertram and gain Nathaniel's attention. 'Kitty!'

'Hush, Clara. Sit down. It is dangerous to stand up.' Miss Bertram scooped Clara's legs from under her and plonked her back on the seat. 'And it is rude to interrupt.'

'Uncle *Naaaaaanniel.*' Clara's appeal was a whine of frustration.

Miss Bertram shot him a wary look from under the rim of her bonnet, then reined Bill to a halt, her expression resigned.

'I had better confess this now, for you shall discover the truth soon enough.'

Every beat of Nathaniel's heart thundered in his ears. What was she about to tell him? Sudden fear gripped him, clenching his stomach. He couldn't lose her. Clara would be inconsolable.

Miaow.

Brack reared up on his hind legs, his front paws on the step as he thrust his head on to Miss Bertram's lap, whining.

'Brack! Get down, sir! My apologies, Miss Bertram, I cannot think what has possessed him.'

'I can.' She brushed at the damp patch on her brown pelisse with a rueful smile.

'Kitty!'

Miaow.

'Oh, heavens! There is no help for it. My lord, Elizabeth… Miss Dunn…gave Clara a kitten.' Her tone rang with defiance, but her expression was wary. 'I know I should have asked your permission first, but—'

'*Kitty.* Uncle Naffaniel. Kitty!'

A kitten! He forced down the relieved laugh swelling his chest. And he had feared—he did not allow that thought to develop. It did not matter what he had feared. He was in danger of allowing his imagination too free a rein when it came to Miss Bertram. Their conversation the other night about romance should be enough to convince him to keep his distance. If she *had* developed a *tendre* for Rendell, so much the better.

'No wonder Brack is so interested in the gig. I assume it is inside the basket?'

Grace nodded.

'See kitty?'

'Not now, poppet. If he runs away we shall never find him. Besides, Brack might eat him for supper.'

'Oh, no. I did not think…might Brack hurt him?'

'Come, let us get home.' The horses began to move again. 'And I do not know, is the honest answer. We have never had cats at the Hall, but he is a hunting dog, so…'

Her face was stricken. 'What have I done? Clara will be devastated if he should get hurt.'

'Then we shall make sure he stays safe.'

'Thank you.'

Her face, as always, lit up with her smile, her mercurial eyes shifting from green to gold and back again. They were as changeable as the play of sunlight through the first leaves of spring, the colour always shifting, reflecting the light, and... Nathaniel tore his gaze from hers.

'It remains to be seen what Mrs Sharp will say.'

Their gazes clashed again—this time with a conspiratorial mix of amusement and trepidation.

'A cat? *Indoors?*' Mrs Sharp propped her hands on her hips. 'It will run riot, up and down the curtains, scratching the carpet. And the *mess*...'

'I am sorry, Mrs Sharp, I did not think of that. But... look at Clara's face...how could you deny...?'

Miss Bertram cast an anxious look at Nathaniel.

'The decision is made, Mrs Sharp. How hard can it be for five adults to keep control of one small kitten?' Nathaniel set the basket on the table as he spoke and unbuckled the strap that held the lid in place.

'My lord! Not on the *table.*'

'I shall not put the cat on the table, Mrs Sharp. I am merely removing it from the basket.'

Sharp—who had jumped guiltily from his favourite chair in the corner as Nathaniel, Grace and Clara had come into the kitchen—peered into the basket as Nathaniel lifted the lid. A reedy *miaow* issued forth, followed by a black-and-white face, whiskers quivering.

Sharp reached in and picked up the kitten. 'You look like you've been a-sweeping the chimneys.' He grinned at Grace. 'Is that his name? Sweep?'

'Sweep!' Clara reached up for the kitten.

'There, little miss.' Sharp put the kitten down and it shot across the room and underneath the large dresser at the far end.

'Causing havoc already,' Mrs Sharp grumbled as Clara let out a wail and toddled after the kitten.

'Oh, dear. I am sorry, Mrs Sharp.' Grace went to the dresser and knelt down to peer underneath.

Nathaniel's eyes were immediately drawn to the shapely round of her bottom, suggestively outlined by her woollen dress. He wrenched his gaze away, irritated he should even notice.

'Allow me, Miss Bertram.'

He crossed the kitchen to kneel beside her and reached under the dresser. Needle-sharp claws raked his hand and he bit back his curse as he scooped up the kitten and dragged it from its hiding place.

'Take the kitten up to the nursery where it is quieter.' He thrust the kitten at Miss Bertram. 'It will be your responsibility to clean up after it and to train it. Is that understood?'

'Yes, my lord,' she said, her eyes downcast.

He felt an ogre, snapping at her like that, but at least no one would suspect the truth of his wayward thoughts—they would blame his sour mood on the kitten.

He hoped Brack would accept it—he made a mental note to introduce them as soon as possible. It was a pretty little thing, with a fluffy coat that was mostly black, with white on its face, stomach, paws, and tail. Sweep. The name suited it, with its white face marred only by a black smear across its upper lip and another around one eye.

He watched Miss Bertram leave the kitchen, the kitten cradled in her arms. Clara bounced alongside, clearly delighted with her new friend.

She would not be intimidated by him. She had moved beyond that stage. She could see past his brusqueness. He would grow to accept Sweep as soon as he saw how much Clara loved her kitten. He would do anything to make Clara happy. Grace brushed out her hair and twisted it into a chignon as she prepared for dinner. Clara was already asleep, exhausted with all the excitement of the day, and Sweep sat on Grace's bed, watching her from wide green eyes.

'You will have to stay in the kitchen at night,' she told him.

She'd thought long and hard about it, but she could not have Sweep disturbing Clara at night, neither did she want him in her bedchamber. Cats, she knew, were often active at night and likely to disrupt her sleep. Now she had only to persuade Mrs Sharp to agree. She smoothed her dress over her hips and scooped Sweep off the bed.

'Mrs Sharp…' she said as she entered the kitchen.

'What is that cat doing here?'

'Now, now, missus.' Sharp came to Grace and took the kitten from her. 'Miss Bertram can hardly leave Sweep upstairs with Miss Clara asleep, can she? And you were complaining about mice only t'other day.' He winked at Grace. 'He'll do grand in here of an evening and Miss Clara can play with him during the day.'

'Hmmph. Just you keep it from under my feet. I'm too busy to have to watch where I'm stepping all the time.'

Grace handed Sweep to Sharp, smiling her thanks, and headed for the parlour. That was her first challenge accomplished and more easily than she had anticipated. Now for the second.

She waited until they had withdrawn to the drawing room, and Mrs Sharp—still grumbling under her breath about *that cat*—had delivered the tea tray. The Marquess, as was now his custom, had carried his brandy glass through from the parlour. Grace poured tea for herself and, ignoring the chess table, she settled into one of the two fireside chairs. Ravenwell hesitated, raised a brow and then joined her.

'Do I detect a desire to talk rather than play?'

'Yes, my lord.' She was committed now. She must do this, for Clara's sake. The worst he could do was refuse.

'When I first came, you said I might make changes to the nursery wing.'

He inclined his head. 'I did indeed. And have you done so?'

'I have, with help from Alice.'

'And did you find everything you need?'

'Yes…'

Grace sucked in a breath, but before she could continue, he said, 'I sense a question coming.'

Grace bristled at the smile teasing the corners of his mouth. He thought her amusing. Someone to be indulged.

'I am only asking for Clara's sake,' she said stiffly. 'I want her to have a home here.' She waved her arm, indicating the room in which they sat. 'The nursery and her bedchamber are now comfortable and cosy, but what about here?'

His brows snapped into a frown. 'Here? This is a drawing room. Not a place for children.'

'Children?' She leant forward. 'We are speaking of your niece. Do you intend for her never to come in here?'

'She does come in here,' he growled.

'Precisely.' Satisfied she had made her point, she sat back. 'Look around you. I am sorry if I speak out of turn, but there is nothing welcoming or homely about this room. And what about Christmas?'

'Christmas?' His brows shot up. 'What about Christmas?'

How could she explain without sounding full of self-pity? She did not want Clara's memories of her childhood Christmases to echo hers.

'What did Christmas mean to you as a boy?'

Understanding dawned in his eyes, and he smiled. 'Stir-up Sunday, delicious smells from the kitchen for days on end, gathering greenery and bringing in the Yule log, going to church on Christmas morning, exchanging gifts.' He gazed into the flames, a wistful look on his face, as he listed his memories. 'Twelfth Night and the Lord of Misrule. Family gatherings with pantomimes and charades…'

He fell silent. He looked…lost and vulnerable. It was the only time Grace had ever seen him with his guard down and her heart went out to him. It had been his choice to live this isolated life but he had been forced into it by the reactions of others. He had only been twenty-one. Such a young man.

He appeared to recollect her presence and his lips firmed. 'It is not the same now. I am happy with the house the way it is.'

'You may be content and you may not relish the thought of celebrating Christmas, but…do you not see? It is our responsibility to make sure Clara's childhood memories are as happy as yours.'

Ravenwell tilted his head as he focussed on Grace. 'And as happy as yours?'

'Some of them,' she admitted. 'The later ones. The Christmases I spent at school, with my friends, are some of my happiest memories.'

'And were your early Christmases *un*happy?'

'Not unhappy, precisely, but then I knew no different. My uncle and aunt were extremely devout and they eschewed anything that smacked of pagan tradition. For them, it was all about church and charity. Laudable, I know, but… for a child…'

She rose to her feet and walked away from the fireplace, away from the warm glow of the flames and the candles on the mantelshelf, to the dark end of the room, then stopped and faced him.

'This room should be the heart of the home and the focus of Christmas.' She waved her arm, encompassing the unlit fire and the bareness of the rest of the room.

Ravenwell looked around the room as if seeing it for the first time. 'I see what you mean. For Clara's sake.'

She smiled. 'For Clara's sake.' She returned to her chair.

'I should like to move some of the furniture back in here, with your permission.'

'I shall not object, as long as Mrs Sharp is agreeable. We kept the furniture to a minimum to lighten her chores. It has never bothered me in the past.'

'She has Alice to help now. And if the work should still be too much, I am sure Annie would be happy to earn a little extra.'

'You may do as you think fit.'

She had not expected enthusiasm; his grudging approval was a step in the right direction. She had vowed to turn this bleak house into a happy home for Clara. Now that vow had widened to include Lord Ravenwell.

Chapter Twelve

Three days later, Clara woke with a runny nose and a sore throat. She was listless and touchy all morning and Grace could do little other than sit and cuddle her next to the nursery fire. Even Sweep was unable to raise a smile or a spark of interest and the morning dragged as Grace remained on tenterhooks, constantly alert for signs of a fever developing. The only bright point was a letter from Rachel, sent all the way from Huria—via Miss Fanworth—which Ned brought back from the village.

Rachel's letter described a very different world to Shiverstone Hall. She wrote of the luxury of the palace she lived in—a *palace!*—the vastness of the surrounding desert and the beauty of the verdant oasis. She had three children in her care—eight-year-old Aahil, his sister Ameera, six, and his brother, Hakim, four—who were slowly growing to trust her. Grace could read her love for the children in the words she had penned. About her employer, the majestic-sounding Sheikh Malik bin Jalal al-Mahrouky, she said but little. There was caution in her words and Grace thought he must be most intimidating.

A little before eleven Mrs Sharp sent Alice upstairs to offer to sit with Miss Clara for a spell whilst Miss

Bertram went to the kitchen for a cup of chocolate. Grace took Sweep with her, putting her next to Brack who, unusually for this time of day, was curled up near the kitchen range. After a hesitant beginning, the two animals had become friends.

'How is she?' Mrs Sharp handed Grace a cup of warm chocolate.

'Tetchy. And most displeased at being left with Alice,' Grace said, sitting at the table. 'Thank you.'

'It is to be hoped you do not succumb to the cold as well. You look pale.'

The housekeeper's concern was unexpected, endearing her to Grace, who cradled the cup between her hands and sipped, then tipped her head back, heaving a sigh, watching mindlessly whilst Mrs Sharp chopped carrots.

'I cannot believe how exhausting it is, sitting and doing nothing other than nursing Clara.'

'Has she slept at all?'

'Not yet.' Grace finished her chocolate and stood up. 'I must return and relieve Alice. Poor Clara, she is so miserable. She does not know what she wants, but she wants it *now*.'

'I have mixed up a remedy for her, to help ease her throat.' Mrs Sharp often treated common ailments within the household with her remedies. 'Give her a spoonful and then, when she does fall asleep, I will sit with her. You'll be bound to have a disturbed night with her and you have missed your walk today. You should go outside for some exercise whilst you are able to. It is a beautiful day.'

Startled by the housekeeper's unusual solicitude, Grace thanked her and, when Clara dozed off shortly after luncheon, Grace took her up on her offer.

Ravenwell had been out since first light, according to Sharp, sitting in his favourite overstuffed armchair in the corner as he sucked on his pipe. Grace lingered, hoping to learn a little more about her puzzling employer.

'Likes to keep himself busy, see. Stops him from brooding.'

'Brooding?' Grace busied herself folding Clara's freshly laundered clothes, as though any answer was of no consequence and she asked merely to be polite. The best way to wheedle information from Sharp was to pretend disinterest.

'Oh, aye. He exhausts himself every day, to stop him thinking about his father. It's the guilt.'

Guilt. Sharp had mentioned guilt before, but always refused to explain.

'Oh, I cannot believe his lordship has anything to feel guilty about.'

'Well that's just where you'd be wrong, missy.' Sharp tilted his head back and, eyes half-closed, blew a perfect smoke ring into the air. 'So you don't know ever'thing, for all yer education.

'No,' he went on after a pause. 'He'll never forgive himself. Feels it here—' and he thumped his chest in the region of his heart '—he does. He ain't the hard man you think he is.'

I don't think him a hard man at all. But she had more sense than to say so to Sharp.

'We tried to stop him going back into the fire, but three of us couldn't hold him back, he was that determined.'

'Was that the fire at Ravenwell Manor?'

'If'n only we could've stopped him, but he were like a man possessed. And his mother. It fair curdled the blood to hear her screams.'

'But…' she had to ask and hope Sharp wouldn't clam up '…why did he go back into the fire? Is that when he got burned?'

'Aye. 'Twas his father. He couldn't walk so well and he was upstairs when it broke out. His lordship…the Earl of Shiverstone as he was then…tried to rescue him. He got as far as the bedchamber, but then the roof caved in and his father was gone. Lord, the nightmares he suffered afterwards. Not to mention the pain. If'n you've ever burned your hand with a candle flame, missy, you'll know the agony. Only multiply that a hundred...a thousand...fold, and you might get nearer the truth.'

Poor Nathaniel. A hard lump of misery lodged in Grace's throat as she imagined his suffering, at only twenty-one years of age. Two years older than she was now. Another piece of the puzzle that was Lord Ravenwell slotted into place. The guilt, as well as the scars, must have been an intolerable burden to one so young.

She donned her pelisse and set off to walk up the hill behind the Hall, her sketchbook under her arm, hoping to capture the wildness and beauty of the landscape with her pencil. She had never ventured up on to the fells before—it was too far for Clara to walk—and she looked forward to exploring this area of her new home.

Her breath grew short as she plodded up the path, determined to reach Shiver Crag, jaggedly silhouetted against the blue of the sky, but she found she had to stop long before then to catch her breath.

She gazed back the way she had come. The day was clear and sharp, and the land fell away below her to flatten into the dale, with its woods and pasture. There was the river she had to drive across to reach the village and... she searched, her hand shielding her eyes...yes, there was the church tower, jutting out amongst the jumble of rooftops. Her chest swelled as she breathed in the cold air, refreshing her lungs and making her blood sing with energy.

She would walk a little further and sketch a little before going back. And she would hope that somehow, miraculously, her nap had restored Clara to full health. Her attention was caught by a huge, golden-brown bird circling lazily in the sky. *Good heavens.* She had thought the bird she saw when she first arrived at the Hall was big, but...this one was gigantic. She watched its mesmerising, effortless glide and marvelled at the span of its broad wings, tipped by feathers that resembled splayed fingers.

She looked back up to the crag. It was further than she first thought. She would have no time to reach it today, but it would be an imposing focal point for her sketches if she walked just a little further, to where the terrain levelled out ahead.

She trudged on until she reached the grassy plateau and there he was.

Ravenwell.

He had not seen her—he stood to her right, half-facing away from her as he delved inside a bag on the ground. What was he doing up here, all alone? Was he…as Sharp had said…brooding? It was odd there were no dogs with him. Nor was there a horse in sight. Did he come up here to this wild, solitary place to think about his father and the night of the fire? Would he welcome company, or would he send her away? The temptation to retreat before he saw her was powerful. She could disappear back down the path and he would never know she had been there.

But…this was her first opportunity to sketch this stark but beautiful landscape and she was loath to waste it. Making her mind up, she tucked her sketchbook more securely beneath her arm and headed towards the Marquess, picking her way across the springy tussocks of grass.

As she drew near to Ravenwell, he raised his left arm, clad in a massive gauntlet, straight out in front of him and let out a shrill cry. Grace's steps faltered. Was it some sort of ritual? A movement caught her eye. The bird—that monstrous bird—had stopped circling. It swooped purposefully and then flew straight at Nathaniel.

It's attacking! No!

Grace ran towards Ravenwell, waving her arms and her sketchbook, shouting as loudly as she could. The bird—surely as big as Grace herself—veered at the last minute, beating its powerful wings as it rose up into the air, its curved claws just missing Nathaniel's head.

Grace grabbed Nathaniel's hand in both of hers, her sketchbook dropping unheeded to the ground.

'Are you all right?' Her breath came in short, heaving bursts.

'What the *devil* do you think you're doing?'

Grace quailed at his fury. He tore his gaze from her and followed the bird's flight.

'Have you any idea how long I...?' He paused.

Hauled in a deep breath.

Looked back at Grace.

Narrowed his eyes.

'Did you ask if I was *all right*?'

Before she could reply, he threw back his head and howled with laughter.

She glared. 'What is so amusing?'

'You!' He gasped for breath. 'Were you trying to *save* me?'

'Well, I did, did I not? That monster attacked you. I frightened it away.'

His chest heaved as another peal of laughter rang out. 'That monster, as you describe her, is an eagle. And she has enough power in those talons of hers to do you some serious damage. And you thought to...'

Their gazes fused, and his words faded. Grace trembled as longing curled through her body and she lost herself in the molten depths of his eyes.

'I...'

At that single word, his gaze, soft as a caress, drifted down to settle on her lips.

Nathaniel's initial burst of rage was, within seconds, quashed by his mirth that this dainty, feminine girl had thought to rescue *him*. Her eyes, glinting in the sunlight, flashed her annoyance and he was drawn into their gold-green depths. And his laughter died. And then her lips parted and, without volition, his gaze dipped to trace their delicate shape and admire their soft, pink fullness. And to wonder how they would taste…

'I…' she whispered again.

Then he was jolted from his entrancement as shock flashed across her face and red infused her cheeks, and he felt the wrench deep inside as she released her grip on his hand. His right hand. His damaged hand, with its coarse and ugly puckered skin. He snatched it away, thrusting it behind his back, out of sight.

'I…I am sorry, my l-lord.' She would not meet his eyes now. 'W-was it meant to fly at you like that?'

She was so pretty. Too pretty, too delicate, for a beast like him. He found the strength to thrust aside his humiliation in order to smooth over their mutual embarrassment.

'Yes, but it is not your fault.' He occupied himself pulling the leather gauntlet from his left hand. 'You meant well.'

He conjured up the image of Ralph Rendell. Now there would be a suitable pairing: the same station in life, both of them young and attractive. Unscarred. That thought had the same effect on his lust as falling in Shiver Beck on a winter's day—something he had done once and never wished to repeat.

'Will it come back?'

He scanned the sky. Amber was very close to being fit enough to return to the wild. Would she return after her scare?

'There. See.' He pointed at the bird. 'She has not gone away. Not yet.'

'How…? Is she tame? Is she yours?'

He told her the tale of how Amber came to his care.

'Her wing is healed now. I've been releasing her for longer each day to strengthen it. She comes back for food, even though she has begun to hunt for herself. One day, she will simply not return and hopefully she'll head north, back to the Highlands where she was born.'

'It sounds so romantic, the Highlands.' Her voice was wistful.

'More romance, Miss Bertram?'

Her lips compressed and a light flush crept over her cheeks. Not the most sensitive comment, following their difference about romance the other evening, and that interlude just now, when he had thought…

What had he thought? For one moment, he had forgotten who he was. *How* he was. He had been a man, looking into the eyes of a pretty girl. It had been a mistake, not to be repeated.

'Have you ever been to Scotland?' he asked.

'No, but I have seen paintings. It is like this but…more so.'

Nathaniel looked around. More so indeed. Very much more so.

'Where is Clara?'

'She is unwell. I have left her asleep, with Mrs Sharp watching over her, whilst I take some exercise.'

'Does she need a doctor?'

'No. We both agree it is only a cold; there is no sign of fever. But she is very miserable, poor mite.'

'I shall come and see her when I go home.' Something caught his eye and he bent to pick it off the ground.

'Is this a sketch book?'

'I thought I might have time to capture the view. I have never been up here before. It is too far for Clara.'

Nathaniel riffled through the pages. 'There aren't many landscapes here.'

'No.' She put out her hand and he whisked it out of her reach so he could continue to look through it.

'They are mostly portraits,' she said repressively, 'and they cannot possibly be of interest to you as you do not know any of the subjects.'

'Oh, I don't know. Here.' He held up a watercolour of three young women and grinned. 'I could be interested in these three beauties. Are they the friends you told me about?'

A light flush stained her cheeks. 'Yes.'

He looked at the painting. It showed skill. 'This is very good. Which one is which?'

She named the three and he said, 'Would you paint Clara for me, when she is better? I should like to have a portrait of her at this age.'

'Yes, of course.'

'Thank you.' He handed her the sketchbook. 'Perhaps you would like to sketch whilst we wait to see if Amber returns?'

Grace perched on a rock and Nathaniel stood behind and off to one side, watching her work. He could watch her all day: her frown of concentration, the pull of her bottom lip through her teeth, the blonde strands of hair that had blown loose and glinted in the sunlight. Rendell was a lucky man, if she had set her sights on him.

All too soon, it seemed to Nathaniel, she closed her book and stood up.

'I must get back to Clara. Oh!' She pointed. 'Amber has come back.'

Sure enough, the eagle was circling out over the dale. Nathaniel hadn't even noticed.

'Stand back,' he said, pulling the gauntlet on to his left hand. 'And for God's sake stay still this time. We don't want to spook her again.'

He waited whilst she retreated several paces, then took a morsel of rabbit from his bag and called as he turned his left side to Amber and extended his left arm, the meat held between his forefinger and thumb. There was the swish of wings, the jolting impact of the landing and the squeeze of the eagle's talons through the stout leather of his gauntlet.

'May I stroke her?'

Nathaniel took a hood from his pocket and slipped it over Amber's head. 'You may now.'

He glanced down at her profile as he spoke. Her brows were bunched across the bridge of her perfect little nose as she stroked Amber's feathers.

'But she would not hurt me. You laughed at me when I thought she was attacking *you*.'

'I laughed at your bold conviction that *you* might protect *me*. I probably should not have laughed, for you showed courage, but please take more care in future, particularly if you have Clara with you. The hood is to keep Amber calm. She is still a wild creature at heart—can you imagine the damage that beak could inflict on a person's face?'

Grace peered at Amber and shuddered.

'It looks so cruel.'

'It is efficient. It helps her survive. Cruelty does not come into it. But she is a powerful predator and should be treated with respect. Come. It is time I returned her to her mew.'

They headed down the hill, to the stable yard.

'Would you care to see my other birds? They are smaller than Amber, but tame. I use them for hawking, as men have done for centuries.'

She hesitated before saying, 'I should love to see them, but maybe another day? I must return to Clara.'

'I shall come and see her once I've put Amber away.'

Nathaniel watched Grace walk away, conflicting emotions churning his insides as he thought back to that moment up on the fell.

That look.

It had fired all sorts of longings deep within him. And she responded—her eyes had not lied. She had been all too aware of that *frisson* that passed between them.

It had been so very long since he'd experienced feelings for a woman—not just the physical need for a woman, but the longing for…more. That most dangerous of random thoughts had taken root in his heart: *What if…?*

She had held his hand without flinching, without even seeming aware… With a harsh sound, he quashed the bud of hope that formed deep inside his heart before it could begin to unfurl.

A beautiful girl like Grace would never want someone as damaged as him.

This yearning inside…it had been stirred up by Hannah and David's deaths…by the realisation that, now, apart from his mother, he was truly alone.

I will adjust to this new reality. I still have Clara. No one can take her from me.

He returned Amber to her enclosure, working without conscience thought, his heart heavy, aching with the burden of loss.

When he reached the house, he found Clara inconsolable—the only place she would settle was on Grace's lap and consequently he saw little of either of them for the rest of the afternoon or the evening. Bored with his own company, Nathaniel went to the book room to work on his ledgers, but he could not concentrate, his wandering thoughts returning again and again to that moment on the fell when their gazes had clashed. Finally, he admitted defeat and, as the clock in the hall struck eleven, he climbed the stairs to bed.

On the landing, a whimper and a cough reached his ears. Praying Clara had not taken a turn for the worse, he headed for her bedchamber.

It's a cold. Nothing to fear. She will recover.

But cold dread gnawed at him. Childhood was precarious; so many died in infancy. He could not bear… Clara was all he had left of his beloved Hannah. He could not lose her as well.

He must set his mind at rest. He entered her bedchamber

quietly, his gaze drawn to the bed, dimly visible in what remained of the firelight.

Clara was asleep, spreadeagled on her back, mouth open as she snored gently. Love for the tiny girl filled his heart. So very precious. A pale shape on the far side of the bed caught his eye—a hand, resting on the coverlet, mere inches from Clara. He tiptoed around the bed, his wavering shadow preceding him, and gazed down at Grace, fast asleep in a chair by the bedside, her head tipped back, the white curve of her throat both seductive and vulnerable. Even in sleep, she was graceful, her lashes fanned against her delicate cheekbones, her honey-blonde hair lying in a loose plait over her shoulder.

Grace. The name suited her to perfection. Ever since that afternoon, Nathaniel had found it impossible to think of her as Miss Bertram.

Grace.

She was clad only in a thin white nightgown that clung to her, softly draping petite breasts and clearly outlining the hard buds of her nipples. Blood surged to his loins. He forced his gaze from her breasts, quelling his inappropriate lust.

She was cold.

A blanket pooled around her feet. He crouched to gather it up and then softly settled it over the sleeping woman. A faint line creased her brow and she turned her head against the back of the chair and shifted her hips. She murmured… a soft, indistinct sound…and then stilled, her brow smoothing over, her lips relaxing, as she sank once more into sleep.

Nathaniel—breath held—tucked the blanket around her so it wouldn't slip again and then carefully, silently, re-fuelled the fire.

Then he tiptoed from the room and quietly closed the door.

Chapter Thirteen

'What do you think, Alice?'

The young maid stood back. 'They look better, miss. They make the room lighter. More…more happy, somehow.'

'I think so too,' Grace said, admiring the new curtains at the windows of the drawing room.

She had found them in a huge old linen press in a spare bedchamber during one of her searches for items to bring a more homely touch to the Hall. The original heavy deep green curtains had deadened the room, sucking the light from it. These, in contrast, were patterned in white and gold and instantly brightened the room. The gold echoed the yellow veining in several of the 'white' squares on the chessboard and in the marbled panels set into the doors of a small decorative cabinet Sharp had carried into the room at her behest.

Thinking about chess set Grace's thoughts in the direction they had taken ever more frequently since her chance meeting with Lord Ravenwell up on the fells three days before. He *had* changed since her first week at the Hall, when they had only met at dinnertime in the evening. Now, he regularly visited Clara in the nursery—where yesterday he had surprised them both with a dolls' house he'd had sent from York—and he spent every evening after dinner with Grace in the drawing room: playing chess or cards or reading, sometimes aloud, whilst Grace applied herself to mending or embroidery. However much Grace adored spending time with Clara during the day, she anticipated the evenings, and Ravenwell's company, with increasing pleasure.

She hoped he would approve of the changes she was making today. She had uncovered the pianoforte and also a pale gold sofa, which she had grouped with the two wingback chairs near the fireplace, and Sharp and Ned had brought in two more upholstered chairs that she had found stored under covers in the dining room. All it needed now was a few ornaments on the mantelshelves and it would be done.

'There's another rug, miss,' Alice said, eyeing the small rug set before the fire where Clara—still a bit snuffly after her cold but with her energy restored—sprawled with Sweep. 'It's nicer than that dull thing, so Mrs Sharp says, with pretty colours in a pattern.'

'Clara. Take care with Sweep's claws, sweetie.' Grace cocked her head at Alice. '*Mrs Sharp* told you that?'

The housekeeper was slowly warming towards Grace, but her reaction this morning when Grace told her she was moving some furniture into the drawing room had been unpromising. Grace had feared a return to their former frosty relationship.

'Yes, miss. She came in when you was out with that cat.'

The entire household, apart from Grace and Clara, referred to Sweep as 'that cat'. Clara was besotted with her kitten, who was running the household ragged, and Grace tried to forestall as much of his mischief as possible. She took him outside several times a day to keep the house clean and in the vain hope of wearing him out. As he grew, he would become easier to cope with. She hoped.

'Did Mrs Sharp tell you where the other rug is?'

'No need, miss. Sharp's gone to fetch it.'

With that, the door opened and Sharp staggered in, a rolled-up carpet—for it looked too big to be called a rug—on his shoulder. They moved the furniture, rolled up the old dingy rug and unrolled the new one, with its symmetrical pattern in white, yellow and green.

'I've given it a good beating,' Mrs Sharp said.

Together, the four of them heaved the furniture back into place, then stood back to admire the effect.

'It looks beaut—' Grace stopped, her heart plummeting. 'Where is Clara?'

She had moved Clara to the other end of the room whilst they were busy, but now there was no sign of her. Or of Sweep. The door was ajar and, cursing herself for getting distracted, Grace dashed out into the hall.

'Oh, no!' Mrs Sharp clutched at Grace and pointed wordlessly up at the landing, her face ashen.

Nausea welled into Grace's throat, her stomach clenching in violent denial of the tableau on the galleried landing above: Clara, standing on a wooden chest and leaning over the balustrade, arms waving as she stretched to reach Sweep, who was strolling nonchalantly along the handrail.

'Sweep! Sweep! *Bad* kitty!' she shouted. 'Danjous!'

Before Grace could move, or speak, a dark shape streaked past the group clustered in the hall. Brack reached the landing, reared up on his hind legs and grabbed Sweep in his mouth. Clara's howl galvanised Grace into action and she tore up the stairs. By the time she reached the landing Brack was back on all fours and had retreated to the far side of the landing, the kitten clamped in his jaws, and Clara had clambered off the chest.

She ran towards Brack, shrieking, 'No! No! No bite!'

Grace swept Clara into her arms before she could reach the dog and turned away, pressing her face, eyes tight shut, into the sweet-scented skin of her daughter's neck, sickened by what had so nearly happened and also by the sight she might see if she looked at Brack. Clara would be devastated if Sweep was injured. The others had followed her—she had heard them pounding up the stairs behind her. Let them deal with the tragedy.

A hand gripped her shoulder, and tugged her around.

'It's safe to look,' rumbled a deep voice.

His lordship. Nooooo. I'll lose my job...no more than I deserve... Clara could have been killed! But, oh, how can I bear...?

Her panicked thoughts steadied. *Safe.* He said it was safe to look. Gingerly, she lifted her head and opened her eyes. A squealing Clara was plucked from her arms. Her gaze darted to Brack, lying by the wall, forelegs outstretched. And Sweep. On his back, between Brack's legs, paws waving in the air as he tried to bat the dog's nose. As Grace watched, Brack lowered his head and swept his tongue along the kitten's exposed stomach.

No blood. No disaster.

Her heart slowed from its frantic gallop to a trot and she breathed again. There was no one else on the landing. Those feet she had heard behind her had been Ravenwell.

'How...?'

'I was in the hall. You dashed past without even noticing me. It was I who sent Brack to fetch the cat.'

Grace dropped her chin to her chest. Sucked in a shaky breath. 'I am sorry. Clara should not...I allowed myself to be distracted.'

'By what, may I ask?'

How could she admit she had been distracted by making changes in his house? How could this be worse?

It would be worse if Clara had fallen. Her knees trembled at that thought and she squeezed her eyes shut again, her neck and shoulders tight with the effort it took not to collapse in a wailing heap.

I have made a mess of everything.

'Well?'

That single harsh word forced her eyes open and her gaze to his. His dark eyes bored into her.

'Alice?' His voice rose, calling down to the hall below. 'Come up here. Take Miss Clara to the nursery. And take that infernal cat with you.'

He raised a brow. 'I'm waiting.'

Grace gripped her hands together. 'We were making a few changes in the drawing room.'

His brows snapped together. 'What changes?'

She forced herself to hold his gaze. 'You did say I might.'

A look of scorn crossed his face. She could not blame him. What happened was inexcusable. Clara had been in her charge.

'I am sorry,' she said. 'I am not trying to excuse myself. We were moving furniture. One minute Clara was playing at the other end of the room with Sweep, the next she was gone.'

Fear shivered through her as she relived the terrible moment when she had run out into the hall and seen her little girl… She bit back a sob.

'We?' That quiet voice bristled with menace. 'You mean to tell me my entire household was present and not one of you noticed Clara leave the room?'

'It was n-nobody's fault but mine, my lord.'

'At last something we can agree upon.' His eyes flashed with anger.

'Wh-what will you do?' Her voice wobbled as the next sob broke free. 'P-please…do not dismiss me. I l-like it here.'

'You cry at the thought of losing your position here, but what of the fact my niece could have been *killed*?'

'I d-do not cry for myself! That picture is burned into my mind…she's so small…so vulnerable… I cannot forget the horror of seeing her…'

Her hands twisted painfully as she tried to interpret his expression through blurred vision.

'The only reason you are here is to look after my niece.' His voice was harsh and uncompromising. 'Yet it appears to me you are more interested in altering your surroundings—*my home*—into your idea of suitably luxurious surroundings for yourself than in Clara's welfare.'

Stung, Grace glared at him. 'That is unfair. And untrue. You *know* my reasons for those changes. You *agreed*.' She hauled in a breath. 'I only wish to make a comfortable and happy home for your niece. She is a *child*. You may choose to live in these cold cheerless surroundings, but Clara deserves better! She deserves a home and a loving family.'

'Instead of which she has me. And a houseful of servants.'

Bitterness infused his words and shame coursed through Grace. She had not intended to wound him but, before she could try to repair the damage, Sharp called urgently from the hall below.

'Milord! Milord!'

'What is it?'

'It's her ladyship, milord. Her carriage is coming up the track.'

Ravenwell's jaw clenched. He shot a hard look at Grace. 'This matter is not resolved.' He reached into his pocket and pulled out a letter. 'Here. Ned brought this back from the village. It is a happy chance that brought me indoors to give you your letter immediately. Had I delayed, Clara might well be dead by now.

'Go. Make Clara presentable and bring her down to greet her grandmother in twenty minutes. And, for God's sake, keep that cat out of the way.'

He ran down the stairs, Brack at his heels, and Grace turned to walk slowly towards the nursery wing, her eyes burning with shame.

'Had I delayed, Clara might well be dead by now.'

He was right. She had never seen him so furious, nor so scathing. What if he persuaded his mother to take Clara home with her? If he did not think Grace a fitting person to care for her, he might very well do that. She must work hard to impress her ladyship. If *she* thought Grace suitable, she might persuade Ravenwell to keep her as Clara's governess.

Before she went to the nursery room to get Clara ready, Grace slipped into her bedchamber, needing a moment of quiet to settle her nerves. She perched on the edge of the bed, still shaken, sick dread swirling through her.

She opened her letter, seeking distraction. It was, she saw with a glad heart, from Joanna. Eager to find out how her friend was faring in her role as governess to the Huntford family in Hertfordshire, Grace began to read, her jaw dropping at Joanna's amazing news: the newborn baby who had been abandoned on the doorstep of Madame Dubois's School for Young Ladies was, in reality, the granddaughter of a marquess. And not only had her grandfather publicly acknowledged her and introduced her into society, but Joanna had also met and fallen in love with Luke Preston, the son of the Earl of Ingham, and they had recently married.

Her happiness shone through every word she had penned.

Pleasure for her friend warred with envy in Grace's breast. Yes, she was excited and thrilled for Joanna, for she knew how Joanna had longed to know about her real family, but she could not help but compare Joanna's happy future to the uncertainties of her own. She did not want to leave Shiverstone. She *would* not leave Shiverstone. She did not know how but she must, somehow, persuade his lordship that he could not manage without her.

Putting the letter aside, she hurried to the nursery to make Clara presentable to meet her grandmother.

Ten minutes later, Grace drew in a deep breath, smoothed a nervous hand over her hair and tapped on the drawing-room door before entering, Clara's hand firmly in hers. The Marquess stood before the fireplace, hands clasped behind his back. His eyes were hard, anger still simmering. She swallowed and crossed the room, surreptitiously towing Clara, whose steps had suddenly lagged. An elderly lady—stoutly built, with the same deep brown eyes as her son—watched them cross the room.

Grace bobbed a curtsy.

'Mother, this is Miss Bertram. Miss Bertram, my mother, Lady Ravenwell.'

'Good morning, Lady Ravenwell.'

Every inch of Grace passed under her ladyship's inspection before, finally, she inclined her head. Her expression indicated neither approval nor disapproval. It was hard not to squirm under such scrutiny, which revived uncomfortable memories of various summonses to Madame Dubois's study for some infraction of the rules.

Her ladyship's expression softened as she switched her gaze to Clara. She held out her arms. 'Come to Grandmama, Clara.'

Grace urged the little girl forward, worried she did not remember her grandmother, but Clara's initial reluctance turned to eagerness and she rushed forward, releasing Grace's hand.

'Ganmama.' Clara allowed herself to be hugged and kissed, then wriggled free. 'Ganmama. I got Sweep.'

'Oh! She is talking again. Oh, Nathaniel, you have worked wonders with her.'

The Marquess cleared his throat. 'I believe you must credit Miss Bertram with Clara's progress.'

'Then I shall. Thank you, Miss Bertram.'

Grace smiled at her ladyship and was once more subjected to a sharp appraisal. Had Ravenwell told his mother about Grace's dereliction of duty? A glance at Ravenwell's rock-like expression revealed no clue. She hovered a moment, unsure for the first time of what was expected of her. She had begun to feel like part of the family, with an established position in the household, but Lady Ravenwell's arrival had underscored her true position. She was neither family nor servant, but somewhere in the middle, and she now felt awkward and out of place. She retreated to a chair by the window whilst Clara remained by her grandmother, pleading with her to come and see her kitten.

The same thought bombarded Grace's head without pause: she had forgotten her place and had crossed that boundary between staff and family. Lord Ravenwell was right to be furious. Furtively, she scanned the room. Her changes might have improved the room, but she understood how they must appear to him. She had been presumptuous, both in accepting the kitten without consulting him first and in initiating changes in *his* home. She was meddlesome and an irritant and she had compounded her error by embroiling the rest of his staff in—

'Miss Bertram!'

His voice, exasperated, penetrated her silent scold. She jerked to her feet. He stood directly in front of her and she was forced to crane her neck to meet his gaze.

'You had better go and fetch that infer… Sweep,' he growled. 'Clara will not rest until Mother has made its acquaintance.'

Chapter Fourteen

Dinner with Lady Ravenwell was an ordeal. Her lady-ship—resplendent in a green satin gown, a matching tur-ban and emeralds—barely acknowledged Grace's presence, talking to Ravenwell about mutual acquaintances in whom he clearly had no interest. It was a relief when the meal was over but, before Grace could excuse herself and disappear upstairs, Lady Ravenwell made clear her expectation that Grace would join her in the drawing room whilst her son remained in the parlour with his brandy.

'You may pour the tea,' the Marchioness commanded as she swept from the room.

Grace glanced over her shoulder at Ravenwell, hear-ing the scrape of his chair on the floor. It had become his habit to drink his brandy in the drawing room, over a game of chess or a hand of cards, but he had merely pushed his chair away from the table. He leant back, stretching his long legs straight. He caught her eye and, for the first time since that afternoon, she caught a glimmer of humour in his expression. She pressed her lips together and stalked from the room. She had no trouble interpreting his amusement.

She was the lamb to be sacrificed on the altar of his mother's chatter.

It was worse than she feared. His mother did not wish

to converse with Grace. Neither did she wish to talk at her, as she had talked at Ravenwell throughout their meal. Her intention became clear as soon as Mrs Sharp had deposited the tea tray and left the room. Grace had barely begun to pour when the interrogation began.

Where was she from? Who were her family? *Where* had she gone to school again? What were her qualifications…if any? Lady Ravenwell's tone clearly expressed her doubts on that last one. And the question that recurred time and again: how, precisely, had Grace found out about the position of governess at Shiverstone Hall?

'The post was advertised in the *York Herald* which is not, to my knowledge, read in Salisbury. How did *you* discover it?'

'My teacher at the school, Miss Fanworth, was told of the vacancy by a friend of hers.'

Grace's hand was tucked down by her side with crossed fingers. A lie was not really a lie if you had your fingers crossed—or so she and her friends had told each other when they were young. Besides, it was very nearly true. It was Miss Fanworth who had arranged Rachel's position in Huria—she could quite easily have done the same for Grace.

'What is the name of this friend?'

'I do not recall.'

'Have you ever been to Harrogate, Miss Bertram?'

'No, my lady.' That, at least, was no falsehood. The stagecoach in which she had travelled to Ravenwell Manor had put her down before they reached Harrogate.

By the time the Marquess came through, close to an hour later, Grace's nerves were in shreds and, as her lady-ship's focus shifted to her son, she begged to be excused.

'Do you customarily retire at such an early hour?'

'I am concerned Clara may have trouble sleeping tonight with all the excitement of your arrival, my lady, particularly after her recent cold. From my sitting room upstairs, I shall hear if she wakes.'

Visions of Clara wandering out on to the landing— even though she knew that chest had been removed—had plagued Grace all evening.

'Very commendable, I am sure. I believe in bestowing praise where it is due, Miss Bertram, and I confess that, despite your youth, you have impressed me with your attention to duty. I thank you for taking good care of my granddaughter.'

Grace blushed as, without volition, her gaze flicked to Ravenwell and fused with his. They both knew that to be a lie.

As she mounted the stairs, the certainty he would now tell his mother the truth churned her insides until she felt sick. Lady Ravenwell's clear suspicions about Grace were troubling enough, but if she should learn of Grace's neglect, Grace would surely be dismissed and then what would she do? She peeped into Clara's bedchamber. Her daughter was sound asleep, on her back as usual, with the blankets kicked askew and her thumb jammed into her mouth. Grace crept in and stood by the bed, love for her child flooding her. Finally, she straightened the covers, bent to kiss Clara's forehead and then retreated to her sitting room.

Grace pondered her uncertain future as she stared into the flames. That future was entirely in the hands of Lord Ravenwell and never had she felt more keenly the divide between her station and his world—a world to which, she realised, both Isabel and Joanna now belonged. She did not begrudge them their good fortune, but how she wished a small piece of their luck might rub off on her.

What could she do? What power did she have?

The answer was none.

She could only wait, impotently, for his decision and then, if he decreed she must go, she must be prepared to fight. For one thing was certain: she would *never* leave her daughter.

We could run away. I could take Clara and go.

For a few minutes, she indulged that fantasy, before reality crashed over her. It was not even remotely possible. Snatch the ward of a nobleman? And how could they live? And then an even greater truth struck her—an insight so startling it near stole her breath. With a gigantic thump of her heart, she understood she would not leave even if she could.

Because taking Clara away from Shiverstone Hall would mean leaving Lord Ravenwell.

Nathaniel.

And not only could she not bear it if she were never to see him again, but she would never, ever—*could* never, ever—hurt him in that way.

Shaken to her core by that revelation, Grace stumbled to her feet and returned to Clara's bedchamber. She stood and gazed at her beautiful daughter, battling against the sick realisation that, somehow, she had fallen for Nathaniel. She had seen beneath the scarred, irascible and reclusive façade he presented to the world to his kind, loving, intelligent heart.

But... Caution screamed through her head. *Remember Philip. You thought you were in love with him and you were wrong. Don't make the same mistake. Nathaniel is a marquess, far above your touch. And right now he does not even like you.*

Finally, lids heavy and stifling a yawn, she knew she must go to bed. She bent over Clara and smoothed her curls gently from her forehead.

'Sleep well, my beloved little girl, and sweet dreams,' she whispered. 'Mama is watching over you.'

A sudden sound from behind her sent her spinning to face the door.

* * *

Nathaniel froze.

All he could take in was the guilt written all over Grace's face.

Mama?

He pushed away from the doorjamb, against which he had stumbled when he heard her words. Her eyes were huge and he saw the movement of her throat as she swallowed. And then she moved, gliding towards him, one finger to her lips, her eyes…her beautiful, gold-green eyes—the image of Clara's, and how hadn't he seen the resemblance before?—stricken.

He barely moved aside and she brushed past him, out into the passageway. The hairs on his forearms rose at her touch and her clean, sweet lily-of-the-valley scent pervaded his senses.

Mama.

He followed her out of Clara's room on to the landing.

'Explain yourself.'

Anger flared, boosted by the vision of Clara in danger that afternoon, and his panic when he had seen her. How very precious she had become to him. What would he do… how would he survive…if he lost her too? His very vulnerability terrified him. And now…what would this new revelation mean for the future for all of them?

Grace had paused to close Clara's door.

'Well?'

She was trembling. He hardened his heart and strode to the door of her sitting room. He held it wide and beckoned. Inside, he stoked the fire and added more wood, willing his temper under control before trusting himself to look at her.

Grace stood inside the door, fingers interlaced, knuckles white. 'Why did you come to Clara's room?'

'Am I not allowed? She is *my* ward. I needed to ensure she is safe after the danger she was put in this afternoon.'

She flinched. 'You cannot know the guilt I feel over my neglect.'

'I am still awaiting an explanation. Do not make me ask again.'

'Clara is my daughter.'

That simple statement crushed any residual hope that he had misheard. The agony in her voice wrenched at his heart, but he could not quash his anger, or his hurt, over her betrayal. He had begun to trust her. Since her arrival, his evenings had changed from something to dread to a time keenly anticipated. How, and when, had the barriers he had built against the rest of the world been breached?

'Why are you here? Did you intend to snatch her away from me?'

Her mouth fell open and yet her gaze skittered from his. 'No! I would never do that.'

'But the thought crossed your mind.'

He watched her intently, noting a blush creep up her neck to her face.

'Only once. You were so angry with me…earlier…but I would never do such a thing. It was a fleeting thought, soon exposed for an idle fantasy. I could never take her from you, nor you from her. I am not so cruel.'

'You said this afternoon that Clara deserves a home and a loving family. You said she deserves better than me and a houseful of servants.'

Her eyes flashed and she crossed the room to glare up at him.

'You twist my words, my lord. It was you who said she only has you and a houseful of servants.'

'But you believe it is the truth.' He grabbed her, his fingers biting into the soft flesh of her upper arms. 'You think she deserves better. That I am incapable of giving her a happy childhood.'

'No!'

She squirmed to free herself and he released her, taking a step back, ashamed he had allowed his anger to prevail. Yet she did not retreat. She moved closer, her gaze searching his.

'Clara adores you.' Her scent enveloped him and her breath was warm upon his skin. Her fingertips caressed his cheek with a featherlight touch. 'You do not see how her eyes light up when she sees you. She has settled here. She is happy.'

Her eyes darkened and her hand slipped to rest against his chest. Without volition, his head lowered and he brushed her sweet, silken mouth with his. His blood quickened, together with the compulsion to sweep her into his arms and taste her again. And again. But doubts nipped at the heels of that compulsion.

Why now?

She must be desperate indeed to contemplate seducing a man like him—desperate to stay with her daughter.

Nathaniel spun away and faced the hearth, propping both hands against the mantel, gripping the wooden edge, grounding himself. She sounded sincere, but could he trust his instincts? He silently berated himself for a fool. He should dismiss her immediately. There was no excuse for her deceit. But he could not utter the words. God help him, he *wanted* to understand. More, he wanted to forgive. He did not want her to go. His very neediness infuriated him, but it was a fury directed against himself, not her.

'That should not have happened.'

'I am sorry.' He had to strain to hear her whispered response.

'Why *did* you come here, if not to reclaim your daughter?'

'I p-promised myself, when she was born, when I gave her away that, one day, I would find her and make sure she was loved and wanted.'

'She was. My sister and her husband doted on her. And now—'

'And now, you dote upon her.'

'Yes,' he said gruffly. 'So why this charade?' He turned to face her. 'Why did you apply to be her governess?'

She hung her head. 'I did not. Not precisely.' A puff of air escaped her and her shoulders slumped. 'I shall tell you the whole story. M-may I sit?'

'Of course.' He waited until she sank on to the armchair by the fire, then dragged over a wooden chair to sit opposite, swinging it around to straddle it, resting his arms across the back.

She told him a tale that was not unique. It happened too frequently: a young girl, her head turned by romantic words and enticing kisses, and a green youth who did not consider the repercussions of his persuasions.

'Seventeen years old.' If such a thing happened to Clara, when she was so young and innocent, he would be after the culprit with a horsewhip. 'What did your uncle have to say about it?'

Her head jerked up, her expression one of horror. 'My uncle did not know. He and my aunt are very devout…they would not…nobody knew, only my three best friends, and I swore them to secrecy.'

'But…surely your teachers must have realised.'

'I managed to hide the change in my shape. My clothes were always loose on me—my cousins are bigger than I and Aunt refused to alter the dresses too drastically. She said I would grow into them and it was not worth altering them twice.'

Compassion blossomed for the child unwanted by her own family. No wonder she needed to ensure Clara was loved and wanted.

'When the babe came…' She fell silent, leaning forward, her elbows propped on her knees, staring at the floor. 'Well…' She hesitated again, then she looked up at him, a blush staining her cheeks but with a look of resolve. 'It was worse than any of us thought it would be. My friends went to fetch Miss Fanworth and afterwards she…'

Her voice had started to wobble and tears brimmed. Wordlessly, Nathaniel passed her his handkerchief.

'Thank you.'

She mopped her eyes before resuming her tale.

'Miss Fanworth thought it best to find a family who would adopt the baby. She knew my own family would not stand by me, so they were never told.'

'But...the principal of the school. Madame Dubois. She must have known. I am surprised she did not expel you.'

'I have no doubt she would have, but she never knew either.'

'And you knew Clara had gone to Hannah and David?'

'No. I did not know who her new parents were until my last day at school. Miss Fanworth told me their name and that they lived in Gloucestershire. That was all I knew. By the time I tracked them down, it was too late and Clara had gone. I was told you were her new guardian and I was even more determined to make sure she was happy. And that you wanted her here with you.'

'Unlike you, with your uncle and aunt.'

'Unlike me.'

She paused, staring down at the handkerchief she kneaded in her fingers, nibbling at her bottom lip. Then she shook her head and looked up, a mischievous glint in her still-watery eyes.

'Those stories I was told about you, in the village... well, suffice it to say they were wild enough to drive me on to come here. I even braved walking through that horrid wood. And then, when I arrived...I was so petrified by the dogs...and then you growled at me that I was late and before I knew it the idea of staying on...of seeing Clara every day...'

She choked on her words, then hauled in a ragged breath.

'Don't send me away. *Please* don't. I know I let you down today and I still feel sick at what might have happened, but I swear I shall take more care in future, only

I *cannot* go…I simply cannot. I'm sorry I did not tell you the truth but, once I was here…how could I?'

Nathaniel held up his hand, hating to hear her beg. Although she had lied, he could not condemn her. She had been driven only by concern for Clara's welfare.

But what about that kiss? She ought to go.

I know. But I do not want her to go.

Then you must confront it. Now.

'I cannot condone what you have done, but I shall not send you away. I, too, am not so cruel. There was no need to try to entice me with…with…'

Dammit. I can't even say the words.

'Understand this, Miss Bertram. If you stay, you stay on as Clara's governess. Nothing more. And no one—ever— must know the truth. Were the truth to get out, it would be too shocking. You must realise the damage such a scandal would do to Clara in the future.'

'Yes. Of course. I understand.' Grace slumped back in her chair, hand to her face, still clutching Nathaniel's handkerchief. 'Thank you.'

Her voice was muffled, her shoulders quivered and he heard a distinct sniff. He suppressed his urge to comfort her. Instead, he stared into the fire, waiting for her to regain her composure. The wood had caught well and tongues of orange, yellow and occasional green reached for the chimney. Eventually, from the corner of his eye, he saw her hands leave her face and she straightened in her chair.

'So,' he continued their conversation, 'the secret will remain between the two of us. No one else must know. I—' A thought struck him. 'Have you told your friends?' He could not recall franking a letter for her, other than the two she wrote on the day she arrived. 'Or your teacher?'

'No. I was too ashamed to admit what I had done and neither do I wish to lie, so I have not yet written to them. I merely told Miss Fanworth that I had tracked Clara down and that she was happy and that I had secured a post here as governess. She does not know the truth.'

Relief, doubt and the still-present anger combined in a stomach-churning mix.

'And, most particularly, my mother must never know.'

'D-did you tell her what happened this morning?'

'No. I did not wish to worry her.'

'That is a relief.'

Her lips quivered in a tremulous smile, prompting a surge of blood to his loins. How he craved a further taste, but he could not take that risk—a beautiful woman like Grace could never truly desire a damaged man such as him.

What about when you met on the fell? There was a spark between you then.

He dismissed that thought with a silent curse. He had not known at the time that Grace was Clara's mother, but Grace knew the truth and she would know the one certain way of remaining with her child was by making herself indispensable to her employer by whatever means necessary. No wonder she felt entitled to alter his home to suit her own needs.

'Where is her father now? Are you still in touch with him?'

'He is dead.'

'I am sorry,' he said.

'I have no need of your sympathy. What I believed to be love was, in truth, infatuation. I was filled with longing for romance and I fell for his sweet words. I am older and wiser now.'

He raised a brow. 'You are? Our recent conversations suggest otherwise.'

Her cheeks bloomed pink. '*I* have not allowed *my* experience to sour me, or to turn me into a cynic about love, if that is what you mean.'

Touché, Ravenwell!

There was nothing to say that would not sound defensive. What if he was a cynic? Did he not have good reason?

'I bid you goodnight, Miss Bertram.' He bowed and left.

Chapter Fifteen

'I have concerns about that young woman, Nathaniel.'

Nathaniel took a second to compose his expression before looking at his mother, ramrod straight on the other side of his desk. He laid his pen aside, rose to his feet and rounded the desk to pull a chair forward for her. Then he crossed the book room to shut the door.

'What are your concerns, Mother?' he asked as he settled back into his own chair, elbows on the armrests and fingers steepled at his chest.

'I am far from convinced of the reason she has come this far from her friends and family to take up a position as a governess. Why would she not choose to stay—?'

'Mother, please do not interfere in my domestic arrangements. Miss Bertram is good with Clara. I do not want to lose her.'

'But it makes no sense, quite apart from the recklessness of a young woman travelling *alone*, from one end of the country to the other, to attend an interview with no guarantee of employment at the end of it. She is hiding something. I am convinced of it.'

'You are allowing your imagination to conjure up unwarranted suspicions.' It was hard to allay his mother's doubts and suspicions when Nathaniel was still plagued by his own. 'I understand her teacher knows someone in the county who read my advertisement.'

'I have a mind to write to this Madame Dubois and—'

'There is no need. I have already done so and have received a satisfactory report of Miss Bertram's time at the school. There is nothing for you to worry about.'

'I am your mother. I am allowed to worry about you.'

'About me?' Nathaniel felt his brows bunch in a frown. 'I thought this conversation was about Clara's governess?'

His mother ignored him. 'I cannot be easy in my mind about Miss Bertram. Fish heard gossip in the village that a young woman had been snooping around, asking questions about Hannah and David and what had happened and whether Clara was at the Manor. What if it was Miss Bertram?'

'Fish should mind his own business.' The butler at Ravenwell Manor had always been a busybody. Nathaniel pushed his chair back and went to crouch by his mother's side. 'There is nothing to worry about. Miss Bertram is good for Clara and she has settled in here well. Why, even Mrs Sharp is warming to her and that in itself is a miracle.'

'Mrs Sharp worries about you too.'

Nathaniel surged to his feet. 'It is neither her place nor yours to worry about me. I am a grown man and I am perfectly capable of managing my own household.'

He stalked back around his desk and threw himself on to his chair, furious he had allowed his mother to rattle him.

His mother's lips thinned and her nostrils flared as though in response to a bad smell.

'She is very young. It would surely be better for Clara if her governess was a more mature woman. Someone more experienced.'

'Better for whom? I believe Clara will benefit from having someone young and lively. And Miss Bertram is schooled in all the accomplishments required for a young lady. She will be an excellent teacher for Clara as she grows up.'

'She is also exceedingly pretty.'

Ah. So now we get to the crux of the matter.

Nathaniel met his mother's scrutiny with a raised brow. Lady Ravenwell sighed.

'Very well, I shall say no more for the time, but I shall keep a wary eye on Miss Bertram whilst I am here.'

Heaven forbid his mother should discover the truth. Or that she might suspect his growing attraction for Grace, or that they had kissed—albeit just a brush of the lips— last night. Nathaniel had lain awake half the night fretting over whether he was right to allow Grace to stay but, in the end, he accepted he could do nothing else. He could not part mother and daughter. And he did not want to lose Grace for his own sake as well as Clara's. He enjoyed her company. She had brought light and hope into his life, just with her presence.

That kiss had been a moment of madness, when both of their passions were roused.

It must not happen again.

'There is no need but, if it will help set your mind at ease, then by all means do so,' he said. 'I am confident you will see that Miss Bertram is very fond of Clara and has her best interests at heart.'

'If you say so, Nathaniel. Now, I must also speak to you about Christmas.'

'Christmas?'

First Grace, now his mother. How he wished the festive season would pass Shiverstone by without any fuss. He'd had no appetite for celebrating since the fire but, last year, Mother, Hannah, David and, of course, Clara, had come to Shiverstone for the full twelve days, refusing to allow Nathaniel to spend another Christmas alone. Now, the happy memories of last year were yet another painful reminder of his beloved sister.

'I wish you and Clara to come to the Manor for the Christmas season as I find I am unable to come here.'

'May I ask why you are unable to come to the Hall?' Would Mother, like him, find the memories of last Christmas too painful?

His mother grimaced. 'Uncle Peter has invited himself and his family to stay at the Manor. He stopped for a few nights on his way up to Scotland and, before I knew what had happened, it appears it was all agreed.'

Her obvious vexation made Nathaniel smile. His father's younger brother was a slippery fellow and, as the years passed and Nathaniel showed no sign of marrying, his uncle's sense of entitlement to the Ravenwell title and estates had grown.

'Oh, no. Poor Mother. What a sorry Christmas you will have, with that flock of vultures eyeing up the furniture. I've a mind to marry simply in order to put his nose out of joint.'

'Oh, how I wish you would, Nathaniel.' Mother leant forward in her eagerness. Then she visibly subsided. 'But I fear you will never give yourself a chance of happiness. I could throttle both Lady Sarah and Miss Havers for the way they behaved.'

'They did me a kindness. Would you really want such shallow sorts as either of them to become my Marchioness?'

'I would like *someone* to have the opportunity. I fear you will never meet anyone out here in this wilderness. Please say you will come to Ravenwell for Christmas, Nathaniel. We could have a Twelfth Night party as we used to.'

He hated to deny her, but he simply could not face it. He did not have to say so; his expression must make his refusal plain.

'Please, Nathaniel? I cannot bear to think of you here, all alone—'

'I am not alone,' he said, more sharply than he intended. 'I have Clara.'

And Grace.

'And do you not think Clara would benefit from seeing her relations?'

'No, I do not. Hannah told me about the first time my uncle saw Clara. He called her a...well, you may guess what term he used. He made no attempt to disguise his disapproval. No, I shall not subject Clara to my uncle's insults. I am sorry, Mother, but we will spend Christmastide at Shiverstone Hall.'

His mother stood. 'Do not think this is the last word on the subject, Ravenwell, for it is not.'

Blast, he'd annoyed her now. She only ever called him Ravenwell when she was angry with him.

His mother stayed a week. By her last day, Nathaniel's patience was stretched to breaking point. Every day had seen a repeat of their conversations about Grace and about Christmas. Finally, his mother had accepted he meant what he said. He would not send Grace away and replace her with an older governess and he and Clara would not be going to Ravenwell Manor for Christmas. The only good part of his mother's visit was that her presence masked the inevitable awkwardness between Grace and him and made it easier to avoid being alone with her.

His final conversation with his mother took place in the drawing room—which, if he was honest, *had* improved beyond all recognition since Grace had changed it. Even his mother had commented on its pleasant appearance in comparison with her last visit. Lady Ravenwell had already visited the nursery to kiss Clara farewell and Nathaniel and his mother were alone, awaiting her carriage.

'Nathaniel.'

His heart sank. He knew that look. 'Yes, Mother?'

'Do not look so hunted. Even I must accept defeat at

some point. I shall not mention Christmas, nor try one last time to persuade you to appoint a different governess.' She crossed the room to peer from the window, then returned to stand in front of him, her expression resolute. 'I hope you will take what I am about to say in the spirit in which it is intended, son. I only ever have your best interests at heart. You do know that, don't you?'

He took her hands. 'Of course I do.' There was no escaping it. Let her say what she must. She would be gone soon. 'What is it you feel honour-bound to say?'

'Nathaniel! There is no need to take that tone of voice.'

'My apologies, Mother.' He deserved that rebuke. 'Please, do go on.'

'I urge you to take care with Miss Bertram. You already know my concerns about her and I shall not repeat them. But you are a wealthy man. A nobleman. You are a good catch for a scheming miss and what better way to inveigle her way into your affections than through your niece?'

Nathaniel's muscles turned to stone as his mother placed a gentle hand against his scarred cheek. Every instinct screamed at him to pull away, but he knew that would hurt her and might even lead her to believe there was some truth in what she said. He released her other hand and folded his arms across his chest.

'I am a grown man, Mother, not a green youth. I can take care of myself.'

'I have seen the way you look at her, Nathaniel, when you think yourself unobserved.'

He struggled to control his dismay as her words sank in. Was he so transparent that even his mother could see through him? What if the servants could see the truth? What if *Grace* could tell? He must take more care.

'Living out here, all alone…take care, darling. Please.' Her voice became urgent as the sound of wheels on the gravel outside heralded the arrival of her carriage. 'She is exceedingly pretty, but no good can ever come of getting embroiled with an employee. I make no doubt she is well aware of the luxuries and comforts that await the woman who ensnares you. From governess to marchioness would be quite an achievement for one such as Miss Bertram.'

No suggestion that Grace might like him for himself and not merely for what he could provide. Even his own mother thought him unlovable. He thrust down his pain.

'You have nothing to fear, Mother.'

Quite apart from the fact a beauty like Grace would never look twice at someone like me, she still visits the village regularly to see Rendell. If she is interested in anything other than being with Clara, it is not me.

'Miss Bertram is here solely to care for Clara.'

Grace put her lips to Clara's ear as she hugged her tight to her chest.

'Shh…' she breathed, willing Clara not to speak.

After Lady Ravenwell came to the nursery to say goodbye to Clara, Grace had made the mistake of saying that Grandmama would be travelling in her carriage. Clara's eyes had widened.

'Wanna see horsies.'

She'd been adamant and Grace had finally succumbed. Although Lady Ravenwell had clearly not taken to Grace, surely she would be pleased her granddaughter had come to wave goodbye.

Now, Grace stood frozen outside the drawing room, absorbing what she had heard, her heart racing. The thud of booted feet approaching the door from within sent her scurrying to the front door. She would think about what she had heard later. For now, it was imperative Nathaniel had no inkling she had overheard his mother's words. The past week had been awkward enough, since that incident with Clara and since he had discovered she was Clara's mother.

And that kiss—she could almost cringe when she recalled how she had invited it.

It had been he who had resisted deepening that kiss. Not she.

Oh, but was her ladyship right? Did Nathaniel watch her? Did he think of her as a woman and not merely a governess?

But then why had he avoided being alone with her since that night unless he, too, suspected her of planning to ensnare him into marriage.

'Miss Bertram.'

She turned, willing her expression not to give her away. Nathaniel, his mother on his arm, approached across the hall.

'I did not expect to see you down here.'

Grace stretched her lips in a smile. 'I made the mistake of telling Clara that Lady Ravenwell was going away in a carriage. Clara is most eager to see the horses.'

'Ah.' He tweaked Clara's cheek, then smiled at his mother. 'Your granddaughter has developed a healthy obsession for horses. Here…' he reached out '… I will take her. You may go about your duties, Miss Bertram, and I shall send Clara to you later.'

Send. Not bring. It is not my imagination. He does avoid being alone with me.

There was nothing Grace could do but relinquish her daughter, drop a curtsy and return upstairs. She tidied the nursery, the conversation she had overheard repeating in her head until she could scream her frustration.

That Lady Ravenwell suspected her of having designs on Nathaniel was no surprise. His mother clearly thought the worst of Grace and her motives in coming to Shiverstone. Grace searched her conscience, but she could honestly say that, despite her own burgeoning feelings, she had never… *never*…dreamed of *catching* Nathaniel or of inveigling her way into his affections as his mother had so vulgarly put it. She had only ever followed her natural urges, inviting his kiss because she wanted him to kiss her, not because she planned to lure him into marriage. And now, with his mother's suspicions planted in his head, would Nathaniel also suspect her of being a scheming miss, out to seduce him for mercenary reasons?

But…his mother's words echoed again: *I have seen the way you look at her when you think yourself unobserved.*

Did he look at her in such a way? Or was it lust his mother saw? Would any red-blooded man not, on occasion, find his baser instincts come to the fore, such as happened that day out on the fell? Surely that was merely a man tempted to succumb to the moment? There had been other instances of tenderness—such as when he had wiped the smudge from her cheek—but his action had been that of a brother, not an admirer.

Images from the past darted through her memory and her stomach clenched. She must not repeat the mistake she had made with Philip. Now, more than ever, she wished her friends were here to talk to or that she could write to them and ask their advice. They would help her make sense of this tangle of emotions: Joanna with her calm good sense and her ability to accept whatever life threw in her path, fun-loving, independent Rachel with her healthy scepticism about love, Isabel, with her love of the dramatic, always ready to distract and entertain whichever of her friends was feeling blue.

Deep down, though, she knew what her friends would say. They would tell her to banish any dreams of Nathaniel as a man. He was her employer.

Nothing more. Two words that prompted an echo from that fateful night.

If you stay, you stay on as Clara's governess. Nothing more.

He could not have been more clear.

She must forget that overheard conversation. Clara would be her focus, no one and nothing else. She would fight her feelings by keeping busy. There was plenty to do with Christmas less than four weeks away. She had used her spare time during Lady Ravenwell's visit productively: knitting mufflers for Sharp and the outdoor men and mittens for Alice and Clara, as well as embroidering handkerchiefs with initials and edging them with lace for Mrs Sharp and Annie.

She had racked her brains for a present for Nathaniel and could think of nothing more interesting than also embroidering his initials on a handkerchief, but her brain was full to bursting with ideas for making Clara's Christmastide a time to remember. There were doll's clothes to sew, a bonnet to knit to match her new mittens and, best of all, a painting of Sweep to hang on Clara's bedchamber wall. Tam—who had a talent for carpentry—had agreed to frame it and Sharp had promised to paint the frame with gilt paint.

A soft knock at her sitting-room door drew her attention and she tucked the handkerchief she was currently embroidering down by her side, out of sight.

It was Alice, holding Clara by the hand. Brack had followed them upstairs and, with a flash of inspiration, Grace knew what she could give Nathaniel for Christmas. He had already requested a portrait of Clara but she could include Brack in the portrait, too, as a surprise.

He might not return her love, but that did not stop her from wanting to make him happy and to brighten his life. His smile would be her reward.

Chapter Sixteen

It did not take Grace very many days to realise that coaxing a smile or, indeed, any indication of pleasure, from Nathaniel was a task beyond her meagre efforts. Clara was the only person who could tease a pleasantry from her increasingly taciturn uncle on the very few occasions he visited his niece whilst she was in Grace's care. Most days, though, upon his return from a day spent outside, Nathaniel sent Alice to bring Clara to him in his book room, leading Grace to the conclusion that, knowing the truth of their relationship, he simply did not want to see her and Clara together.

Their former easy friendship was no more and Grace mourned its passing. After overhearing his mother's warning, Grace had feared she would analyse Nathaniel's every word, look and gesture for his true feelings but, in actuality, there was no mistaking his opinion of her. His rejection of her—even as a friend—resurrected all her old insecurities. Her uncle, aunt and cousins had not wanted her. Philip had not wanted her. Now Ravenwell could barely stand being in the same room as her. Clara's very existence confirmed Grace's lack of moral character and she supposed she should be grateful Nathaniel hadn't cast her out on her ear immediately.

Her life at Shiverstone Hall would be lonely indeed if not

for Clara. Clara was a constant joy: the shining star around which Grace's life revolved. She gave Grace the strength to endure the shards of pain that pierced her heart every time Ravenwell looked right through her.

A week after his mother's departure, Grace and Clara returned from a visit to Elizabeth and, after handing Bill to Ned to unharness, Clara spied Tam.

'Doggies?' She ran up to him, her eyes beseeching. 'See doggies?'

He tweaked her cheek. 'Might I take Miss Clara to the kennels, Miss Bertram?'

'Yes, of course, Tam. I believe I might wait here for her, if you do not mind.'

Tam grinned. 'We'll not be long.' He knew very well Grace's dislike of facing the dogs all at once.

Grace could hear Ned whistling in the barn as he rubbed Bill down. She leaned against the barn wall, her mind drifting, thinking of nothing in particular. The ring of a boot heel on stone jerked her back to awareness and she straightened just as Nathaniel strode around the corner, coming from the direction of the mews where he kept his birds.

He stopped short, his brows bunching, and Grace's heart sank even as her breath caught at the mere sight of him. She could not bear this. How was she ever to mend this distance between them? It was as though he hated her. His mother could not have been further from the truth if she had tried. She stretched her lips into a smile.

'Good afternoon, my lord.'

'What are you doing here? Where is Clara?'

'She has gone with Tam to the kennels. I am waiting for them to return.'

'I see.'

He began to move away. There was a time when he would have teased her about her nervousness around the dogs. Now he could barely look at her. Rebellion warred with caution in her heart and won. How dare he treat her like a pariah?

'My lord, you did offer to show me your hawks. Might we go and see them now?'

He stared at her, expressionless. 'I am busy.'

She'd risked thus far. She would not back down. 'When might I see them, then?'

'When I invite you, Miss Bertram.' He lifted his hat. 'Good afternoon.'

He strode away before she had any chance to reply.

Following that encounter, Grace made no further attempt to break through his reserve. She could not afford to alienate him. She was here, with Clara. That was the most important point of all. Any further tension between herself and the Marquess could only jeopardise her future at the Hall—a risk she must not take.

Her trips to the village—whether to visit Elizabeth or to attend church—provided some respite to the increasingly fraught atmosphere at the Hall, but even those were lost to her when day after day of heavy rain confined them all to the house.

Almost two weeks after Lady Ravenwell's departure, Grace pulled open the curtains in Clara's bedchamber and folded back the shutters. At last! The rain that had fallen incessantly for the past week had stopped and given way to the sun: pale and weak, maybe, as it hung in the washed-out blue of the sky, but without doubt the sun.

'Look, sweetie,' she said to Clara. 'Ned was right. It *has* stopped raining. We shall be able to go out today.'

And what a relief that would be. With everyone confined indoors, unable even to attend church on Sunday, tempers had begun to fray, with snapped remarks and frowning faces on everyone. She turned to Clara, who had scrambled from under the bedcovers and was jumping up and down on her bed.

'Clara. Do not bounce on your bed. I have told you before.'

'Sweep! Sweep!'

'Yes, we will go and find him, as soon as you are dressed and have eaten your breakfast. Come, quickly now, or your porridge will be cold.'

She dipped the washcloth in the warm water Alice had brought up and washed Clara's hands and face, then dressed her in a warm, woollen dress. She then uncovered the serving dish of porridge and served up a bowl each for herself and for Clara. They would need something warming inside them if they were to drive to Shivercombe today, as she planned. The thought of visiting Elizabeth buoyed her spirits.

Hand in hand, Grace and Clara went to the kitchen.

'Sweep!' Clara ran to her kitten, who promptly disappeared under the dresser—his favourite refuge.

'Clara. I have told you. You must move slowly and not shout. You have scared him.'

Grace laughed, looking at Mrs Sharp to share her amusement. She was busy slicing ham from a joint and had not even glanced up when they came in the room. There was a large basket on the table, half-full, and the set of her mouth suggested she was not in a good mood.

'His lordship wants food sent out,' she grumbled. 'I told him, I did, Ned'll have to come back after it. I haven't got time to spend traipsing all over the fells a-looking for them and Sharp's rheumatics are playing him up, with all the wet weather.'

'Could I take it for you?'

Mrs Sharp paused, then shook her head and resumed slicing. 'No. You've got Miss Clara to watch and I can't have her under my feet today. Alice is helping Annie with the laundry. Got to make the most of the weather while there's a chance of drying them sheets.' She shook her head. 'His lordship's got no idea. He can only think about them animals. Setting that bird to fly today, they are, then seeing to the sheep. He doesn't understand what it takes to keep this place running. And with Christmas just around the corner, too.'

She wrapped the slices of ham in a clean cloth and put the bundle into the basket, then wrapped thick slices of bread and some hunks of cheese and piled them on top.

Grace watched her in silence, chewing at her lip. 'Is there anything else I can do to help?'

She got the answer she hoped for. 'No. You're better off taking Miss Clara out for a breath of fresh air. And take that wretched cat out of here too. Although…' she paused again to wipe her brow on her sleeve '…he did take after a mouse this morning. Didn't catch it, mind, but I dare say he'll get better when he grows. At least then he'll be some use.'

Grace ignored the housekeeper's grumbles. It was plainly one of those days and the less said the better. 'I thought I might drive to the village and call upon Elizabeth,' she said. 'If you are sure you do not need me.'

'That is a…oh, drat! I forgot to put in the pickles.'

The housekeeper rushed to the larder, returning with a jar of pickled beetroot and a bowl of apples. Grace didn't linger. Mrs Sharp was clearly preoccupied. She put on her cloak and bonnet, then helped Clara with hers and then they headed for the barn where Bill was stabled.

Some time later—hands chilled following her struggle with stiff straps and buckles—Grace climbed aboard the gig and gave Bill the office to proceed. She felt inordinately proud of herself. It was the first time she had harnessed Bill to the gig without help. She had checked and double-checked each fastening and she was confident nothing was amiss. She smiled down at Clara, tucked in by her side, a blanket around her legs.

'This is fun, is it not, sweetie? We are off on an adventure, after being stuck indoors for so long. It will be nice to see Miss Dunn again, won't it?'

'More kitties?'

Grace laughed, tilting her face towards the sun and breathing deeply of the clean, fresh air. 'No more kitties,' she said. 'I think one is enough, don't you?'

She drove the gig down the track and into the forest. It still gave her the shivers, but she felt much braver driving the gig than she had when she had walked through it all alone, scared of every sound and terrified of what might await her at Shiverstone Hall after the villagers' lurid stories.

Her confidence soared. She had been a town girl through and through, but now she had learnt about the countryside and the animals. She had climbed the fell and touched an eagle. She could harness a horse and drive a gig. She had even grown to like the dogs. Well... She liked Brack on his own. She was still wary when they all ran loose at once, leaping and barking. How her friends would stare at what she had accomplished and how brave she had become.

The only dark cloud in her life was Nathaniel.

She no longer deluded herself that he harboured feelings for her and she could only pray they might soon regain their former easy-going companionship, with its games of chess and cards, and accompanying smiles and laughter. Since his mother's visit all of that mutual ease had fallen away and, at dinner every evening, they each fumbled for the right words to say.

Heartsore. She had heard the word before, but hadn't known such pain could be real.

Bill plodded placidly on through the wood and, very soon, they emerged from the cover of the trees and followed the curve of the track down to the ford. Bill stopped. Grace frowned.

'Get up, Bill.'

She shook the reins. Bill took two steps, then jibbed

again, his front hooves at the water's edge. Grace slapped the reins on his back, clicking her tongue in imitation of Ned, but Bill would not budge. The ford was wider than usual, but the water—murky and brown instead of its normal crystal clarity—did not look much deeper. Grace doubted it would reach Bill's knees, let alone swamp the body of the gig.

She flicked the whip across the horse's broad back. He laid back his ears and shook his head, setting his bit jingling.

Stupid animal, frightened of a bit of water.

'Stay here, Clara, and do not move. I shall be back in a minute.' Grace tilted Clara's chin so she could look her in the eyes. 'Promise?'

The little girl nodded and tugged the blanket tighter around her legs. Satisfied Clara would stay put, Grace climbed from the gig and walked to Bill's head.

Nathaniel scanned the sky to the north. He had set Amber free as soon as he had reached the high fell. She had circled above him and his men for a long time, waiting, he knew, for him to call her in with a reward of food, but he had ignored her. Instead, he and his men had concentrated on locating their sheep after all the rain, rounding them up ready to drive them off the fells to the lower pastures for the remainder of the winter. Finally, Amber appeared to give up and she flew north in a steady line until now she was a mere speck in the distance.

Even though it was the right thing to do, Nathaniel was sad seeing the giant bird go. He hoped Amber would soon regain her mistrust of man—she had already successfully hunted for herself, so hopefully she would have no reason to seek out humans.

'Your lordship.'

'Yes, Tam?' Nathaniel answered absently, still watching

that increasingly faint speck. They had stopped for a brief rest, on the edge of the fell above Shiver Dale.

'My lord!'

His interest caught by Tam's urgent tone, Nathaniel joined him on the edge, where he gazed out over the dale to the south.

'Look.'

Nathaniel followed Tam's pointing finger, down the slope to the dale where the beck flowed. A horse and gig had emerged from the wood, heading down the track that led to the ford.

'That's Bill,' Nathaniel said. 'And Miss Bertram.'

Grace. Off to visit that damned curate again.

Jealousy flooded through him, turning him rigid with anger even as his common sense reminded him he had done everything possible in the past two weeks to keep her at arm's length. Then his brain caught up with what his eyes were seeing.

'What on earth does she think she's doing? The river isn't safe to cross after all that rain.'

'Ay, but will *she* know that?' Ned said, from where he held their three horses. 'That's Miss Clara in the gig 'n' all.'

'Bill's sensible; he won't attempt to cross.' Nathaniel tried to believe it, but he knew how deceptive the beck was after rain. What if she persuaded the cob to go forward? The power of that current... Sick anxiety twisted his gut and he walked across to Ned and took Zephyr's reins, pulling his head up from the grass. 'I'll go down and turn them back.'

He tightened Zephyr's girth and mounted before looking down the hill again. Sure enough, Bill had planted his feet on the edge of the river and was refusing to walk on. He headed Zephyr down the slope, in a direct line to the ford, leaning back to help the horse with his balance. The ground was slippery and, more than once, Zephyr's hooves slipped and only the stallion's great strength prevented them tumbling. It took all of Nathaniel's concentration to pick out a safe path.

Then he heard a shout from behind him. He looked up and a spasm of fear clutched his belly. Grace had climbed from the gig and was pulling at Bill's bridle, trying to persuade him into the river. Nathaniel swore loudly and, heedless of the danger, he dug his heels into Zephyr.

The stallion responded gallantly and they bounded down the slope, his hooves skidding perilously as Nathaniel offered silent prayers for the surefootedness of the stallion and the continued stubbornness of the cob. They reached gentler ground and Zephyr transitioned into a gallop, but it was heavy going across the sodden ground. Then time appeared to slow as Nathaniel saw Grace try once more to tug Bill forward. Bill threw his head up, knocking her off balance.

'Noooooooooooo!'

Nathaniel crouched low over the stallion's neck, urging him ever faster, but there was nothing he could do to prevent the tragedy unfolding. He could only watch, helpless, as Grace toppled backwards, arms windmilling, into the water.

Chapter Seventeen

Five seconds later Nathaniel reined Zephyr to a halt as a black-and-tan shape streaked past and launched itself into the river. Bill again stood, statue-like, facing the water. The river swept on. No sign of Grace. Or Brack.

I must find them. He looked at Clara: eyes huge, huddled in a blanket in the gig. *I can't leave her alone.*

He wheeled Zephyr around, staring back across the dale. Tam had already reached the bottom of the hill; he would reach the gig in a matter of minutes. Nathaniel waved at Tam, then pointed to Clara. Tam raised his hand in acknowledgement, then leaned forward over his horse's neck, urging him faster.

'Do not move,' Nathaniel called to Clara.

No time for more. No time to stop and reassure her. Heart in mouth, he kicked Zephyr into a canter, following the beck downstream. He trusted the stallion to pick a safe path as he scanned the river, trying not to despair at the speed and strength of the roaring, churning mass once they left the comparative calm of the ford. They weaved around bushes and trees, always sticking as close as possible to the riverbank. Finally—he hauled on the reins—a flash of white, a face, two arms wrapped around a sturdy branch protruding from the beck.

Nathaniel leapt from the saddle and raced to the water's edge.

'Grace!' Her eyes were screwed shut, lips drawn back to bare clenched teeth. 'Grace!'

A tree had toppled into the beck, its trunk disappearing under the surface some ten feet before that branch emerged from the swift rush of mud-coloured water. Nathaniel shrugged out of his greatcoat, pulled off his boots and clambered on to the trunk. He cursed freely at the rough bark that cut into his knees as he crawled along and again when he reached the place where the trunk sank from sight under the frigid water. The tree's bulk helped steady the rush of the beck at this point, but it was still fierce enough to knock him off balance. Nathaniel manoeuvred around to sit astride the submerged tree, then steadily pulled himself closer to Grace.

'Grace! Hold on, sweetheart. I'm coming.'

Her eyes opened. *Thank God.* They stared uncomprehendingly. Her lips were blue and now he could see her teeth chattering. He must get her out of this and fast. He pushed himself to go quicker, aware—even as he neared her—that she was rapidly weakening. Her head lolled on her neck and her arms were losing their hold, gradually slipping.

'Hold on! Think of Clara! You can't leave her!'

She made a visible effort to rouse, forcing her head up and opening her eyes. Nathaniel dragged himself along the submerged truck, ever closer.

You can't leave me.

His father's face... Hannah's... David's...they floated through his mind's eye and his throat thickened.

'Stay with me, love. Hold on. I'm coming.'

I cannot lose you as well.

A sob erupted from his chest. He clamped his teeth against the next.

No time to fall apart, Ravenwell. Get on with it. Get her.

She was so close. Just like his father. He had seen him, through the flames, but he could not save him. He had failed his father. Left his mother a widow. He would not fail Grace and leave Clara an orphan. As if in a nightmare, he saw Grace's head slump and in a final, desperate lunge, he reached her at the moment her hold on the branch slipped. He hauled her into his chest with one arm and snatched at that same branch with his free hand. Immediately, the power of the flow lifted him and tugged at his legs until he was stretched out, feet pointing downstream. He fought the greedy suck of the river, gritting his teeth against the screaming agony of his arm and shoulder, hauling them both against the current until he was close enough to link his arm around the branch.

Gasping, he stared at the bank. So near and yet so far. But failure was not an option. Clara needed them both. He kicked out with his legs, struggling to bring them back under him until, at last, he could feel the trunk beneath his feet. He could not risk turning to face the bank. Sending a heartfelt prayer heavenwards, he shifted Grace into a more secure hold and dropped into the water, one leg each side of the trunk again, gripping it with muscles honed from years of riding. He inched backwards along the trunk, desperation fuelling him, until he reached the bank. Near-exhausted, he dropped to the ground, Grace's inert form cradled in his arms, and staggered away from the river.

Six feet from the water's edge, his knees buckled and he collapsed, cushioning Grace against the fall. He set her down and she immediately rolled to her side and began to cough, water dribbling from her mouth. He rubbed and patted her back, scraping wet strands of hair from her face.

I must warm her. He forced his stiff muscles to move, turning to scan the riverbank upstream. *Surely Tam or Ned will come soon.*

He struggled to his feet, juddering with the cold, stripped off his wet jacket and shirt, picked up his discarded greatcoat and rubbed it briskly over his chest and arms. Then he fell to his knees next to Grace and pulled her into a sitting position. He must warm her and he could not do that whilst she was clad in soaking wet clothes. Her cloak had already gone. She moaned as he struggled to remove her dress.

'What…?'

'Help me, my love.' He placed his cheek against hers and rubbed skin against skin. 'We need to get you warm.'

She scrabbled at his arm with weak fingers. 'Clara!'

'Hush. She is safe. The men are with her.'

Her entire body was shaking as he tugged again at her dress.

'Wha…no! You…you…'

Her words were slurred and weak, but still she managed to struggle as he worked the sopping woollen dress up her body and over her head.

'Miss Bertram!'

She stilled momentarily at his command, then thrashed her head from side to side. 'No, no. *Noooo*…'

Grimly, Nathaniel continued to disrobe her, until she was clad only in her shift. He lifted her to his lap and reached for his greatcoat, wrapping it around her, pulling her wet hair out from the collar. He rubbed her with brisk movements, praying the friction would warm her, talking to her to keep her awake.

'Stay with me, my darling. Don't leave me. Think of Clara.'

The welcome thud of hooves eventually sounded and Tam appeared. He slid to the ground.

'Thank God, milord.'

'Miss Clara?'

'Ned's driving the gig back to the Hall. Is Miss Bertram…?' He paused and peered more closely. 'I don't like her colour, milord. We need to get her home.'

'We do, Tam. I'll take Miss Bertram on Sammy and you can ride Zephyr to the Hall.' The stallion would never tolerate a double burden. 'Tell Mrs Sharp what's happened and to heat plenty of water ready for us.'

He wrapped his coat more securely around Grace and handed her up to Tam before regaining his feet and pulling on his boots. It took him two attempts to mount Sammy. His legs were about as much use as lengths of string and agonising pain ripped through the muscles of his right arm and shoulder as he dragged himself into the saddle.

'Where's Brack?' Tam asked.

A hard lump lodged in Nathaniel's throat. 'I've not seen him since he went into the water after Miss Bertram.'

Tam hoisted Grace up in front of Nathaniel, then he stripped off his own heavy coat.

'Here, milord. No good you coming down with the ague on top of all else. We'll come back out and search for the dog once Miss Clara's safe and I've spoken to Mrs Sharp.'

He swung up on to Zephyr and galloped away. Nathaniel blinked back hot tears, then muttered yet another curse. He was getting soft. But… Brack had been with him a long time. A loyal companion.

Grace stirred and he wrenched his attention back to the matter in hand. He flung Tam's coat around his shoulders, blessing the immediate warmth as it blocked the chilly December air from his still-damp skin, and then shifted Grace into a more secure position on his lap.

She was so very delicate. How would she survive? He pressed his lips to her temple, willing her to keep fighting. Her shivers were ever more violent. He must warm her. He loosened the coat around Grace and pulled her close into his bare chest, skin to skin. They would warm each other. He rearranged the coats around them and nudged Sammy into a walk, leaving the reins lying slack on his neck. He could not risk going faster and cause either of the coats to slip off.

His arms encircled Grace beneath the tent of the coats and he rubbed her slender limbs in turn. The delicate bones of shoulders and hips, elbows and knees revealed the lack of flesh beneath her skin. She weighed little more than a child.

'Stay with me, my darling. We will soon be home.'

Home.

Her presence had changed the Hall into a home for him after nine long years of it being nothing more than a roof over his head. She belonged there, with Clara and with him, and yet he had done everything in the past fortnight to make her feel unwelcome and unwanted, using his anger to hide from reality. He had seen the pain in her eyes and he had ignored it, more concerned with protecting his own heart and peace of mind.

They settled into a rhythm, with Grace huddled against his chest, his chin resting on the top of her head, his thoughts ranging free. He had not failed this time, as he had with his father. He relived his terror when he had seen her tumble into the river. His muscles tightened without volition, nestling her closer into him, willing the heat of his skin to warm her.

Cold killed. He saw it happen every spring, when an ewe lambed earlier than expected. If the weather was unkind and the lamb couldn't get dry and warm, it would soon succumb, the cold numbing it, slowing everything down until it sank into death.

He would not allow that to happen to Grace. That terror he had felt…he knew, with heart-stopping certainty, that it had been more than the horror he would have experienced had it been Tam or Ned who had fallen.

A low moan reached his ears and again his arms tightened reflexively. He could not lose her now. She felt so frail in his arms, but she had a strong will. She would survive.

She *must* survive.

For Clara's sake.

For his.

'Stay with me, my darling Grace. Stay with me.'

He had thought that by keeping her at bay his growing

feelings might wither and die, but he had been wrong. They had continued to twine around his heart until he could no longer ignore the truth.

He was in love with Grace Bertram.

Fool that he was.

He needed to say the words. If the worst should happen, he needed her to know.

'I love you,' he whispered and pressed his lips to the cool skin of her forehead.

He had fallen in love with her, even though he knew she could never love a damaged soul such as he, and even though she deserved all the things in life he could not provide: friends, fun and laughter, parties and dancing.

It seemed the heart did not respond to logic.

He cringed at how he had treated her since his mother's visit.

God, please. Let her live, and I promise to change my ways. Even though I can never tell her how important she is to me, I will show her. I will make her happy. Every single day. I swear.

He rode right up to the back door. Everyone piled out, faces creased with worry, and Mrs Sharp and the other women carried Grace off to get her warm and dry.

'Tam's gone out to look for Brack,' Sharp said, as Ned took charge of Sammy.

'I must go, too. I need to find him.'

His legs buckled as he turned to follow Ned and he stumbled. Sharp was by his side in an instant, tugging Nathaniel's arm across his shoulders.

'Yer in no fit state to go anywhere, milord. There's a tub of warm water a-waiting in your chamber—best you get yourself warm and dry and some food inside you before you think about that. There's nothing you can do that Tam can't.'

'I'll go out, too, once I've settled Sammy, milord,' Ned called over his shoulder. 'Don't 'ee fret. We'll find 'im.'

Sharp helped strip Nathaniel, who could not even summon the energy to shield his scars as he normally would. Sharp took his wet clothing away, leaving Nathaniel to his thoughts. He closed his eyes and rested his head against the rim of his bathtub, feeling the heat of the water seep through his flesh and thaw his chilled bones. He had nearly lost her. Grace. She smiled in his imagination, her clear, soft skin radiant, her expressive gold-green eyes warm and sparkling, her blonde hair as fine and delicate as strands of silk. Then another picture took its place—river-drenched hair straggling across her face in dirty strands, lips blue and pinched, pale eyelids, fragile as a moth's wing, closed in utter exhaustion.

He exploded from the bathtub, unheeding of the water that sloshed on to the floor. A towel was draped over a chair near the fire, warming. He grabbed it and scrubbed at himself, then pulled the waiting shirt and trousers on to still-damp skin. He shrugged into his banyan and strode from the room towards the nursery wing.

He tapped at Grace's bedchamber door. Annie—Tam's wife—answered.

'How is she?'

'Sleeping, my lord. She—'

'Stand aside. I want to see her.'

He must see her. He needed reassurance. He needed to know she was safe. That she would survive.

'But—'

'You will be here the entire time. There can be no impropriety.'

He pushed the door wide, leaving Annie no choice but to move out of his way. He crossed to the bed and stood staring down at her.

So small. So fragile. But her cheeks were pink, as were her lips, and her breathing was even and regular. The fear that had seized him loosened its hold and the tight band around his chest eased.

'Has the doctor been sent for?'

'No, my lord. She is bruised and battered, but Mrs Sharp is certain she will recover.'

He had faith in Mrs Sharp's experience in treating injuries and illnesses.

'She said Miss Bertram's chest sounds clear,' Annie continued, 'so she doesn't think she breathed in any water.'

'That is good. Has she regained consciousness at all?'

Nathaniel laid the backs of his fingers against the silken skin of her cheek. It was warm. As it should be.

Reassurance.

There was a graze on her forehead that had begun to swell, but otherwise she appeared unscathed.

'She came round when we bathed her, as she warmed up,' Annie said. 'But she didn't make much sense. She was gabbling about Miss Clara. And Brack.'

At her words, a crease appeared between Grace's eyebrows and her lips pursed. 'Brack.' Her voice sounded hoarse. 'Where's Brack?'

Annie came to stand beside Nathaniel. 'We told her Miss Clara was safe. Alice brought her before Miss Bertram went to sleep,' she whispered. 'But we didn't know about Brack.'

Grace's lids slitted open and she fixed her gaze on Nathaniel. She ran her tongue along her lips.

'Is he safe?' She pushed her bedcovers down and held her hand out to Nathaniel.

Annie tutted and pulled the sheet and blankets up, tucking them around Grace, but she resisted the woman's efforts to fold her arm back under the covers.

'Nath…my lord.' She spoke with urgency. 'He saved me. Brack.' Her lids drifted shut, then she sucked in a deep breath. He could see the effort it took to force her eyes open again. 'Tell me. Is he all right?'

He could not lie, not when those green eyes were fixed on him so beseechingly. He took her hand in both of his, resisting the urge to press his lips to her skin. Never, by word or deed, would he embarrass her by revealing the extent of his feelings for her.

'I do not know. Ned and Tam are out looking for him now.'

Her fingers clutched at his. 'He saved me. He pushed me towards the bank and I grabbed a branch, but he…he was swept away.'

She gulped, her eyes sheened with tears and her anguish wrenched at his heart. He wanted nothing more than to protect her from anything and everything bad in this life. He stroked her hand, cursing the inadequacy of his efforts to comfort her. Unbidden, an image of Ralph Rendell arose in his mind's eye and a silent growl vibrated in his chest.

'I saw him…I could not…' Her voice trembled.

'Hush.' Nathaniel smoothed her forehead. 'We will find him.'

Somehow. Alive or dead, we will find him.

'You must sleep now. Please, do not worry.'

'You will tell me the truth?'

'I will.'

That image of Rendell would not go. Nathaniel knew he should only care about what was best for Grace, but still he hesitated. He did not want the man here. But…the curate had the right to know what had happened. He must set aside his feelings for Grace's sake.

'Shall I send for Mr Rendell?'

Her eyes widened. 'Am I dying?'

'No!' He gripped her hand. 'Of course you are not dying.'

'Then why…?'

'He is your…friend. I thought you might want to see him.'

Her lids lowered. 'No. There is no need.'

His spirits rose. Was she not as smitten as he thought?

Grace stifled a yawn. 'I am so very weary.'

'Sleep then. I shall see you later.'

After I have found Brack.

He headed for the door.

Chapter Eighteen

Nathaniel rode out on his bay hunter, Caesar, dread clogging his throat and that tight band once again clamped around his chest. He was afraid of what he might find but, at the same time, he could not rest until he knew what had happened to Brack.

The sun was low in the sky, the shadows lengthening and he reckoned he had an hour before it would become too dark to search. He aimed straight for the place where he had found Grace, and began to follow the course of the beck, scouring the bank and the undergrowth for any sign of his faithful dog. The failing light did not help his search. Brack's black-and-tan colouring would be easily camouflaged by the dark earth and fallen leaves under any bushes, unless he was out somewhere in the open. That was not likely. He would hole up somewhere, as long as he had an ounce of strength when he got out of the water. Nathaniel refused to accept the dog might not have succeeded in getting out.

After five minutes of riding Nathaniel muttered an oath, reined Caesar to a halt and slid from the saddle. He'd not been thinking straight. From a nearby hazel he cut a long, straight stick and, pulling the reins over the horse's head to lead him, he began to walk. His entire body ached, but he ignored the pain. There would be plenty of time to recuperate after he found Brack. He trudged on downriver, poking the stick into and under every bush, whistling and calling from time to time, ears straining for any reply.

He had searched maybe a quarter of a mile of bank when two figures on horseback materialised out of the gloom.

'Well?'

'Nothing, milord.' Ned touched his finger to his cap. 'Sorry.'

'We've ridden up and down this stretch twice, as far as the bridge, and we've seen no sign, milord.' Tam said. 'But we did meet Gil Brown from the Braithwaite estate and he promised to alert their men to keep an eye out. I doubt there's more we can do tonight.' He cast a meaningful look at the sky, darkening by the minute. 'It's going to be a cold one, by the looks of it.'

It felt hopeless, yet Nathaniel couldn't give up. Not yet. Not while there was still light to see by.

'You two get off home,' he said. 'I'll just walk on a bit further.'

The two men exchanged a look.

'We'll stay and help.' Tam started to dismount.

'No!'

Tam slowly swung his leg back over the saddle.

'Sorry. I did not mean to snap.' The men's stares burned into Nathaniel, shaming him. 'Thank you both for your efforts.'

He knew the men were concerned about him, but he needed to be alone. Hope had faded. If the worst *had* happened…he wanted to face that alone.

'You have ridden this stretch. I'll walk it, until it gets too dark. It will not take more than one of us to do that.'

Their hoofbeats faded into the distance and Nathaniel resumed his lonely search, praying silently even as he called Brack's name. He needed to know. He could not bear to imagine his faithful Brack injured and in pain. He would rather he was already dead than lying somewhere alone, hurt and slowly dying.

Finally, the night had drawn close all about him. He knew he must abandon the search. Heart a lead weight in his chest, throat aching with unshed tears, he flung the stick away into the darkness, threw the reins over Caesar's head and put his left foot in the stirrup. He had bent his right leg ready to propel himself into the saddle when Caesar threw up his head, his ears pricked as he stared at something off to their right, away from the river.

Probably a fox. Or a rabbit. He had nothing to lose, though, so he took his foot from the stirrup and walked towards whatever had caught the horse's attention. Caesar followed without hesitation. Nothing too strange then, or he would plant his hooves in the ground and refuse to move. Nathaniel swallowed, nerves playing havoc with his insides. *What if...?*

Feeling foolish for that sudden upwelling of hope, he called, 'Brack? Are you there, boy?'

He strained his ears. Nothing. He glanced round at Caesar, still on high alert, staring...staring...not wild-eyed, but focussed and intent. Nathaniel walked in the direction of Caesar's gaze. Ten yards. Fifteen. Caesar halted, snorting quietly, soft nostrils vibrating. Nathaniel stroked his nose, looking around, trying in vain to see...something.

He whistled.

The barest scuffle sounded from the undergrowth in front of them. He dare not drop the reins, for fear Caesar might finally take fright. He pulled the reins over the horse's head again and moved towards the sound. When his arm and the reins were at full stretch, he stopped, trying desperately to penetrate the darkness, wishing he had not discarded his stick.

Then he heard it. A low whimper. Heart in mouth, he cast around for somewhere to tie Caesar. If it was Brack he would need the horse—well accustomed to carrying deer carcasses—to get him home. He tied Caesar to a sapling and then ran back to where he had heard that sound.

'Brack?'

A rustle. He honed in on it and moved forward with care. A bush loomed in front of him. Dropping to his knees, he felt beneath. His fingers met with damp, matted fur and another whimper.

'Thank you, God.'

With both hands, he felt along Brack's body, eliciting several whines. Hopefully they were bruises and not broken bones. He was horribly aware that Brack—stretched full-length on his side—had not even raised his head. He could not leave the dog here all night; he had no choice but to move him. He eased Brack from under the bush, closing his ears to his whines and one weak yelp. Dogs, unlike horses, were always vocal at the slightest hurt; he must trust that was the case this time. Nathaniel stripped off his coat and wrapped it around Brack, who was now panting in distress. Nathaniel's nerve almost failed him. What if he caused lasting damage?

I must. He can't survive out here. And I can't see to examine him properly.

'Sorry, old lad,' he muttered, 'but I've got no choice.'

He lifted Brack as gently as he could, then carried him to Caesar. Mounting was awkward—he had to search for a fallen tree first, to make it possible—but they were soon on their way home, Brack's inert form lying across Nathaniel's lap.

He'd found Brack but would his faithful friend survive?

When Grace roused, the house was quiet and her room dark, just a residual glow from the banked fire to penetrate the gloom. She shivered, closed her eyes again and wriggled around, snuggling deeper under the covers, vaguely conscious of aches and pains in various parts of her body. Eyes still shut, she lay cocooned in the warmth, her mind scrambling its way from the depths of sleep, remembering her sense of achievement in harnessing Bill to the gig, and—she sat bolt upright, the covers falling unheeded to her waist.

Oh, dear God! Clara! She is safe... I'm certain she is safe. I saw her...they brought her in to see me.

Didn't they?

She threw back the covers and—*ouch*. What had started as a leap from her bed turned into a crawl. She had never felt so battered and bruised. She gritted her teeth against the pain and felt around for her slippers. She slipped them on and then found her chamber candle on her nightstand and took it to the fire to light it with a spill. Her shawl was draped at the end of the bed. She snatched it up, flung it around her shoulders—it was so large it almost reached the floor—and went to the door that connected her bedchamber to Clara's. She raised the candle to light the room and her terror subsided at the tiny form sleeping peacefully. Her pulse steadied. A movement caught her eye and she realised someone else slept in there, on a truckle bed. It was Alice, presumably to attend to Clara if she woke, so Grace wouldn't be disturbed.

Grace stood watching her daughter, digging into her memory for what she could recall of the day before. She remembered Mrs Sharp giving her a dose of laudanum to help her to sleep. She relived the moment she had tipped backwards into the icy water and the unexpected strength of the flowing water that swamped her clothes and tumbled her along until she was beyond the ford and in the deeper water. She shivered, nausea squeezing her throat as she remembered swallowing mouthful after mouthful of filthy water, desperately gasping for air every time her face broke the surface, and Brack...

She backed out of Clara's room. Had they found him? She frowned, the action prompting a pain in her temple. She touched her forehead, feeling the swell of a lump and the rough soreness of abraded skin. She should return to bed and yet, even as that thought crossed her mind, her stomach rumbled. She would give anything for a warm drink and something to eat. She would go down to the kitchen— the range would have been banked for the night, but there would be enough heat to warm some chocolate and, besides, she could not sleep without discovering Brack's fate. If they had found him, he would be in the kitchen, where he slept every night.

Grace left her bedchamber and descended the stairs, wincing as she put her weight on her left leg. As she crossed the hall to the door that led to the servants' domain at the rear of house, the longcase clock struck two, making her jump, thereby setting the shadows cast by her candle to dance across the panelled walls. She shivered, pulling her shawl tighter around her.

She followed the passageway to the kitchen and lifted the latch, pushing the door open to reveal the soft glow of a single candle on the dresser. Stepping lightly, Grace rounded the table. There, stretched out on a folded blanket before the range, was Brack. His ear flicked and he thumped his tail gently against the floor, but did not lift his head, his neck being pinned down by a loudly purring Sweep, who was draped over it.

'What are you doing out of bed?'

The soft query came from the gloom at the far end of the kitchen. A tall form unfolded from Sharp's favourite overstuffed armchair, leaving a huddle of blanket behind. Nathaniel stepped into the light. The sight of him…the memory of what he had done for her… Grace shook her head, mutely, swallowing down the surge of emotion that threatened to overwhelm her.

'What is it, G… Miss Bertram? Are you unwell?'

He was by her side in an instant. Large, safe, comforting. Heat radiated from him and his scent—citrus soap with an undernote of warm male—invaded her senses. He slipped his arm around her waist, supporting her weight.

'You should not be down here. Come. Sit down.'

He urged her towards the chair. She resisted.

'No. I am well, I promise you, apart from a few bruises. It was only that I...' She turned within the circle of his arm and tilted her head, capturing his gaze. 'Thank you. From the bottom of my heart, I thank you.'

His eyes darkened as they searched hers. His lips parted as his head lowered, but then his shoulders jerked and he raised his head, breaking eye contact. She searched his expression. His lips were now a tight line. A frown creased his brow and a muscle bunched in his jaw.

'You have no need to thank me.' His voice was gruff as he removed his arm from her waist and shifted a fraction, putting space between them. 'Anyone would have done the same.'

She knelt by Brack, stroking him to cover the slap of humiliation.

'And you, handsome, steadfast Brack.' She leant over to press her lips to his domed head. Her eyes blurred with tears. 'Without you, I would certainly not be h-here.'

She gulped back a sob. Giving way to her emotions would achieve nothing other than to embarrass both her and Nathaniel. She would not have looked up at him so... so *invitingly*...but...had she imagined those tortured pleas? Those endearments? She brushed those unanswered questions aside. Whether she remembered truly or not could make no difference. She had acted without thought and Nathaniel's rejection was plain. And painful.

She would focus on the reality. She had survived. Her terror would fade and she would continue with her life. Much as she had after she had given up Clara. Grace had learned the value of resilience then and she would use that lesson now. She would survive Nathaniel's rejection.

Grace smoothed Brack's head, giving her time to compose herself. Sweep had by now roused, seeking some of her attention, and Grace tickled him under the chin.

'Is he injured? Will he recover?' she asked.

'We think that, like you, he is battered and bruised and shocked, but nothing broken. He should be back to his old self within a few days.'

Sweep set himself to wash Brack's ear and then moved on to his eye. Brack seemed not to object. Grace patted him.

'Where did they find him?'

'About half a mile down river from where you were.'

'I am so relieved.'

Grace regained her feet, stumbling slightly. Nathaniel cupped her elbow—no supporting arm around her waist this time.

'I came down to find out if Brack was safe,' she said, keeping her gaze on the dog and the kitten, 'but I am a little hungry. Do you mind if I—?'

'Sit down and I will find something for you.' Nathaniel ushered her, again, towards the chair in the corner.

Weariness settling in her bones, Grace sank into the chair, folding her legs and tucking her feet under her as she snuggled into the still-warm, still-smelling-of-Nathaniel blanket. Nathaniel watched her until she was settled, an unfathomable expression in his dark eyes. She heard the vague noises of food preparation and soon found a plate with a slice of Mrs Sharp's fruit cake thrust into her hands.

'Thank you.' She nibbled at the cake, the plate balanced on her legs, until Nathaniel returned with a cup of chocolate. She drank it gratefully, her lids growing heavy with the effort of trying to stay awake. Vaguely she felt the bowl and plate being removed and then she remembered no more.

'Ooh, miss! Such goings-on yesterday.'

Alice was wide-eyed as she lit the fire in Grace's bedchamber. Grace winced at the protest of her sore muscles as she rolled over.

'How is Miss Clara? Is she awake yet?'

'Not yet. She was awake in the night for a while, so she is making up for it now.'

Which meant Alice, too, had been awake but she was as cheerful as ever this morning, despite her disturbed sleep, as she cleaned her hands with a damp cloth and dried them on her apron. Grace felt like nothing more than snuggling back down and sleeping the day away, but it was time she got up. Clara would wake soon, wanting something to eat... Grace sat up abruptly, her hand to her mouth.

'What is it, miss? Have you got a pain?'

'No. No, I am all right. I had a recollection of something...' *Or was it a dream?* 'Alice. Did the men find Brack yesterday?'

'No, miss.'

Oh, no. Poor—

'But his lordship did.'

'His lordship?'

He had brought her home and then gone out again for his dog? Her heart swelled with admiration for his loyalty and courage.

'Yes, miss. Half-dead he was. The dog, I mean, not his lordship, although he didn't look much better.' Alice bustled over to the bed and handed Grace her shawl. 'I've never seen him so...so...*anguished.* Nothing would do for him but to sit up all night in the kitchen in case Brack took a turn for the worse.'

So it wasn't a dream. She *had* gone down to the kitchen and talked to Nathaniel. And invited him—albeit wordlessly—to kiss her. An invitation he had refused. Nausea churned her stomach. But how had she got back to her bedchamber? She had no memory of anything after drinking that chocolate...

Alice walked to the door and opened it, then paused to look back at Grace. 'That's the trouble with animals, isn't it, miss? They can't tell you what hurts. Not like people.'

Not like people... Grace flopped back against her pillows. *But people can choose not to tell you what is wrong. And not all pain is physical.*

Nathaniel...

Alice was still speaking.

'I beg your pardon, Alice. I'm afraid I missed what you said.'

'I said, Mrs Sharp said you must stay in bed and she will bring you some breakfast directly.'

'But...' Grace levered herself up to a sitting position.

'Now, miss, you'd best do what Mrs Sharp says, or...' Alice rolled her eyes, then laughed. 'I'll look after Miss Clara. Mrs Sharp said to take her to the kitchen for her breakfast today.'

'Bring her in to see me first, Alice. Please? I need to see she is all right.'

'Oh, bless you. Miss Clara's bright as a button. It's you that needs looking after.' And with that Alice bustled from the room, shutting the door behind her.

Grace relaxed back into the pillows again, picking over the events of the day before, her thoughts circling and circling...avoiding...too afraid to confront the truth...too terrified to admit, even to herself, the awful thing that *could* have happened yesterday as a consequence of her actions when Bill had jibbed at the water's edge.

What if...?

The sound of the door opening dragged her from her thoughts. She plastered a smile on her face. But it was not Clara, or Alice, who appeared.

It was Nathaniel.

Chapter Nineteen

'Good morning, Miss Bertram.' His dark brown eyes were filled with concern. 'Alice said you were awake. How are you feeling this morning?'

'Sore.' Her burgeoning guilt forced her to admit, 'And ashamed.'

He came closer. 'Why ashamed?'

She sat up, hugging the covers to her chest. 'For the trouble I have caused. For the danger I p-put you in.' Her eyes swam as she finally confronted her worst fear. 'When I think…if you had not been there…what might have happened t-to…Clara…'

Her daughter's name strangled in her throat as she choked back a sob. This was the first time she dared to put that dread into thought, let alone words. Until this instant, it had remained a black spectre hovering around the edge of her consciousness. She had put her precious daughter in danger through her own stupidity. Tears burned her eyes and stung her nose.

Nathaniel perched one hip on the bed, facing her. 'You are not to worry about something that did not happen. It was an accident.'

'But she might have…she could have…' The tears spilled from her eyes, and she covered her face with trembling hands. 'I was so proud of myself,' she muttered through her fingers. 'Stupid! Stupid! I had proved I could harness Bill without any help and I did not want to turn back. My own pride almost cost my life. And yours. And Brack's. And Clara's…'

She ended on a wail. Strong arms came around her and she was hugged close to his solid chest, the steady thump of his heart in her ear as she cried out her guilt and her distress.

'Do not blame yourself. The fault was ours.' The rumble of his words vibrated through her, soothing her. How she wished she could stay cocooned in his arms always. 'We should have warned you the current is treacherous after heavy rain, even though the ford appears shallow enough to cross safely. We all know you are not used to country ways.' His hands cupped her shoulders and he moved her away, ducking his head to peer into her eyes. 'If it will make you feel better, Mrs Sharp is, even now, in her kitchen worrying herself sick that she had said nothing.'

'Mrs Sh-Sharp? B-but she does not even l-like me.'

A handkerchief was pushed into her hands.

'She is becoming accustomed to you.' There was a wry note in his voice. 'I thought you knew that.'

'I had begun to hope it was true.'

Grace dried her eyes and blew her nose, then tucked the handkerchief under her pillow.

'I might have need of it again,' she said in response to Nathaniel's raised brow.

'I can see I shall have to replenish my store of handkerchiefs. I recall you promised me at your interview that you would not succumb to your emotions again.'

Grace's heart lurched. 'You cannot…do you mean to send me away?'

'For crying? Or for depleting my stock of handkerchiefs? It was but a jest, Miss Bertram, albeit a poor one.'

I no longer even recognise a joke at my expense. I am useless.

The vague recollections that had plagued her since waking suddenly came into sharp focus. She could not contain the gasp that escaped her as she remembered Nathaniel carrying her from the river. Disrobing her...

'My dress.'

The words blurted out before she could stop them. Better she had waited to ask Alice, but it was too late and Nathaniel waited for her to expand that comment with raised brows.

'I...that is... I wondered...I remembered...' The sick feeling in her somach invaded her throat as she felt her face burn.

All the planes of his face seemed to harden. 'You remember correctly, Miss Bertram. Please understand that you were dangerously cold when I pulled you from the beck. You needed to be warmed and that was impossible with your clothing sodden with icy water.'

'Oh.' She plucked at the fringe of her shawl. 'I see. I do understand. Is... Did you... Are my clothes here? At the Hall?'

'Ah. No, they remain where I discarded them. On the riverbank.'

'But I will need—'

'You will not wear those garments again. Not whilst you are in my employ. I do not wish to be reminded of—'

He fell abruptly silent, a scowl upon his face, and Grace's heart sank. Of course he did not wish to be reminded of her stupidity and how it had almost killed him and Brack, not to mention the risk to Clara. But she needed her dress and her cloak.

'But I only have—'

'Enough.' He raised his hand, palm facing her. 'I will replace your clothing. There are lengths of fabric stored somewhere—you may choose whichever takes your fancy and make…or, no. Speak to Mrs Sharp. I believe there is a seamstress in the village who will make up some dresses for you. You will hardly have the time, with Clara to care for. And, for God's sake, do not choose brown or grey or any of those other dull colours you are wont to wear.'

Grace stared, flummoxed. 'But, my lord, I am a governess. I should wear clothing suitable to my—'

His gaze snapped to hers. 'And I, Miss Bertram, am your employer. If I choose to order my employee not to wear dresses that transform her into a drab, then I expect to be obeyed. Without question. Is that clear?'

The warmth in his voice belied his harsh words. Her heart lifted; he was not so very angry with her after all.

'Yes, my lord.'

She smiled tentatively. Truthfully, it would be no hardship to accept his offer. Dark colours always drained her complexion. She should not really care about her appearance, but she was woman enough to want to look her best, especially in front of Nathaniel.

'Thank you. And—and I am pleased Brack is safe. I did not know, last night, that it was you who found him.'

He raised a brow. 'Does it matter who found him?'

'I meant…that is…you went out again for a dog when you must have been as exhausted as me.'

'Not quite,' he said, with the glimmer of a smile. 'And Brack is not just *a* dog. He is *my* dog. I look after my own.'

'And you love him.'

'You think it strange that I care for my animals?'

'No! I think it admirable.'

It was not only his animals he cared for. He cared for Clara and for the people who worked for him too.

For her.

'Thank you, again, for saving me yesterday, my lord. And for looking after me last night.'

His eyes crinkled at the corners. 'You are very welcome, Miss Bertram.'

A suspicion suddenly struck her. 'Did you put laudanum drops in my chocolate last night?'

A bubble of laughter rose inside her at the face he pulled, reminiscent of a small boy caught out in mischief.

'Guilty as charged. I apologise, but you needed to sleep, not lie awake fretting, so I thought you could use a little assistance.'

'No wonder I could not remember returning to my bed.' She willed her cheeks not to grow pink. 'I… Did you…?'

'I carried you upstairs, if that is what you are wondering. You did not stir. And you cannot—' he fleetingly brushed her cheek with one finger '—be embarrassed after the events of yesterday afternoon. I was the perfect gentleman, I can assure you.' A faint smile stretched his lips and was gone.

'I did not doubt it, my lord. Thank you.'

The bed rocked as he stood up. 'I am relieved to find you on the road to recovery and will leave you in peace. Mrs Sharp has prescribed rest for you today, so please ensure you do as she says.'

He turned on his heel and left the room, leaving Grace to ponder her growing feelings for a man who did not return them.

Or does he?

His mother had seen enough in his behaviour to prompt her to warn him off Grace and most successfully, too, to judge by his behaviour since her visit. There was a definite softening in his attitude today, though, and she would swear she had not misremembered those frantic endearments when he rescued her.

But…her doubts about her own judgement were still powerful.

Look what happened last time I believed a man cared for me.

She conjured up the memory of the night before when she had gazed up at Nathaniel. He *had* been tempted to kiss her, but then he had ignored her silent invitation. He was her employer. A marquess.

Miss Fanworth's warning against dalliances with employers whispered in her memory. The teacher had joined the four friends as they waited in their shared bedroom for the carriage that would whisk Joanna away to her new life.

It never ends well, she had said. *Look at poor Madame...* and then she had blushed, pursed her lips and shaken her head when urged to tell the girls more.

Grace and her friends had often speculated about what had happened to Madame in the past. Rumours—passed down from each generation of schoolgirls to the next—told the tale of a newly qualified governess who had fallen in love with her high-ranking employer's heir. It was said that Madame had been paid off with the school in Salisbury, but that she had been left broken-hearted.

Grace struggled to believe the stern Frenchwoman had ever been so ill-disciplined as to allow her heart to rule her head—a trait of which she had accused Grace on more than one occasion—but then, the night before Rachel had finally left the school, she had discovered a little more of the truth. Unable to sleep, Rachel had gone downstairs and happened upon Madame reading a pile of old letters with tears in her eyes.

'*Surtout, garder votre coeur,*' Madame had said, before sending Rachel back to bed with a warm drink. *Above all, guard your heart.*

Rachel had told Isabel and Grace—Joanna had already left the school—and they had come to the conclusion the rumours about Madame's lost love must be true.

With a sigh, Grace wriggled down under the covers and rolled on to her side. Henceforth, she would make sure it was her head that ruled her heart. Madame had spoken wisely. At least she would still see Nathaniel every day. Perhaps now they could return to their chess games and their former, more comfortable relationship and forget the cold, unhappy atmosphere of the past fortnight.

She would encourage him to spend more time with Clara and she would focus on making them both happy.

It was four days since Grace's accident. Sunday morning. Everyone had gone to church, taking Clara with them, but Grace had declined to go, unable to face the inevitable questions about her ordeal.

As soon as the carriage disappeared from sight, Nathaniel said, 'Would you care to see the hawks today? The weather is perfect. We can fly one if you would like to.'

Grace beamed her pleasure, causing Nathaniel to burn with shame at the memory of his brusque rebuttal the last time she had asked to see the birds.

As they soon reached the top of the fell—the place where Grace had thought the eagle was attacking him—Nathaniel said, 'Are you certain this is not too much for you?'

Grace laughed, her eyes sparkling, her cheeks flushed with their walk. She wore an old black cloak of Mrs Sharp's—he had ordered her a new cloak, but it was yet to arrive—and a serviceable brown bonnet, but Nathaniel swore he had never seen any fine lady as beautiful as Grace Bertram.

'I am not tired. How could I be when you have walked up here at a snail's pace to accommodate my woefully short stride?'

He stopped anyway. 'Here is a good place. There is no need to go further.'

His kestrel, Woody, was on his arm. Next to the other birds of prey—the buzzard and the peregrine falcons—he was dainty and colourful and Grace had fallen in love with him, admiring the black-spotted, chestnut-brown plumage on his back and wings, and his slate-grey head and tail.

Nathaniel removed Woody's hood and set him free to

fly. Grace watched, awe and delight on her upturned face, and Nathaniel watched Grace.

'He is staying in one place now,' Grace said.

'He is hovering. It is how kestrels hunt. They have sharp eyesight and they watch for the movement of mice and voles, or for small birds. It is hard to see it, but if you watch very carefully you can see that his head stays perfectly still whilst his wings and his body absorb the currents of air.'

'Will he come back to you?'

'Yes, of course. I've had him from a chick. He could not survive out here on his own. Here, we will call him in.'

He stripped the gauntlet off his left hand and passed it to Grace. 'You are right-handed so you must wear the glove on your left so you can replace his hood and change his jesses over without fumbling.'

'What if I hurt him?'

Anxious eyes searched his and his heart flipped in his chest. How he resisted the impulse to take her in his arms there and then he did not know.

'Do not worry. I am here. I will do it.'

Her trusting smile set his blood on fire.

'Stand like this…' with his hands on her shoulders, he moved her so she stood sideways to where Woody flew '…hold your arm out in front of you, like so, with your fingers straight…' he raised her left arm '…and stay still.'

He stood close, his hand behind hers, holding a sliver of fresh meat. He let out a call to the bird, who, knowing there would be food as a reward, flew in, straight as an arrow, and landed on the side of Grace's hand. She gasped.

'I did not think I would feel him through the leather, but I can feel his grip.'

Nathaniel gave Woody his reward and folded Grace's fingers around the thin strip of leather—the jess—which was secured to the kestrel's anklet.

'There,' he said, Grace's lily-of-the-valley scent filling his senses, she was so close. 'Now you have control of when he flies again.'

They flew Woody several more times, then Nathaniel slipped on his hood and they started for home.

'Thank you, N…my lord,' Grace said.

He bit his tongue to stop himself from giving her permission to call him Nathaniel. How could that help in his efforts to keep her from his heart?

'I am pleased you enjoyed it, Miss Bertram.'

'Do you think…might I come with you again? I should like to see the bigger birds fly as well.'

As she spoke, she stumbled against him and he caught her, pulling her close. He looked down. She looked up. He was so tempted to succumb to the desire sizzling through his veins, but he could not. He stiffened his resolve and, with a pang of regret, he put her from him. She had accepted the scars on his face and his hand, but she was young…naïve…she could not possibly realise the full extent of the damage that damnable fire had wrought. Imagining her horror at the sight of his naked body sent shudders of dread rippling through him. How could a beautiful woman like Grace ever accept—be intimate with—a ravaged man like him?

'Thank you for catching me,' Grace said, after a few seconds of uncomfortable silence. 'I should take more care.'

She sounded completely unconcerned and relief flooded Nathaniel that he hadn't followed his desire to kiss her.

'I should like to ask you about the Christmas decorations,' she then said.

'Yes?'

'I should like to cut some evergreens in the woods. Mrs Sharp said there is holly and ivy, and…and…well, some other trees, that I could use to make garlands to decorate the Hall.'

'You mean such as laurel and juniper?'

'Yes.' She didn't sound sure. 'I think she said those sorts.'

Nathaniel suppressed his smile, love filling him at the effort she was making to fit into this alien—for her—place.

'You do not need my permission to cut branches in the woods.'

'No. But I do need your permission to ask Ned or Tam to help cut them. And carry them home.'

Home. He liked the way she said home.

'Of course you may ask them. And I will help, too. When is it you wish to start?'

'A few days before Christmas. And then we shall make garlands and decorate the Hall on Christmas Eve. It would be nice…' her voice became wistful '…if we might have a Yule log, too. Do you think—?'

'The wood has all been cut for the winter. I doubt we have anything big enough.'

But he would move heaven and earth to find one, just for Grace.

Chapter Twenty

Two days later, Nathaniel appeared in the doorway of his book room as Grace descended the stairs carrying Clara—already dressed to go out—and her own new cloak and bonnet. She put Clara down when they reached the hall and the little girl ran straight to Nathaniel, arms aloft. Love, tinged with melancholy, laced her veins as she wished the three of them were a real family.

'You are going out?' Nathaniel swung Clara up and kissed her before putting her down again.

'Yes.' Grace avoided his gaze, draping her cloak over the newel post whilst she donned her bonnet. 'We are going into Shivercombe to consult with the seamstress and take her the fabric I have selected for my new gowns. I shall also visit Miss Dunn.'

'Are you sure about driving, so soon after your accident?'

Grace paused in the act of tying her bonnet ribbons under her chin. She adopted a light tone. Nathaniel didn't need to know the full extent of her nerves. 'I have to cross the beck again sometime, so why not today? I *must* replace my dress and I long to see Elizabeth.'

She had missed attending church on Sunday and Elizabeth had sent a very concerned note, via Mrs Sharp, enquiring after her health and inviting her to visit soon. Grace swung her new cloak around her shoulders and fastened the silver clasp at her neck.

She hesitated. She had already thanked Nathaniel for her new cloak, but this was the first time she had worn it. And she was very conscious of him watching her, his gaze sending shivers dancing across her skin.

'Thank you again for this beautiful cloak.' She stroked the fur trim.

'The colour suits you.'

His voice was gruff, as though he were embarrassed. The cloak was emerald-green velvet, lined with fur, and Grace had gasped with delight when she opened the package Ned had brought back from the village yesterday. It was the finest garment she had ever worn.

On impulse, she said, 'You could come with us, if you are worried.'

He stared. 'To the village?'

'Indeed. We will not stay above half an hour with Elizabeth and if it will set your mind—'

'Take one of the men.' He pivoted on his heel and shut the book room door firmly behind him.

Grace bit her lip. It had been a foolish thing to suggest. Of course he would refuse.

'Come, sweetie.' She took Clara's hand. 'Let us go.'

Her bravado lasted until the final part of the track that led down to the ford. As it came into view, her heart began to thump and she clenched the reins, inadvertently pulling Bill to a halt. How she wished Nathaniel was by her side, but no sooner had that thought surfaced than she quashed it. She glanced down at Clara, sitting quietly on the bench seat beside her. A pair of solemn green eyes gazed back at her, giving her the strength to overcome her nerves and drive on. The water was back to its normal level and flow and Bill did not hesitate to plod across the ford, but still

Grace held her breath the whole way and only breathed easily again once they were safely through.

She called upon Mrs Campbell, the seamstress, and was measured for two round gowns, before calling at the rectory where a grand fuss was made of her. All the Dunns were present, as was Mr Rendell, and they demanded every detail of her accident, exclaiming with horror at her ordeal.

'I am grateful for your concern,' she said, finally, after the Reverend and Mrs Dunn had left the room. 'But I wish now to put it behind me. I know now not to attempt the ford when there has been heavy rainfall, so it was a valuable lesson.'

'A lesson? My dearest Grace, you have no need to put on a brave face for us.' Elizabeth reached down to pluck Clara from the floor and sat her on her knee. 'Your Miss Bertram is *very* brave, is she not, Clara?'

Mr Rendell flashed a sympathetic smile at Grace. 'Eliz...er... Miss Dunn, I believe Miss Bertram means to convey the message that she does not wish to be continually reminded of her ordeal.

'Let us instead discuss Christmastide, for it is a week tomorrow, and I have traversed the length and breadth of Langthrop Wood this morning in order to discover where the best holly berries grow, only to return somewhat disheartened.'

'It is a little early to cut greenery.' Elizabeth spoke somewhat absently, engrossed by now in a game of pat-a-cake with Clara. 'We do not decorate the church until Christmas Eve as a rule.'

'I know, but last year it took us so long to locate the best berries, we were decorating the church until well after dark, if you remember. I thought to save us time on the day if I knew their location, but now it looks as though we shall have to be content with nothing brighter than green leaves.'

'But I noticed an abundance of berries on my drive into

the village today,' Grace said. 'I may not recognise many
trees, but I do know holly.'

An image flashed through her mind of Isabel, the previous Christmas, a sprig of holly with bright berries tucked
into the red ribbon she had tied around her best bonnet.
A wave of nostalgia hit her. How different this Christmas
would be from last.

'But that is Shiverstone Woods, Grace. It is on Lord
Ravenwell's land, and we could not...he does not...' Elizabeth's voice drifted into silence.

'I shall ask his lordship for permission,' Grace said. 'He
may choose not to attend church, but the rest of us do and
I am sure he will not object—'

'I do not need you to petition his lordship on my behalf,' Mr Rendell said, firmly. 'I shall ask him myself. In
fact, with your permission, Miss Bertram, I shall accompany you back to Shiverstone Hall today in order to settle
the matter.'

'But Ralph... Mr Rendell...what if Lord Ravenwell is
angered?' Elizabeth's voice rang with fear. 'Why do you
not allow Grace to—?'

'Hush, Elizabeth.' He leaned over and patted her hand.
'There is no need to upset yourself. The village rumours
are built on fear of the unknown. His lordship was perfectly civil when last I called at the Hall and I have no fear
of him. It is only right, as it is for the church, that I ask
him myself. He can only refuse, but I hope he will find it
harder to refuse me face to face than through the medium
of an employee.'

Ralph? Elizabeth? Grace barely paid attention to their
words—she was too busy speculating over the meaning of
her two friends calling one another by their given names.
How romantic it would be if they were in love, and they
married, and had a baby...

She came back to the present with a start, her own name
having penetrated her thoughts.

'I beg your pardon?'

'I said, I shall saddle my mare and then, when you are ready to leave, I shall ride back to the Hall with you. You can point out the hollies on the way. I am aware this must seem a trivial matter to you, but it is important to our congregation that the church be festively decorated to celebrate Our Lord's birth day. And, traditionally, the villagers use any leftover greenery to decorate their cottages.'

'I do not think it trivial, Mr Rendell, and I shall welcome your company on the journey home.'

'That is settled then.' Mr Rendell rose to his feet. 'I shall leave you ladies to your gossip and I shall be ready whenever you are, Miss Bertram.'

He bowed and left the room. Elizabeth's gaze followed him, lingering on the closed door as though he were still in sight until, with a visible start, she appeared to recall her visitors. She glanced at Grace, a becoming flush colouring her face, and then she ducked her head, burying her face in Clara's curls.

'Mr Rendell is a very pleasant young man, is he not, Elizabeth?'

'Oh, he is. He is so...oh! I simply must tell someone, but I must swear you to secrecy, Grace, for Ralph has yet to speak to Papa, but...we have an *understanding*.'

Grace clasped Elizabeth's hands. 'I am so happy for you. I hope...do you believe your father will give his permission?'

Elizabeth beamed, her dark eyes sparkling. 'I do hope so.' Then her smile faltered. 'But until Ralph gets a living of his own, we will have to remain here. It would be so wonderful to have a home of our own,' she concluded in a wistful tone.

'I am sure it will not be long before he is able to progress.'

'You will not tell Ralph—or anyone—that I told you?

We did agree we must keep our love to ourselves until he speaks to Papa. I only hope it may be soon.'

'I will not breathe a word, Elizabeth, but I am delighted for you.'

'Ralph.' Clara looked from Elizabeth to Grace and back again. 'Ralph.'

'He is Mr Rendell to you, sweetie.' Grace tickled Clara under the chin, then held out her arms. 'Come, Clara. It is time to go home.'

'You call that place home, Grace, but does it truly feel like home to you? I heard it was—oh! I am sorry, that was most indiscreet of me.'

Grace did not need to think about it. Despite the occasional longing for her old friends, she could not imagine living anywhere else.

'Yes, it does feel like home. I make no doubt Mr Rendell told you the house is sparsely furnished and dark, but his lordship has allowed me to make a few changes and I think it is an improvement.'

'Well, I think you are very brave, living there.'

Anger stirred. 'Lord Ravenwell is not an ogre and I have no need of bravery, I can assure you.'

'I did not mean—'

'And I did not mean to snap at you.' Elizabeth's stricken expression roused Grace's remorse—she was only reacting to the stories that circulated about Nathaniel. 'His lordship is kind to me and he loves Clara; how can people say such cruel things about him?'

'They tell their stories to fit the facts as they see them, Grace. If his lordship came into the village on occasion, they would base their opinions on what they see, not what their imaginations conjure forth.'

'If only they knew him as I do—'

Grace bit her tongue, her cheeks scorching as understanding dawned in Elizabeth's eyes.

'Oh, *Grace*... I did not suspect you had developed feelings for him. Please, do take care. You are a lovely young woman, but even if he did return your...your *affection* you surely would not wish to spend the rest of your life in such an isolated spot, cut off from everyone.'

'I have no expectations beyond my present position.' Grace stood up, preparing to depart.

'Now I have angered you. I am sorry for speaking so bluntly. It was unforgivable in me.'

Grace had no wish to leave Elizabeth on bad terms. 'No, it is I who must apologise. You spoke out of concern for me. And I truly have no expectations, Elizabeth, but... people can change, can they not?'

'Only if they truly want to, my dear. Do not forget, his lordship has lived his chosen life for several years now and therefore must be content. If he did crave a more sociable existence, do you not think he would have shown some signs of change by now?'

Grace hesitated. How could she put into words what she wished for, deep in her heart? She longed to cry: *Love can conquer all*, but she knew such a sentiment would worry Elizabeth and embarrass them both. No, she would keep her own counsel. And hope she was right and Elizabeth wrong.

'We must go now, Elizabeth. Goodbye.'

It was pleasant to have Mr Rendell's company on the drive home. He tied his horse to the back of the gig—much to the delight of Clara, who spent the entire journey on her knees, facing backwards, and chattering to the animal—and rode in the gig with Grace and Clara. They pulled up in the stable yard, handed the horses over into Ned's care and walked to the house.

'I will go and find his lordship,' Grace said, showing Mr Rendell into the drawing room.

'This room is much improved since my last visit.' He

turned a circle. 'Is that your doing, Miss Bertram? You
have an eye for colour, I see.'

Grace felt her cheeks heat with pleasure at his compliment.

'She certainly does.'

Grace spun round. Her heart gave a tiny lurch at the
sight of Nathaniel, his brown hair windswept, filling the
open doorway.

Nathaniel scowled. That delicate blush told its own tale.
Her beau had escorted her home and Grace could not disguise her pleasure.

'I was up on the fells and I saw you driving up the track.'
The eruption of jealousy when he had seen them had threatened to overwhelm him. It was contemptible. He must learn
to be pleased for her—for them both. 'Good of you to see
Miss Bertram safely home, Rendell.'

'It was my pleasure.' Rendell strode over to Nathaniel,
his right hand thrust out.

From the corner of his eye, Nathaniel noticed Grace's
gaze drop to his hand. It was gloveless and her expression
revealed her qualms as clearly as if she spoke.

She is afraid I will snub him.

As she lifted her gaze to his, he raised a brow, stepped
forward and clasped Mr Rendell's proffered hand, conscious of the whisper of relief that escaped her lips as he did
so. When had she become such an important part of his life
he was constantly aware of her and what she was feeling?

His instincts urged him to leave now, but his pride forced
him to stay.

'I have asked Mrs Sharp to send in refreshments. You
will take tea with us before you leave, Rendell?'

Nathaniel gestured towards the cluster of seating around
the fireplace. 'Please, take a seat.'

He followed the curate across the room, but did not
sit. Instead, he poked at the fire, stirring the flames into

life. Mrs Sharp carried in the tea tray and departed again. Grace then poured the tea whilst Rendell made a fuss of Sweep—who had jumped on his lap—exclaiming over how big he'd become. Nathaniel accepted a cup from Grace and finally sat down.

The minute he did so, Rendell spoke, as though he had waited for the right moment. 'I had an ulterior motive in escorting Miss Bertram home, for I have a request to make of you, my lord.'

Random thoughts and suspicions darted through Nathaniel's head. Chief amongst them was that Rendell meant to ask his permission to court Grace.

Nonsense. Why would he need my permission? I am not her father.

But there was Clara. Nathaniel swallowed. Hard.

What if he knows the truth? What if he wants them both? What if...?

He slammed a door in his mind against those increasingly frantic conjectures.

'Go ahead.'

Clara bustled over to Rendell. 'Ralph,' she said, gazing up at him. ''n Sweep.'

A punch to the gut could not have stolen Nathaniel's breath more effectively. *Ralph?* He stole a glance at Grace, who was struggling not to laugh.

'Clara! This is Mr Rendell. You must not call him anything else. Can you say Mr Rendell for me?'

'Mr Wendell.'

'Good girl. That is better. I apologise, Mr Rendell, I fear Clara must have overheard something she should not have done.'

The curate's cheeks had bloomed red. 'It is of no matter, Miss Bertram,' he said hurriedly. 'Now, your lordship, if I might move on to the purpose of my visit—I am here to request permission for myself and some of the villagers to gather holly in Shiverstone Woods.'

'Holly?'

'Er…yes. I have searched the woods on the other side of the village, and the holly there has barely any berries and—'

'And the berried holly is needed to decorate the church for the Christmas services,' Grace said. 'You should blame me if Mr Rendell's request has angered you, for it was I who told him of the abundance of berries in Shiverstone Woods.'

Nathaniel hastily smoothed his frown away. If only he could admit to them it had been incredulity that creased his brow, not anger. Holly…he had worked himself into a panic, and all Rendell wished to discuss was holly? Although there was still the small matter of Clara calling him by his first name. She had heard that somewhere.

'Yes. You have my permission.'

Grace beamed. 'Thank you.'

'We will gather it over the next few days,' Rendell said. 'And we will then decorate the church on the afternoon of Christmas Eve. It is quite an occasion. Most of the village helps and then we have a short service, with carols.'

'It sounds magical.' Grace's eyes shone with enthusiasm. 'Might we… It would be lovely to take Clara, if you will allow it, my lord?'

'Your entire household would be welcome to come along, my lord.'

'I understood it was your intention to decorate the Hall on Christmas Eve, Miss Bertram?' She had told him of her plans over dinner the night before.

'It is, but we shall collect the greenery in advance, to give us time to make garlands, and then all we need do on Christmas Eve is bring them indoors and decorate the rooms. We should be finished in time to help at the church.'

He could not resist the plea in her eyes. He had sworn not to stand in the way of her having friends in the village, even if those friends did include the handsome curate.

'Of course you may attend. I am sure Clara will enjoy it.'

She beamed again—a smile that tore at his heart. If only she might always smile at him like so. He did not want to lose her, even though it seemed inevitable. His mind shied away from the complication of Clara. He would not let her go. But could he part mother and daughter? Clara, he knew, could be the means to keeping Grace at Shiverstone Hall even if she fell in love with another, such as Rendell. But... could he be so cruel? So selfish?

Loving Grace meant he wanted her to be happy. Always.

Impatiently, he thrust aside his conjectures. He would deal with these issues if...when...they arose. In the meantime, he would do everything in his power to keep Grace and Clara happy and content. And if that meant throwing himself into preparations for a Christmas he saw little point in celebrating this year, then so be it.

Chapter Twenty-One

'Not one, but two letters, Miss Bertram. You *are* popular.'

It was four days before Christmas and Ned had been to the village as usual to collect the post. Spying them on the table in the hall, Nathaniel used them as an excuse to pay a visit to his niece and her governess in the nursery.

'Two?'

Grace held out her hand and he gave her the letters before swinging a clamouring Clara up into his arms and spinning around with her.

'Oh, how lovely.'

Grace's cheeks were pink with pleasure and Nathaniel found his thoughts wandering in a completely inappropriate direction: Grace…hair wild and unrestrained…beneath him…pink with a completely different kind of pleasure. He forced his attention from Grace and to Clara, bending to tickle her face with his hair.

'They are from Joanna and Isabel,' Grace said. 'Is it not kind of them to write again, even though I have not yet replied to their letters?'

Her pleasure from something so simple humbled him. She had been through a difficult childhood, a heartbreaking experience, and she was in effect all alone in the world—he had not failed to notice her uncle had not replied to her letter—and yet still she saw the good in people and remained full of positivity. Was that due to her youth? Would she, like him, grow more cynical over time? Or was it simply in her nature to see the goodness and kindness in everything? Her attitude was contagious. It had changed his household, and for the better. Even Mrs Sharp had shed her misgivings about Grace.

Grace placed the letters, unopened, on the mantelshelf.

'Are you not going to read them?'

She shook her head, her blonde hair escaping from her pins in delightful tendrils that caressed her neck. 'I shall wait until I may give them my full attention, when Clara is asleep.'

'Read them. I shall play with Clara, so you will not be distracted nor feel you are neglecting her.' He sat on the floor next to his niece and began to stack brightly painted wooden blocks one on the other.

Grace smiled her thanks and reached for the first letter. From the corner of his eye he watched the expressions chase across her face. When she had finished, she looked thoughtful.

'I hope it did not contain bad news?'

'I beg your…? No. No, not bad news. It was from Isabel. Do you recall…my friend who married William Balfour, Viscount Langford's son?'

Clara, crowing in delight, dashed Nathaniel's tower of blocks to the floor.

'Indeed, I do.' Nathaniel scooped the scattered blocks into a heap. 'You were worried about her, I remember.'

And we disagreed about the need for love in marriage.

'I need worry no more, it seems. They have been to stay with Joanna and her new husband, Luke, at his family home in Hertfordshire. Isabel seems much happier than last time she wrote. Indeed, she talks of her husband in glowing terms…and, yet, still it feels as though there is something she is hiding. Oh, how I wish I could see her face to face and know that everything is all right.'

'If the other letter is from Joanna, could that shed some light?'

Nathaniel grabbed Clara and tickled her. She squirmed, giggling. When he released her, she scrambled to her feet and ran to the other side of the nursery. Nathaniel promptly started to rebuild the tower.

After a silence whilst Grace read Joanna's letter and during which Clara charged at Nathaniel and demolished the tower once more, Grace set the second letter aside with a sigh and a look of longing on her face.

'You miss your friends, don't you?'

She started. 'Yes. But it is not that. It is…they have both moved on with their lives. That, somehow, more than anything, brings it home to me that there is no going back. Our childhood is over and two of the four of us are already wed. And Joanna is so very happy, I—'

She fell into silence. Had her thoughts drifted to Rendell? Was she envious of her friends' happiness? Did she hope…wish…the curate would speak and give her the same joy?

'Again! Again!' Clara hopped from foot to foot and Nathaniel began to gather the blocks once more.

'Joanna says Isabel and William have settled into their marriage,' Grace continued after her pause, 'and they are happier than they were at first.'

'See. I told you a successful marriage has no need of love or romance.'

She frowned, lips pursed. 'She *also* believes that Isabel has fallen in love with William, but not he with her. Or, at least, he is denying his feelings.'

Nathaniel found he could not hold her gaze and he focussed on Clara.

'Now, Miss Bertram, I shall build my tower again and, this time, woe betide any young lady who tries to knock it down.' He wagged his finger at Clara, who squealed excitedly from the far side of the room.

Miss Bertram, it appeared, was not to be deflected. 'I cannot believe that will make a happy life for Isabel.' Her lids lowered, as did her voice, and he had to strain to catch her final words. 'Unrequited love, surely, must be the most painful cross of all to bear.'

This conversation needed to end. It was drifting too close to reality for Nathaniel's comfort.

'There is nothing you can do about it,' he said, 'so I suggest you put it from your mind.

'Whooooaaaaa!' Clara had launched herself across the nursery, straight at Nathaniel, landing with full force on his chest, knocking him backwards. He used her momentum to lie on his back and swing her up above him, face down. 'Clara is flying, like a bird.'

He happened to glance across at Grace and he caught her watching them with that same look of longing. If it wasn't for Rendell, he might think…but no. To complete that thought would lead to madness. He had only to look at her and then at himself in the mirror. No, that yearning expression was no doubt a wish that it was Clara's father playing with her. Not him.

He sat up, standing Clara on her own two feet, and then stood up, brushing his hands over his breeches and coat. Again, Grace watched him, following the movement of his hands and Nathaniel's pulse quickened, stirring his blood. If only…

'I must go,' he said.

Grace also rose. 'We are due down in the kitchen,' she said. 'I said I would help Mrs Sharp make mince pies and gingerbread, and I promised Clara she might play with Sweep.'

'Sweep? Play Sweep?'

'Yes.' Grace picked Clara up and kissed her cheek. 'We shall go and see Sweep now. He has taken to staying in the kitchen,' she added to Nathaniel. 'I suspect Sharp feeds him titbits and Mrs Sharp is happy, now he is keeping the mice at bay. But Clara is not so happy, because she wants to play with him.'

'Let us hope her new toys at Christmas will help take her mind off the cat,' Nathaniel said as they left the nursery, side by side.

Tam had made Clara a wooden Noah's Ark and he and Ned were busy whittling animals to go inside it. Grace, too, had been busy making gifts. Some—her knitting and embroidery—he had seen, for she had taken to bringing it to the drawing room after dinner and working on it whilst he read aloud. But her painting, for the nursery wall, she said, was allowed to be seen by no one until Christmas Day. Her busyness had prompted him to set aside a little of his indifference for Christmastide and to purchase gifts for Clara and for Grace. In accordance with custom, the servants would receive their Christmas boxes on Boxing Day.

They were at the head of the staircase. 'Here, let me carry her downstairs. She is getting heavy; I have the bruising on my chest to prove it.'

He reached to take Clara and his hand brushed against Grace's. A faint gasp reached his ears, even as they jerked apart, Grace quickly relinquishing her hold on the child. Nathaniel's heart pounded and heat flooded his veins even as the hair on his arms and the nape of his neck stood to attention.

Grace's cheeks had taken on a tinge of colour. He saw her swallow as she raised both hands to lift her hair and repin it. Then she smoothed her hands down the skirt of her gown and finally she looked at him, with a strained smile.

'Thank you.'

Nathaniel rode Caesar into Shiverstone Woods and yelled Tam's name.

A faint shout came from deep within the trees and he

turned the horse in that direction. Five minutes later he rode into a small clearing and reined Caesar to a halt with a vicious but silent curse.

There were others here. Strangers.

Tam, Ned and Grace were watching him and all he wanted to do was wheel the horse about and gallop away. He regretted riding Caesar. Had he been on Zephyr, he could have excused himself on the grounds the stallion would not wait quietly whilst he helped to cut and gather branches for Grace's garlands. As it was, he had no excuse.

Caesar sidled beneath him, tossing his head, reacting to Nathaniel's tension. He could not leave, not with Grace's eyes upon him as she walked towards him with such a welcoming smile. He gathered his courage and dismounted. How many others were here? How many eyes to gawp? How many fingers to point? How—

'Thank you for coming to help.'

She was by his side. She laid a tentative hand on his sleeve. He resisted the urge to shake her off.

'The villagers are here today to gather decorations for the church as well.'

'So I see.' What else could he say? It mattered what Grace thought of him.

He scanned the clearing and the nearby trees. Most of the people continued with cutting and bundling holly, ivy and other evergreens. There were a few surreptitious glances but, in the main, the villagers were getting on with the task in hand.

His heartbeat slowed. It would take an hour or so of his life. He could do that for Grace. He need not speak to anyone else and, if he did not speak, he knew they would leave him alone.

'Where do you want me to start?'

Christmas Eve dawned bright and cold. Clara woke Grace early, so she took her down to the kitchen for her breakfast. It would be warmer there. She went in, Clara on her hip, to find Sharp in his chair, sucking on his pipe, Sweep curled on his knee. Mrs Sharp was nowhere to be seen.

'Good morning, Sharp. Do you think it will snow?'

Sharp removed his pipe. 'Don't 'ee go wishing for snow, missy. It makes life very hard way up here.'

Grace sighed, knowing Sharp was probably right, but today she did not wish to be practical. She wished today and tomorrow to be fun-filled and romantic and beautiful, and a covering of snow would be perfect. It had snowed last Christmas in Salisbury. It had covered the ground and painted the rooftops and the bare branches of the trees glistening white, turning the school and its surroundings into a magical place for the four friends who had remained at the school for the Christmas holidays—their last Christmas as schoolgirls and their last Christmas together.

Grace pushed down her memories and the yearning that arose in their wake. She was here now. She had Clara. Surely she was worth any sacrifice? And if her love for Nathaniel must remain unrequited, then she must learn to accept it.

Madame had survived *her* lost love,

Isabel's recent letter, in addition to writing about her marriage, had also contained extraordinary news about Madame who, sadly, was gravely ill with pneumonia. During a conversation about girls' education with the Duke of Wakefield, Isabel happened to mention Madame Dubois's School for Young Ladies, and the Duke had been quite overcome. The tale that emerged was of two young people who had fallen in love but, out of duty to his poverty-stricken estates and his family, the Duke had put aside his own desires and married for money. He did finance the school—just as those old rumours had always claimed—but he told Isabel he had made sure he was never told its location.

The Duke had then rushed away, to travel to Salisbury and visit Madame in her sickbed.

Poor Madame. Grace hoped she would recover and that she and the Duke were now reunited. No wonder she had warned her pupils against forgetting their station and falling for the seductive wiles of employers, or employers' sons. But Madame had never mentioned the danger of falling in love. Grace did not even have the excuse of being seduced. She had succumbed to the man himself—not to whispered compliments, adoring looks or tempting kisses.

'You are very quiet, missy.'

Grace started. She had pulled out a chair and sat at the kitchen table as though in a dream, a still-sleepy Clara on her lap.

'Sorry. I was thinking about decorating the rooms. The garlands—'

'The missus and Alice have already fetched them indoors.' With Mrs Sharp adamant that not one sprig of greenery should cross the threshold until Christmas Eve, they had made up the garlands in the barn, with a brazier to keep them warm. 'They're in the dining room, ready to be hung up after breakfast.'

Later that morning, a shadow fell across Grace as she placed the final candle in the garland that swathed the huge carved stone fireplace in the hall.

'The house looks very festive. Well done, Miss Bertram.'

She smiled at Nathaniel, the little leap of her heart at the sight of him now so customary as to barely register. 'Thank you. I have enjoyed it, but it has been a joint effort.'

'I know. Come…' he crooked his arm '…I have a surprise for you. Outside.'

He led her to the front door, which was rarely used. They stepped out into the porch and Grace gasped. Bill stood stolidly in front of the house, a massive log attached with rope and chains to his harness.

'A Yule log?' She beamed up at Nathaniel. 'But…you said…'

'It would not have been a surprise if I had told you my plan, would it? And there is something else.'

He pointed to the side of the porch. There, on the ground, lay a bundle of green, forked branches festooned with white berries.

'Mistletoe!' Grace felt a blush build in her cheeks. She could make a kissing bough. Would Nathaniel…? She covered her sudden embarrassment by saying, 'Where does that grow? I could not see any in the wood.'

'There is a lime tree in the park at Ravenwell. I sent Ned over a few days ago to fetch some.'

'He certainly brought a large bundle.'

With lots of berries…that is a lot of kisses. Grace knew all about the tradition of kissing beneath the mistletoe and plucking off a berry for each kiss. A swirl of anticipation tightened her stomach. *Will he kiss me? If I stand beneath the mistletoe, later, when there is no one else there, will he kiss me?*

She sneaked a look at Nathaniel as he directed Ned and Tam in unchaining the log. The three men heaved the log off the ground, but Grace had eyes for no one but Nathaniel as his shoulders bulged with the effort and his strong thigh muscles, clearly outlined by his breeches, flexed.

In no time, the log was positioned in the huge, open fireplace and Tam and Ned left, closing the front door behind them, leaving Grace and Nathaniel alone.

Grace had carried in the bundle of mistletoe. Nathaniel turned and she saw his eyes smoulder, like a banked fire, and she felt again that tug of anticipation deep inside her. Her blood quickened and, certain she must be blushing, she moved away, putting the mistletoe on to the floor by the round mahogany table that now graced the centre of the large hall.

Then Sharp came into the hall, followed by Mrs Sharp, Alice and Clara.

'I've brought the kindling, milord.'

Sharp set to work laying the small, dry twigs and split logs around the Yule log whilst Nathaniel disappeared towards the kitchen. He soon emerged again with a smoking lump of charred wood on a shovel.

They all gathered round as he placed the wood on to the twigs already laid and piled more on top. They soon caught and flames began to lick around the Yule log. There was a cheer, and then the Sharps and Alice—with Clara, who wanted to play with Sweep—retreated to the kitchen, leaving Grace and Nathaniel alone again.

Chapter Twenty-Two

'Why did you light the fire that way?' Grace asked Nathaniel.

'It is tradition,' Nathaniel said. 'Every year, a piece of the Yule log is saved and then, the following year, it is used to light the new one. That was a piece we saved from last year.'

'I thought you never celebrated Christmas?'

Grace felt absurdly let down. Nathaniel had shown no enthusiasm for Christmas and she had congratulated herself on changing his mind about celebrating this year.

'I do not,' he said. 'Not since...well...' He touched his cheek, fleetingly. It was the very first time he had ever referred to his scars and Grace was touched by this evidence of his trust. 'Then my family came to Shiverstone for Christmas last year and it was almost like old times. But...this year...I've been dreading...the memories...without Hannah and David...it did not seem...' His voice faded into silence, a muscle bunching in his jaw.

Poor Nathaniel. Any festivities would be bound to raise painful comparisons with last year.

'This Christmastide will not be the same, but I hope you will enjoy it in a different way.' Grace silently vowed that she and Clara would help him make new happy memories.

'I will. You have helped me see the importance of enjoying the Christmas season, for Clara's sake.' He indicated the mistletoe. 'Where shall I hang this?'

Grace eyed the mass of green. 'In here?' She indicated the hall. 'I shall tie a bunch with red ribbon. I doubt we will need all of it, however.'

She looked up and their gazes fused, sending heat spiralling once again through her body, making her skin tingle. Then, because it was nearly Christmas, and because she had offered a kiss—more than once—and been resisted, and just because she felt a little like the rebellious Grace Bertram of old, she bent, snapped off a branch and then straightened, holding the sprig of mistletoe above her head.

He stilled. Not a muscle twitched as he looked deep into her eyes. No smile. No frown. He could not refuse this time. Could he?

His eyes flared and then, with a heartfelt groan, he crushed her to him, his mouth covering hers: hot, hard, demanding. Her lips parted and he took possession, exploring every inch of her mouth. She clung to his shoulders as their tongues entwined, shivers of desire racing through her as she pressed close, the evidence of his arousal hard against her. Even as she melted into him, however, she sensed his change: like someone slowly awakening, as though his brain was catching up with the actions of his body.

He lifted his mouth from hers. She clung closer, but it was no use. Gently, he eased her back, then took her hand—the one that still clutched the mistletoe—and plucked a berry, holding it up between thumb and forefinger.

'You are right,' he said. 'Such a large bundle will be wasted here. Tell Mrs Sharp and Annie they may take what they need before you dispose of the rest.'

Grace loathed this confusion of emotions. How could he kiss her as though his soul depended on it, then dismiss her as easily as he would the leftovers of a meal once his hunger was assuaged?

'I shall take what is left over to the church this afternoon. I am sure there are plenty of men in the village who will be pleased to make use of it.'

Goading him was a risk, but she was cross and she *wanted* to provoke a reaction.

He scowled. 'You still intend to help decorate the church?'

'I do.' She raised her chin. 'You should come too. It would not hurt you and Clara would be thrilled.'

His eyes narrowed as a low growl rumbled deep in his chest. 'I never said it would hurt. Be ready at two.' And he stalked into his book room and slammed the door.

He did not want to go into the village, but that challenge was a provocation too far after that kiss. Until then, he had successfully carried the moment: breaking their kiss, despite the insistent clamour of his body for more, and faking a detachment so far from the truth it was ludicrous. He had goaded her. And she had goaded him right back. And then his pride stopped him backing down. Now, as the carriage rumbled across the ford and followed the lane to the village, it was too late to change his mind. He would not appear a coward in her eyes.

He could not believe it when she had snapped off that mistletoe and tempted him to kiss her. It was tradition: a bit of fun, a quick kiss under the mistletoe. And he, poor deluded fool that he was, had lost control and kissed her like a starving man at a feast. But...she *had* kissed him back. He had not imagined that. And now, he was more confused than ever. He thought her heart belonged to Rendell, but then why would she return his kiss with such...*passion*?

Grace sat opposite him, with Clara. She was beautiful, wearing her emerald cloak and, beneath that, the new blue-sprigged muslin dress that Mrs Campbell had made for her. Her eyes had shone when Ned had brought her two new gowns back from the village. She made the best of the hand life had dealt her. Unlike him. Her courage humbled him: she had travelled hundreds of miles to find Clara, for no reward other than to ensure her daughter was happy and loved.

Was *that* why she kissed him in return? Was her love for her daughter the motive for everything she did? Was she acting a role, intent on securing her future with Clara?

They walked up the cobbled path to the church door, the murmur of voices within getting louder with every step. As they entered, there was a sudden hush from the occupants. Nathaniel stiffened as he felt every eye upon him, but took courage from Clara's tiny hand in his. A symphony of whispers reached his ears, but how could he blame them for their curiosity when it was he who had fostered his own reputation?

A familiar figure emerged from the throng. Ralph Rendell strode down the aisle, hand outstretched.

'My lord, Miss Bertram—how good of you both to come. And little Miss Clara too.'

Despite that kiss, Grace showed no trace of awkwardness on greeting the curate, who appeared unsurprised by Nathaniel's presence. The villagers, one or two of whom Nathaniel recognised from collecting greenery, soon returned to their tasks. Such an enormous step for him seemed of scant importance to everyone else.

Nathaniel's head ached.

'Good afternoon, Rendell.' He made himself smile. 'We had some greenery left over from decorating the Hall: holly, mistletoe and so forth. We thought you might find a use for it.'

They were joined by a fleshy, older man, dressed in black with a white stock, and an attractive, dark-haired young woman.

'Thank you, that is most generous,' Ralph said. 'Now, Lord Ravenwell, might I introduce the Reverend Dunn and his daughter, Miss Elizabeth Dunn?'

Nathaniel shook hands with the clergyman and bowed to his daughter, who dropped a curtsy, tensing under the latter's open appraisal.

'The additional greenery is most appreciated, my lord,' Reverend Dunn said, 'but I must request that you do not bring mistletoe into the church.'

Nathaniel raised a brow. 'You have some objection to mistletoe, sir? I recollect seeing it in York Minster in the past.'

'That is an old tradition and the Dean there might do as he pleases. *I* do not believe it has any place in the House of God, with its links to the druids and paganism. However, it will prove most welcome in the Rectory.'

The vicar grinned and Nathaniel relaxed somewhat.

'Papa! May I tell Grace our news?'

'Rendell?' The vicar looked to his curate, who smiled. 'I have no objection.'

Elizabeth took Grace's hands. 'I am bursting with happiness.' Her cheeks bloomed pink as her dark eyes sparkled. 'You must be the first to know. Mr Rendell has spoken to Papa and he has given his consent. Our betrothal will be announced tomorrow.'

Shock reverberated through Nathaniel. His gaze flew to Grace, but she revealed no hint of distress as she hugged her friend and congratulated the curate. When the others at last moved away, Nathaniel placed his hand briefly at the small of her back. She stiffened. He dipped his head.

'That was unexpected. Are you all right? We can leave if you wish.'

Her puzzled frown seemed genuine. 'I was not surprised, for Elizabeth confided in me on my last visit. Come, let us fetch the greenery from the carriage.'

They brought in the branches of holly and ivy, laurel and juniper, and helped to decorate the church. Then the Reverend Dunn donned his vestments and read a short service before leading the congregation in singing carols. Clara, too young to know the words, warbled away happily and Grace's sweet voice rang out.

Hark the Herald Angels Sing... Nathaniel sang by rote as his mind wandered.

Not by a single word or look had Grace shown anything other than pure delight for her friends, but she *had* been forewarned. She'd had time to prepare for the announcement. Grace was resilient and self-reliant, but Rendell's choice of another woman must surely open the wounds from her unwanted and unloved childhood, and from Clara's father's rejection. Nathaniel recalled his own despair when, despite the understanding between them, Lady Sarah Reece had accepted another man's proposal after Nathaniel's disfigurement.

He knew the pain of rejection.

Without volition, he rubbed at his right cheek. Two women—Sarah and Miss Havers—had rejected him on the strength of his facial scars alone. He'd never had the courage to reveal the rest of the damage wrought by the fire. He'd spent his life since then alone, apart from his servants and his family.

Until now. He looked around the congregation: happily singing, the odd few meeting his eyes with a smile. They already seemed to accept his appearance. Had his experiences as a young man—newly injured and facing the shocked stares and unkind remarks of strangers and the avoidance of former friends—driven him to wrongly believe all people would react in the same way?

He turned his gaze to Grace. She glanced up, smiling, her eyes warm. There was no one he would rather be beside, he realised, but that insight terrified him. He could never expose himself to rejection again. Those past memories were too strong; they still held the power to hurt. As, no doubt, Grace's memories of her lonely, unloved childhood could still hurt her.

Had Rendell's betrothal to Miss Dunn revived those

childhood insecurities? Could that be why she had returned his kiss under the mistletoe? Had she been seeking comfort? Did she crave assurance that she belonged and was capable of being loved? Was that why she had fallen so readily for Clara's father's sweet words?

Well, he could offer comfort, he could provide a home. He could offer no more and, sooner or later, a woman such as Grace would want more. He had seen her pleasure as she interacted with the Dunns and the rest of the villagers and, although the danger posed by Rendell had passed, there would be other men.

She needed people around her, and happiness and laughter, and that he could not offer.

The singing ended.

'My lord. Miss Bertram. Would you care to join us for a bite of supper?' The Reverend Dunn stood before them. 'It will not be very grand, but I know Elizabeth and Ralph would welcome the opportunity to celebrate with their friends.'

'I am not sure,' Nathaniel said. 'It will be dark soon…'

From the corner of his eye, he saw Grace's smile fade and he was helpless to resist.

'…but…on the other hand, the sky is clear and, although not a full moon, there should be enough light to see us home.'

Ralph Rendell joined them. 'It would mean a lot to us if you can stay a while.'

'Very well. We shall accept. Thank you.'

Grace looked thrilled. And he was happy to make her happy.

Chapter Twenty-Three

It was late by the time they arrived home. Ned drove the carriage away from the front of the Hall with a rattle and a clatter of hooves, and then there was silence. The landscape was frosted, sparkling like a hundred thousand diamonds in the moonlight. The night air was still, scented with wood smoke, and Grace—pleasantly light-headed from the combined effects of the mulled wine, the infectious joy of the newly betrothed couple and the intimacy of that slow carriage ride in the dark, with Nathaniel and Clara, like a proper family—was convinced there was magic in the air.

It was a night when anything seemed possible. Nathaniel had visited the village and met his neighbours for the first time in nine years. He had helped decorate the church and he had accepted the vicar's invitation to supper at the rectory. He had already begun to change, thanks to her. How much further might he change, with her help?

Her future suddenly seemed full of promise and boundless possibilities and, for the first time, settled.

She had found a place to call home: a place where she belonged and a home where she was not only wanted, but where she was valued and valuable.

Clara was already asleep, cradled in Nathaniel's arms, and Grace opened the front door to allow him to carry her through. Brack, tail whipping back and forth, was there to greet them, as was Sharp. Grace put her finger to her lips and pointed to Clara.

Sharp nodded, sliding the bolts home quietly as he secured the front door.

'Will you be needing me for anything else tonight, milord?'

'No. You may go to bed, Sharp. Thank you.'

Sharp disappeared towards the back of the house. Nathaniel turned to Grace and her stomach flipped. Surely she was not imagining the heat in his gaze.

'I will carry Clara to bed,' he whispered.

Clara barely stirred as Grace undressed her and put her in her nightgown, then tucked her into her ready-warmed bed, after removing the warming pan with its load of hot coals. She kissed her little girl's forehead, smoothing her unruly curls, and then Nathaniel, too, kissed her goodnight. They left the room, Nathaniel holding the door for Grace and then closing it softly behind her.

Nathaniel hesitated. 'Shall you retire immediately?'

She shook her head, mute. She wanted to be with him. She longed to surround him with her love and to heal him and to help him return to the life he should be living.

If only he would take me in his arms.

She felt emboldened—by the night, by the hush of the house around them, by the wine—but not so emboldened that she could take the first step towards the intimacy she craved. She was sure the desire that smouldered deep in his eyes every time he looked at her was not mere wishful thinking on her part, but still she could not risk making the first move.

She played a little game in her head: *If he does not care for me, he will send me to my room. But...if he does care...*

'I am not tired,' she said, 'but if you do not wish for company, I shall retire to my sitting room.'

He half-bowed. 'I shall enjoy your company.'

They walked downstairs side by side, Grace's stomach dancing with butterflies. Was she wilfully allowing her imagination to lead her into the wrong decisions? Was it just because she longed for him that she imagined he felt the same? She, of all people, knew what the outcome of this night might be. She had Clara to prove it. And yet, her heart was so full of love for Nathaniel, so full of the yearning to take him in her arms and soothe away the years of hurt and loneliness, that she would face that risk with her eyes wide open and no regrets.

In the drawing room, the fire was still alight. Grace sat on the sofa whilst Nathaniel poured two glasses of wine from a decanter. He sat on a chair. Grace stared at the crystal wine glass in her hand, fiercely concentrating on the play of firelight through the ruby red of the wine, quelling her disappointment. She had been so sure he would sit by her side. Doubts now dominated, where only moments before she had been so full of hope. She sipped the wine, the spicy, fruity tang teasing tongue and throat, and cautioned herself not to get this wrong...not to make a fool of herself.

Her lips tingled with the effects of the wine. She glanced up as she soothed them, saw his gaze follow the movement of her tongue and her pulse leapt in response.

She had to break the silence—had to say something, no matter how inane, before she blurted out the truth she held in her heart.

'Thank you for coming with us today.'

He lifted his glass in salute, but said nothing.

'It must have been hard for you.'

A faint line etched between his brows and then was gone. If she hadn't been watching so closely, she would have missed it. He placed his glass on the side table and leaned forward, reaching to capture her hands. She stilled, her heart racing as their gazes locked. Her head whirled. She could drown in the brown depths of those beautiful eyes.

'It *was* hard, but not as hard as I anticipated.' His fingers firmed around hers. 'And I have you to thank for that. You have helped me face my fears.

'Before today I would have let the stares and the whispers of those strangers bother me and I would have walked away from those that stared. I have allowed my fear to dictate my life, but you have taught me to give others the chance to accept me for myself and not judge me by how I look.

'You have taught me there are more important things in life, such as Clara's future.' He hauled in a breath. His eyes darkened. 'I owe you so much, Grace.'

Grace turned her hands within his grasp and curved her fingers around his.

'You owe me nothing. Allowing me to stay here with Clara is reward enough. I am happy here. This is my home, now, for as long as you will allow me to stay.'

'Then that will be for ever, for I have promised you I will never part you from Clara.'

'Thank you. I cannot tell you how much that means to me.'

She willed him to kiss her, striving to communicate her love and her desire by a look alone, but that smouldering heat still did not flare into passion.

Why does he hesitate? Does he fear I will reject him?

Could she, by loving him, banish the pain of the past and show him the way to a brighter future? She could not be mistaken…this lost soul in front of her needed her. She had it in her power to heal his hurts and to restore his pride. She must find the courage to take the first step…

'Grace…I…'

'Hush.' Holding his gaze, Grace slid from the sofa to her knees before Nathaniel. She placed her fingertips to his lips, then slowly, gently, she stroked her hand over his face, caressing his damaged cheek, registering the uneven texture, as though knotted pieces of rope lay beneath the surface of his skin: tangible evidence of the fire that had changed his life for ever.

He stilled, every muscle tense, his eyes haunted.

She could not put into words how proud she was of him, for facing the villagers and for his willingness to change; such words would surely injure his masculine pride. No, she could not tell him, but she could *show* him all those things, and she could show him, by her actions, that in her eyes he was both beautiful and lovable.

She leaned into him, pressing her body between his muscled thighs as she placed her lips on his.

It was akin to kissing a statue. Hard lips, rigid jaw. She pressed closer still, raising her other hand so she cradled his face, her lips soft as they moved against his mouth. Every muscle appeared to wind a notch tighter, if that was possible, until, with a groan and a gasp, he took her in his arms, moulding her to him, as he angled his head, his lips softening and moving under hers. His mouth opened and their tongues met, igniting a fire deep inside.

She poured her heart and her soul into that kiss, molten fire sizzling through her veins until she could no longer tell where she ended and he began. Her body had melted, sinking into him like honey on warm toast. A strange ache spread through her, rendering arms and legs heavy with need.

She wound her arms around his neck, pulling his head closer, fingers threaded through his hair, losing all sense of place and time. He slid to the rug, holding Grace close to his chest as he lay on his back, hands roaming freely over her back, bottom and thighs, stoking her passion.

She fumbled at the knot in his neckcloth. His hands covered hers in a vice-like grip. Grace raised her head, studying his tight expression.

'What is wrong?'

'I…I cannot…'

She covered his lips with hers. 'Yes, you can,' she whispered. 'For me.'

His grip tightened momentarily, and then, with a growl, he released her wrists to tear the cloth from around his neck and cast it aside. Grace had no need to see his neck to understand his sudden doubt. Her fingertips, and then her lips, discovered the same bumpy texture as on his cheek and she feathered the entire surface of his neck and jawline with tiny, butterfly kisses: the soft, lightly stubbled undamaged side as well as the tight, uneven, stubble-free area that bore the scars of the fire.

She pulled away, raising her upper body by bracing her hands on his chest.

'Can you feel my lips on your neck?'

His hands tightened at her waist. 'No. Your touch is too gentle.'

He groaned then, as she lowered her body to his once more and pressed her lips more firmly to his neck.

'Can you feel that?'

'Yes, but only as pressure. It is like eating food without being able to detect the nuances of taste.'

She arched her upper body away from his again, capturing his gaze. 'Then tell me what gives you pleasure.'

A wicked light crept into his eyes. Large hands stroked over the globes of her bottom and squeezed as he rocked his hips, pushing the hard ridge of his erection against her.

'This.' He rocked again. 'This gives me pleasure.' He raised his head from the floor and captured her lips again in a slow, drugging kiss. 'Infinite pleasure.'

In one swift movement that wrung a gasp from her, he rolled her on to her back and settled on top. His weight on her sent delicious swirls of anticipation throughout her body and her thighs parted of their own volition, the sensitive flesh between a yearning, hollow ache. She sighed, closing her eyes, succumbing to pleasure as gentle hands skimmed her neck and body and questing lips followed.

She clutched his shoulders with urgent fingers, arching beneath him as he nibbled the exquisitely sensitive bud of her nipple through her muslin gown.

A hand skimmed up her leg, then pushed her stocking and garter down to caress her bare flesh even as he seized her lips in another scorching kiss. In feverish anticipation, Grace reached for the buttons of his waistcoat, then slid her hands inside, stroking his broad back, revelling in the play of honed muscles through the fine linen of his shirt. He was so big, so male...*all* male...and she wanted him with an urgency she could barely contain. She squirmed beneath him, vaguely aware that she moaned as she did so, and then his weight was no more. Her eyes flew open. He had propped himself up on his arms.

'Are you sure, Grace? You will not be...my appearance...' His uncertainty was tangible.

'Hush.' She pressed her fingertips to his lips. 'I am sure.'

She dared not say more. More words might turn into a plea, she wanted him so much.

He rose to his feet in one fluid motion and then gathered her into his arms, carrying her much as he had Clara earlier. He hugged her tight to his chest.

'I will not take you on the floor,' he said, before taking her lips again.

He strode for the door and they were up the stairs and in Grace's bedchamber in a flash. He placed her on the bed and immediately followed her down, pushing the neckline of her dress low to free one breast. He drew her beaded nipple into his mouth, sucking and nibbling until she was on fire.

Their clothes were gone—she barely noticed how and when—and finally they were flesh to flesh and he was moving over her and inside her, and she was arching to meet him, the urgency building, digging frantic fingers into his back...snatching at the sheet beneath her...clutching his hair as he dipped his head again to her breasts—

striving for—reaching for—and then finally…finally…she was there and soaring free, her body pulsing with pleasure as Nathaniel withdrew and, with a heartfelt groan, spilled his seed.

Panting, Nathaniel drew her close to his chest and hooked the blankets up to cover them. He pressed his lips to the top of her head and—happy, contented and replete—Grace sank into a satisfied sleep.

Chapter Twenty-Four

Grace opened her eyes to the vague awareness that a new day had dawned and there was a moment when she could not fathom what was different. Her mind felt—not unpleasantly—fuzzy and she lay still, warmly cocooned, fleeting images of the day before darting through her memory, like butterflies flitting in and out of patches of sunlight.

The day before… Christmas Eve…which meant today was—her idle thoughts stuttered to an abrupt halt. Those wavering memories steadied and coalesced as she became conscious of a slight soreness between her thighs and the presence of a large, warm body in her bed, nestled into her back. Panic flowed and then ebbed and her lips relaxed and stretched in a spontaneous smile. Nathaniel. Her dream had come true. Carefully, she wriggled around until she faced him. She watched him sleep in the dim light of the early morning, love flooding her heart.

They could be a proper family now. Her and Nathaniel and Clara. And even, in the future, maybe they could have more children. Brothers and sisters for Clara. And he would no longer feel the need to isolate himself here at Shiverstone Hall. And—

Nathaniel's eyes opened. He blinked and she leant over and kissed him, tracing the sculpted muscles of his hair-roughened chest. She breathed deeply. He smelled wonderful and she snuggled closer. He smoothed her hair away from her face and kissed her, a wonderful, slow, drugging kiss. His hand skimmed her breast, then settled, and the flesh between her legs leapt in response.

'Good morning, Grace,' he murmured as he bent his head.

He circled her nipple with his tongue, then drew it deep into his mouth. She gasped and bit his shoulder.

'Do you like that?'

A wicked smile hovered on his lips and then he trailed his tongue down her body to the apex of her thighs. She sighed her pleasure, opening for him, giving herself up to the wonderful sensations spiralling through her body as Nathaniel loved her.

'We will be so happy, the three of us as a family,' she murmured later, as Nathaniel rolled off her and lay on his back.

He stared up at the ceiling, a deep line grooved between his brows. 'Family?'

'Why…yes. You and me and Clara…' Grace propped herself up on one elbow, and traced his lips with her fingertip. 'Just think how she will benefit as she grows up. You will no longer have to bury yourself here at Shiver—'

He turned his head to stare at her. 'I *like* it here at Shiverstone.'

'Well, yes, of course. I know that. But, with me by your side, it will be different. We could live some of the time at Ravenwell; we could invite friends to stay—'

'I *have* no friends.' He sat up, scrubbing his hands through sleep-tousled hair.

Grace's spirits floundered for a moment before she rallied. If only she could make him see how much better his life could be. How much happier.

'Maybe not, at the moment, but you will love Joanna

and Isabel when you meet them and I am sure their husbands are—'

'*No!*'

He leapt out of bed, keeping his scarred side facing away from her. He snatched his discarded shirt from the floor and tugged it over his head.

'But... I will help you. You must not fear—'

He stared at her, his eyes cold. 'I do not need your help. Nor your pity. I must go. Clara must not see me here.'

'No, of course not, but...she will know eventually, w-won't she?' She could not prevent disquiet threading through her voice.

'Know that we slept together? That would hardly be appropriate for a two-year-old. Last night should never have happened.'

Instinct leapt to the fore; Grace knew intuitively what he was doing. He was retreating into himself. He was so used to protecting himself he did not see he no longer need do so. Grace flung the covers back and rushed to him, heedless of her nakedness.

'Nathaniel.' She grabbed his arms. 'Do not say so. Last night was...do you not see? We can be a family now. Think of Clara, how lovely it will be for her to have a new papa and mama.'

With every word she said, his expression hardened. How could she get through to him? Make him see how wonderful their future could be?

'With us by your side, you can take up your rightful place in society again.'

He shook her hands from him. 'I do not want to take my rightful place in society again. Last night was a mistake. We were both under the influence of too much wine. We were two lonely people seeking comfort. Nothing more.'

Grace snatched her shawl from a chair and flung it around her.

'It was *not* just the wine. That was not the only reason

you made love to me.' Tears crowded her throat, choking her voice, and she kept swallowing in an attempt to contain them.

'I never offered anything other than comfort. I cannot be what you want me to be. I have no wish to change my life. I want you to go.'

The breath left Grace's lungs in a whoosh and her legs went to jelly. 'Go? What do you mean?'

'Leave. I don't want you here. I cannot bear to see you or to have you under my roof.' He tugged on his breeches, gathered the rest of his clothing and stalked to the door.

'But…you cannot mean that. Nathaniel…my lord…you *promised* you would never send me away.'

He spun to face her, his lips curled in a snarl. 'I do not want you here. I want you gone. Today.'

'But…I have nowhere to go.' Grace hauled in a ragged breath. She must stand up to him. This could not be happening. 'No. I won't go. I will not leave you and I will not leave Clara.'

He stilled, his brown eyes hard as they raked her. 'Go to Ravenwell. Take Clara. It is her you really want and, God knows, you have more right to her than I.'

Hot tears scalded her eyes. 'But—'

'Take her. I do not want you here. You presume too much, Miss Bertram.'

Fury now rose up, overwhelming her misery. 'Presume?' She all but spat the word. '*I* presume too much? And you, my lord? What of your presumption? Did you presume that, because I made a mistake once, I would be content for my body to be used to slake your lust? Do you now presume that your two-year-old niece's needs are of no account when they do not happen to coincide with your own whims?'

'I will never neglect Clara's needs. I will provide you with a house on the estate at Ravenwell and an income. Neither of you will ever want for anything.' He opened the door.

'Except love!' Grace tried one last time. 'What about my heart? How can I be happy without you?'

'Love? You already know my view on that, Miss Bertram.' His bitter laugh was cut short as he slammed the door behind him.

Grace's anger sustained her all through the soul-destroying packing of her belongings and the leave-taking of the staff, telling them she was taking Clara on a previously arranged visit to her grandmother. There was no way on earth Grace would leave her daughter with that heartless monster.

Nathaniel was conspicuous by his absence—riding out on Zephyr over the fells, according to Sharp, who handed Grace a pouch containing coins.

'His lordship said to take it to cover your expenses.'

Grace resisted the urge to throw it in Sharp's face. This was none of it Sharp's fault. Besides, she would have need of the money. A plan, born of desperation and fury, had begun to form in her mind. Her heart was in pieces, but she hid every hint of despair, concentrating instead on efficiency and practicality as she packed Clara's clothes and a few toys in a bag, including all the presents Grace had so lovingly made for her. She distributed her gifts to the servants and received some lovely scented soap from the Sharps and Alice in return, and then—the very last thing before she left—she went to the empty guest bedchamber where she had concealed the picture of Clara and Brack she had painted for Nathaniel. Her first impulse was to burn it, but she carried it to Nathaniel's bedchamber and left it lying on the bed. She hoped he would suffer every time he looked upon it. She had poured her heart and soul into making love with him and he had flung it back in her face.

She had been taken for a fool. Again.

Ned had agreed to drive Grace and Clara to Ravenwell and by eleven they were on their way, a lengthy drive ahead of them. Grace waited until both Shivercombe village and the Hall were behind them, then called to Ned to stop.

'Yes, miss?'

'There has been a change of plan, Ned. Please drive me to Lancaster.'

'Lancaster? But, miss, I were told—'

'Who told you, Ned? His lordship?'

'Why, no, miss. You did.'

'I instructed you to drive to Ravenwell, Ned, and now I am instructing you to drive to Lancaster instead. It is quite all right. I have merely changed my mind about visiting Ravenwell…that is all.'

They would stay tonight in Lancaster and then head south. She felt guilty hoodwinking poor Ned, but she flatly refused to be sent off to Nathaniel's disapproving mother. With the money in the pouch she had calculated there would be just enough to get her and Clara to Salisbury. She did not much care what might happen to her after that, but what she needed now was a familiar place and a friendly face.

Miss Fanworth would know what to do.

Four days later, after a tortuous journey of jam-packed, rackety coaches and of further overnight stops at dubious coaching inns in Manchester, Birmingham and Bristol, Grace and Clara were set down in Cathedral Close, outside the stately façade of Madame Dubois's School for Young Ladies. Grace gazed at the familiar surroundings with a painful lump in her throat. Here were such memories. She had not expected to return so soon, nor under such circumstances.

The sheer obstinacy that had kept her going through the last four days faltered. Miss Fanworth might well be sympathetic, but she would not condone what Grace had done. As much as she had told herself Nathaniel deserved to lose Clara, she knew, deep down, she was wrong to bring her here without his knowledge or permission. And what of

Madame? Her heart sank at the likely reception she would have from the formidable principal of the school.

A whimper from Clara triggered renewed resolve. They had come this far. They were both exhausted. She tightened her hold on Clara's hand, picked up their bags with the other and mounted the front steps to knock on the door. Many of the pupils and staff would have gone home for the Christmas holiday, she knew, but she also knew some would remain. Neither Madame nor Miss Fanworth had any other home.

The door swung open, its hinges well-oiled as ever, to reveal the sombre features of Signor Bertolli. His eyes widened above his magnificent moustache.

'Miss Bertram!' He gestured for Grace to enter and to sit on one of the sturdy chairs set against the walls of the spacious, brightly lit entrance hall, with its classical cornices and stately staircase. 'I will tell Miss Fanworth you are 'ere.'

He hurried across the hall towards the closed door of Madame's office and a sudden fear hit Grace, remembering Isabel's last letter which had said Madame was ill.

'Wait! *Signor!*'

The art master paused, looking back over his shoulder. 'Where is Madame?'

'She 'as been unwell with the pneumonia, but she is getting better. Miss Fanworth 'as been running the school.'

Two waves of relief hit Grace, the first at the news of Madame's recovery and the second at the realisation she would not yet have to face Madame. Could she and Miss Fanworth, between them, concoct a story to explain Clara's presence? Her little girl's wan appearance tore at her heart. The journey had been tiring for Grace, let alone for a two-year-old who did not understand why she had once again been uprooted from familiar surroundings and taken from the people she loved. The guilt had nearly overwhelmed

Grace at times during that interminable journey when Clara had asked for her *'Uncle Naffaniel'*, but it had been too late to turn back and, besides, Grace could not summon the courage to face him again.

Thus, by the time Signor Bertolli showed her into Madame's office, and there was Miss Fanworth—plump, motherly Miss Fanworth—coming towards her with hands outstretched and a kindly yet concerned smile...

Grace burst into tears. Clara wailed. Miss Fanworth fluffed around, like a mother hen.

'Ask Cook to send up tea,' she said to the art master. 'And close the door behind you, please.'

She bade Grace sit on a fireside chair and she sat in the other, picking Clara up and settling her on her lap. She waited until the maid had brought up the tea tray and poured each of them a cup of tea, and then said, 'Tell me all, my dear.'

Between sobs and hiccups, Grace poured out her heart, finally ending with, 'Please don't tell Madame. She'll send us away. Please let us stay for a few days until...until...oh, Miss Fanworth, what am I to do?'

Miss Fanworth shook her head, wisps of light brown hair escaping from her cap. 'I do not know, Grace, my dear. You ever were an impetuous girl, but I really thought *that business* had taught you more caution. Still, we do not have to decide now. Little Clara looks exhausted. You both do. Let us discuss it further in the morning. I am sure it will all seem brighter then. Would you like to sleep in your old room with Clara? It is empty for the holidays.'

'Thank you, yes. And you won't tell Madame?'

'I won't say anything other than to tell her you are here, but you must examine your conscience as to how much *you* decide to tell her. She is not an ogre, you know. She cares very much for all her pupils, past and present.'

Suitably chastised, Grace hung her head. Miss Fanworth

stood, lifting a now-sleepy Clara, who whinged at being moved. 'Come. I shall send a light supper for you both up to your room. You will feel much better after a good night's sleep and I am certain you will soon see the right road to follow.'

Nathaniel sat on Zephyr on the high fell by Shiver Crag, staring unseeingly over the land that stretched below him. He was dry-eyed, but there was a hollow inside him as big as the dale. Not just his heart had shrivelled and died, but every last cell had withered until all that remained was an empty, ugly husk.

Why had he sent her away? To punish her? To punish himself? He had told himself he did it for her own good— to set her free, as he had set the eagle free—but the truth was that her vision of their future had completely unnerved him. He had convinced himself he could never make her happy and that she would, sooner or later, reject him.

Their final exchange still haunted him.

'Neither of you will ever want for anything.'

'Except love! What about my heart? How can I be happy without you?'

'Love? You already know my view on that, Miss Bertram.'

She had said nothing about love until then. Did she mean it? *Could* she love a man such as him?

The answer was as clear as the view before him. Yes. She could and she did. She looked at him and she did not see his scars. She saw *him*. She loved *him*. Her unflinching courage humbled him.

He had been a fool.

An utter fool.

Stubborn. Heartless. Cruel.

A coward. And, shamefully, he knew that last to be the truest of all. He had been panicked by her expectations and too afraid to expose the truth in his heart in case she rejected his love.

He had been scared of losing her, so he had sent her away.

Could any man have got it all so very wrong?

He turned Zephyr's head for home.

The following morning dawned grey and cold. Clara—heavy-eyed and snuffling and asking for Uncle Naffaniel—could not be placated and by early afternoon, when Madame sent for Grace, she was almost relieved to hand the care of her beautiful little girl to Miss Fanworth.

What kind of mother am I?

Heartache, guilt and inadequacy plagued her as she climbed the stairs to Madame's bedchamber, her steps slowing as she neared the door. How could she face the all-seeing, all-knowing Madame when her thoughts and emotions were so utterly confused and raw? She tapped on the door.

'Come.'

That familiar voice was as imperious as ever. Heart in mouth, Grace entered, shutting the door behind her.

Chapter Twenty-Five

Grace had never before seen the inside of Madame's bed-chamber. It was as graceful and tasteful as expected, furnished in elegant rosewood, the walls papered in rose and ivory stripes.

Madame reclined on a rose-coloured *chaise longue* set before a window, her dark, silver-streaked hair draping, loosely plaited, over one shoulder. Madame herself was pale, but her grey eyes were as sharp as ever under her dark brows and as Grace approached her the familiar apprehension fluttered deep in the pit of her stomach.

There was something different about Madame, though—something Grace could not quite pinpoint: a gentler cast to her features that was not solely due to the absence of her customary tightly scraped bun. There was a softening in the lines around her eyes and mouth that made her appear less harsh.

Madame beckoned, indicating a chair near the *chaise longue*. 'Come, Miss Bertram. Sit here and tell me why you have returned, for I cannot think it is because you pine so very much for your old school.'

Grace sat down and haltingly confessed to Madame all that had happened, omitting only the fact that Clara was her natural child.

'This man. This Marquess. He sounds an unhappy man. He is, I think, scared. He rejects you before you reject him.'

'But…I would not reject him. I love him.'

'And you tell him this?'

'He does not believe in love.'

Madame shrugged. 'He says he does not believe in love, but he is a man. He wants to feel loved. He wants to be the centre of your world. He is more complex than many men, but at heart that is what he needs, even if he does not see it.'

Grace cast her mind back to Christmas morning. 'But… I told him we could be a family. I tried to make him see how happy we could be: how Clara would benefit, how we could have friends come to visit, how he could take his rightful place in society again.'

'Ah. And did you pause to consider he might not wish to change his life? That your Marquess—who has cut himself off from everyone for so many years—might need time to adjust to a new future?'

'No.' Grace bit her lip as she confessed, cheeks burning as she realised for the first time how thoughtless she had been.

'I thought not. You have not changed, Miss Bertram, you are as impetuous as ever, never stopping to think about consequences. But…still…I find I do not understand the role of this Clara. Have you grown so fond of her in such a very short time?'

'She is easy to love. Everyone at Shiverstone Hall loves her.'

'But her uncle—he sends her away with you. Why did he do so? Does he not love her? Is he not a man of honour? Is *he* not the child's guardian?'

'He adores her! And she adores him.' Grace felt her face flame at the passion in her reply.

'And yet he is prepared to lose her. And you take her from the man you profess to love, even though you know he will miss her.' Her voice grew stern. 'Tell me the whole truth, Miss Bertram, for how can I help you otherwise?'

Tears prickled. 'She is my daughter.'

'So...' Madame's tone gentled '...*this* is what happened to your baby. I did wonder but, of course, I could not ask.'

Grace's head spun. 'You *knew* about my baby?'

'But of course. I know everything that goes on in my school. Did you doubt it?'

'But...' Grace stared at Madame, and everything she thought she understood about the Frenchwoman shifted, re-forming into a very different picture.

'But...why did you never—?'

She fell silent as Madame raised an imperious hand. 'My position was such that, had I acknowledged your foolishness, I should be forced to take an action I did not wish to take. And so I chose to turn the blind eye.'

Grace hung her head, ashamed her stupidity had forced Madame to compromise her principles.

'You will bring Clara to visit me,' Madame said, 'but I find I am weary now. We shall talk again.'

Grace descended the stairs, her mind whirling. Madame's words helped her view Nathaniel's actions in a different light; she had much to think about.

Below her, Miss Fanworth had just admitted a distinguished, broad-shouldered gentleman. He removed his hat to reveal thick, silvery hair, there was a murmured exchange, and then he headed for the stairs, nodding to Grace in passing.

She reached the entrance hall. Clara ran to her, crying, the minute she saw her.

'She has been very fretful,' Miss Fanworth said. 'I think she fears you will leave her.'

Those words hit Grace with the force of a lightning bolt. What had she done to her daughter?

'And she keeps talking of a sweep, or I think that is what she said.'

'Sweep is her kitten.'

'Sweep? Brack?' Clara's sorrowful plea wrenched at Grace's heart.

Grace did not know how to console Clara. She could not promise she would see Sweep and Brack again. She did not know what the future held. She hugged her daughter tight.

'Who was that gentleman?' she asked, in an effort to distract herself.

'That is the Duke.'

'The Duke?'

'Of Wakefield. He visits Madame every afternoon at three o'clock.'

Grace gazed up the stairs, but the Duke had already vanished from sight. 'Is it true what Isabel wrote to me about him? He told her that he and Madame...well, that they had been in love, many years ago.'

'Yes, it is true. And now they have found one another again. Oh, it is so romantic.' Miss Fanworth's eyes misted over. 'His visits have done her the power of good; the change in her is astounding. And he has vowed to come every day until she is fully recovered.' Miss Fanworth sighed, one hand pressed to her ample bosom. 'Such devotion. Would that I might so inspire a man.'

Would that I might, also.

Nathaniel. Just thinking his name turned Grace's knees to jelly and set up a wanting, deep down inside, that gave her no respite. Madame's voice repeated through her head and the conviction grew that she must go back.

The very thought terrified her, but how could she not? She must face up to the mess she had made of her life. And of Clara's.

On New Year's Eve Grace was reading a story to Clara in the library when Miss Fanworth bustled in, waving two letters.

'They are from dearest Rachel,' she said. 'One for each of us. I dare say she had not received my letter with your address in it by the time she sent these. That is fortunate, is it not?'

She sat opposite Grace and they opened their letters at the same time. Grace read the joyful announcement of Rachel's betrothal to her employer, Sheikh Malik bin Jalal Al-Mahrouky and of their plans to marry in the spring, then stared unseeingly out of the window.

'Well…what splendid news.'

Grace started. 'Yes, indeed. I am thrilled for Rachel.'

Then why was her heart leaden with self-pity? What kind of person envied a friend's happiness? Her three friends were now settled and she was truly happy for them, but…

I am the only one alone and unloved. As I always have been.

Even as a child she had been unlovable. Tears scalded her eyes, and she stood abruptly.

'Would you mind…could you finish Clara's story for her? I will not be long.'

She ran from the room and up the stairs, unsure of where she was going until she found herself outside Madame's door. She did not allow second thoughts. She knocked.

'Well, Miss Bertram? Have you made your decision?'

'No. I do not know what to do.'

'Listen to your heart. It will tell you what to do for the best.'

The best for me? Or for Nathaniel? Or for Clara?

Grace thought of the Duke, with his silver hair and his dignity. Madame had faced heartbreak.

All those years apart.

'Did you listen to your heart, Madame?'

'Ah.' Madame closed her eyes, lost in thought.

'Non, ma chère,' she said, eventually. 'I listened to my

conscience. I gave him up without a fight, because I loved him and because I could offer him nothing. I ignored my heart, believing it was for the best. Perhaps, if he had come after me…if he had tried to persuade me…but he did not. He is honourable, and he put his duty first.

'I have regretted it every day of my life. Now, we have another chance and we both know that love, it does not die. It hides away. It bides its time, until it may shine again.

'You have the chance I did not have: to fight for your love, to reassure your Marquess that what he can offer is enough and that you will be content. He is afraid he will be unable to make you happy. If you are sure he can, go back and tell him what is in your heart. That is my advice. What is the worst that can happen?'

'He might reject me again.'

'He might. You must learn to accept that you cannot mould others' lives to suit your own purposes. And if he does…you are a strong woman; you will survive. Would you be any unhappier than you are now?'

Madame's words haunted Grace as she returned to the library and to Miss Fanworth and Clara, whose woebegone face lit up when she saw Grace.

'I think,' Miss Fanworth said, 'that Clara is scared you will vanish too. She needs a great deal of reassurance.'

My little girl is unhappy and it is my fault.

Could she risk returning to Shiverstone? If Nathaniel did not love her…if he sent her away…she would lose Clara too.

But she is no longer mine. I gave her away and I cannot support her on my own. Whatever the risk, I must return her to Nathaniel. He loves her and he will care for her whatever comes of him and me.

'Miss Fanworth.'

'Yes, my dear?'

'Please, will you look after Clara? I am going to buy a ticket. To go home.'

The teacher's kindly face wreathed in smiles. 'I am so pleased, but I will miss you, and Clara. When will you leave?'

'The day after tomorrow,' Grace called, as she rushed out of the door.

New Year's Day, 1812

Grace was in her bedroom with Clara, packing in preparation for their journey the next day, when she heard a carriage draw up outside the school. It must be three. She peered out of the window for one last look at Madame's Duke.

The carriage outside was mud-spattered. The horses' breath clouded in the chill air and the driver was... *Ned*! Joy erupted through her. She snatched Clara from the bed.

'He's here, Clara. Uncle Nathaniel is here.'

Nathaniel tapped his foot as he waited on the doorstep of Madame Dubois's School for Young Ladies. The door finally opened to reveal a matronly woman with kind eyes and a welcoming smile.

'Good afternoon. May I help you?'

'Miss Grace Bertram,' he said. 'I have come for her and for my niece.'

Her smile faded and she made no move to allow him entry.

'This is a school for young ladies, sir. Might I enquire as to your purpose in seeking Miss Bertram?'

She reminded him of nothing more than a mother hen fluffing up to protect its chicks and, despite his irritation, he warmed to her.

'I have come to take them home.'

She visibly subsided and opened the door wider. 'They are upstairs. Please, come in.'

Nathaniel strode towards the stairs. At the foot, he became aware of several whispering and giggling girls staring at him over the balustrade. He had faced worse on the journey south, but soon discovered that if he ignored people's reactions, they quickly lost interest. A few silly girls would not stop him.

Nothing mattered more than finding Grace and Clara.

He ran up the stairs and there they were. What could he say? What words would heal the hurt and mend the chasm between them? But words were not needed. Her smile shone out and she ran to him, and then his arms were full.

Grace and Clara.

Back in his arms, where they belonged.

They parted, Clara now in Nathaniel's arms, her pudgy arms locked tight around his neck.

'Uncle Naffaniel.' She kissed his cheek.

'Did you miss me, poppet? I missed you. And so does Sweep.'

While he talked to Clara, his eyes were on Grace, devouring every inch of her, oblivious to their audience.

'How did you know where to find us?'

'Ned heard you enquire about a stagecoach to Salisbury when he dropped you off in Lancaster.'

The mother hen arrived at the top of the stairs, puffing. 'Girls! Go to the common room immediately.'

The girls scurried down the stairs and out of sight.

'My lord, this is Miss Fanworth,' Grace said. 'Miss Fanworth, the Marquess of Ravenwell.'

Even Nathaniel, with all his personal misgivings, could hear the pride in Grace's voice and his heart swelled with hope.

'Shall I take Clara whilst you talk?'

Miss Fanworth reached for Clara, who tightened her hold on Nathaniel's neck. Only when she had possession of Nathaniel's hat would she consent to go with Miss Fanworth, satisfied her Uncle Naffaniel would never leave without his hat.

'She has been miserable without you,' Grace said. 'I am so sorry.'

'You have nothing to be sorry for. It was I who sent you away. And I have regretted it every day since. I missed you so much.'

He must say the words out loud. He would not continue to live in fear of rejection. 'I love you, Grace Bertram.'

Grace stepped close, gazing up at him, her green-gold gaze intense. 'I love you too, Nathaniel. And I *am* sorry because you were right. I did presume too much. I never questioned whether the life I *thought* would make you happy was what you truly wanted.'

'With you by my side, sweetheart, I can change. I *will* change.' He brushed her lips with his, stroking a tendril of hair from her face.

She leant into his hand, turning her head to press a kiss to his palm. 'There is no need to change: it is *you* I want, Nathaniel, not the life you can provide. As long as we are together, I will be happy.'

'But I *want* to change. I have had time to think…to adjust…and I no longer wish to hide myself away at Shiverstone. You have helped me to accept myself, scars and all. You have given me the courage I lacked. With you by my side, I can face the world again.'

Her familiar lily-of-the-valley scent weaved through his senses and he crushed her to him, taking her lips in a scorching kiss, losing all sense of time and place as their tongues tangled and he caressed her curves, aching with need.

The bang of a door downstairs roused him.

'Is there somewhere we can go?' he whispered against her lips.

'My bedchamber.' She took his hand and led him to a room containing four beds and a half-packed portmanteau. 'This is my old room: the one I shared with my friends,' she said. 'It no longer feels the same, despite the memories. We have all moved on.'

Nathaniel took her in his arms. 'You have moved on to make new memories. The old ones are still there, to be treasured, but you cannot go back in time.'

'I no longer have any desire to go back in time. All I desire now is a future with you, however you will have me.'

Gentle fingertips stroked his face. He captured her hand and kissed those fingertips, one by one.

'I am sorry I doubted you,' he said. 'I loved you and I wanted you, but I was afraid and I fought my feelings for you with every ounce of my strength.'

'Shh, my love. No more apologies, no explanations.' Her breath whispered across his skin as she pressed her soft curves against him. 'We have no need of words. Come.'

She urged him to a bed. He sank on to the mattress and she settled on his lap, cradling his face as she kissed him. He stroked her lips with his tongue and she opened to him. Silence reigned for several minutes as lips, tongues and hands expressed their love.

Nathaniel wrenched his lips from hers. 'I could never believe a beautiful girl like you would look at an ugly monster like me.' He feathered kisses over her face and neck, the blood pooling hot and heavy in his groin.

She touched his cheek. 'You are so very far from being ugly or a monster. You are a beautiful man, inside and out.'

His vision blurred and he blinked as he forced a laugh. 'Beautiful? Now that is coming it too strong, even for you, my darling.'

She shook her head, loose wisps of blonde hair framing her face. 'Beauty means nothing.' She placed her hand over his heart. 'It is what is in here that counts. Always.'

With a groan, he tilted his head and nuzzled her neck. She squirmed and giggled, fuelling his blood all the more, and he lifted her, laying her back on the narrow bed, crushing her lips with his as he covered her with his body. She was warm and pliant beneath him as she returned his kiss, reaching beneath his jacket to pull his shirt free. Warm hands slid under his shirt, over his bare chest and a quiet sound of satisfaction hummed deep in her throat.

She reached for the fall of his breeches, desire burning in her eyes as her fingers closed around him. The last vestiges of his restraint flew away. He tugged at the hem of her gown. She raised her hips to assist him. He skimmed her satin thighs to play amongst the soft folds between, his touch eliciting a breathy, *'Yes'*. She writhed beneath him, widening her legs, urging him on.

He settled between her legs and pushed into her slick, welcoming heat, then stilled, savouring the sensation as she tightened around him. He took her lips in another searing kiss as he slowly withdrew. Then he thrust, hard. She gasped into his mouth even as her hips rose to meet his and then they were moving together in glorious rhythm.

He knew instinctively when she was ready: he felt the tension build within her, felt her teeter on the edge. He drove into her again, sending them together into a starburst of ecstasy.

Some minutes later, Nathaniel cranked open one eyelid and took in their surroundings. He looked at Grace, still lying beneath him, eyes closed, a satisfied smile curving her lips. She was utterly beautiful. He longed to pull her into his arms and drift into sated sleep, but they could not take that risk. Not here. Not now. He forced himself to his feet, tucking his shirt into his breeches as he crossed the room to peer out of the window.

'Nathaniel?'

The worry in that one word had him whirling to face her. The uncertainty in her eyes near unmanned him. *Hell and damnation!* He reached the bed in two strides, pulled her to her feet, and folded her into his arms.

'I am here,' he murmured. 'I will never let you go again.'

Her tension dissolved and she relaxed into him. She

fitted against him perfectly. He rested his chin on the top of her head, content for the first time in nine long, lonely years.

'I love you, Nathaniel.'

He lifted her chin with one finger. 'And I love you, Grace, very, very much.'

There was something he must do. A question to ask. But…first…he lowered his head and kissed her again, tenderly, worshipfully, the smooth perfection of her lips soothing his soul.

A tap at the door had them springing apart. Miss Fanworth peered in, her cheeks pink.

'Clara started to get upset so I thought I should bring her up to you.'

Nathaniel took Clara from the kindly teacher, thanking her, then ushered her from the room, shutting the door behind her. He turned to Grace and, still holding Clara, heart pounding, he dropped to one knee. Grace's eyes widened.

'It seems fitting Clara should be a part of this,' he said. 'Grace Bertram, I bless the day you came into my life. You have unlocked my heart and my soul and I love you more every day.

'Please, will you do me the honour of becoming my wife?'

'Yes! Oh, yes!' Grace fell to her knees and wrapped her arms around Nathaniel and Clara.

'Me too, Uncle Naffaniel?'

Nathaniel and Grace laughed as one and Nathaniel hugged Clara a little tighter.

'You too, Clara, poppet, you too. We will be a proper family, and you will be our adopted daughter. But we will never forget Hannah and David.'

'No, we will never forget Hannah and David,' Grace said. 'Even though I never met them, they will always hold a very special place in my heart.'

Nathaniel bowed his head, the memories of his sister and her husband still painful, but no longer as raw.

'When they died, I railed against the Fates for taking away my only friends and for forcing my life along a different path. But love and hope and a new future have sprung from that tragedy and I bless the day you both came into my life, my beautiful Clara, and my dearest, darling Grace.'

'Me too, Uncle Naffaniel.'

Epilogue

Ravenwell Manor—23rd December 1812

'Milady!' Alice rushed into the drawing room, her plump cheeks quivering. 'Milady!' She skidded to a halt, hand pressed to heaving bosom. 'There's carriages a-coming. *Three* of them.'

'All three together? How wonderful.'

Grace jumped to her feet, then froze, her hand to her mouth. Alice reached her side in an instant.

'Oh, milady. Again?'

'No.' Grace shook her head. 'No, it is not the sickness. I rose too quickly and felt light-headed, that is all. Now, come. We have visitors to greet.' She cast a swift glance around the room. All was neat and gleaming. 'Will you ask Fish to tell his lordship—?'

'I am here.'

The deep voice came from the doorway and Grace pivoted to face Nathaniel: handsome, inherently masculine, *hers*. Her heart gave its customary somersault and then melted at the sight of Clara, holding his hand. She was growing so tall, her soft brown curls falling down her back in ringlets. Grace could not wait to introduce her new family to her friends.

'Alice, will you alert Cook that we shall require luncheon in an hour, please? Are all the bedchambers prepared? And the servants' quarters?'

'Yes, milady. Shall I take Miss Clara now?'

'No. She will come with us to greet our guests.'

Alice, who had moved back to Ravenwell Manor with Nathaniel and Grace after their marriage, scurried from the room. The Sharps had elected to stay at Shiverstone Hall as caretakers and Ned, Tam and Annie had also stayed behind, to care for the animals and Nathaniel's beloved hawks. Every few weeks, Nathaniel rode over to the Hall to fly his birds and stay the night and, in the spring, they planned to return as a family for a longer visit.

If I am able to. Grace smoothed her hand over her gently rounded stomach, and a warm glow of contentment suffused her.

Nathaniel's gaze tracked the movement of her hand, then lifted to her face and she saw the heat banked in his eyes. Anticipation tugged deep within her, but there was no time to dally.

'How are Ralph and Elizabeth? Have they settled into the vicarage?' she asked, to distract him.

Nathaniel and Clara had been to visit the newly married Rendells in their new home, taking with them a bunch of freshly gathered mistletoe. The elderly incumbent of the local church, St Thomas's, had recently retired and Nathaniel had gifted the living to Ralph Rendell.

'They have and they are as happy a pair of lovebirds as ever I did see—except for us, my darling, irresistible wife.'

He cradled Grace's face and brushed a kiss to her lips. Then his eyes darkened and he lowered his head again, and kissed her until her insides were molten. But, this time, she must resist and, hands on his chest, she pushed him away.

'Nathaniel! Our visitors will be here any minute.'

He chuckled and kissed her again. 'It is precisely because their arrival is imminent that I am taking advantage whilst I may. You must not begrudge me a little sustenance to see me through the next few hours.'

'Papa! Mama!' Clara tugged at Nathaniel's sleeve for attention.

Grace's heart swelled. Clara might never discover that Grace was her natural mother but, once she and Nathaniel had wed, they had agreed Clara would be their adopted daughter and they would be her father and mother from that day forward.

Nathaniel scooped Clara high. He put his lips to her cheek and blew, making a rude noise that had Clara giggling and squirming in his arms as they all made their way to the front door. Their servants were beginning to congregate in the hall, ready to conduct the visitors to their bedchambers.

'The Reverend Rendell was most appreciative of the mistletoe,' Nathaniel said, with a grin, as they reached the double entrance door, standing wide in readiness. 'In fact…' he tipped his head towards Grace, lowering his voice '…nothing would do for our new vicar than to test it out with his bride. I don't know…' he shook his head, his brown eyes brimming with merriment '…if that is the way a man of the cloth sees fit to behave in full view of his benefactor, what hope is there for society?

'They send their pleased acceptance of our invitation to join us for Christmas dinner, by the way.'

'How lovely it will be to have our friends all here,' Grace said. 'Mother is delighted at the prospect of seeing a full dining table at the Manor once again.'

Nathaniel's mother—after a distrustful start with her new daughter-in-law—had soon accepted Grace and they were now firm friends. She now lived in the Dower House on the estate, but she visited almost every day.

The rumble of the carriage wheels and the hoofbeats of eighteen horses—three teams of four, plus six outriders—grew ever louder as they reached the end of the long, straight carriageway that led from the road and negotiated the turning circle that would bring them to the front steps of the Manor.

The sky was uniformly white, with not a hint of grey, and the air was still—almost as though it held its breath in anticipation. Nathaniel had predicted snow and Grace breathed a silent thank you that it had held off until the travellers arrived.

The carriages halted and the silence—punctuated only by the occasional jingle of a bit or stamp of a hoof—was deafening in its own way. A sudden attack of nerves assailed Grace. It had been almost a year and a half since she had seen her beloved friends.

Will they be different? What will they think of me? What will their husbands be like? What if—?

She felt Nathaniel's hand at the small of her back, large and reassuring. She glanced up at him.

'Don't be nervous. You will be fine. You'll see.'

His eyes met hers, steady and confident with no sign of apprehension, and Grace marvelled at the change in him since the day they met. And then there was no more time to worry, for carriage doors were being flung wide and there they were.

Joanna. Rachel. Isabel. Three dear, familiar faces.

Tears blurred Grace's vision and she blinked rapidly, so as not to appear an emotional fool and yet...

They came together in a rush: hugging, kissing and exclaiming.

And tearful—even Joanna, who had never, ever been seen to cry before.

All four of them, in a laughing circle, with tears rolling unashamedly down their cheeks.

Isabel peered out of the window. 'Now that we are safely arrived, I declare it may snow to its heart's content.'

They were gathered in the drawing room after a delicious luncheon.

Grace joined her. 'I believe you will get your wish.' She lowered her voice. 'You will tell me if there is anything you need, will you not, Isabel?'

'Thank you, Grace, darling, but you must not worry about me. I feel exceedingly well. Blossoming, you might say.' Isabel smiled, and placed her hands either side of her swollen belly with a sigh of contentment.

It was chilly by the window and they moved nearer to the warmth of the fire.

'Do you really think it will snow, Lady Ravenwell?'

Grace smiled at the handsome young boy's serious expression. Rachel's stepson, Aahil, had never seen snow in his life. Neither had his younger sister and brother, Ameera and Hakim, who both sprawled on the floor next to Clara, playing with her Noah's Ark.

'I think it will, Aahil. And then…' Grace eyed each of her friends in turn '…we will build a snowman. Do you remember—?'

'The Christmas before last!' Isabel's blue eyes sparkled. 'We all stayed at school and we built the *biggest* snowman…'

Joanna, sitting on the sofa, newly born Edward cradled in her arms, smiled. 'That was such a happy Christmas.'

'This one will be better.' Rachel sat next to Joanna and leaned over to admire the babe. 'He is *soooo* sweet, Joanna.' There was a note of longing in her voice. 'May I hold him?'

'Of course.' Joanna passed her son to Rachel, who crooned softly until he settled again.

'Our snowman will be bigger and better.' Hakim, hopping from foot to foot in his excitement, joined Aahil. 'Will it snow, Lady Ravenwell? Will it snow, do you think?'

Hakim had seemed timid on first arrival, but had soon lost his shyness with all these new people. His father,

Malik—exotically dark and impossibly handsome, with piercing eyes—broke off his discussion with Nathaniel about hawking, a popular means of hunting in his beloved Huria.

'Calm down, Hakim, or I shall send you to the nursery,' he said. 'If the Fates smile upon us, it will snow. Bombarding her ladyship with questions will change nothing.'

'He is excited, Malik. And full of energy after spending so many days cooped up in the carriage,' Rachel said, as she cradled Edward.

'As am I.' Luke, Joanna's husband, stood up and stretched. 'I beg your pardon, ladies, but I need to work off some of this energy. Ravenwell, I believe you mentioned a couple of new hunters? Any chance of putting them through their paces?'

All four men perked up and Grace found herself exchanging knowing looks of amusement with her three friends.

'Indeed. However, before that...' Nathaniel turned to Aahil. 'How would you like to help us bring home the Yule log, young man?' He cocked a brow at Malik. 'I don't know if you're familiar with the tradition, Al-Mahrouky, but the Yule log is specially selected to burn the full twelve days of Christmastide. It is brought indoors on Christmas Eve and lit and then, if possible, a piece is saved on Twelfth Night to light the following year's Yule log.'

'But it is not Christmas Eve until tomorrow,' Joanna said, from her seat on the sofa. 'Will that not bring bad luck?'

'We will not tempt fate by bringing it indoors until tomorrow, but we must drag the log closer to the house before it snows. We can leave it in one of the outbuildings overnight. What do you say, Aahil? Are you feeling strong?'

'May I, Father?'

'Very well, son.'

'Me too!' Hakim bounced up and down.

'May I come too?' Ameera stood up.

'Me, me, me!' Clara shouted, scrambling to her feet, lining up with Ameera and Hakim in front of Nathaniel. 'Papa. Papa. Pleeease.'

'Clara, I do not think—'

'*Pleeeaaase*, Papa.' She turned beseeching eyes to Grace. 'Mama, please.'

Grace raised her brows at Nathaniel. She saw him bite back his smile and she knew he would be helpless to refuse those three pleading faces.

'Al-Mahrouky?' Nathaniel directed his question at the Sheikh, who nodded.

'Very well,' Nathaniel said to the three. 'If you promise faithfully to do exactly as you are told, you may come.'

'Thank you,' they chorused.

Ameera, tugging Clara with her, moved closer to Nathaniel. 'Does that hurt?' She pointed to Nathaniel's scarred cheek.

There was the sound of indrawn breath and Rachel straightened as though to remonstrate with Ameera, but Grace caught her eye and shook her head.

Nathaniel smiled down at Ameera. 'No. Not now,' he said. Then he crouched down before the three youngest children. 'But it hurt a great deal at the time and that is the reason you must always be very careful with fire.'

'I am pleased it doesn't hurt,' Ameera announced. 'May we go outside now, please, Lord Ravenwell?'

Nathaniel laughed as he stood up. 'Yes, Ameera, we will go now.' He winked at Grace. 'We'll take a couple of footmen to help with the children. It will give you ladies a chance to catch up with the gossip.'

William, his light brown eyes creased with amusement, said, 'Judging by the non-stop chatter since our arrival, I cannot credit there is any subject still uncovered. They already appear to have catalogued the happenings of every single day since last they met.'

'You, Mr Balfour, are a tease.' Isabel slapped her husband playfully on the arm. 'Run along and play, you men, and leave your womenfolk in peace. We still have many important matters to discuss.'

'Important matters! Ha!' Luke stooped to kiss Joanna on the cheek. 'Children and babies, I'll be bound.'

'Are you suggesting that children and babies are *not* important, my dear?' Joanna regarded her husband quizzically.

He laughed. 'You have me there, my sweet. Children and babies are, of course, the most important of all things. I stand corrected.' He reached out and tickled Edward's pudgy cheek with a gentle finger. 'I fear you must wait a year or two to join us, my son, but at least you shall stay nice and snug indoors whilst we men brave the elements.'

After the men and children had gone, Edward's nursemaid whisked him off to the nursery and the four girls were left together.

'Ravenwell Manor is wonderful, Grace. It is so modern, so beautifully appointed, and this room is exquisite,' Isabel said.

Rachel and Joanna nodded their agreement.

'It was completely rebuilt after the fire.' Grace gazed around the drawing room, her favourite room in the house, decorated in shades of green and cream. 'Nathaniel's mother planned the décor.'

'Is that the fire that injured Nathaniel?' Joanna asked in her soft voice.

'Yes. He went back inside to rescue his father, but he was too late.'

Pride swelled at his bravery and at his courage in facing a full life once again, for her sake and for Clara's, and now...she placed her hand against her stomach...for their future family as well.

Grace looked up and found Rachel watching her, an unfathomable expression on her face.

'Are you quite well, Rachel?'

Pink suffused Rachel's cheeks. 'Are you...are you increasing, Grace?'

Isabel's head jerked up, her copper curls bouncing. 'Really? Are you, Grace? Why have you not told us? How exciting. We shall all be mothers together.'

'Isabel! Really. Calm down,' Joanna said, with a laugh. 'Grace has not answered Rachel yet and you are already three jumps ahead of us. You do not change.'

They all laughed.

'I'm sorry, Grace. But...is it true?'

'Yes! We will have a brother or a sister for Clara by the early summer, God willing.'

Then she recalled Rachel's expression. Would her news upset her friend? There had been something...that longing in her voice, earlier, and the look in her eyes when she held baby Edward...

Hoping and praying there was nothing amiss, she said, 'Your time will come, Rachel. You have only been wed nine months and—'

'I think I am with child.' Rachel blurted out her news with a blush.

The gasps were audible, then they all spoke at once.

'Are you sure?'

'How do you know?'

'But you never wanted children.'

'A lady can change her mind,' she said primly, in reply to that last comment from Isabel, and then she burst out laughing. 'I am not certain, but I'm fairly sure. I haven't even told Malik yet... I did not dare, for fear he would stop me journeying here for Christmas.'

A contented glow suffused Rachel's face as she added, 'He is very protective.'

'So we will truly all be mothers. With children by the men we love. How glorious is that?' Isabel stood, flinging her arms wide, and then twirled in a circle. 'Two years ago, we were all dreading our futures as put-upon drudges and now…look at us. Married ladies all and with children we never expected to bear.'

'Except for Grace,' Joanna said. 'Do you know, Grace, for all it was such a terrifying ordeal for you, in a way I envied you. You would be the only one of us to be a mother. Even though you had to give Clara away, still you had experienced the most wonderful thing that can ever happen to a woman.'

Grace clasped Joanna's hands, understanding the pain of her childhood with no family to love her. They had that in common.

'I never knew you felt that way, Joanna. I never believed anyone could envy what happened to me. But I see, in a way, what you mean. I always knew that somewhere in this world there was a part of me. I bless the day Miss Fanworth told me the names of Clara's adopted parents.'

'We have both found true families now, Grace. Although…' Joanna paused, her brow wrinkled with thought '…I eventually came to realise that Madame Dubois did love me, in her own way. She and the rest of the teachers were a kind of family to me, but I was too busy envying the other girls and their conventional families to realise it.'

Rachel laughed. 'No one could ever accuse *my* family of being conventional but, speaking of Madame, it is fortunate she never found out about the baby, Grace, or your life might have turned out very differently.'

'Ah, now that is where you are mistaken,' Grace said. She told them what Madame had told her the previous Christmas. 'She turned a blind eye because she knew my uncle would cast me out.'

'So the sly old thing knew all the time. Well, well.' Isabel subsided into an armchair.

'Talking of Madame,' Joanna said, 'I have some *marvellous* news about her and also about the school and Miss

Fanworth.' She paused for effect, a mischievous glint in her eyes.

'Hurry up and tell us.'

'Stop teasing, Joanna.'

'Tell us quickly before I burst!'

'We-e-e-ll…' Joanna eked out the moment, clearly enjoying being the news bearer.

'Joanna!' Isabel, sitting next to Joanna on the sofa, nudged her. 'Tell us. I am in a delicate condition, don't you know, and I must not be stressed.'

Joanna laughed. 'Oh, very well. Do you remember the Duke of Wakefield?'

'Yes, of course. *I* told *you* about him at that soirée last Christmas Eve and I wrote to Grace and Rachel about him.'

'And he visited Madame last Christmastide, when Clara and I were there,' Grace said, 'and Madame told me her tragic love story. I wrote to all of you about that. And I do know Madame fully recovered from her illness, for Miss Fanworth wrote and told me so.'

'Yes, she has recovered. In fact, she has so far recovered that she wed her Duke last week, and Madame Dubois is henceforth to be addressed as her Grace the Duchess of Wakefield.'

'A *duchess*?'

'How do you know?'

'Why did you not say before?'

'Yes, a duchess. And I know because Luke and I attended the wedding. And I did not say before because we had so much else to share.'

'So Madame has her happy-ever-after as well,' Rachel said. 'I am so pleased for her.'

'And the school?' Grace asked. 'You said you had news about the school.'

'She has gifted it to Miss Fanworth, who is now the principal.'

'So, we four and Madame get our handsome princes, and poor Miss Fanworth gets a pile of bricks and mortar.'

'Isabel!'

'Anyway,' Grace said, with a sly glance around her friends, 'there is always Signor Bertolli.'

She mimicked his Italian accent and twirled an imaginary moustache and the others burst into fits of giggles. They had long speculated over the Italian art master and his apparent liking for the plump, motherly Miss Fanworth.

Without Madame and her iron discipline at the school, who knew what that feisty Italian gentleman might get up to?

Christmas Eve

Grace awoke the following morning and rolled over to face Nathaniel. He still slept, warm and tousled and *delicious*. Stealthily, she leaned over and kissed his lips. He stirred and reached for her, eyes still shut.

'You are insatiable, woman,' he grumbled as he drew her close.

She snuggled against him, reaching between them as his hand delved for the hem of her nightdress and trailed up her bare leg.

When they eventually surfaced, they discovered a world transformed. The expected snow had fallen—so much snow it shrouded the land as far as the eye could see, thickly distorting every familiar feature. The sun shone in a cloudless sky, and the snowcovered landscape glistened and glimmered invitingly.

Somehow—and Grace was not sure quite how it happened—it was arranged that the men would take the excited children outside to build a snowman before bringing in the Yule log, whilst the women stayed indoors to dec-

orate the house with the garlands Grace and the servants
had crafted over the past week.

Hmmph! Stay indoors where it's nice and warm, indeed.

She did not voice her frustration to her friends, however. After all, they were not children any more and Isabel, in particular, might not wish to risk going outdoors in
her condition.

They had finished decorating the dining room and were
about to start on the drawing room when the door flew
open to reveal Isabel, clad in her sky-blue velvet fur-lined
cloak and twirling a matching bonnet in her hands. Grace
had not even realised she had disappeared.

'Why should the men have all the fun?' Isabel said. 'I
want to go outside in the snow. We can finish decorating
the house later. Grace has done all the hard work already.
What do you say, girls? Will any of you join me?'

Grace, Rachel and Joanna, as one, dropped their garlands and chorused, 'Yes!'

Grace rang the bell and sent maids to fetch their cloaks,
hats and gloves. Whilst they waited, Isabel continued to
twirl her bonnet until, with a sudden exclamation, she
stopped, plucked out the short plume tucked into the hat-
band and discarded it. She then broke a forked branch of
mistletoe from a kissing bough and put it in place of the
plume.

'There.' She grinned saucily. 'Three berries, as well. I
shall have fun in the snow.'

They tumbled out into the garden, where Luke and William were rolling a snowball for the body of the snowman
and Nathaniel—with Brack by his side—was helping the
three smallest children roll another for the head. Malik and
Aahil stood aside, watching.

Rachel tutted. 'Aahil needs to play. He tries to emulate
Malik, but he is nine years old. If he cannot be a child now,
when can he?'

And, with that, she scooped a handful of snow and threw

it straight at Malik, hitting his head and knocking off his hat. He spun around, his dark eyes flashing with an anger that soon melted when he saw Rachel.

Luke, meanwhile, had seen what happened. 'Come on, men,' he yelled. 'War is declared!' And he grabbed a handful of snow and lobbed it at Joanna.

Malik's aloofness lasted all of ten seconds. With a sudden laugh, he joined in, and then they were all throwing snowballs, laughing and shouting, whilst Brack gambolled around, barking and snatching at mouthfuls of snow.

A truce was called only after Joanna slipped flat on her face in a snowdrift. Luke was by her side in an instant.

'Enough,' he panted, grinning widely as he lifted her up. 'You, my beautiful lady wife, are coming indoors right now to get changed out of these wet clothes.' He strode towards the house, carrying Joanna.

'Can we finish the snowman?' Aahil gazed up at Nathaniel, dark eyes wide, hair sprinkled with snow.

Nathaniel patted his shoulder. 'Of course we can. You fetch the head whilst we set up the body.'

Malik helped Nathaniel manoeuvre the larger of the two balls into place outside the drawing-room windows and Ameera scampered through the snow to help Aahil whilst Clara and Hakim chased Brack.

Grace, Rachel and Isabel were content to watch, catching their breath after so much laughter. William joined them, his brows raised suggestively as he looked his wife up and down.

'New bonnet, my dear?'

Isabel preened a little. 'Oh, this old thing? I have merely retrimmed it, Husband.'

He wrapped his arms around her and kissed her soundly, then plucked a berry from the mistletoe. 'Only two more? You disappoint me.' He kissed her twice more, removing a berry after each kiss. 'That is better, for no one else gets to kiss *my* wife.'

The snowman was soon completed and Aahil, as the eldest and tallest of the children, crowned him with an old hat of Nathaniel's. Ameera wound a scarf around his neck and, together, they made his face with coal for eyes, a carrot for a nose and a row of hazelnuts to mark his mouth whilst Hakim and Clara stuck lumps of coal in a crooked line down his body, for buttons. An old clay pipe completed the transformation.

The children stood back, eyes and smiles wide.

'Is he magic?' Hakim whispered. 'Will he come alive and have adventures when it is dark and we can't see him?'

Rachel crouched by his side and hugged him. 'He will if you believe in him, Hakim.'

They were all warm and dry, congregated in the drawing room, when Luke and Joanna eventually reappeared.

'At last,' Isabel cried. 'We are waiting to light the Yule log.'

Two of the footmen had brought the log indoors earlier, setting it in the drawing room grate—only just big enough to accommodate it.

'Sorry.' Luke looked entirely unrepentant.

'We were playing with Edward,' Joanna said, with a blush and a stifled giggle.

'We're all here now,' William said, with a merry glance. 'I have been looking forward to this.'

The fire was lit, using a blackened lump of wood saved by Sharp—bless him—from last year's Yule log, and then all the adults helped drape garlands around the room, adding candles, whilst the children played with Sweep, who was fascinated by all the greenery. Isabel fashioned a dainty headdress for Ameera, using sprigs of juniper, interwoven with red ribbon and tiny fir cones. Clara and Hakim then wanted their own headdresses, so she made two more whilst a delighted Ameera danced around the room.

Finally, all that was left was to hang the kissing bough.

After some dispute amongst the men as to who was the tallest—Malik won, by an inch, over Nathaniel's six foot two—the bough was hung from the chandelier in the centre of the room, just high enough that Malik could stand beneath without it brushing against it.

Then the maids brought in mulled wine and fruit punch and warm mince pies, and cleared away the remaining greenery.

Isabel, her rich copper hair shining in the candlelight, sang a carol, filling the room with her exquisite voice. And then they were all singing, their voices rising and falling in a rich blend, and Grace found herself blinking back tears. Nathaniel, next to her on the sofa, hugged her close and before long, Clara clambered up to join them in a singing, laughing, loving heap.

As the singing came to an end, Malik held up his hand for silence.

'I thank you for inviting myself and my family to join in celebrating Christmas at your home,' he said.

He stood straight and solemn, but Grace was sure she detected a twinkle in his eyes.

'I have found enjoyment in all of your traditions,' he continued, 'but the one I most appreciate—' he grabbed Rachel's hand and tugged her to stand beneath the kissing bough '—is this one.'

He bent his head to kiss Rachel, who wound her arms around his neck and kissed him back enthusiastically.

Malik plucked a berry from the bough and then kissed Rachel once more. There was a moment's stunned silence as the rest of the room watched and then William, with a wink at Isabel, stood up.

'I say, Al-Mahrouky. Leave some for the rest of us to enjoy.'

Malik lifted his dark head. 'You had your fair share of berries in the garden, Balfour. Do not think it went unnoticed,' he said, to a round of laughter.

Nathaniel then stood, raising his glass, and a sudden hush fell over the room. One by one, those still seated rose to their feet.

'I should like to propose a toast.'

Nathaniel's deep voice sent a *frisson* of desire chasing up Grace's spine. As if sensing her reaction, he captured her gaze with his, the faintest of smiles tugging at the corner of his mouth. The angle he stood, next to the fire, highlighted his damaged cheek, but Grace barely noticed it now. It was a part of him and loved and adored by her as much as, or even more than, every other inch of him.

'To Christmastide—a time for friends and for family and a time of joy—to beloved friends from our past and to firm friends in our future, and to happy families, those who are present and—' his fiery gaze lowered to Grace's belly, leaving a scorching trail of desire in its wake '—those we have yet to meet.'

From the corner of her eye Grace saw Malik place his hand, fleetingly, on Rachel's belly. Rachel's gaze jerked to his. He nodded, then slipped his arm around her waist and hugged her close into his side.

So he does *know.* Grace caught Rachel's eye and they shared a contented smile.

Luke and Joanna stood close together, with eyes only for one another as they drank their toast.

'And, last but not least,' Nathaniel continued, 'to the newly wed Duchess of Wakefield, whose discretion and whose sage advice is greatly appreciated by *this* husband at least.'

'And by this one,' Luke said, raising his glass again as he smiled into Joanna's eyes.

'To Madame, for all she has done for me and for sending me away. She was wise, indeed, for if she had granted my wish of staying at the school to teach, I should never have met you, darling Luke.'

'And to Miss Fanworth,' Grace added, 'for if it was

not for her, I should never have found Clara, nor you, my dearest love.'

'Yes. To Miss Fanworth, without whom I would never have travelled to Huria and met Malik and my beautiful stepchildren,' Rachel said.

'To Madame, Miss Fanworth, and their School for Young Ladies,' Isabel cried, raising her glass high as William snaked his arm around her waist.

A quiet bubble of contentment swelled inside Grace. 'To us, to friendship everlasting, to happy memories, and to the brightest of futures,' she said as she raised her glass for the final time.

'We all have so very much to be thankful for.'

* * * * *

LET'S TALK

For exclusive extracts, competitions
and special offers, find us online:

f facebook.com/millsandboon

𝕏 @MillsandBoon

📷 @MillsandBoonUK

Get in touch on 01413 063232

For all the latest titles coming soon, visit
millsandboon.co.uk/nextmonth

JOIN US ON SOCIAL MEDIA!

Stay up to date with our latest releases, author news and gossip, special offers and discounts, and all the behind-the-scenes action from Mills & Boon...

 @millsandboon

 @millsandboonuk

 facebook.com/millsandboon

 @millsandboonuk

It might just be true love...

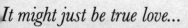

GET YOUR ROMANCE FIX

Get the latest romance news,
exclusive author interviews, story
extracts and much more!

MILLS & BOON

HISTORICAL

Awaken the romance of the past

Escape with historical heroes from time gone by. Whether your passion is for wicked Regency Rakes, muscled Viking warriors or rugged Highlanders, indulge your fantasies and awaken the romance of the past.